ONLY
DAUGHTER

SARAH A. DENZIL

Bookouture

Published by Bookouture in 2019

An imprint of StoryFire Ltd.

Carmelite House
50 Victoria Embankment
London EC4Y 0DZ
www.bookouture.com

ISBN: 978-1-78681-711-2
eBook ISBN: 978-1-78681-710-5

PROLOGUE

If you were here with me now, I'd say sorry for everything.

I know I've let you down, disappointed you, and it hurts. This is how it ends for me, isn't it? Alone with my thoughts, with my pain, all the regrets about who I am and how I acted coming back to haunt me. I let you down more than anyone else. Maybe one day you'll be able to forgive me, but I know I'll never forgive myself.

It hurts so badly. I'm crying as I watch the blood seep through my dress. Red spreads across the yellow, like spilled paint. My body is cold all over and I'm starting to shake. I'm certain that my face is as pale as the thin sliver of moon above me.

Perhaps I can get out of this pit, if I can remember how. Wind whistles through the rocky depths of Stonecliffe Quarry. Otherwise known as the Suicide Spot. Aren't there steps built into the cliff? A half-finished attempt at transforming the old quarry into a park; now a place for the dying to claw their way back to life. A rebirth.

My hands grope the cold, slippery surface around me. I landed here with a thud and broke my bones. I wish you were here to guide me, to tell me where to go. I wish I could tell you how you were the one I looked up to, who made me want to be a better person. Always.

What will you think when you find my dead body?

I remember the man who jumped from this cliff five months ago. He probably fell close to where I am now, landing with a crunch, breaking his neck. No one found him for a week. Will that be me?

A scream escapes from my throat, sharp like a dagger against my vocal chords. *Help me!* Desperate, rasping with all the air in my lungs, but what comes out is barely a whisper. My throat is raw. Fight harder. Scramble, pull yourself forward. Grasp the rock. My fingers dig into dirt and a sharp pain from my left wrist makes me dizzy. When I lift my head, the stars dance, and I know I'm beginning to lose consciousness. If I do, then this is over and I will die, and I'll never be able to see you again and tell you I love you. And I'm sorry. My tights and dress are soaked through with blood, damp from hip to ankle.

My head is a heavy weight, swollen and foggy, interrupting my concentration, but I grit my teeth together so hard that my jaw starts up a dull throbbing. The smell here is of sweet blood mingled with the damp earth. It stinks of death, and I expect my life to begin flashing before my eyes like it does in the films. Your smile pops into my mind. Other people I love, too. That's when I know I'm starting to give up, but I can't, I have to keep going.

It's here, the first ledge; I touch it with scratched fingertips. A cloud passes over the moon as I cry out in pain at my first attempt to pull myself up. Is my wrist broken? I can't support my weight. *Come on.* A fingernail peels from my skin as I make a second attempt. My eyes roll back in my head as a wave of throbbing pain washes over me. My hands are slick and slippery, leaving my life's blood all over the stones. When I grasp the first step, my fingers can't find purchase, and before I know it I'm falling again, this time a mere few feet, and my head hits the cold surface of the quarry floor.

If you were here now, I'd apologise for everything.

But I wouldn't just say sorry; I'd warn you, too.

Because they're coming after you next…

CHAPTER ONE

My most overwhelming emotion is in fact a colour. Blue. Chipped blue nail polish on her fingers. Blue lips. The bluish tint to the hospital lights, and the way the white sheet appears blue under their glow.

There's a strand of blonde hair over her face, which I brush away and tuck behind her ear, half expecting her to roll her eyes and say 'Muuuuuum' with a crooked smile. But that would require her eyes to be open, and they're not.

It surprises me that there have been no tears yet. Perhaps it's the smell of the hospital clogging my feelings, blocking them with the sour tang of disinfectant. Or perhaps it's the coroner hovering politely in the doorway, waiting patiently for us to make an identification. Waiting to tick a box, to start the paperwork, to move on to the next step. But we can 'take our time' with her. As long as we need. That's what grieving parents do, isn't it? They take time. They become sponges for bereavement, soaking it all up and then washing everyone else with their grief. I can already tell that Charles will be that kind of mourner as he stands beside me whimpering softly.

But *I* can't find the tears. Instead I concentrate on Grace's fingers, on the chipped blue polish and the scratches on her skin. The dirt under her nails. When Grace fell into the quarry, she was still alive, and she clawed against the ground, trying to climb up the stone steps. She'd suffered a compound fracture of the tibia and bled out as she pointlessly scraped her fingers against the dirt.

There is no nail left on the little finger of her left hand, and I can't stop staring at that finger. It's making me angry. It's making me so furious that not even the disinfectant smell, or the well-meaning coroner, or the strand of blonde hair, or the puckered, dead lips of my daughter can block it out. A simmering rage is stirring because my daughter, my seventeen-year-old, beautiful daughter, should not be lying lifeless on a gurney in an understaffed hospital. She should be awake, rolling her eyes, flipping her hair, ignoring me in favour of the phone she can never be parted from. That's what my daughter should be doing.

'It's her.' Charles's voice cracks and a strangled noise escapes from his throat. Almost instinctively, I place a hand on his arm, without moving my transfixed gaze from that missing fingernail.

'Your daughter? Grace?' the coroner asks.

'Yes,' I reply, as Charles begins to crumple in on himself.

He becomes greedy, pawing at me, grasping the collar of my shirt and burying his face into my neck. Soon hot tears wet my skin and his body pulsates against mine. I cling to him, too, stroking his hair, comforting him. Why am I not the one breaking apart? Shouldn't it be the mother to break down crying? To scream and rip her hair out at the roots? To beat her breast and wail? The truth is I'm too angry for pain. The pain hasn't begun yet, but it will.

I hold my husband as the lights above us flicker twice. His fingers dig into my shoulders, but that's good, because it gives me some real physical pain on which to concentrate, to help control the rage stirring within. The coroner is trying not to watch, but I can tell she is, and I worry whether I appear stiff, unemotional or strange. I don't always react to situations the way other people do, but I know that. I know who I am.

'I'm sorry.' Charles straightens himself, smoothing his hair back. He removes his glasses and wipes his eyes with a handkerchief. A few seconds later there are fresh dewdrops on his mousy-grey eyelashes. He steps back and stares down at our daughter, which redirects my focus back to her.

She's still; lifeless. I try to imagine what life will be like, not making her breakfast, not being woken from a nap by the sounds of her violin practice, not picking her up from school, not hearing her snap at me when I tell her to put her phone away or ask if she has a boyfriend. For seventeen years this person has been the centre of my universe. Every waking hour has been in some way linked to this person, who *I* made, who was pulled from my body. And now, within a few short hours, that link has been severed, permanently.

There. There's the pain. And I welcome it.

We were given as much time as we needed to identify Grace's body, but I couldn't tell you how long we stayed in that room. Charles held her hand for a while. Towards the end I began to pace back and forth, thinking about her death, the violent and unexpected nature of it. I couldn't stop thinking about the nail torn from her finger. For some reason the broken leg ended up pushed to the back of my mind. Perhaps it was because of the sheet covering the injury. Grace was a girly girl – she once cried when she broke a carefully manicured nail. The idea of one tearing from her flesh… She must have been in so much pain.

And that's what makes this tragedy even more unfair, what makes me furious instead of sad. She suffered, right to the end. She suffered more than a *good* person like Grace ought to. A seventeen-year-old girl with talent and beauty and kindness should not be torn away from the world in this manner. Where is the justice? It isn't right.

But then I remember that justice doesn't exist in the way we want it to. The universe isn't at our beck and call to right our wrongs. The universe is indifferent to us; we're just too arrogant to see it.

'What happens now?' I ask.

Charles and I are sitting in a waiting room, speaking to the police officers dealing with Grace's sudden death. PC Mullen strikes me as too young and inexperienced to be dealing with a case like this. In order to find out why my little girl died, I want to make sure that every possibility is explored – by someone with the wherewithal to turn every stone. He has the kind of baby face that should be downing snakebite at a university club night. The other one, DS Slater, is older and hopefully wiser. He has a sharp chin and a neutral expression. I imagine he gets straight down to business. DS Slater first liaised with us when Grace didn't come home from school yesterday. He coordinated the search that ended when Grace was found in the quarry. I'm sure I'll always remember his calm voice as he informed us over the phone that a body had been found.

As he speaks to us now, he uses some of that same composure. 'There will be a post-mortem to uncover the cause, but we aren't treating your daughter's death as suspicious.'

I find myself sitting up straighter. 'Not suspicious? She was missing for hours. Someone could have taken her and…' My hands, resting on my knees, grip both legs, fingernails digging in.

'I know,' he says gently. 'But I'm very sorry to inform you that a note was found in Grace's pocket. We believe that Grace may have committed suicide.'

As Charles says, 'Suicide?' my arm stretches out towards the detective, palm open.

'I'd like to read it.' I leave my hand out, waiting.

Charles begins to cry again, and DS Slater glances at my husband's tears before directing his attention back to me. He nods once. 'That's fine. We have a copy here.'

I make a mental note to ask for the original back once the post-mortem is over. I'll need to see it, to touch it, to know it's real.

It's PC Mullen who offers me the sheet of paper. With every ounce of willpower, I refrain from snatching it greedily from his hand. If my daughter killed herself, I need to see the proof.

Charles leans over my shoulder as I smooth out the note. Even in the photocopied version, I recognise Grace's handwriting. The way she loops the tail on her y is ingrained in my memory. The dots on her i's are always slightly to the left. Her letters never fail to hit the line as she writes, keeping her prose perfectly straight. I helped her with that when she first learned how to join her letters.

'Do you recognise the handwriting?' DS Slater asks.

'It's Grace's handwriting,' I confirm.

I know that Grace wrote this letter, and yet I see nothing of my daughter within the carefully drawn loops and dots. It's a short note, devoid of emotion, with a hint of desperation that sickens me.

Mum and Dad,

I'm so sorry. Everything is becoming too much. I don't think I can go on.

Love,

Grace

There's no goodbye, no declaration of love, no explanation of what might have caused this sudden need to exit life. There's nothing of who I thought my daughter was. It's almost boilerplate. I don't know what I expected from a suicide note, but this isn't it. It doesn't feel real.

I'm in shock, which means my judgement may be slightly off. I've lost my centre. There's a gaping black hole where the purpose of my life should be, and perhaps I can't trust the emotions running through my body. But this note does not ring true to me. For one thing, an entire line has been scribbled out, completely obstructing the letters underneath. What did it say? What does it mean?

Because the note has been photocopied in colour, I can see that the line has been blocked out in a different colour to the ink of the original note. That strikes me as odd. Why would Grace do that? Why would she use a different pen?

'Oh God,' Charles moans. 'I didn't know she wanted to die. She was *seventeen*. This isn't right. Kat?' He looks to me as though he wants me to make everything better.

'Did you notice any change in Grace's behaviour over the last few days?' PC Mullen asks.

I shake my head. 'No. Grace wouldn't kill herself.'

'I know this is difficult—' DS Slater begins.

'This doesn't even sound like Grace,' I insist, tapping the photocopied note with the back of my hand. 'Grace wouldn't kill herself. She had everything to live for.'

'It may seem like that, but unfortunately teenage suicide isn't uncommon. Teenagers are under a lot of stress with exams and personal relationships.'

'I know that,' I snap. 'But I knew my daughter. Look at this. Why would she strike through an entire line in a different pen?'

'There are many possible reasons.' DS Slater speaks slowly, as though to someone whose grasp of English is inferior. 'Her original pen may have run out. She may have written words she later regretted and thought would hurt your feelings.'

'Then why didn't she rewrite it?' I ask. 'What time did she die?'

'We won't know for certain until her post-mortem,' DS Slater replies with a frown. 'But we believe that she died sometime around midnight.'

'Then what was she doing all that time?' I demand. 'Where did she go? Who was she with?'

'The short answer is we just don't know,' DS Slater says. 'But given the evidence – the note, the location… We know the quarry attracts suicidal people. I'm inclined to believe that there was no foul play here.' He pauses and raises his hands slowly, as though placating a crazy person. 'I'm so sorry for your loss, and I know this is difficult to accept, Mrs Cavanaugh, but you identified the suicide note yourself.'

'It doesn't matter if she wrote it,' I say, refusing to back down. 'What I'm saying is that maybe someone forced her to write those words. The Grace I know wouldn't commit suicide. She was happy.'

'Kat.' Charles places his hand on my knee.

'No, Charles, listen to me. You don't believe this, do you? You don't believe these lies?' I snatch up the note and hold it aloft with trembling fingers.

His hand squeezes. 'I don't want to believe it. But that's Grace's handwriting. She was stressed with school, and you know that sometimes she suffered with mood swings.'

I shake my head in disbelief, unable to understand why my husband is so quick to believe this, and then turn back to DS Slater. 'Have you checked CCTV? Witnesses? Who was she with all that time?'

DS Slater clears his throat and talks in that same soothing tone. 'When Grace first went missing, we asked around at the school, and no one had seen her leave. I'm afraid there isn't much CCTV in a small village like Ash Dale, but we will certainly be checking.'

I'm well aware that they're all talking to me like I'm a child, and I can't bear it. I can't be with anyone in this room anymore. Forcing Charles's hand from my knee, I get to my feet and pace from wall to wall. DS Slater's promise is lip service, designed to pacify me, but it's a start. No one is going to listen to me now, not this soon after identifying the body. They think I'm emotional, that I'm hurting, that I'm a grieving mother to be coddled. I loved my daughter more than anyone. She was my one true connection to this world, the one part of me that tethered me to everyone else. The truth is, I don't care about anyone but Grace and I never have. DS Slater, PC Mullen, the ever-so-patient coroner, even my husband, are little more than people orbiting my life. Grace was the one person I truly cared about and now she's gone.

If DS Slater can't or won't find out what happened to her, then I will.

CHAPTER TWO

The birth did not go well. Grace was breech, the umbilical cord wrapped around her neck, and the midwife was sweating through her scrubs. In the rush to get her out, the cord was tugged too hard and ruptured. I lost enough blood to put me in a hazy, confused state while Grace was checked over and cleaned up. The gory chaos of the birth was followed by a blood transfusion which had me hooked up to a machine while Charles placed Grace on his chest and stroked her soft head with his fingertips. I watched through tired eyes, and in that moment I felt jealous of him, of the easy way he soothed her, of the obvious love he felt for the tiny human I had grown inside *my* body and almost died pushing out. I wanted to hold her in my arms, rest her head against my chest and watch her fall into a contented sleep. I wanted the perfect moment I had been led to believe all mothers experienced.

In the days that followed the birth, part of me resented this tiny baby for the pain she'd put me through. And as if that wasn't enough, there was barely a second in the day where Grace's small face wasn't bright red and scrunched as she howled at me. She refused my nipple. On the rare occasions she did breastfeed, I had terrible cramps that shuddered through my body. She never wanted to nap and I was completely exhausted, barely able to shuffle to the bathroom for a few seconds of agonising pain. She only ever softened when Charles walked her up and down the corridor at the hospital. She didn't want me, and a paranoid voice in my head told me that it was personal, that she saw every flaw I had. She knew who I was and she spurned my affections because I wasn't worthy.

But Grace's initial rejection made me more determined to win her over. After I'd recovered from the blood loss and regained some strength, I laid her on my chest and let her sleep. I placed my finger inside her tiny fist and allowed her to squeeze it as hard as she could. When she was crying, I stroked her head, touching the smoothness of hair over her soft skull. She yawned to reveal a pink mouth and I was fascinated. I even came to enjoy the funny noises she made, and I watched the spit bubbles emerge from her lips.

It was during this gradual shift in circumstances that I discovered I was falling in love with my daughter, not because I was supposed to, but because I liked being around her. She was part of me. She was the good part. I wanted to keep her safe, and, more than anything, I wanted to be a better person for her.

But as hard as I tried, I'm not sure I ever truly became a better person.

When we arrive back at our empty house after the long, tortuous identification, Charles heads straight to the kitchen and slops whisky into a glass. Georgie and Porgie, our two ever-enthusiastic black labs, bound into my legs, licking my hands, before moving on to Charles, most likely sensing his distress. Through a foggy haze, I hear one of them begin to whimper. I can't watch.

There is a cloud around me of poisonous gas, sapping all the energy from my body and disconnecting me from Charles and the dogs and from our beautiful home: a sprawling Victorian mansion of a house. Rather than spend more time comforting my husband, I find myself stepping heavily up the wide staircase, shedding my jacket and shoes as I go, leaving them where they fall. Oil paintings shake in their frames as a stiletto hits the wall.

The old floorboards groan under my step. My hand grips the oak railings until my knuckles turn white.

Her room is at the end of a long corridor of doors. There are seven bedrooms spread out through Farleigh Hall. Grace, in effect, had the entire first floor to herself, because the master bedroom is on the second floor, converted from the old ballroom. Now, as I walk down the corridor towards her room, it hits me how utterly empty this house is going to be without her. I'd coveted Farleigh, longed to live here. After the first time I'd visited the sprawling estate, I'd gone back to my tiny flat and practised writing the address as if it were my own: *Kat Cavanaugh, Farleigh Hall, Ash Dale, Derbyshire.* No house number. No 'Flat 3B'. No woodlice in the kitchen. Charles had provided me a ticket out of poverty and I'd yanked it greedily from his chubby fingers. What I hadn't anticipated was Charles giving me a treasure even better than money: Grace.

But now, after longing for the kind of luxury Farleigh Hall could give me, I run my fingers along the mahogany-panelled walls and feel nothing but the chill of the wood. This house is a shell without her voice, without the sound of music blaring out of her room. I close my eyes and I still hear her violin practice echoing down the corridors. The grief swells up like a tornado, threatening to knock me from my feet.

When I reach her room, I hold my breath as I swing the door open. Surely there should be a change in atmosphere. Grace's room should be unrecognisable. The sight of an apocalypse. Scorched earth, never the same again. But nothing has changed since she left for school yesterday morning. The cleaners haven't been in since Grace went missing, which means it still smells like her. Her clothes have been left dangling over the ottoman at the end of the bed. Her bedding is tangled in a ball, as it always is. Her violin rests against its stand in the corner. She could come bursting out of her bathroom with a towel wrapped around her hair and a sheet mask sliding down her face. I stand in the doorway and wait for her, a smile on my face, expectant. *What are we trying today, Grace? Relaxing honey mask? Cooling cucumber? Pedicures in the village?*

But she will never step out of that bathroom again.

I can't get the colour blue out of my head.

I wrap my body around the ball of bedding and close my eyes, inhaling what's left of her scent.

It has to be done and it has to be done alone. There is someone who needs to be told about Grace. Charles offered to drive me, but he was barely coherent by the time I navigated my way back down the stairs with bleary eyes. Besides, I never drive there. I either book a taxi or I take the bus. Today I book a taxi. Charles always thinks that this behaviour is endearing, because I came from nothing and he's old money, but I don't want these people to know my change in circumstances. I don't want them to know anything about me. If I could, I would never go to that place again, but the person I'm about to see is stubborn. I worked hard to get out of where we're from, but she refused to leave.

Before the taxi arrives, I chug down a large measure of Charles's whisky, sending my mind into a pleasant haze that will surely get me through the journey. Then, because Charles begins to weep again, I find my shoes, snatch up my handbag and wait outside, no longer able to bear the greedy, tearful husband inside the house. It's not fair for him to take comfort from me when I'm dried up and hollowed out. What comfort do I have for him? What's left of me?

When I climb into the hybrid, a low whistle sounds from the front of the car. 'Some place you have here.'

'Yeah, I know.' I reel off the address and the driver programmes it into his satnav. The whisky sits sourly in my stomach, and every time I close my eyes, I see Grace's chipped fingernails and the cuts on her flesh.

'Not driving today?' he asks. 'If I were you, I'd take that Jaguar out for a spin. And on a glorious spring day like this? With the top down?' He shakes his head as though I'm a crazy woman for not continuously rejoicing in my own wealth.

'No,' I say. 'My daughter died yesterday.'

I watch through the rear-view mirror as his face pales before I lean back against the seat. There are dull aches in my skull and abdomen, radiating out to the rest of my body. Good. Give me pain. I close my eyes and picture Grace on the gurney. If I'd drunk more whisky, maybe I could have blocked it all out. Charles has the right idea, crying and drinking, reaching out his hands like a baby waiting to be held. Why haven't I been doing that? Why haven't I broken down and made everyone around me step up to console me?

No, the mother has an obligation. Here I am, doing what needs to be done, and trying to do it right. Though I have to admit to myself that it isn't all from a place of altruism. The truth is, I have an ulterior motive. I know my daughter didn't kill herself, and there are certain people in my life that I need to be sure didn't harm my child. I'm about to confront one of those people. I want to see the expression on her face when I tell her that Grace has died. Perhaps I'll learn what really happened to her that day.

CHAPTER THREE

The taxi drops me off at the end of the street and I hand the driver the cash. He says he's sorry for my loss as I'm closing the door. Coming here usually involves shedding my wealth like a second skin. I wear nondescript clothing and tie my hair back in a tight ponytail. She's the only one from here who knows about my circumstances, and she's ashamed of them. Of me. Today, though, I completely forget about my usual ritual and arrive wearing the clothes I threw on this morning, which happen to be the same expensive clothes I wear day in, day out: a cashmere cardigan, Louboutins, a soft leather tote from Mulberry. I'd usually avoid all of these brands, because it gets me off to a bad start with her. But there's nothing that can be done about it. A shudder runs through my body, and I consider calling the taxi back.

'Katie, is that you?'

A familiar voice calls to me from the concrete garden outside a small terraced house. A woman limps over to me, her polyester leggings rubbing between her thighs to make a *swish-swish* sound, and leans on the back fence.

'Look at you. I hardly recognised you. Oh, I *love* that bag,' she says, the pink flesh below her chin wobbling up and down.

'Hi, Mrs Nash. It's fake.'

'On your way to see Susan?' she asks.

'Yes,' I reply, trying to move along.

'Oh good. Give her my love, won't you?'

I brush a lock of ash-blonde hair away from my face and nod. Everyone on the estate loves Susan, as Mrs Nash calls her (I have another name for her), which is no surprise seeing as Susan gave them all a load of cash to share between them. Lucky, lucky Old Barrow residents. It was Charles's money, obviously, and it was supposed to be put towards her moving *out*, but she decided to tell all her friends she'd won a few grand on the lottery and split the whole lot with them.

My heels click-clack against the pavement. I'm on the road behind the terraced houses, looking in on the washing lines and plastic garden furniture. Every step taking me closer to that house makes my heart beat faster. A horrible thought consumes me: what if *now* is the moment I lose control and break down? What if Grace's death hasn't hit me yet because I haven't said it out loud to anyone except a random taxi driver?

After a few more steps, there it is: my childhood home. I take a deep breath to steady myself, as I always do. The two-up two-down terrace should've been adequately sized for one woman and one daughter, but Susan, my mother, is a hoarder. I don't come here very often, and I've certainly never brought Grace with me. When Mum wanted to see Grace, I'd offer to pay for a taxi to bring her up to our house, but she would always take the bus. It was never too often, either. Mum frequently forgot Grace's birthday – she never remembers mine – and Christmas was hit-and-miss depending on whether she had plans with the neighbours or not. Not that any of this bothered me, except that I hated to see Grace disappointed when Grandma hadn't bothered to send her a birthday card.

It's Grace's disappointed face on her eighth birthday that I hold in my mind as I knock on the door. Mum had been to visit the Christmas before her birthday and, for once, they'd had a nice time together, playing with Grace's dolls. Mum has always loved dolls. She keeps a collection of the pasty-faced things in the lounge, sitting upright amidst all the other crap, with their eyes that follow me through the room. Come February, when Grace's birthday came along, my poor, naïve daughter thought that Grandma would want to spend it with her, so she invited Mum to her birthday party. I called Mum and begged her to join us, using as much charm as I could muster, but none of that works with her. She'd already arranged to cat sit for Nadia Patel at number 45. That's how it is with Mum.

'What are you knocking for? Where's your key?'

A waft of stale house stink hits me as soon as she opens the door. I'm surprised by how old she looks. Mum always said I got my attractive features from my dad, and I believe that may be the only true thing she's ever said to me.

'I forgot it.'

'How did you manage that?' she says, shuffling away from the door to allow me into the home.

I follow her in, dodging the stacks of magazines and trying desperately to ignore the overflowing bin. No part of me wants to close that door and shut myself in this house, but I have to. No part of me wants to be here in this place, where I used to eat my toast leaning over the sink in the mornings, sit on the sofa and watch soaps with my silent mother, put myself to bed when she was in a drunken stupor. No part of me wants to remember any of that, especially not today, but I had to come. I need to be face-to-face with her as I deliver the news.

Despite being in her late sixties, Mum is still sprightly. She's always been a slip of a woman, because she doesn't particularly enjoy food. The pleasure of chocolate cake is lost on her. She'd be just as happy with a plate of kale. That, and the fact that she's always out and about in the community, means that she's managed to stay fit.

'Well?' Her eyebrows shoot up as she waits for my response. As she moves a bag of clothes from an armchair, placing it on top of a leaning stack of newspapers, her gaze travels over my body, taking in my outfit. 'Why are you dressed fancy? What, did you want to rub it in, did you? Show everyone on the estate that you're rich now? Is that it? You think you're better than us, flashing your cash? Is that husband of yours with you? Driving around in that *ridiculous* car like he's the "big I am"—'

'Mum.'

She ignores me. 'It's disgusting is what it is, parading around in expensive things when there are people starving on the streets—'

'Grace is dead.'

'What?'

'Grace is dead.' I take a deep breath. 'She didn't come home from school yesterday. I rang the police and they searched for her. They found her at the bottom of a quarry this morning. She fell and broke her leg – bled to death.' Another deep breath. 'I had to identify her… body.' My legs are wobbly, but I'm getting through it. 'She died, Mum. She's gone.'

The gold mantelpiece clock continues to tick as anger and injustice swell up inside me again. I long to knock it onto the carpet and smash it to smithereens, grinding the glass into the stained carpet. It's ticking song mocks me, reminding me that time carries on while my daughter will not. And as it ticks on, my mother continues to stand there in complete silence, gawping at me. Twenty ticks later, a low moan emits from her open mouth and she starts to fall.

Alarmed, I reach out to try and steady her, but she bats away my hand with surprising force before collapsing on the carpet. She begins to wail, loud and obnoxious, like a siren that I can't physically stand to hear. Awkwardly, not knowing how to comfort this woman who never comforted me, I place an arm over her shoulder and make soothing noises.

'Come on, Mum. Try and sit on the chair. Come on.'

'She's… gone?' Her eyes connect with mine, and not for the first time in my life I think about how much she resembles a child. 'My poor baby.'

No. *My* baby. Mine. No one else's. Anger floods back into my veins and I get to my feet, withdrawing myself from the woman on the floor. None of her wailing and moaning strikes me as genuine; instead it seems to me that she wants to make my daughter's death about her, which is pretty much exactly what I thought she'd do. The dull ache in my skull begins to throb almost unbearably and I gaze across the room, searching for a bottle. Locking eyes on the bounty I need, I pick my way through the mounds of belongings to get to the glass cabinet, then open the door, snatch up a bottle of gin and take a long swig.

'Give me some of that, will you?'

Miraculously, my grief-stricken mother has perked up at the sight of the alcohol. She climbs to her feet and reaches for the bottle.

As she drinks, I sink down in one of the chairs and rub my temples. My martyr mother, the woman who lives like an angel outside the house, who changes as soon as she's within these four walls. I expected nothing more from her and the whole encounter has left me with an unpleasant taste in my mouth. When I'm unhappy, I usually go to Grace to cheer me up. Happiness, for me, has always been fickle and fleeting, but Grace's smile has certainly helped through the years. Her goofy jokes too. Charles bought her a book of jokes when she was eleven and she never stopped reading from it. Those memories are helping me get through this moment with my own mother and her manipulative histrionics. Now that she has the gin, she sits happily sucking it down like a baby from a bottle.

'What happened?' Mum asks, mollified by alcohol.

I shake my head; nothing about this feels real. 'I don't know. The police… Well, the police found a suicide note in the pocket of her dress. They believe she killed herself.'

A long silence draws out while I stare at my fingernails. She'd tried to claw her way out of that pit after falling. She'd tried with enough exertion to rip off her own fingernail in the process. Was that suicidal? Would she fight back to such an extreme?

Mum breaks the silence with a voice low enough to reverberate through the glass door of the cabinet. 'What did you say to her?'

I lift my chin to meet her gaze. 'What?'

'You must have said or done something to her. A young girl like that doesn't kill herself if she has a loving mother.' She sets the gin bottle down next to the electric fire, avoiding eye contact.

'You think that *I* made Grace suicidal?' My voice is barely audible over the sound of the ticking clock. But I don't whisper in anger; rather shock. Out of all the ways I'd imagined this conversation, *her* blaming *me* hadn't made the cut. However, now that I'm here in front of her, the woman who barely gave a shit about me my entire life, somehow it all makes sense.

She snatches up the bottle and takes another swig. 'That girl was perfect. It's you who ruined her.' One more glug. 'You were never right. You came out wrong. Too much of *him* in you.'

'Him' is my father, the man who had the indecency to leave my toxic mother when she was pregnant with me. It was probably the best decision he ever made.

'Grace didn't kill herself.' I stand. 'I don't care what the police think. Someone made her write that note and then they pushed her over the edge.'

'Who would want to do that?' Her words are beginning to slur from the quarter bottle of gin she has drained.

'I don't know. Either someone who wanted to hurt Grace or someone who wanted to hurt me.'

She lets out a humourless laugh. 'You're already making her death about yourself, aren't you? Poor Katie. You must be loving this. How many people have you told already?'

'I haven't told anyone,' I lie.

Her eyes narrow and she nods knowingly. 'I feel sorry for Grace, I do. In fact, I always have felt sorry for her. You might have the money, but that's all you've got. At least I have a real family here.'

'That's right, Mum. You chose your family, didn't you? And that family never included me, did it?'

'You never wanted family, Katie.'

'That's not true.'

She takes another swig and stares at the fire.

'You've never forgiven me for what I did; that's the real truth,' I say.

She swallows the gin before responding. Her voice is low, emotionless, and her eyes never move from the fire. 'Well, not everyone has a child like you, do they? A violent, twisted piece of shit.' Finally, her eyes meet mine. 'How do you sleep at night, Katie?'

CHAPTER FOUR

I've not been Katie Flack for a long time. The name still carries a bit of infamy around Old Barrow, certainly at my old school, and that's one of the reasons why I never go home. Running into people from that part of my life is never a pleasant experience.

I was ten years old when I first started acting out. My school had a reputation for being rough, with plenty of troubled kids coming off the council estates nearby. Out of a bad bunch, I was one of the worst. There was barely a day that went by without me getting into a fight. I broke Lucy Bates's nose, gave Kevin Clarke a black eye and kicked our PE teacher in the shin, among other misdemeanours. My violence was the beginning of a conduct disorder. It led to what happened with Annie Robertson. It led to nightmares, and more violence, and an event so appalling that my mother never forgave me.

'I'll let you know when the funeral is arranged.' As I open the back door, letting some much-needed clean air into the kitchen, I can hear Mum shuffling behind me. She's quick enough to reach me before I leave.

'So that's it then? You're going to drop this news on me and go?' Mum places her hand on the door to hold it open.

'I won't stay here and be insulted by you. For one thing, you insinuated that I was responsible for my daughter's death.' I step into the wasteland of her back garden, completely devoid of anything green.

'It was the gin talking,' she replies.

That lifts my hackles, because I know it's a barefaced lie. I rotate on my heel to face her. 'Did Grace ever visit you?'

When a slow smile spreads across her lips, all the blood drains from my face. 'Yes.'

'On her own?'

'Yes.'

She knows I hate this and she loves it. Now she has the upper hand. I wish I could slap away that smug expression.

'Well? When? Recently?'

'Two weeks ago.'

I shift my weight from one foot to the other. Though I'd come to my mother all guns blazing – after all, when bad things happen in my life, it's usually connected to my mother – I hadn't expected this. The last time I saw the two of them together was at a disastrous Christmas dinner three years ago. Charles had hoped to repair our relationship by inviting Mum as a surprise to us both. It was his first Christmas since his mother had passed, and it had awakened the romantic notion in him that family must appreciate each other no matter what.

I can't stop myself from asking, 'What did you do? What did you talk about?'

'We talked about you.' Her voice is soft; she is relishing the power this new information has given her. 'Among other things.'

'Was she upset about anything?'

'They were private talks, Katie.'

My hands ball into fists of frustration. 'Well now she's dead, so I don't think her secrets matter anymore.' My chest tightens, like elastic wound into a knot. *Grace is dead. My daughter is dead. She's dead.* Every time I say it, it doesn't sound real. A bizarre combination of words that string together to make no sense whatsoever. Standing in the garden of my childhood home, facing my childhood bully, I feel too far away from my daughter. I need to go home and be in her room again. Why did I leave? Why did I come here?

'We talked about school, what she was up to, that kind of thing.' She shrugs. 'Maybe you didn't know your daughter as well as you thought you did...' Mum backs away from the door. There's a hint of a smile on her face, slowly turning into a smirk, because she's won the game, she's rattled me to my core. A question runs through my mind: *Did you ever even care about Grace?* But I can't muster up the strength to say the words out loud.

And with that, the door closes. A fleck of old, dry paint flutters from the door frame, mere inches from my nose. Before I walk away, I peel another long, crumbling piece of paint from the wood, giving myself a moment to stop shaking.

Did you make me who I am, Mum? And, in turn, did I affect who you were, Grace?

On the journey home, I long for Mum's bottle of gin to warm up my freezing insides. This driver is thankfully a silent one, and we pass through the rolling green hills of Derbyshire without a peep between us. There's nothing left in me for idle conversation. If I'd thought I was hollowed out after the hospital this morning, the meeting with my mother has destroyed what was left. I find myself scrolling through my phone, because when my fingers are at rest they quiver like an alcoholic's.

What did you do, Grace? Why would you willingly go to that woman? Didn't she know that my mother is nothing more than a spider waiting for prey?

But Mum could well be lying about those visits. It might be one of her cruel games to twist the knife. She never laid a finger on me when I was a child, but I don't remember her smiling unless I was crying. There's no doubt in my mind that every bit of badness in me I owe to my mother. Every manipulation, every time I lash out, it's because I learned it from her.

All the good parts of me were shaped by Grace. Not even my mother can take that away from me. I won't let her.

The closer we get to Farleigh Hall, the more the memories of Grace come flooding in. Charles's family estate is a few miles out of a small village called Ash Dale, between Bakewell and Buxton. The taxi swings through the village, following the path of the Wye, with views of the Peak District all around us. It's in Ash Dale that Grace went to primary school, where she learned how to read and write, how to add up numbers and make friends with other children. She went orienteering in the woods behind the mining museum. If you take a right out of Ash Dale village instead of following the main road to the left, you reach the Ash Mills, part of the industrial landscape that Charles's ancestors helped to shape. I once made a Victorian-style outfit for Grace to wear on a school trip there. She learned all about Geoffrey Cavanaugh, the man who built Farleigh Hall: a great Victorian industrialist who owned several paint factories in and around the area, along with, of all things, Stonecliffe Quarry. The thought has me reeling, my belly full of gin flipping over like it's on a spin cycle, but the driver doesn't notice as I briefly close my eyes to steady myself.

The taxi travels up the hill from Ash Dale, moving away from the Wye, bending with the roads as they narrow and narrow. Finally, we come to a wider area with a flat expanse of never-ending green, and in the middle of all that green is Farleigh Hall. The taxi veers right onto the driveway, gravel crunching beneath the tyres, through two wrought-iron gates built in 1885. How many times did I drive Grace through these gates after collecting her from school? How many times did I ask her to turn the radio down as she bopped along to One Direction, her hair swinging from side to side? How many times did I roll my eyes as she formed a heart shape out of her fingers to express her love for Zayn?

She'd been a bubbly girl before the teenage years set in. While there were fewer hearts and not as much One Direction, my Grace was still a cheerful soul all the way up to seventeen. She'd never donned black eyeliner and Doc Martens and grunted like the girls I went to school with.

We pass the stables (empty since Charles's deceased mother, Emily, stopped riding), the aged and battered Land Rover (because old money doesn't need to shout about it), the woodshed, the tasteful cherub statue on the drive and, finally, we reach the house.

Grace called it the 'cross house' when she was four years old. Rich, romantic Geoffrey built the house in mock Tudor style, with black beams criss-crossing over the whitewashed walls. Climbing ivy loops over the archway of the front door. This brings back memories of Grace at that age, trying to grasp the leaves dangling down whenever Charles carried her into the house.

Both Georgie and Porgie are whining at the door when I enter, tails wagging, eyes big and confused. I've learned to recognise that these are their hungry faces. I head into the old pantry, now converted into a utility room, to feed them.

'Don't bother.' A stumbling Charles approaches, stops and leans against the door frame. 'I already fed them.'

Idly stroking one on the nose, I examine the two dogs more closely. 'They're looking for Grace.'

Charles nods and his head bobs up and down, chin hitting chest. 'Do you think they know?'

Charles shrugs. 'Maybe. I think they knew when Mum passed. I still take them to her grave every week and they sit there for a few minutes.' He leans down and scratches the ears of one of the dogs. I think it's Porgie, judging by the slightly more amber tint of his eyes.

'I didn't know you visited Emily's grave every week.' Would a good wife know that her husband visited his mother's grave every week? *Should* a good wife know?

'I'll have another grave to visit soon. So will you. Unless we decide on a cremation. What do you think?' Despite slurring his words a smidge, Charles seems to have pulled himself together. He crouches down, staring up at me with bloodshot eyes, Porgie licking his fingers.

'I don't… I hadn't.' The thought of Grace in the cold ground repulses me, makes me feel dirty. But if we cremate her she'll burn away to nothing. 'I need some air.' The utility room is too small and musty, stinking of wellies and damp umbrellas. Grace never did air out her umbrella after the latest downpour like I asked.

'We need to decide, Kat. We need to arrange the funeral.' He follows me out of the room and into the kitchen, the sound of the dogs pattering behind. 'Oh.' He stops and sighs. 'I forgot to ask how it went.'

'How you'd imagine. Where's that whisky you were drinking?' Cupboard doors open and slam shut. My head continues to throb – not that alcohol will help that. Grace's mug, with a large gold G on it, stares at me from the middle shelf.

'Is she going to come and stay with us? Help out with the funeral?'

'No.' I close the cupboard door, turn to him and lean against the counter.

'I'm sorry, Kat,' he says.

But I'm shaking my head. 'What for?'

His eyes are wet again. He pulls me into a hug, but for once it doesn't feel like it's meant for him.

Charles and I aren't a touchy-feely couple. He knows that I hate most body contact. We certainly don't go walking down the street hand in hand like a couple of teenagers. Yet I lean in to him and I hold him close. He's soft and warm, smelling like lemon and sandalwood.

'How are you holding up?' he asks. 'Because I'm a total fucking mess.'

'I… Well…' Before I can answer, the house phone shrieks. Usually one of the maids would pick up the phone, but they haven't been here since Grace failed to come back from school yesterday.

Charles moves across the room to take the call, leaving me with an oddly cold aftertaste. At least I find the bottle of Scotch on the breakfast bar. I grab a tumbler, pour a large measure and promise myself that this is my last one. We've both had too much to drink; I'm aware of that. But what else will take me away from the grim reality? Every time I close my eyes, I see her face. I see blue fingernails and blue-tinged skin.

'Yes. Right. Okay.'

Is it our first condolence call? There's been no announcement yet. Soon an outpouring of grief will begin, because Ash Dale is far too small a village not to mourn the bright and beautiful. They'll mourn Grace and cry for her and they'll send us food, but none of them will want to help uncover the truth. I'll be on my own for that, mark my words. Luckily, I have enough simmering anger at my disposal to make sure whoever hurt her will pay. Because there's no way Grace killed herself. No way.

'Are… are you sure? No, that's not possible.' Charles's voice begins to tremble.

I set down the glass and move closer to my husband, until we're face-to-face and I can clearly see the pallor that has spread across his skin. There are tiny droplets of sweat on his upper lip.

'What is it?' I mouth.

Could it be the police calling to inform us of a development? Evidence that someone pushed her, perhaps? Bruise marks on her skin, or… or worse? Was she hit? Did she suffer?

He hangs up, drops his gaze. Won't look at me.

'What is it?'

A shiver of fear snakes down my spine.

'Grace was two months pregnant at the time of her death,' he says at last.

I don't react, simply stare at him silently, every part of me still. *Grace was two months pregnant...* The sentence sounds alien. I have no emotional connection to what he's saying to me; it's nothing more than a jumble of words that don't belong together.

'What? But that's not possible. She was just a kid!' Her Ariana Grande posters are still on the wall. There's a stuffed bear on a shelf. Her nail-polish colours range from pink to bright yellow. How could that same girl, my *child*, be pregnant?

'They're sure, Kat. Grace... she was... she would've had a baby.'

The betrayal of what he's saying to me hits me hard in the abdomen, like two short, sharp punches. I take a moment before I draw air back into my lungs. It's as I take a second breath that I become fully awake. *She would've had a baby...*

I open my eyes and allow my anger to take shape, to give me the strength I so desperately need. Whoever hurt my daughter has no idea who they are dealing with or the lengths I will go to in order to find out what happened to my child.

My mother did not exaggerate my past. There are certain things about me that no one in my carefully crafted, perfect life knows. I'd put my previous behaviour behind me for one person: Grace. Now Grace is gone.

CHAPTER FIVE

Silently, Charles and I make our way to the nearest chairs, by the kitchen table, and sink into them. We sit next to each other, neither one of us looking at the other. Both sickly, pale versions of ourselves, like two crumbling statues. He has no idea of the decision I've made. He thinks I'm taking in all of this, slowly, like him. What I'm actually doing is trying to figure out where to start in order to find out who impregnated my little girl. To find out what happened to her. Did she even know she was pregnant?

'Did she have a boyfriend?' Charles asks. 'I… Why didn't I know about any of this?'

'She did,' I reply. 'But… I didn't know about the baby either, you know. She never told me.'

Yes, I knew about the boyfriend, but I hadn't even entertained the idea that Grace was having sex. The boy she'd once brought to the house was short with mousy-brown hair, struggling to grow a moustache. He never came across as much to worry about. I'd thought she could do much better, but that was about it. Teenage girls tend to develop differently to boys. Girls are beautiful in a gangly, giggly way at that age, whereas the boys are awkward creatures, in-between any kind of identity, sporting patchy facial hair and dousing themselves in terrible aftershave.

But what if I'd fallen into the same trap so many other mothers fall into? *Everyone else's kid is having sex and drinking and staying out late, but not* my *kid. My kid is special.* My child is – *was* – perfect, at least to me, and the idea of contemplating anything other than that perfection hurts almost as much as the fact that I'll never see her again.

'What's his name? I'm going to kill him.' My usually mild-mannered husband is on his feet in half a heartbeat, red blotches spreading from chin to chest as though he's been tie-dyed. His mad eyes roam, find my glass of whisky; he lifts it and lobs it into the oven door, breaking both.

'Fuck!' he yells. 'Fuck. This.'

'Come here, sweetheart.' I gesture to him with my arms out wide. This is what he needs – more comfort. For once I wish Emily was here, to take some of the comforting responsibility. In life, I resented her closeness to my husband, but now I wish she was here to help carry this *weight* that's pressing down on me. 'You're not going to kill Grace's boyfriend.' He folds into my arms. His head rests on my shoulder and I stroke his hair.

He's not going to kill Grace's boyfriend – not if I have anything to do about it. If that mousy-haired man-child had anything to do with her death, I will get there first. Because I can do it without remorse. It won't be the first time I've watched the life fade from somebody's eyes.

What no one understands is that Grace was the one who kept me sane, who kept me *good*, because I'm merely pretending to be an upstanding member of society. I take my bins out on time, I smile at people walking their dogs and I follow the Highway Code, but the real reason I do these things is to fit in without drawing attention to myself.

I have antisocial personality disorder, diagnosed during my troubled and violent teenage years.

The reason I've behaved myself for all this time is Grace, because I wanted my daughter to be raised by good people who loved her. I had to *learn* how to be a good wife and mother. Now that she's gone, I don't have to worry about any of that anymore. And where does that leave me? Do I quit my therapy sessions? Do I stop trying to be good? Here are my claws, retracted and blunt from lack of use, waiting for me to make a decision.

Grace was not suicidal. She didn't have any darkness in her; she was bright and happy. But maybe her pregnancy had something to do with her death? If I'm going to figure this out, I need to be open to all possibilities. Not only did she suffer at the bottom of that quarry, her fingernails clawing the muddy ground, but there was a life slowly dying inside her. What size was Grace when I was two months pregnant? The size of a bean, I remember them saying.

Why didn't she tell me she was having sex?

Charles falls asleep on the sofa, the whisky finally catching up with him, and I slip away up the stairs to Grace's room. I should be calling people – Grace's friends, Charles's aunt, my lunch friends. The truth is, there are painfully few people to call, and I want to focus on getting some answers first.

That smell hits me again as I open the door. She used special purple-coloured shampoo to lighten her blonde hair and that's the scent I first notice. I walk straight into the bathroom, open the bottle and inhale. It's like she's in the room with me. Lavender and patchouli. A laugh, a hair flick, a sing-song voice mocking my outfit.

This is the first time I've been in her bathroom for months, and I'm rather in awe of being here. I'm not a prying mother. I've always given Grace her personal space, partly because that is what a *good person* would do, and partly, after seeing the way my own mother snooped through my belongings, because I didn't want to subject Grace to the same treatment. But maybe I should have snooped? Maybe that would've kept her alive.

I open the cabinet on the wall, crammed full of face masks and body lotions. After every sleepover Grace attends, she always comes back with more. I have a hunt through the mess but there's nothing of interest in here. Grace will never go to a sleepover again, never have fun, laugh, cry. It takes all my self-control not to smash the mirror on the cabinet door.

There's nothing in the bathroom that will help me. No pregnancy tests or birth control items. I'd understood that Lady Margaret's was a school with a decent sex-education programme. Charles and I were far too squeamish to bring up the subject at home. There's another big strike against our parenting skills. My mother's cutting words ring in my mind. Did I cause this? Is it all my fault?

I'm lightheaded as I make my way back into Grace's room, throbbing pain radiating from my temples. But I've come to appreciate it. Why shouldn't I be hurting when Grace is cold, blue and missing her fingernail? I don't want to feel anything other than pain and anger, because that's what I deserve for failing her.

I'm tempted to crawl onto her bed and sleep, but I force myself to search for clues, starting with the boyfriend, Ethan. What happened there? Is he the father? Who else could it be? Does he know about the pregnancy? Did *she*? You hear stories of teenage girls giving birth in the school toilets because they didn't understand their bodies enough to recognise the signs.

There are too many unanswered questions and I'm not sure where to find the answers I need.

Grace's laptop is on the desk, still plugged in and charging from yesterday. Charles doesn't like it when Grace leaves things charging in her room; he doesn't trust electronics not to burst into flame. I unplug it and then sink into the bed, pulling the laptop onto my knees. It smells even more like Grace here: the patchouli mixed with the tang of her sweat. One day these sheets will stop smelling like her and then nothing will smell like her again.

The laptop boots up, but it's password-protected. Grace loves the dogs, so I type in Georgie, then Porgie, then georgieporgie. None work. Next I try Georgiep0rgie – and I'm in. If there's one thing I know about my daughter, it's that she could while away hours on this machine. Often I'd walk into the family room and find her curled up on the sofa with headphones on, watching another YouTube star shouting at the camera. None of it made sense to me, but Grace would giggle away. She even started her own YouTube channel, which is where I start. I want to hear her voice.

'Hi, everyone. So, today I want to show you my super quick-and-easy guide for playing "Shake It Off" on the violin…'

It takes my breath away, seeing her moving, talking, being. Her hair is more honey than white here, imitating my own shade of blonde. This is her most viewed video, filmed before she started transitioning into the platinum locks sported by her friends at Lady Margaret's.

I pause the video to steady myself, but as I do, the image of her blue lips jumps into my mind. Every memory is tainted by the sight of her dead body. My abdomen aches from missing her, the pain starting to overtake my headache. God, I long for this day to be over, for it to be a cataclysmic glitch in the overarching plan of life. This is all a terrible mistake. Grace didn't die. The universe fucked up. Here she is, alive and well, ready to yell at me for snooping around on her laptop.

I press play. There's an awkward silence as she lifts the bow, ready to play her first notes. Then the sound of her violin fills the room, slow and deep and beautiful. Listening to it makes me want to hear her perform the classical pieces she often rehearsed before orchestra practice. Those were the ones that haunted the house, seeping into every room and making it warmer than before. Those are the pieces I hope to dream about when I finally rid my memory of her blue lips.

Grace.

Instead, I'll probably dream of her in the hospital. Another dead body in my nightmares.

I pull my thoughts away before they spiral out of control and force myself to concentrate. There are many videos to choose from on her channel, which is much more popular than I'd realised while Grace was alive. Not all of them are about the violin; some were filmed with a GoPro as she took the dogs for a walk, running through the meadows at the back of the house. There are other excitable girls in her videos, all of whom I recognise from parties, shopping trips, sleepovers and outside the school gates. There's Alicia, picking daisies and placing them in Grace's hair. She's silver-haired and beautiful, tall and slim enough to wear a crop top and leggings. Then there's Sasha, another violinist from the school orchestra, with olive skin and curly dark hair – a quiet girl who played duets with Grace. I begin to make notes. What was it that DS Slater said in the waiting room? Teenagers are under a lot of pressure from exams and personal relationships. Could one of these people have contributed to Grace's death?

Ethan, however, does not feature on the YouTube channel, and I deliberate why. Perhaps he's the odd kind of teenager who eschews social media, preferring to be incognito. I should try her Instagram or Facebook account to see if he pops up there.

But for some reason, she doesn't have autofill set up for Instagram or Facebook. I try her YouTube password but that doesn't work, so I get up from the bed, move over to her desk, and begin to go through her drawers, trying to remember if Grace had a place she kept her passwords. I know there was a notebook she often wrote in, but was it where she kept a password log?

And why wouldn't my tech-savvy teenage daughter, who used to set up our gadgets, not have autofill installed on her web browser? That in itself is odd. Who did she think would log on to her computer? Was she deliberately hiding information from me?

It's as I'm rifling through Grace's drawers that it hits me. I don't know where Grace's phone is. The police never mentioned her phone during the interview. They haven't released her belongings yet, but they showed us the alleged suicide note. Why wouldn't they tell us if her phone had been recovered? And why wouldn't they check her messages? Did they check it and find nothing relevant? Or was the phone not found at all? There is no way that Grace would ever leave the house without her phone. That's my next step. I need to find that phone.

CHAPTER SIX

At home, the condolence calls have started coming through, but where I am now is silent and still. There's no chair – only a table, where a cold, lifeless body lies. Just me and her. Moving slowly, so as not to interrupt the quiet, I reach out and push Grace's blonde hair away from her face, wishing that she hadn't dyed it such a bright platinum. I miss the honey highlights and the brown lowlights. I miss the way she once resembled me as a teen, with blue eyes that held a warmth, like seas in hot countries. But the platinum colour bleached away all the highlights and lowlights and somehow changed the colour of her eyes.

Now that Grace has been through the post-mortem, the blue tinge of her skin has been airbrushed away by the funeral home, but I still can't stop thinking about that day in the morgue when Charles and I identified her body. I stroke my fingertips against hers; the dirt is gone and her nails are bare.

I called DS Slater as soon as I realised that Grace's phone was missing. They had an update for me, too. The coroner's office had decided not to investigate following the post-mortem. Grace's injuries were consistent with her fall and there was no sign of a struggle. DS Slater promised me, earnestly, that he had personally spent the last few days checking the quarry, examining CCTV from the few cameras in Ash Dale and asking around to find out if Grace had been alone. He told me that no one had seen Grace with anyone else. He believes she acted alone. He believes that Grace threw herself from the top of Stonecliffe Quarry, the Suicide

Spot. She then bounced against the jagged rock edge, broke her leg, punctured the skin and bled to death as she desperately tried to drag herself back up the steps carved out of the stone with one of her wrists broken. The suicide note survived, tucked away in her pocket. Inside her school bag there were exercise books, a pencil case, a make-up bag and a purse. There was no sign of her mobile phone.

'She would've had her phone,' I'd insisted.

'I agree,' he'd replied, again with that soothing, calm tone, 'because I don't know of any seventeen-year-old who leaves the house without a phone. But there are many possible explanations. She might have lost it. Has she ever lost her phone before?'

'Well, once,' I'd admitted.

'That could be it.'

But I'd hung up unconvinced.

Now that the investigation is over, we can arrange the funeral. But the thought of burying her… As I grip the edge of the cold metal table, fingertips a centimetre from Grace's left shoulder, I can't imagine watching her arrive at the house in a hearse.

The condolence calls began this morning because Grace's death has been reported by the news: MISSING TEENAGER GRACE CAVANAUGH HAS BEEN FOUND DEAD. POLICE ARE NOT TREATING HER DEATH AS SUSPICIOUS.

No, there's nothing suspicious about Grace's death, I think bitterly. She was a seventeen-year-old pregnant girl. She was a promising violin player, working towards her A levels. Her father is a businessman – rich, busy, high-powered. Everything about Grace, on paper, points to a life of high stress, high pressure. But no one knew her like I did.

If she weren't dead on this table, she would be clinging to my side, arm looped in mine. Grace was the opposite of me, needy and empathetic, often demanding more of me than I thought it possible to give. She stretched me to my limits in terms of affection and love, and yet the more she demanded, the more I found within myself.

Grace wasn't highly strung, she was relaxed and well-adjusted. There was a learning curve when she first started secondary school, but she eventually became popular because she had an easy way with people, not just because she was pretty and clever. I watched her, I saw her with her friends and I knew her.

'But you were pregnant.' The part that doesn't fit in my picture of Grace. 'You didn't tell me. I was right there, Grace, right under your nose, and you didn't tell me what had happened to you. How did it happen? Did you make a mistake? Did someone hurt you?' For all I know, this *Ethan* isn't even the father. But I can't allow my mind to spin out of control with conspiracy theories. Grace had a boyfriend, they both decided to take the next step and they made a mistake. It's a familiar tale told around family dinner tables across the world. *Mum, Mom, Ma, Mama, I'm pregnant.*

But not for me. You never let me in.

'Did I ever really know you, Grace?' As I speak, my jaw aches and my fingers are sore, all from the tension in my body, from gripping the table, from clenching my teeth together.

And did *she* ever know *me*?

When Grace rejected me after her birth, I thought it was because she sensed who I was. Perhaps it emanated from me like a pheromone, detected only by animals and babies.

There are seven billion people in the world, all connected in some way. We're related to each other, we love one another, we irritate each other, we say hello on the street and recognise faces from our local shop, we hold hands, we fight, we eat together, we drink, we give each other gifts at Christmas, we throw parties for colleagues and celebrate the birth of a new baby. But is this picture of the world as one big happy family nothing more than a fantasy? Is this the tale we tell ourselves at night? We understand that wars and serial killers exist, but we also tell ourselves that world peace is possible. What we don't understand is that four per cent of those seven billion people don't care about anyone else but themselves. They are sociopaths, and they can live however they like because they lack a conscience. They aren't connected to anyone else on this earth. They don't love, and they only give you a gift at Christmas because they want to play pretend.

When I was thirteen years old, I saw several child psychologists because of my behaviour, and one of them suggested that I suffered from antisocial personality disorder. A sociopath. I believed I was part of that remorseless four per cent until Grace came along and I began to feel what I thought was love.

My relationship with newborn Grace didn't form right away. I didn't have an epiphany while watching a tiny fuzzy jelly bean on a screen. My ice-cold interior didn't melt the first time I heard her heartbeat inside me, and I didn't cry tears of joy when I felt her kick from within. For the majority of my pregnancy, Grace was a means to securing a better future. She was my ticket out of hell.

I don't believe that a mother's love is strong enough to destroy the effects of sociopathy with one magical unicorn horn to the heart. There are far too many bad mothers in the world to suggest that. However, the way I came to feel about my daughter can only be described as unconditional love. No one was more shocked than I was. But her existence made me *want* to love. For the first time, I *wanted* to love her like non-sociopaths love their children. I even sought professional help, and together with my therapist, I discovered that I could love and nurture her. I'd assumed, because of what I am, that I wouldn't be able to.

Because of Grace, I learned to live in this society without leaving oily footprints wherever I stepped. At first I wasn't sure how to be a good force in the world. At the age of twenty-two, after living for several years without caring about anyone else, I had to learn what it is that makes someone *good*. It was at this time that I decided to adopt the 'fake it till you make it' philosophy to life. If I could pretend to be a good person every single day, then maybe one day I'd wake up and I truly would be a good person.

'I'm sorry, Grace,' I whisper to her. 'I can't be good anymore.'

I'm too tired to be good. Now, all I can do is run with anger towards whoever hurt my daughter. My grief started out uncertain and unformed, but I've twisted it into an arrow with a purpose. That arrow points to a problem I must solve: who murdered my daughter?

CHAPTER SEVEN

There are flowers on our doorstep. White lilies. Once again, I think of how Grace loved colour: pinks, purples, reds and yellows. All of this *white* and all of this *blue*. I will hate white lilies until the day I die.

'White lilies would be perfect for the service, don't you think?' Charles says. 'Who are they from?'

I search the bouquet for a card. 'I guess the florist forgot to attach the card. I don't know.'

'Maybe there's one inside,' he replies.

Sure enough, there is a pile of envelopes on the doormat, each containing a card of condolence, most featuring lily photography on the front. We make our way through them at the kitchen table, a bottle of whisky in the centre.

'I still can't accept it, Kat,' Charles says, wiping away tears and standing the cards up in a gaudy display that curdles my stomach. 'She was too young. She shouldn't have ever, *ever* wanted to take her own life. Why didn't we see it?'

I pause, remaining cautious. Charles has already dismissed my convictions that Grace was not suicidal. He believes and trusts the police, accepting their ruling of suicide without so much as a second thought. If I continue to push my beliefs, he might actively try to stop my own investigations.

'She hid it from us,' I say. 'If she knew, she chose not to tell us she was pregnant, and with A levels and everything else, maybe it was too much for her to cope with. What if she thought she'd let us down?' All of those things are true, and yet I don't believe for one minute that Grace would kill herself over any of them. She would have been nervous – afraid, even – to tell us about the baby, but to take her own life? No, I won't accept it.

'*We* let *her* down if she couldn't tell us.'

There's something about the way he regards me that makes me question whether he believes I was the one who truly let her down, not him. I'm the mother. I'm the one who should double up as the 'friend' for 'girl troubles'. This was my domain and she didn't tell me.

'We failed her.'

He's right: I failed her.

My personality disorder can make social clues tricky to decipher, but after almost eighteen years of living with Charles, I have a good read on his subtle put-downs. His long, hard stare tells me everything I need to know.

Then, with a sudden change of heart, he reaches across the table to take my hand. Perhaps the expression on my face revealed my thoughts and he felt guilty. 'But we won't fail her again. We have one last chance to do right by her. And we will.'

On the day Grace died, I was annoyed that she was late home from school. Whenever she was meeting a friend, I almost always got a text message – *Getting food with Alicia. Back by eleven!* – followed by a long line of smiley faces. On the day she died, I didn't get any texts. I phoned her friends and she wasn't with them. I called Charles and he said she'd probably gone into the village for a hot chocolate. Or maybe she'd lost her phone.

It wasn't until she didn't come home that night that fear set in. It was the first time I'd felt real fear since I was six years old and I'd smashed my mum's favourite china doll. She'd loved that thing more than me. When she found out, she didn't speak to me for a week – and she didn't make me any food either. I lived on toast and butter because the toaster was all I could use.

None of that – not the fear that kept me awake the night she didn't come home, or the week-long silence at my mother's house – compared to the fear Grace must've felt when she was in the dirt at the bottom of the quarry. I stand above it now, staring down into the void, trying to experience what she must have felt. Putting myself in another person's shoes is never easy for me, but when I close my eyes I can picture my fingers deep in the crevices of the rocky wall, trying to pull myself up out of the hole I'd fallen into. My throat aches from screaming. My white-blonde hair sticks to my forehead.

I walk away from the Suicide Spot with the stench of rot lingering in my nostrils. The rain-drenched earth is slippery as I return to the Land Rover. I push my damp hair away from my eyes as I speed away, chills running through my arms and legs, a dull ache in my abdomen.

The Suicide Spot. A man threw himself over the edge some months ago. He was there a week. Alone. Dead. Body frozen from the cold weather. Even if Grace was suicidal, why would she choose a place like that, knowing that she might not be found right away? Why would she want us to see her battered, bruised body? Why did she leave us with nothing except for that unemotional note? With parts of it scribbled out rather than written again to at least make it neat.

I'm shaking my head as I drive back to the road. What I'm supposed to be doing is going to the florist to choose the flowers for the service while Charles calls his aunt, his one remaining living relative. What I'm actually about to do is pay a visit to another person who may or may not have hurt my daughter, because the longer I leave it, the easier it is to bury the truth.

None of Grace's friends have called the house, only their parents. That makes a lot of sense. Dealing with grieving parents is an adult's job. But it means that I haven't spoken to any of the people who saw Grace most often – her friends who sat next to her in class, went to the library with her and ate lunch with her at the canteen. It's the students in Lady Margaret's sixth form I should be talking to, and the first teenager I'm going to see is Ethan Hancock, Grace's boyfriend.

I take the road back down to Ash Dale village, chasing the Wye, stopping for the midday cattle movement between the upper and lower fields of the Buckland Farm. David, the owner, leaves his farmhand to it and comes over to the car, leaning on the door when I wind the window open.

'How are you holding up?' he asks.

'I'm up, I suppose,' I reply.

'She was a lovely girl. Carol always said how nice she was. If you need anything, pop on over. Carol will have food and a cuppa if you want one.' He tips his flat cap and goes on his way.

The word is spreading around the village. David slaps one of the dairy cows on its backside, the border collie nipping at his heels, and my foot hovers over the accelerator, desperate to get away from them all. I wind the window back up, block out the scent of cow dung and lean back against the headrest.

That's what they'll all say to me, words that don't mean a thing. *Lovely. Nice. Bright. Smashing. Wonderful.* Christ, that's how Grace will be remembered. How long will it take them to forget her?

The last of the cows shits out a long spray of brown liquid as it waddles through the five-bar gate to the next field, making its slow way down to the milking barn. David and his farmhand speed off in the Land Rover, the collie running alongside the cows, barking joyfully.

Further into the village, I pass the church and notice flowers placed on the entrance steps. Are those for Grace? No one has placed flowers at the quarry. If she had died in a car accident, there would be supermarket bouquets taped to lamp posts, but this is a 'suicide'. Maybe no one wants to sully themselves by heading to the spot where a girl threw herself over the edge. Maybe they're praying for her unfortunate soul at the church instead.

Because I've never been to Ethan Hancock's home before, I need to keep one eye on the satnav as I make my way through Ash Dale and out towards Bakewell. His house is five minutes outside of the village on a road called Ivy Lane. I never quite know what to expect when driving around this part of the countryside: sometimes the roads are wide, busy and taken over by tourists towing their caravans; other times they are narrow dirt tracks leading between farm estates. This one is somewhere in-between, on a flat stretch outside the village containing identical semi-detached properties with neat front gardens.

I pull up next to number fifteen. This house is where Grace spent many an evening or Saturday with another family, and yet this is the first time I've been here. As far as I know, Grace and Ethan had been seeing each other for around three months. I have spoken to Ethan's mother, Louise, on the phone, but I'd never noticed her at the school gates when Grace was younger. This will be our first face-to-face conversation.

The house is very regular, with a rose bush in the front and a Vauxhall on the drive. The first time I saw Ethan, I figured that Grace could do better, and the sight of this house isn't convincing me otherwise. I press the doorbell and wait. Am I about to meet the boy who could've been my son-in-law? If Grace hadn't died, would she and Ethan have married to raise their baby together? As I stand and wait, that familiar anger builds up again. What will he be like, the boy who impregnated my daughter? The boy who possibly killed her, too.

CHAPTER EIGHT

When the door opens, the woman behind it greets me with an expression of pure horror. 'Mrs Cavanaugh. I didn't... I mean... I was devastated to hear about Grace.' She blinks at me, her pale face in shock.

'I'm intruding, aren't I?' It's clear that Ethan's mother wasn't prepared for dealing with a grieving parent today. 'It's Louise, isn't it?'

'Yes,' she says. 'I mean, yes, it's Louise, but you aren't intruding at all. Come in.'

I've never seen a picture of Louise before, but it doesn't surprise me that she recognises my face. Even before Grace didn't come home from school she would have seen pictures of us at some point. Charles and I feature on the display boards at the school as donors, as well as appearing in the pages of magazines like *Tatler* when we organise charity functions in Ash Dale and London. I should probably recognise Louise from those days of collecting Grace at the school gates, before she started catching the bus or meeting friends to walk home, but the truth is she's not noticeable to me. She has one of those mousy, small-featured faces that all blend in with each other.

She leads me through a very beige hallway to an even more beige lounge. A sign on the wall tells me to 'Live, Laugh, Love'. I desperately want to give Louise the name of my interior designer. But that would be inappropriate and mean. That's not the kind of behaviour I would set as an example for my daughter.

'Tea?'

Louise catches me as I'm lowering my head and sighing, in contemplation of the choices I made when Grace was alive. Do I still need to live by example? Has that ended now? Do I stop trying to be a better person?

'Tea would be lovely.'

Louise's eyes have widened a little. She sees a broken woman before her and she doesn't know how to act. I'm not sure I blame her for that; I know I wouldn't want someone like me turning up on the doorstep.

'I won't be a moment,' she says, brightening her smile to cover up the awkwardness. 'Make yourself at home.'

The deep cushions of the sofa are perfect for making myself at home. While cupboard doors open and a kettle boils, the fat family cat wanders in and sits itself down on a very hairy armchair. Both cats and teenagers claim their own spots in the family home, which makes me consider moving Grace's chair to another room when I get home. The thought of sitting in our family room staring at an empty chair makes my breath catch in my throat.

'Would you like milk?' Louise bustles into the room with a tray. 'Oh, I see you've met Marmaduke. That's his chair – he always sits there.'

'Milk is good, thank you.'

She spills a drop as she pours, mumbling to herself as she cleans it up. I take the mug and place it on a coaster on the coffee table.

'I was just distraught to hear about Grace,' she says at last. There's a wobble in her voice, a catch of emotion. 'She spent some time here with Ethan over the last few months. She was a lovely girl and I, well, all of us, can't believe it. Ethan has been very quiet; he's obviously very upset about it all. I think they were… close.'

She knew they were boyfriend and girlfriend then. And yet she's reluctant to say the words; I wonder why that is. Does she suspect that her son had something to do with Grace's death? Louise's eyes flit from mine to the black rectangle of the TV, to the window, to Marmaduke and back to me. This is not unusual and doesn't faze me in the slightest. Maintaining eye contact is very easy for me, but it can be uncomfortable for others. I've read that this is typical of someone with antisocial personality disorder. It's the way I take the measure of a person, figure them out – how strong or weak a person is, how easy they are to manipulate.

Louise seems nervous and uncomfortable. Her home indicates that she's very regular, not someone who strikes me as a deep thinker. But she's a mum and she has a son to protect, which makes her dangerous.

'Did you get our card?' Louise asks. 'Ethan picked it himself. He wanted one with flowers on it because he said she liked flowers.'

'Grace loved nature,' I say. 'Is Ethan home? In fact, it's flowers that I'd like to talk about. I'm arranging Grace's funeral and I'd like to chat to some of the people closest to Grace…' I clear my throat, glancing down at my tea. Then I lift my chin up and look her squarely in the eye. 'Us parents never quite know our kids, do we? I mean, do you even know Ethan's favourite band right now?'

Louise rolls her eyes. 'It changes every week.' She sips her tea and allows herself the tiniest of chuckles. She's beginning to relax, which is what I want.

'Grace was the same. I can't believe she's gone. I keep expecting her to walk in through the door and throw her bag down on the table like she always did.' I shake my head.

Louise puts down her tea, frowns and pulls a few tissues from a box by the fireplace. 'I'm sorry.' She dabs at her eyes. 'She was such a beautiful girl. You must be heartbroken.'

I recognise some of the posters on Ethan's wall because they're the same bands the kids at my school hero-worshipped when I was a teenager. The circle of idolisation has found a new audience with the next generation of young people who think they're outsiders, when in fact they're going through the exact same awkward phase as thousands of kids have already been through. Alongside a black-and-white still of Rage Against the Machine in concert is an artistic shot of Billie Joe Armstrong from Green Day, and alongside Billie is a large poster of a cannabis leaf. Che Guevara watches me from above Ethan's bedside table.

Below all the posters, Ethan is sitting on his desk chair, one leg tucked underneath the other, his free leg swinging back and forth. His eyes are cast down, which results in me having to stare at the top of his head as I perch on the edge of his single bed. His hair is stiff with gel. The room is stuffy and the lingering scent of dirty underwear fills my nostrils, but at least here I can talk to him alone, which is what I wanted. Louise allowed me this because I asked her for it. Who can refuse a grieving mother?

'How are you holding up?' I ask, taking it slowly. Inside, I'm raging, bulging with questions that demand answers. Did this spotty idiot make a baby with my daughter? Did they argue about the pregnancy? Did he push her into the quarry because she wanted to keep the baby?

He sniffs, pokes at his jeans, doesn't meet my gaze. 'I'm okay. Just miss her, I guess.'

'I do too.'

The screensaver on his computer is a colourful photograph of Snoop Dogg smoking a spliff. I'm curious to know whether Louise thinks these are all ironic statements. More likely she's lost control over her wayward son. When I was a teenager, no one would have cared if I was hanging out with a stoner. In fact, you could chuck a pebble into a classroom at my comprehensive school and it would inevitably land next to a kid who was using some form of illegal substance. But I can't believe I became the parent who didn't notice that her strait-laced daughter was involved with someone who may be going down the wrong path.

My gaze travels across the room, searching for signs of Grace. Did she give him that snow globe of New York City? Or maybe the poo-emoji keychain? I can imagine Grace finding that amusing. Where else is my daughter? Was she in the bed I'm sitting on? The one that hasn't been made?

When my skin grows hot with anger, I try to keep my thoughts calm, in the way that my therapist has taught me. Emotions don't tend to be a problem for me, but I do sometimes find other people frustrating. My therapist, Angela, has helped me deal with those everyday frustrations, but what she hasn't prepared me for, however, is what it's like to lose a child.

'Can you help me, Ethan?'

I let the question hang in the air until he raises his head to look at me. Do I imagine some insolence in the way he lifts his eyebrows?

Finally, as he meets my eyes, I smile. 'I'm planning Grace's funeral, but it's tougher than I ever could've imagined. The Grace I knew loved daisies and tulips, but parents don't always get to know their teenagers as well as they'd like to. You spent a lot of time with her, and your mum mentioned that you knew she liked flowers. What kind of flowers do you think I should get?'

Ethan picks at a loose thread on his hoody while I try to ascertain whether there are tears in his eyes. 'Tulips. Yellow ones.'

For some reason his answer hits me harder than I expect. Maybe he knew my daughter after all, because I would have ordered yellow tulips for her too. My eyes sting and I clear my throat, forcing myself to concentrate. 'What about music?'

Ethan brushes away a tear and stares out of the window. 'Taylor Swift, "Love Story".'

Again, I'm surprised. That's the song I would have chosen for her myself. Maybe, after finding out that Grace was pregnant, I'd convinced myself that she was some other person, a secret person that had been hidden away from me. But it's possible I was completely wrong.

'Thanks, Ethan. I really appreciate it. Would you like to speak at the funeral?'

He shakes his head. 'I can't. Sorry.'

The anger hits me again. She was your *girlfriend*, I think.

'Did you spend much time with Grace before she died? Did you see her at school that day?'

'I saw her,' he says. 'We hung out at lunch a bit.'

'Did she seem upset?'

He pulls the thread a little harder. 'She'd fallen out with her squad.'

'Her squad?'

'The mean girls. Alicia and them lot.'

I nod. The girls from the YouTube video. 'Did they fall out a lot?'

'I guess so,' he says. I can tell he's beginning to speculate why I'm asking him all these questions.

'I never thought Grace would hurt herself,' I say. 'Charles and I had no idea she was depressed. What about you, Ethan? Did you see it?'

'No,' he says, his voice rising slightly. 'No, of course not.'

'Because you would have helped.'

He nods. 'Yeah.' And then he looks away.

'What is it?' I prod.

He's gone back to not meeting my eyes, directing his gaze away from me out of the window, back to the desk, back to the window again. 'We had a stupid fight. I wish we hadn't. It was those stupid girls, they were being bitches to her. I guess I didn't say the right thing or whatever. She doesn't... she... she gets so *irrational* sometimes.' He pauses, aware of his mistake. 'Got.'

'Irrational?' I ask.

He just shrugs. The clock on his wall, adorned with the Derby County football badge, ticks away the seconds, and for a few heartbeats I'm taken back to the stale room at my mother's house. I clear my throat and pull myself together.

'Were you the father, Ethan?'

He's still staring out of the window, with one tear in the corner of his eye. He frowns, then his head snaps towards me. 'What?'

'Were you the father of Grace's baby?'

'What?' His mouth drops open and his eyebrows knit together. He shakes his head slightly, as if in disbelief. 'What? I don't understand.'

'Grace was pregnant when she died, Ethan. Didn't you know that?'

The blood drains from his face. 'That isn't… That isn't possible.'

'It is,' I say calmly. 'She was pregnant. Why do you think it wasn't possible?'

'Because we didn't…' He rubs his eyes with the sleeve of his top. 'She wouldn't…'

'You didn't have sex?'

He can't meet my eye as he shakes his head again.

'But you were her boyfriend and she was pregnant when she died, so I find that a little hard to believe.'

A rasping noise escapes from his throat and his head bobs up and down, still with his sleeves balled into his eye sockets. When he speaks, it's muffled but high-pitched. 'We promised we'd wait. That's what she told me before…'

'Before what?' I ask.

'Before we decided to just be friends. We've not been going out for quite a while now. But she didn't want to tell anyone we weren't together anymore, so we kept it between ourselves and hung out as normal.' He rubs the palms of his hands on his jeans. 'I thought we might get back together, but we… didn't.'

'Are you telling me the truth?'

Ethan pulls a signet ring from his finger and flings it onto the carpet. I reach down and take it. It's gold, plain, boring. 'When we were still together we had promise rings. She gave me this. And then suddenly she wanted to be friends. I didn't get it. But we never… That's what the ring was for. To say we'd wait.'

I find myself surprised that I believe him. The idea of a promise ring is strange to me, but this generation is different, more sensitive perhaps. Did Grace have one that matched? I can't remember her ever wearing anything with such a dull design. Grace's jewellery usually involved some sort of nature symbol: bumblebee earrings, unicorn necklace, hummingbird ring.

'Is everything all right?' Louise appears at the door, half in, half out. Perhaps she has been listening to our conversation. I don't particularly care if she was. Charles might, though, when the gossip spreads throughout the village.

'I must get going, Louise. Thank you for the tea. And thank you, Ethan, for letting me know which flowers were her favourite. I'm sure Grace thought very highly of you.'

As far as I know, Grace did think highly of this boy, who is currently sitting on his desk chair sniffling, but I don't. I know bitterness when I see it and he's full of it. How long has he been angry with Grace for wanting to be friends rather than a couple? Though I don't trust Ethan, I do believe, until I'm proved wrong, that he didn't know about Grace's baby. But when he told me that Grace was upset, he dismissed her problems as insignificant and irrational. Perhaps he had an opportunity to save her and let it go. I'm not sure how great a part this boy played in my daughter's death, but I am sure that he wronged Grace, and I might have to find a punishment for that. Could I ever live with the loss of my daughter if I didn't?

CHAPTER NINE

A silver-haired girl laughs at the camera, while my Grace, still honey hued at this point, plays the theme to *Star Wars* on the violin. Occasionally Alicia joins in with her flute, making pretty eyes at the camera. The clip has been watched over fifty thousand times. How did I not know that Grace's videos were this popular? Her face has been seen by strangers all over the world. I scroll through the comments and find disturbing opinions about her appearance, the way she talks, how young she looks. From creepy to bitchy to downright strange, people word-vomit up their feelings about a three-minute clip of two teenage girls messing around in someone's bedroom.

Since the meeting with Ethan, I've been racking my brain in an attempt to decipher all the confusing aspects of Grace's death. Ethan appeared genuine to me, even if I didn't like him, but that means nothing. If he was telling the truth, then he isn't the father of Grace's baby. But if the father isn't Ethan, then who is? Now, a week after first identifying the body, I find myself leaving Charles alone with his demons while I invade Grace's space, immersing myself in her videos, watching her over and over, hoping the answers will hit me.

The video with the *Star Wars* theme wasn't recorded in Grace's room. The walls are a violet shade, there are posters of Little Mix on the wall and a black cat stretches lazily on a bed with pink sheets. This must be Alicia's room, the clip filmed there and then posted on Grace's vlog.

How many of these internet weirdos have sent a private message to my daughter? Had she been barraged by phallic imagery from perverts across the globe? Should I have banned my daughter from an activity that appears on the one hand an innocent pastime, and on the other a dangerous and reckless pursuit? At seventeen years old, Grace could have moved out and lived on her own if she wanted to. Then I wouldn't have been able to police anything at all. But while she resided here, under my roof, should I have done more? There's a line that every parent haphazardly walks: the line where we give our children enough freedom to allow them to evolve, while at the same time guarding them from danger. I always wanted to provide Grace with safety – because I never had it – but I also wanted her to grow, to make mistakes and to keep her heart open. It didn't work. Now here I am, hoping that if I watch this video over and over again, it might reveal the secrets Grace was hiding away from me before she died.

Yet again, my mind drifts back to the conversation I had with Ethan yesterday. He pointed the finger at Alicia and Sasha, suggesting that there'd been some sort of falling-out, but without Grace's phone, or her passwords to Facebook or Instagram, it's hard to know what happened. I need to see them, to be face-to-face when I ask them what happened. But first I want to see my daughter again. Not this clip of her laughing, which I've watched twenty times on a loop, but my actual daughter. She's alone. I need to be with her.

Perhaps it's morbid, but while I stand with the body of my daughter I listen to her last voicemail on repeat. It's a boring message. *Hey, going to orchestra rehearsal after school. Totally forgot about it so don't have a cow, okay? Bye.* It makes me sound like an ogre of a mother who yells at her kid for barely any reason, but it's clearly an exaggeration. When Grace turned thirteen I swiftly learned that teenagers are prone to them.

Her cold body has no answers and the voicemail is a fantasy I'm playing to myself to ease the pain of her absence. But nothing good can come of obsessing, of weeping over her lifeless corpse. Will the question of what happened to you keep me going, Grace? I hope so.

On the way back from the funeral home I take a left rather than a right, drive out of the village, up a narrow, winding road surrounded by wild garlic, and come to a sprawling house that I'm more than familiar with. While Uber drivers will come to Ash Dale, the teenagers here can't rely on them. Mum and Dad are the taxis until the kids pass their driving tests. I've spent many an evening ferrying Grace to Alicia's house, but I've never come here without her, or without collecting her.

There's a keypad next to the gate, a security feature that Emily Cavanaugh eschewed when she was alive. 'Oh, it's too "new money", darling,' she'd rasped to Charles. 'We're perfectly safe here.' And, honestly, she was probably right. I'd seen far more crime in poverty-stricken Old Barrow than in Ash Dale. Poor people steal from each other because it's easier. Stealing from the rich requires planning and smarts. If someone wants to rob us, a gate with a telecom probably isn't going to stop them.

'Jenny, it's Kat,' I say when the small silver box comes to life.

There's a pause, and then the gate opens. When I park up on the drive, she's waiting on the front steps with two spaniels scurrying around her feet. She's dramatically clutching a shawl about her shoulders despite there being no chill in the air, and I can already see that she's crying, her mouth gaping open and her eyebrows high up her forehead, like a clown imitating sadness.

Stop grieving for me.

'Kat!' Her arms open expectantly and a fat tear rolls down her cheek. I fold dutifully into her, inhaling her floral scent, placing my head down on the cashmere shawl. She withdraws, holds my shoulders and says, 'But I didn't expect to see you today. You must be in bits.'

'I need to ask Alicia a question,' I reply.

She nods. 'Of course you needed to come to Alicia and me. We were a unit, weren't we? I'll put the kettle on.'

The phrasing catches my attention because it isn't strictly true. While we are friends, we weren't a group of bezzie mates eating ice cream and watching sitcoms together. Warning bells ring in my head, as they often do when I'm around Jenny. Too often, Jenny exaggerates situations in a dramatic fashion. The thought of her doing the same with my daughter's death ignites that spark of anger I'm continually carrying with me. But at the same time, I might find answers here.

Jenny calls out Alicia's name as we enter the kitchen. I take a stool at the breakfast bar, leaning on the marble surface. Charles and I have known Jenny and Malcolm Fletcher for several years. They're the couple we'll arrange dinner with or bump into at a function. Both Jenny and Malc come from money, and both have careers that are mostly for show. Jenny writes a column for a newspaper no one reads anymore. Malc owns an investment company that someone else runs for him. Still, Charles and Malc do some business together every now and then.

One of the spaniels nips at my ankle but I ignore it. Jenny comes around the bar to shoo him away.

'Sorry,' she says. 'He reacts to strong emotions. I think he can smell them emanating from people. When I cry he sits on the floor by my leg and growls at me. He hasn't left my side since Grace died.'

There are a lot of statements like this from Jenny. She gave me healing crystals at Christmas and has a wellness guru instead of a therapist. But not all of her endeavours are altruistic. She makes money via social media using affiliate links to the same healing crystals and gurus. Often her 'gifts' are a subtle way of attempting to get me to endorse them too. The more endorsements she gets, the more sales she makes.

'You must be in so much pain.' As the kettle boils, she reaches over and grasps my hand. 'We haven't stopped crying since we heard the news. Malc tried to call this morning to speak to you both.'

'I was out,' I reply. 'I went to see her again.'

'Grace?'

'Yes.'

'Have you seen her a lot?' she asks.

'I guess this is the third time now.'

Jenny's eyes widen and she lets go of my hand. Her reaction suggests that it's strange for me to visit Grace for a third time. I decide to break the awkwardness by explaining, 'I don't like the thought of her there alone.'

Jenny begins to cry as she pours boiling water into mugs. 'Oh, I'm sorry. I keep thinking about it being Alicia and I can't stop myself.'

Does she want me to comfort her? I don't have the energy. Her outpouring of emotion is draining me, and that familiar thudding headache returns. In the absence of alcohol, I rub my temples, praying for it to leave me be.

After a long, dramatic sniff, Jenny walks over with the two mugs and then places a milk jug and a bowl of sugar next to them. 'You're so brave. I don't know how you're even walking and talking right now.'

'I think I'm still in shock,' I reply. Perhaps it's true, I don't know.

'Of course.' She takes my hands again. 'You mustn't blame yourself, you know. I had a long talk with Alicia when we heard the news. Neither of us saw anything in Grace that would make us think… well…'

I pull my hands away.

'What I mean is, not one of us saw this coming,' she continues. 'So you couldn't…' She falters, the ghost of an awkward smile on her lips. Then she places a hand on her chest. 'Oh, that poor girl, in all that pain.'

What did you say to her? My mother's words come back to me like an echo. Grace was fine, she was normal, she was a regular teenage girl. She wasn't suicidal and she wasn't like me. There wasn't anything to notice, because she didn't kill herself.

Before I can react to Jenny's statement, Alicia steps into the kitchen, humming to herself. She glances at me and falters. In the brief moments that follow, I make a mental note of everything I see. Firstly, there are no tear tracks or red eyes. Her black eyeliner is either freshly applied or she hasn't been crying. According to Jenny, '*we* haven't stopped crying'. Unless the 'we' refers to her and Malc. Secondly, Alicia appears shocked to see me, which isn't surprising, but what is surprising is the worried expression on her face.

'Kat's here,' Jenny says. 'She has a question for you.'

Alicia stops between the kitchen door and the counter. She holds her hands together in front of her body and her expression is somewhere between nervous and neutral. Is she trying to rid her face of emotion? Is she scared of me?

'Hey, Alicia. I wanted to stop by and see how you were.'

She moves her hands from the front of her body, plunging them into the pockets of her shorts. 'I miss her,' she says quietly.

'I know how close you were with Grace, so this must be hard for you. But I wondered whether you'd consider speaking at the funeral? You were like a sister to her, Alicia. She would've wanted to hear what her best friend had to say about her.'

As I watch Alicia process this information, there's a yapping from one of the spaniels, followed by a mewing. As Jenny scolds the dog, Alicia scoops up the same black cat that I saw in the YouTube video, stroking its head.

'Bloody Jasper keeps going for the cat,' Jenny says, exasperated. She runs her fingers through her messy strawberry-blonde hair. 'What do you say, Lissie? Do you think you would be able to say a few words?'

Alicia's hand makes its way down the cat's back. 'I… It'll be hard.' She doesn't look at me. 'But yes, I'll do it.' Her silver hair ripples as she shakes her head a little.

'Were you and Grace okay before she died?' I lightly drum my fingers against the breakfast bar, drawing out the moment. 'I spoke to Ethan yesterday and he said you'd had a falling-out. It's okay if you did. Grace loved you no matter what, you know that. I wanted to let you know that it's okay.' I turn to Jenny. 'Teenagers fall out all the time, don't they? I don't want Alicia to feel even worse than she already does.'

'You okay, chick?' Jenny walks over to her daughter and hugs her, making the black cat squirm between them both.

'Don't squash Marshmallow,' Alicia cries, as the cat leaps out of her arms with a hiss. 'Mum, look what you did!'

'It's okay, Lissie—'

'No, it's not.' There's an expression of pure thunder on Alicia's face as she backs away from her mother, spins on her heel and runs out of the room.

Jenny faces me with a sheepish expression on her face. 'She's struggling. She's young; she doesn't understand what grief is.'

'It's not any easier when you're older either.' My voice is quieter than I thought it would be. Smaller. I'd come into this house with the intention of uncovering the truth, of keeping an emotional distance from the situation, but yet again my grief has caught up with me. 'I should go.'

'No, stay and finish your tea. I just need to have a chat with Alicia. She'll come down again and we can talk it through.'

'It's fine. I'll give you a call about the funeral arrangements.' The word 'funeral' leaves a bad taste in my mouth.

'Whatever is best for you.' Jenny begins to rub my shoulder as I walk with her to the door. 'Kat, can I make a suggestion?'

'Okay.'

'Do you want me to put you in touch with my psychic? Look, I know it's… Well, it might be too soon. But she's an excellent medium.' Before I can speak, she holds up a hand. 'No, don't say anything yet. Think about it. Wait until you're ready. Wait until you need closure.'

There's nothing I can say to that. While Jenny can be offensive in an ignorant way, her blunders are in character with the woman I know. Alicia, on the other hand, is acting like she has something to hide.

CHAPTER TEN

She wasn't a clingy toddler at all. Her first day at nursery was a breeze; she didn't even glance back. The primary school remarked on how independent she was – even went as far as to say she was a natural-born leader, bossing the other four-year-olds around in the playground. But when Grace hit her teenage years, I noticed an insecurity that hadn't been there before. She was still bouncy and sweet at home, but out in public, she'd changed. During her short life, she'd smiled through her puppy-fat years, grinned her way through braces and chatted inanely with anyone and everyone who had a spare five minutes. But as soon as secondary school started, I noticed a difference.

She would curl up on the sofa with me, insisting that we watch movies together. Suddenly her wardrobe wasn't good enough, and Charles suffered through an internet-shopping binge to get her what she needed. I'd insisted on a budget, and it was a good thing I had. In the evenings, I'd shout her down for dinner, only for her to watch make-up tutorials on her phone as she sat at the table. She'd hover in the doorway to our bedroom and watch me do my hair.

One memory stands out: her finger twisting a wispy blonde lock as she said shyly, 'Will you show me how?'

At thirteen years old, she sat next to me on my ottoman and I showed her how to curl her hair.

Later that week, we'd smothered coconut oil onto our scalps and sat together watching reality TV. Now, when I sit on the same sofa, the coconut wafts over to me and I almost expect her to be next to me.

All of that – the insecurity, the sudden focus on her appearance – I'd put down to hormones and the usual peer pressure among girls of that age. I'd never experienced it myself, because the world I'd grown up in was vastly different. Gossip and mean girls weren't much of a concern, whereas fighting on the sports field and casual shoplifting were. I haven't tended to worry about the opinions of other people, but I'd needed to learn how the world worked for my daughter's sake. I thought Grace's experience of school was *normal*. What if it wasn't? What if Grace was being bullied and I hadn't seen it?

Georgie and Porgie almost knock me over when I go down to the kitchen. I quickly pour their kibble into their bowls and open the back door to let them run around the garden. As I return to the kitchen through the utility room, Charles walks in, showered, shaved and wearing a suit.

'You're going to work.'

He takes an apple from the fruit bowl, eyes me swiftly, bites into it. 'You don't approve.'

'It's a bit soon, isn't it? It's barely been more than a week.'

'If I stay in this house, I'll drink it dry. I need to get out, Kat. Besides, you've been gallivanting around God knows where. Why can't I get out, too?'

'I've been visiting our dead daughter and her friends, not to mention arranging her funeral.'

'Stop it. Don't say it like that.' He throws half the apple back into the bowl and sighs heavily. 'This house is suffocating me.'

I take a few steps forward, closing the gap between us, ready to fold him into me like a good wife does and absorb his pain. But I sense from his rigid posture that he doesn't want comfort right now, which gives me an excuse to hang back. 'All right, you should go then. Will you be in Derby?'

He nods. 'I swear I won't go too far afield. And I'll stay in touch. Are you going to be okay?'

'Of course.' It's what he wants to hear, and I provide that for him, but I don't open up and let him in because this is how our relationship works. This is as much as I can give him. I don't blame him for getting out of this house. There's no comfort here; only memories, and me.

There are phone calls to make, condolence calls to receive, services to hire. My mind is never allowed to rest because there's always another chore to complete. And yet... there's one task I can't bear, that I keep putting off: choosing clothes for Grace to be buried in. From underwear to shoes, Grace needs to be clothed. Despite not having an open casket for her – the thought makes me sick – she needs an outfit.

Trying to choose this outfit forces me to admit the truth to myself: I didn't know her. We spent time together, we talked, we preened each other, but when it comes down to it, I didn't know my own daughter was pregnant, that she was sad, that she was alone.

There are clothes all around me, torn from hangers, piled high on a blanket box, dumped on the carpet. When did she buy this set of lacy underwear? Have I seen these before? What about this red crop top? When did she sneak out of the house wearing that?

Here is the teal ballgown, nipped in at the waist, that she'd worn to her school prom last year. Perhaps she would want that night to be immortalised. Charles had welled up at the sight of his beautiful daughter before she, Alicia and Sasha had piled into a limo, the driver sweating at the thought of navigating the tight country roads. If there was ever a moment in time to immortalise, that would be a good one. Sixteen, beautiful, celebrating the end of GCSEs with a stunning gown and dancing the night away.

She'd stayed at Alicia's that night – at least that was what she'd told us – and the next morning, when I asked how prom had gone, she'd answered 'Fine'. To me, that had been a perfectly acceptable answer. I never pried or prodded for extra information. Now, when I think back, I question whether the night had ended as full of good spirits as it had begun. Was that the night she lost her virginity? That's what happens in all the Hollywood films – the girls finally put out for their boys on the night of the prom. But in Britain it's different. The kids are usually younger. The prom isn't as much of a milestone here. Maybe I'm overthinking this.

Still, the ballgown is a bad idea. Perhaps the tea dress that Grace wore to a vintage charity night at the school would be better. I think of how beautiful she was, with her red lipstick and hair like Veronica Lake. But that was Grace playing dress-up. What about the halter dress she wore to a sweet sixteenth? Nothing is quite right. Before I know it, I'm throwing the whole lot back into her wardrobe.

Being alone in the house is doing me no good, and yet I can't bring myself to leave. With the mood I'm in right now, I'll end up back at the funeral home, replaying that voicemail. I'm wired, stalking the rooms, avoiding both food and drink, living on fumes and old messages from Grace. I found another one: *Tell Dad he left his watch at home.* There are hundreds of WhatsApp messages to choose from, too. We often communicated that way. Is that because I'm too cold and distant for a phone call?

Part of me wishes Charles hadn't gone to work. I've grown accustomed to the formless shape of him on the sofa, inhaling whisky and weeping into the cushions, grieving harder than I ever could. But I have to face the fact that since Grace died, we have been living separately in the same space, not connecting, merely existing. If he needed to get out, then that is what he should have done.

I find a casserole on the doorstep. According to the attached card, Jenny and Malc left it for us. But eating it means accepting the status quo. It means getting on with my life as though nothing has happened. I tip the contents into the bin. I can't think straight. Last night I had a nightmare about hitting Ethan in the skull with a rock.

Back in the hospital, sitting across from PC Mullen and DS Slater, I'd told myself that I would find out what happened to my daughter, that I'd uncover the truth. And yet her funeral is almost here and I still have no answers. Neither Ethan nor Alicia gave me much information, and it would come across as odd, maybe even suspicious, if I visited them again. I don't want everyone to raise their guard around me. There's no point isolating people when I need them on my side.

In a whirlwind of activity, I pull all the condolence cards from the shelves and spread them around me on the family-room carpet. Perhaps there is some sort of clue within these messages that I've overlooked.

I'm so sorry for your loss. Grace will be missed— someone at Charles's company.

We love you Grace. Sleep tight – signed by several members of Grace's form at school.

There are no words. Love you all. Love Grace. Her light can never be dimmed – signed Jenny, Malc and Alicia.

Our hearts go out to you both, Kat and Charles. We'll miss Grace deeply – Rachel, Chris, Sasha and Oliver.

Goodbye, Grace. Thank you for everything – Lily.

I don't remember a Lily. Perhaps it's someone from school? There is something unusual about the message, so I set the card aside.

Thank you for the music – Daniel and everyone from the orchestra.

There are several signatures on this one, but I don't remember a Daniel. Was he one of the musicians?

Sending our deepest condolences. Grace was a beautiful girl. Heaven gained another angel – Louise, Gareth, Ethan and Billy.

I've seen the same sentiments pasted across Facebook too. It all feels impersonal and clichéd. The one message that seems real is from this Lily person. There's nothing directly from Alicia, Sasha or Ethan, only their parents. Should I mark this as suspicious? I'm sure it's normal for the parents to take control in times like these; Charles or I would have done the same if one of Grace's friends had died.

Reading the cards coaxes my anger back to the surface, but that's exactly what I want. I want to be fuelled by fury, walking a path of justice no matter how hot it gets underfoot. These cards are empty and useless. These words mean nothing.

There's one left. I open the card, prepared to read another pointless message.

She deserved it.

I blink in shock. Who would send such a message?

Where is the envelope for this card? Perhaps there's a clue in the postmark? But then I remember that I gave all the paper to one of the maids for recycling. I'd also thought that Charles had already read these cards, but he would have mentioned this one. He probably set all the cards up in a drunken haze and failed to read through every single one.

Staring at the message, I decide that I need to know more about Grace's friends, and the best way to do that is try her social-media accounts again. Chances are someone from Lady Margaret's sent this card. I shove everything away except for the nasty card, grab my phone and try the Georgiep0rgie password for Instagram. I put her email address into the bar, then try a few more variations of her password, switching from the names of the dogs to our cat, Whiskers, who was put to sleep last year. Finally, Wh1skers works and I'm in. A sudden headiness washes over me at the surprise of finally being granted access. I hadn't actually expected this to work.

Her username is GracefulGirl and her profile picture is of both the Labradors jumping up to her waist while she grins. There are fifteen new messages. When I tap the icon, the inbox pops up and I see yet more outpourings of grief:

We miss you.
I can't stop crying.
Maggie's will never be the same. (Referring to the school by its more popular nickname)
Why did you do it?
Why didn't you ask for help?
You're selfish for killing yourself like that. Pathetic.

Another horrible message. The username doesn't strike me as familiar, and the profile doesn't contain any pictures of the person behind the account, only motivational posts about exercise. Perhaps it's the same person who sent the card, or perhaps it's nothing more than an internet troll. Suicide is an inflammatory subject, and I can't rule out the possibility that the person who sent the card has suffered their own personal tragedy related to suicide.

I scroll down the inbox until I reach the messages that came in before Grace's death. It's there that I find the final conversations between her and her best friends. My eyes are searching for boys' names, but there's one direct message that stands out among the others. It's in all caps for a start, demanding attention.

HOW COULD YOU DO THAT TO ME? I'LL GET YOU BACK YOU FUCKING BITCH.

The username of the sender is not anonymous this time, nor is the profile picture: a slim face with bright pink lipstick surrounded by shiny silver hair. Alicia sent the message to Grace the day she died.

CHAPTER ELEVEN

The dress is Roland Mouret, a figure-hugging number with the right amount of modesty. Last night I pulled a hat with a veil out of the back of my dressing room and placed it next to the dress in our bedroom. Then I tossed the hat aside.

The dress hangs on a hook by my dressing table where I always organise my outfits for the day ahead. Underneath the dress are my Marc Jacobs kitten heels. Everything is black, but I think I'll wear a string of white pearls with matching earrings.

The room is dark, on account of the fact that the sun hasn't risen yet, and next to me in the bed, Charles is snoring. A sliver of green light from the thermostat's digital face hits his cheekbone, and I hope he'll shave today. It's three thirty in the morning; soon I will need to get up, put on that dress and leave this house.

There will be all eyes on me today – examining what I wear, how I act, counting the tears that fall down my cheeks. I will be judged as a mother, as a woman and as a person, and I will be found wanting.

The ones who don't judge me will pity me instead. They will cry for me from the back pews, imagining what it would be like if it happened to them. Right now, my daughter is all they can think about. A teenage girl is dead and that's a tragedy to obsess over. After the funeral they will forget her name. But I will be forced to get up and make breakfast as though the world is the same as it ever was.

For me, the world will never be the same.

There is one reason why I have arranged my outfit with care and attention, and why I'm sitting up in bed at 3.30 a.m. thinking about what people will do and say at the funeral, and that is Grace. The funeral is more than a burial, it's a way to find answers about what happened to her. It's an opportunity to see the expressions on people's faces, and to watch their reactions as the day goes on. Who has a guilty conscience? And yes, I want them to see me and see everything I have and everything I am. The dress on the hanger across the room is armour. Behold my power and influence. This is who I am, and I am watching you.

I should be asleep, but every night I dream of Grace sitting next to me watching reality TV with coconut oil slathered over her hair. Legs over my legs, woollen socks bundled at her ankles, condensation running down the cardboard carton of ice cream. For anyone else, that dream would be beautiful – a moment of bliss, frozen in time. But for me it's a nightmare, because it reminds me of who I am, and of what I'd felt that day with Grace. I'd been bored, but I'd forced myself to stay focused on her, to grit my teeth and ignore the tedium in order to play the perfect mother.

Boredom explains the high rate of suicide amongst people with antisocial personality disorder. We crave conflict and excitement. We can jump out of planes with barely an adrenaline spike. We often want to hurt people in order to exert our power over others, like every serial killer that has ever existed. But when we play nice and try to fit in with the rest of society, we are forced to deal with the boredom that comes with it. There's no room for power play when you're acting like a good citizen. The mind-numbing boredom never ends, and it tortures the mind – an itch that can't be scratched.

Now, as I stare across the room at the dress on the hook, I long for the days when boredom was all I had to worry about. If I could trade a thousand years of that boredom for Grace's return to the world then I would do it willingly, and that surprises me. Perhaps my therapy with Angela is finally kicking in.

*

There's a handwritten note on the sideboard detailing the time that Grace will arrive in the hearse. I'd scribbled it down as a reminder, and now I find the sight of it ridiculous. How could I forget?

People are in the house, spread out through the ground floor. Jenny, Malc and Alicia stand awkwardly in the kitchen, nursing mugs of tea. Charles is slumped over the kitchen table, with Malc occasionally rubbing his shoulder. Grace's former nanny is sitting in the grey armchair in the morning room, dabbing her eyes with a damp tissue. It was Grace's favourite armchair in this room, but I don't have the energy to ask her to move. And worst of all, my mother is here, sitting next to me on the antique sofa, outdoing Grace's nanny by wailing into a handkerchief. This is the most contact I've had with her since the day I told her about Grace's death. She hasn't called me or asked me how I am, and yet I'm sitting here with my hand on her knee in an attempt to provide comfort. At the same time, I can't stop myself from staring out of the window, waiting for the hearse to arrive. My hand doesn't move, it doesn't grip; it's simply there, limp and lifeless. Inside and out I'm a statue carved from marble, so cold my extremities are like ice. I'm waiting to be shattered into a million pieces by one fatal blow.

We're in the morning room because it has the best view out the front of the property, and I see the hearse as it slowly comes up the driveway. My stomach heaves. This is it. I'll never touch her face again, because it's going into the ground today. Charles and I had one last visit to the funeral home yesterday. We held hands and stared at her, memorising as much as we could, but I'm not sure the memory of her cold skin and missing fingernail is a good one.

'Oh no. No no no no,' wails Mum. *What did you say to her?*

Charles hurries into the room. 'It… She's here.' There's stubble around his chin. He didn't shave after all.

The hearse pulls us all to the window one by one, Mum last. Her legs are shaking and she has to lean against me, forcing me to inhale the mothball scent of her old black dress. That smell is a familiar marker of death. Whenever anyone dies within a few miles of the council estate, Mum attends the funeral in that thing, crying, gripping the loved ones of the deceased and generally acting the martyr. But mostly I remember this dress from my uncle's funeral, and I remember the way Mum's tears dried up as soon as we arrived back at the house and she opened the gin.

Her nails dig deep into the flesh on my forearm, but I don't care. There's that pain I'm forever longing for.

'Oh, Grace.' Jenny begins to cry, clutching Alicia with one arm hooked around the girl's shoulders.

I know I should be watching Alicia after finding that unpleasant message, but I can't tear my eyes from the convoy of black cars navigating the driveway in front of our house. Early-morning sun catches the glass of the back window of the hearse. Inside, a wooden box lies still, covered in yellow tulips. All the air leaves my lungs. A buzzing noise cuts me off from the rest of the room and for a split second it's simply me and the hearse. The yellow of the flowers… My mind fills with the memory of honey-hued hair. I place one hand on the window pane, close my eyes and imagine the scent of her lavender shampoo.

We arrive at St Vincent's, the tiny Catholic Church next to Ash Dale community centre, a small squat building with a few faded stained-glass windows of red and green. The same location and priest were used for Emily's funeral three years ago. Throughout the short, silent car ride, I watched the coffin travelling in front of our vehicle, never taking my eyes from it, hoping her cold body was comfortable against the silk lining we chose for her, and then feeling like an idiot for having those thoughts.

Mourners gather outside the church, some clutching bouquets of flowers, others holding tissues in closed fists, their red eyes seeking me out as I exit the car. After a cursory glance at the group of faces, I turn back to the coffin. The pall-bearers lift her gingerly from the car. Am I imagining a gentler touch than at the other funerals I've attended? Perhaps the directors have been moved by Grace's young age, by the light weight of her body.

As the coffin moves towards the church, I lead the procession into the building, but my legs feel as though they're about to buckle beneath me. My marble-like extremities have now transformed into jelly and all the blood has left my limbs. Trying to catch my breath, I bend over for a second, but that makes me dizzy and nauseated. While I steady myself, Mum catches my elbow with her arm, trips and falls to her knees with a loud gasp of surprise. Charles is the one who hurries over to us. Acting quickly, he hooks his hands underneath her armpits, heaving my mother back to her feet.

'Come on, Susan,' he says gently.

She lets out a low moan and slumps limply into his arms. I flash Charles a grateful smile for dealing with her.

Mum's behaviour may be a childish attempt at getting attention, but in all honesty I'm grateful for it. All eyes are on her, judging her, forgetting all about me. I smooth my dress, check the clasps on my shoes are still fastened and follow my Grace as she enters the church.

CHAPTER TWELVE

Organ music plays to cover up the sounds of sobbing and the awkward shuffle of the pall-bearers. Charles and I have chosen to let the professionals carry Grace's coffin in the absence of physically strong friends and family. Charles's aunt Sylvia unfortunately isn't well enough to attend, meaning my mother is the one close family member we have in attendance. Too many only children.

As Grace's coffin is placed at the front of the church, someone forces a hymn book into my stiff, unyielding fingers. I begin to sing the words on the page. Did I choose this hymn? I'm not even sure there is any sound coming out of my mouth as the organ drones on and on. All around me, voices chime together and a melody rises. I allow my eyes to drift away from the hymn book, away from the coffin and instead focus on the people in the church.

Alicia's silver hair stands out from the crowd, especially as her head is bowed. Jenny still has her arm around her daughter's slight frame, acting the mama bear today, her long, dark shawl spilling over Alicia's lacy blouse. I quickly scan Alicia for signs of genuine grief, but with her head bowed it's difficult to tell. She's wearing a tight pencil skirt, very tasteful, and her hair is straight and shiny, not a dark root in sight.

In the row on the opposite side sit Sasha and her parents, Rachel and Chris. Sasha isn't singing at all; instead she stands wringing her hands and staring at her feet. Ethan is two rows behind, his mouth moving but his eyes staring straight ahead, unfocused and red. His skin is pale, which could be a sign of anxiety. It could also be because he, like most people, hates funerals. Maybe this is his first one? Among the rest of the congregation, I see a few familiar faces: parents, teenagers, teachers. Grace's music teacher is here; I recognise him from parents' evening as one of the few staff members who stood out, largely because he seemed like the kind of teacher who wanted to be everyone's friend. A young guy that all the girls had crushes on.

Charles tugs on the hem of my dress and I finally notice that the singing has stopped. Everyone else is sitting except for me, standing there in the front row, body twisted, staring at everyone in the church. The grieving mother, spaced out and unaware of her surroundings. They probably think I've taken a bunch of pills to get through the day.

When I sit down, the priest begins to talk, listing a selection of Grace's achievements, which I sent him by email two days ago: her local award for music composition, her A grades in her GCSEs, the mentoring she did for younger students, the followers she had amassed through her vlogging channel. He talks about God's love and protection. Charles's hand rests on mine, slightly damp from where he's brushed tears away with his fingertips. The congregation sniffs collectively. Am I the only one in the room who isn't crying? I could fake it, force a blurry sheen of moisture over my corneas. But no, I won't fake it. My daughter deserves more than crocodile tears. What I feel inside is worth more because it's real. Let them judge me. Let them whisper behind my back as I walk out of this church without a mascara smudge in sight.

We pray. We sing. We stand. We sit. The congregation obeys the priest in every command. There are times when I consider flinging myself at the coffin, and others when I want to run out of the church. At one point I'm afraid I might vomit on my shoes, but I don't, I get through it.

'And now we will hear from friends and family who would like to say a few special words about Grace,' the priest says.

It's important that I watch Alicia stand up from the pew and walk down to the pulpit, so I crane my neck to see her. Jenny almost doesn't allow her daughter to get to her feet; she clutches Alicia's hand tightly and takes a few moments to let go. But the teenager picks her way through the crowded row and continues to the pulpit, her heels clicking on the stone slabs. She's handling the attention like a pro, but what else would I expect from the most popular girl at school?

She flicks her hair, rests a few pieces of paper on the lectern, glances up at the ceiling then down to her feet and blinks several times.

'When I was younger, I used to beg my mum and dad for a sister. I wanted someone to dress up with me, to play dolls with. I wanted someone to share my secrets with.' She pauses and sucks in a long, deep breath, blinking again. Is she trying to force out tears? 'I never thought I would find my own sister as I made my own way through this world. Sometimes I think Grace chose me. Perhaps she was searching for someone too. Grace was someone I could share everything with. She was my best friend.' Now she does begin to cry, twisting her face into a contortion an Oscar-winning actress would be proud of. 'I remember the last thing she said to me…' She pauses to shuffle her papers and I lean forward, eager to hear what she has to say. 'It was silly, really. We sent each other messages every day.' She dabs her eyes with a tissue, making me wait. 'It said, "I love you, sis."'

Alicia leans forward dramatically and her silver hair cascades over the wooden lectern. Jenny rushes to her side, placing that protective arm back over her daughter's shoulders. They whisper to each other on the way back to their seats, Alicia nodding while wiping tears from her eyes.

'That was very brave,' Charles says, rubbing Alicia's arm as they pass.

But I don't think it was brave at all. I think it was all a lie.

To my utmost horror, my mother is the next to stand. We hadn't arranged for her to speak; in fact, Ethan changed his mind and is supposed to read a poem. But now my mother is striding towards the pulpit and panic rises in me. She gets to the lectern and blows her nose far too close to the microphone.

'She was an angel,' Mum says. 'I've never seen such a beautiful child. Such perfect features. I remember the day she was born, with those bright eyes and ruddy cheeks.'

My teeth grind together in anger. My mother was nowhere near the hospital on the day of Grace's birth. I hadn't even invited her.

'I held her in my arms and rocked her back and forth while she cried and cried. I was the only one who could comfort her. It was me who—'

'No.'

Her eyes seek me out and the church falls silent. My fingertips tremble and the thud of my pulse is the one sound I hear clearly. There's another tug on my hem but this time I ignore it. For some reason I have taken to my feet and now everyone is gawking at me, including my mother. I shake my head three times, never moving my gaze from the woman whose 'grief' has briefly given way to disbelief.

'No,' I say again, quieter this time. 'Stop talking.'

'Honey.' Charles stands, trying to guide me back to the pew. 'Sit down, honey.'

But I wait, the moment dragging on as my mother stares me down, until she finally steps away from the pulpit. She stumbles again and Charles moves forward to help her, but this time she bats his hand away. I remain standing until she is back in her seat, and then the priest continues with the service.

'I'm sorry for your loss, Mrs Cavanaugh.'

The afternoon continues in a blur of thin smiles and sniffles. My hand is grasped and shaken more than I would usually like, but my mind is elsewhere so it doesn't really matter. It has been elsewhere since I watched the coffin slowly descend into the dark grave. I have been split apart, creating two Kat Cavanaughs: one who is tough enough to block out the pain, and a traumatised little girl rocking back and forth in the corner of a dark room.

'It was a lovely service.' DS Slater smiles in that grim way that people do when they want to lighten the mood but not appear happy. 'How are you holding up?'

'It was nice of you to come, Detective,' I say, still feeling disconnected from my body.

'I wanted to pay my respects,' he replies. 'I never had the privilege of meeting Grace, but it sounds like she was a very bright girl.'

'She was. I'm just sorry that there wasn't more of an investigation. I made my doubts very clear.'

'You did. But even still, I believe we made the right choice, given the circumstances.' He pats my hand again. 'Thank you for your hospitality this afternoon. Unfortunately, I need to go back to the station now.'

'Yes, you must catch those murderers.'

He nods, no trace of a smile left on his sharp face.

A small part of me comes floating back and I grasp it, determined to stay focused. No matter what the detective says, I still have my instincts to rely on, and they're telling me that Grace was murdered. That is what I need to concentrate on.

'Do you think we need more wine?' Charles must have walked over while I was distracted by DS Slater. 'We're getting through it rather quickly.'

'That's because my mother is here. I'll tell the caterers to open two more bottles of the red.'

As I begin to leave, Charles touches me on the elbow. 'Hey, what you did in the church...'

'I know, I shouldn't have. I ruined the service.' It wasn't what a good person – a good mother – would have done. A good person wouldn't have made a scene.

'No, I wasn't going to say that. I'm glad you did. I hated hearing her lies, too.'

'I'm sorry.'

He regards me curiously, head tilted to the left. 'What for?'

'For her. Of all the mothers to have' – I roll my eyes to the right, where my mother is talking loudly to a group of parents from the school about how close she was to Grace – 'I had to come out of that one.'

Another piece of me makes its way back out from the fog of grief.

'This day was always going to be the worst day we've ever had,' Charles says.

'I know.'

'She couldn't have ruined it. How could it be any worse?'

We grip on to each other, both thinking of our daughter. But I can't bear it for too long. I pull away.

'The caterers…' I mutter.

'Kat.' He keeps hold of one arm. I stop, move a step closer to him. 'After all of this, we should talk. You're… you're not grieving, Kat. You need to let it out. I know you're holding it all in, trying to be brave.'

'No, that's not—'

'You had a tough upbringing.' His eyes flit across to my mother. 'And that's made you a bit harder than others, I get that. But you haven't even *cried*.'

'That's not true. Let me go, Charles, people are staring.'

'So what?' His eyes widen, but he lets me go. 'Let them. Oh, fuck this, I need a drink.'

Speaking in a low but forceful whisper, I say, 'I might be holding it together, but have you ever thought that it's because I have to? We can't both fall apart, Charles. You have the luxury of getting drunk and crying into the sofa cushions. I have to keep things going around here. Have you thought of that?'

'I'm already back at work. I *am* holding it together.' I stare at his wide, pinstriped back as he walks away from me, blustering through the dining room towards the kitchen.

'Keep thinking that,' I mutter. Let him drown himself in whisky. I can't be his mother, which is what he wants me to be. If I've got to pull myself up on my own, he can do the same.

'You married a weak man.' Mum's voice is like a viper at my ear. 'I told you so.'

'I married a weak man to get away from you,' I reply.

There's no need for me to turn and see her smirk; I sense it as the tiny hairs at the nape of my neck prickle.

'What do you really know about him anyway?' she says. 'How close were Grace and Charles before she died?'

This time I do turn around to stand face-to-face with my mother. 'What do you mean? They are – *were* – father and daughter. Of course they were close.'

'How much time did they spend alone together?'

I shake my head and move away, disgusted. I know what she is insinuating. She follows me, sipping her wine, her tongue stained red.

'Do you remember how young you were when you met him?' she prods. 'He was an older man. And he only married you because you fell pregnant, didn't he?'

'I was a grown woman,' I snap.

'You were not! You might not have been a teenager anymore, but you had the face of a child, I always said that.'

'Don't be ridiculous.' We make our way through the mourners, out of the French doors and into the garden. Mum is on my heels, her clunky shoes making a racket on the paving slabs of the patio. 'I was a fully grown adult, and Charles hadn't married because he still lived with his mother and had commitment issues. It was nothing sinister.'

Though I dismiss her words, I can feel the dark tendrils of her poison worming through my veins, infecting me from heart to extremities. I can't let her in. But at the same time, my mind wanders back to when I first met Charles, to the things I would do that his other girlfriends wouldn't, to the way we solidified our relationship, and I feel slightly sick.

'Are you sure about that, Katie? Don't you think you should find out? There are rumours, you know.'

What kind of rumours is she talking about? There are things about my sex life with Charles that she couldn't possibly know. What *rumours*?

'Get out, Mother.' It doesn't matter what she says or thinks; this is my daughter's funeral. A hot flash of anger heats my face. Why did I allow her to come? She doesn't care about me or Grace – everything is a cruel game to her. Perhaps this is it. This is the moment we finally cut ties.

I watch her slink back into the house, where the rest of the mourners are eating the food I paid for. While I'm here, on the outside, I watch them all. I see Ethan take a sandwich, make his way over to a group and stand very close to Alicia. He got to recite his poem in the end, stuttering over his words while the rest of the church sat rigid, still in shock from my outburst. Sasha is on the other side of Alicia, with a glass in her hand. The liquid looks suspiciously like wine. Ethan puts down his plate on my antique dining table, reaches into his suit jacket and removes a flask. The three of them put their heads together as he distributes liquor into their glasses.

On the other side of the room, Jenny and Malc have plates of food and are talking to Ethan's mother. Someone makes a joke and they laugh. My husband stumbles through this scene, a glass tumbler in his hand, already drunk. Why hadn't I noticed that he was drunk earlier? He passes a group of teenage girls, stops and begins talking to them. I move away. I can't watch any longer.

CHAPTER THIRTEEN

'Hi, Grace. It's Mum. I wanted to call yesterday, because I wanted to talk you through everything that was about to happen to you, but I didn't, and I'm sorry. I know that you'll never hear this message. This is entirely for me. I suppose I can't help myself; I need to talk to you.' I lift up my knees, crumpling the bedding and clutching it to my chest with my free arm. In my other hand I press the mobile phone even closer to my ear, until the corner digs painfully in. Anything to keep me grounded.

'I know you had secrets – I guess all teenage girls do – but I wish you'd told me yours. I just… I never thought you were the kind of daughter to keep things from me. Was I a bad mother? Is that why you never told me about the baby? Or maybe you didn't even know yourself… I wish you could speak to me. If I could look you in the eye and hear you explain what happened, I'd… I…

'Where's your phone, Grace? Why didn't you have it when you died? No one believes me when I say that you didn't do this to yourself. I'm alone, and I think you were alone too, weren't you, at the end?

'I have to go now. Dad just left for work. I need to feed the dogs. I love you.'

Quietly, I place the phone down on the bedside table, lift the duvet and swing my legs out of bed. There are mascara stains on the pillow, and the Roland Mouret dress lies in a crumpled heap on the bedroom floor. Armour broken. It's the day after the funeral and the house is silent again.

After showering and drying my hair, I make breakfast, accidentally taking a second bowl out of the cupboard. The dogs whine, their tails wagging low to the ground. Maybe Jenny was on to something when she said that dogs sensed moods.

I dutifully feed the dogs and let them into the garden for their morning run. The maids are bustling around the house, completing the last of the cleaning following Grace's wake. Michelle, the housekeeper, orders them around in a hushed voice, trying not to disturb me after the stress of yesterday. They seem surprised that I'm out of bed, and I am too. I hadn't intended on doing anything today. And then my mother whispered her poison in my ear. Now I need to see my therapist.

'I'm surprised to see you, Kat.' Angela adjusts her weight, an action she tends to perform frequently throughout our sessions. Her large frame is never quite contained in the high-backed armchair she uses. Whenever I come for my session, I always wonder why she doesn't buy a bigger chair. 'I'm sorry about Grace.'

'Oh, you heard? But you didn't come to the funeral.'

'That's right.' She leans back and her light brown hair catches on the velveteen material. 'Has that upset you?'

I have to think carefully about that, as I do with most of my emotions. While I often experience anger or annoyance, deeply hurt feelings don't come naturally to me. After twelve years of therapy, she knows exactly how I process my emotions, which means I don't have to pretend. 'No.'

'Well, I'm sorry that I didn't come. I wanted to, but I didn't think it would be appropriate given our professional relationship. That doesn't mean that I'm not extremely sorry for what you're going through, Kat. Our sessions have often focused on how much you loved your daughter, and I know those feelings were genuine.'

'Are,' I correct. 'My love hasn't stopped.'

'You're quite right. My apologies.' She smiles. 'I think you did the right thing, coming in for a session today. This must be a difficult time for you, and it's good to talk through how you're feeling. Can you tell me about your emotional response to Grace's death?'

I try to compose myself. The green walls of the room are supposed to be soothing, but today they make me shiver. All I see are the fields surrounding Farleigh Hall and the lush woodland where Grace and I used to walk the dogs.

'Take your time,' Angela says patiently.

I nod, still thinking about Grace. 'When she was younger, she wore red wellingtons and jumped in puddles.' Red: the same colour as Angela's top. 'I find it hard to concentrate on anything but memories of her, but...'

'But?' she prompts. Despite her words, she's now gently tapping the top of her pen against her notebook, betraying the serene smile on her face.

'I'm angry at the injustice of it all. Grace was young – she had her whole life ahead of her. I know that sounds like a cliché, but it's true. Now I understand why everyone always says that after the death of a child. She was all set to have a *good* life, too. I don't know if that makes it more or less tragic. Charles and I have plenty of money, and we were both generous with it when it came to Grace. Charles was almost too soft with her. He gave her whatever she wanted.'

'Daddy's little girl,' Angela says, raising her eyebrows.

The phrase makes me cringe.

'Sorry,' she says quietly, noticing the way my expression freezes. 'That sounded a bit flippant.' She pauses before continuing. 'Do you think you're getting enough support from others? Do you want more support from others?'

Again, I have to think about it. 'No. I'm capable of taking care of myself. If anything, people want comfort from me, or they grieve for me. They stare at me, pity me. They cry.'

Her eyes narrow a touch. 'Are you sure? They don't hug or console you? They don't listen to you when you speak?'

'Well, yes,' I say. 'But it's more for them than me.'

'How do you know you're not imagining this need for others to be comforted by you? This could be the personality disorder making you feel on the outside looking in.'

'I suppose that's true,' I admit.

'Kat, you know you're doing very well. Your love for Grace has kept you from behaving in a destructive manner all these years. But there might be some triggers to watch out for, and isolating yourself from other people is one of them. Have you cried?'

'Not much. Only while alone. I thought I'd cry at the funeral but I didn't.'

She nods, and I try to figure out if she thinks that's good or bad. 'And how is your relationship with Charles since Grace died?'

'He's needy and clingy one minute, angry and distant the next.' I shrug.

'How does that make you feel?'

There's a spot of dirt on the green wall above Angela's head making me think of the mud we would track in after a long family walk with the dogs. I wish she would clean her office more often. 'Annoyed, mostly.'

'Marriages are always give and take,' Angela says. 'Perhaps you need to open up in order for him to open up to you.'

'He hasn't' – I use air quotes – '"opened up" with me in months.'

'Is this the lack of sex you've been telling me about?'

'Yes. Obviously it started before Grace died.'

'Is there a reason why you're focusing on that right now?'

'Because I'm a self-serving sociopath?' My hands clench. Perhaps it was a mistake to come here. Perhaps I should have stayed at home and wallowed in grief like a normal person.

'We both know that isn't true, Kat.' Angela leans closer to me, stomach bulging a little over her trousers, hair falling over her face, half-covering the bad nose job that I often find distracting. 'You may be suffering from *antisocial personality disorder*' – she puts emphasis on the words in a gentle chastisement of my use of 'sociopath', which she doesn't like – 'but you have not been self-serving for a long time now. Could it be that you want *comfort*? Sex is a form of comfort for many people.'

'I guess.' I haven't thought about sex in that way before. To me, it's a necessary part of life, a bit of enjoyment in this mostly bland world. It has never been anything emotional.

Angela picks up her pen and makes a few notes. Very quietly, she mutters, 'It is odd, this lack of intimacy with Charles. I mean, given his preferences in that area…'

With those few words, my mind snaps back to the insinuations Mum whispered with her forked tongue. *There are rumours.* What rumours? About the way Charles and I met? About our sex life? About… Grace?

'Kat?'

But in my mind, I'm wrapping my fingers around my husband's throat, and the look in his eyes begs me to squeeze even harder. I flex my hands, feeling the tension all the way from my wrists to my fingertips, and when I notice Angela observing me, a hint of curiosity in the curve of her smile, I ball them back up before tucking them between my legs like a child hiding evidence of disobedience.

'You seem agitated. I've never known you this agitated before.' She bends over her notebook again. 'Perhaps we could go over some stress-relief—'

'Antisocial personality disorder is genetic, isn't it?'

She lifts her head. 'That's a very complicated question, and one that scientists have been trying to answer for years. There's certainly a biological component to the disorder, and there may be a genetic connection, but environment plays a big role, too. You, for instance, had a difficult relationship with your mother, which had a huge effect on your development.'

I half smile. 'So, no matter what, it's the mother's fault?'

'No, that isn't what I meant. The relationship you have with your mother may have played a role. From what you've told me about her, she has her own sickness to deal with and in effect neglected you from a young age. Attachments are very important to a child and their developing conscience.'

'Can a sociopath love?'

Angela sighs. 'Not usually.'

'Do you think I loved her?'

'Grace? It's impossible for me to say. Only you know that, Kat.'

'But if I never truly loved her, she might have picked up on that, mightn't she?'

'It's possible,' Angela admits, making another note in her book.

'Everything I did affected her,' I say, half to myself. 'Everything *Charles* and I did affected her. We created her.'

'That's right.'

'Then we're the murderers, when you think about it. We both killed her.'

CHAPTER FOURTEEN

I should go home. There's nothing to do, exactly, but I should be there, wallowing, drinking wine, burying myself in Grace's bedclothes. But I'm officially drawing a line under that kind of behaviour. I'm no longer allowed to judge myself for not spending every waking moment bawling my eyes out. There are more important things to focus on, and I know Grace would approve of me spending my time trying to uncover the truth about what happened to her before she died.

First, I make several phone calls while driving. It takes some persuasion, but I manage to get everyone I need. I have no qualms about using the grieving-mother card to get people to do what I want; they all owe me a few moments of their time.

I have an hour to kill, and I find myself driving around, thinking about the funeral. Is it my imagination, or had Ethan's tightly knitted facial expression given the impression of fear? Any one of Grace's friends could have had some sort of involvement in her death or even been there when she died.

What I've come to understand is that if I want to learn more about Grace's circle of friends at Lady Margaret's, I need to get to know the parents better. That's what I'm going to do this afternoon. They are the obvious 'in' to figuring out their children. Right now, I have everyone's sympathy, and I'm not afraid to use that to my advantage. That's why I suggested Jenny, Louise and Sasha's mother, Rachel, all come to Lady Margaret's for a quick meeting about a school memorial service for Grace.

Grace's tutor, Preeya, cornered me at the wake to discuss arranging a memorial at the school, but at the time I'd been too lost in my own distress to give it any thought. She believed that the kids at school would find it easier to move on if they could say goodbye to Grace. Some had obviously come to the funeral, but most hadn't, and they needed closure.

Even if none of those vicious little teenagers killed my daughter, I know someone is keeping secrets. Alicia sent Grace nasty messages; Ethan neglected her when she was in pain. I need to rectify those wrongs and find out what they're hiding from me.

After I've parked the Land Rover, I switch on the radio and sit for a while, listening to the pop music Grace used to like. Different songs bring different memories. There are some that fill the car with the scent of her body spray, others that come with the sound of her voice. After about fifteen minutes have passed, I get out, hook my bag in the crook of my elbow and make my way through the gangs of students hanging out at the school entrance, heading for the faculty office at the back of the school. Preeya was right: the students need this memorial. Most of them don't recognise me, and that's a good thing. They're largely standing around in groups, heads bowed, sniffing. Some of the girls are crying and others are describing Grace's funeral. I hear 'That's so sad' more than once.

It's the kind of mass hysteria I remember well from my own school days, except we weren't dressed in formal school uniforms; instead we refused to tuck in our shirts and wore striped tights beneath miniskirts. The sight of these distraught young girls makes me cringe. The last time I saw students standing around in groups, sniffing and crying, it was all because of me.

There's no time to linger on history now. I push those memories away, because when I let them take hold, I find I can't concentrate on anything else for the rest of the day. Angela says this is guilt trying to fight its way through my broken mind and starved conscience, but I'm not so sure. It just happens to be a moment in my life that I can't forget. I did what I had to do, and guilt never came into it. Despite what my mother calls me. Despite the long discussions with child psychologists about my violent temper. Despite the life that was taken.

I'm the last to arrive, as I'd planned. The others have gathered around Preeya's desk. As head of English, Preeya has her own office, though it's rather small for the number of people in the room. I scan the faces of the others and see someone who surprises me.

'Malc! I thought Jenny was coming.'

He rises to kiss my cheek. 'The dog threw up on the carpet.' He rolls his eyes. 'She's taken him to the vet.'

'Was he picking up on her emotions again?'

Malc lets out a frustrated breath. 'Something like that.'

He sits back down in the chair, casually leaning against one of the armrests. I briefly catch Rachel checking him out. Malc is a rich man with a lot of charm and a glint in his dark eyes, always on the lookout for a pretty face. Every year or so, Jenny discovers evidence of an affair, they spend a few days apart and then he crawls back to her. I glance at Rachel, tall and well-dressed in a red cashmere cardigan, and wonder if she will become his next fling.

As I move closer to Rachel, she pulls her gaze away from Malc and stands to give me a quick peck on the cheek. 'Kat, how are you holding up after yesterday? It was a beautiful service.'

'Coping, I think.' I position myself closest to Preeya. 'Except for the wobble during the eulogies.'

She takes my hand for a squeeze. 'Oh, honey, you're more than entitled to one. I'm surprised to see you today, though.'

'Honestly, I think it's what I need right now. If I stay in that house on my own… well…' I pause, remove my phone from my bag and then say, 'Charles is back to work, you know.'

'I do,' Malc replies. 'He told me yesterday.'

'You think it's too soon as well?' I ask.

'Maybe. But he knows himself, so…' He shrugs.

Louise gives me a little wave from the back of the room and I nod to her. She opens her mouth as though to speak before stopping. Sensing her awkwardness, I decide to move on.

'Shall we get the kids in?' I say to Preeya. 'It would be good to have their input. Actually' – I pull a notebook from my bag – 'I have a few questions to ask them. I'm going to jot a few things down, if that's okay.'

'They're on their way,' Preeya says.

While we wait, I take off my jacket, set my notebook on my knee and think about all the notes *I'd* received during my school days, usually telling me to go to the headmaster's office. In those meetings, I was regularly told in a clipped tone that I'd never amount to anything. I had potential but I was wasting it all. Why did I keep lashing out at the other students? Didn't I feel any remorse for what I'd done? I'd sit in silence and wait until I was either sent back to class or suspended. Sometimes I had to sit even longer until my mother arrived. She'd cry during those meetings. She'd hug me and ask where she'd gone wrong. Then, when we were at home, she'd put a lock on the fridge and refuse to make me my dinner. I lived on dry crackers and old bread until I could find the key.

Ethan enters first, still tense, his gaze not meeting mine, moving straight to his mother. Alicia holds her head up high, exchanges a glance with her dad and sits down next to him. Sasha offers me a nervous smile before going to her mum. The extra bodies in the small space make the room claustrophobic and hot. Alicia's perfume wafts over, bringing with it memories of Grace, and I'm forced to remind myself of the nasty message she sent to my daughter: *HOW COULD YOU DO THAT TO ME? I'LL GET YOU BACK YOU FUCKING BITCH.*

My voice cracks as I say, 'Thanks so much for coming, everyone. Today, as well as yesterday. I know you're hurting right now, and that's why I want to do this.'

'You okay?' Preeya asks.

I nod my head and clear my throat. 'Let's talk about the memorial. Should it be for the whole school or just the sixth form?'

'I think it should be open for anyone to come,' Preeya says. 'I had a chat with the head and she has agreed to block out the first period for the memorial. The sixth formers will definitely all come and I think a lot of the younger kids will want to. There's been a huge outpouring of grief. Grace really made an impact on the younger girls – you know how they look up to the sixth formers. I think it'd be a good idea to get someone in from a suicide-prevention charity to speak after the memorial...' She drifts off after noticing the expression on my face.

Every wall of the room seems to close in on me. My chest tightens. That slumbering, flickering rage stirs inside, and I'm forced to push it back down as I take a moment to compose myself. 'I'm sorry. I still find it difficult to accept that Grace killed herself. But you're right. It is a good idea.' Though it's hard, I manage to force out a thin smile.

Preeya fiddles with the sleeve of her dress, suddenly full of nervous energy. This isn't the best start. I'm supposed to be making myself approachable. Natural charm is one of the few perks of having a personality disorder like mine.

'I, um...' I pretend to fiddle with my notebook in an attempt to garner more sympathy. 'I was thinking that it might be a nice idea for Grace's best friends to share their favourite memories of Grace. I know it's putting you on the spot a bit, but if any of you could talk about that today, I can jot it down and we can incorporate it into the memorial somehow.'

'That's a wonderful idea,' Preeya says enthusiastically.

'I'd like to put together a memory book for myself, so I might need a few extra details for that, too.'

'Whatever you need, Kat,' Malc says.

'Thanks, everyone. I mean that. This is… Well, it's brilliant that you've come together like this.'

Preeya reaches out to take my hand, squeezing my fingers gently. This is what Angela was talking about, these moments of comfort. Maybe she was right about people genuinely wanting to help me, and maybe she was right about my broken brain ascribing selfish ulterior motives to the good intentions of others.

And for a moment I falter, because my plan involves manipulation, which means being a bad person. The kind of person Grace wouldn't want me to be.

She's not here anymore, I remind myself.

'Sasha, I'm sorry, sweetheart, but would you mind going first?' I gently extract my fingers from Preeya's and open my notebook. What none of them know is that my phone has a voice recorder app, which I have running in the background. It was a hasty download, though, and I haven't tested it yet. Hence the backup notebook.

'You okay, hon?' Rachel asks her daughter.

Sasha nods, and as she composes herself, I examine her for the first time. Both Sasha and Alicia are part of the school orchestra. Sasha is the second chair violin, while Grace was first chair. Alicia plays the flute. Lady Margaret's is well known for their orchestra, putting on a few local shows throughout the year. Sasha would often come to the house to practise with Grace before these shows, and Grace had featured Sasha on her YouTube channel, the two of them giving instructions on how to play Ed Sheeran or Imagine Dragons songs on the violin.

She's a pretty girl, though not as stunning as Grace or Alicia. Her hair is dark, curly and shiny. She's always struck me as very proper, saying please and thank you, sitting straight at the table. I've always assumed that her father is strict, encouraging her talent to the point of living through it vicariously – a dangerous line to tread in the family dynamic.

'I don't know.' Sasha's heavy eyelashes flick up in her mother's direction. At seventeen, she should've developed a bit more confidence by now, but that's none of my business. 'I guess it was when we took the dogs for a walk around the fields. We had a picnic and it was a nice day.'

'I'm sorry to ask, Sasha, but could you tell me a bit more? It's incredibly useful to know these things. You know, for the memorial.'

'Well, we were chatting a lot.' Her face becomes bright red, which tells me they were talking about boys. Her gaze flickers to Ethan and her flush deepens. They were talking about Ethan then. The poor girl can't hide it at all. She'll need more armour if she's going to get through this life unscathed. 'We saw a pheasant. Later we walked to the—' Almost immediately, the red fades from her face and Sasha becomes off-white, like the eggshell wallpaper around her.

'What is it, sweetheart?' I ask gently.

'We went to the quarry.' She looks at her mum again. 'It wasn't long after the man killed himself there and Grace wanted to see.'

I nod slowly. 'Thank you, Sasha.' I scribble down a note: *Insecure. Quarry.* 'What was it like at the quarry?'

'Quiet. There wasn't anyone around. I don't think anyone apart from schoolkids ever goes there, to be honest. Not since the man…' She worriedly glances towards her mother for more comfort and reassurance.

'Grace knew it was called the Suicide Spot?' I ask.

Sasha nods. 'She wanted to see the place where he jumped.'

Malc shuffles uncomfortably in his chair and Rachel inhales sharply as the atmosphere changes. Thinking about the quarry sends a chill through my body. Wanting to move on from my daughter's fascination with death, I continue on to the next friend. 'Ethan? Would you mind going next?'

He rubs his hands underneath the table and sniffs deeply. There are no tears in his eyes and I speculate as to whether the sniffing is the symptom of a drug habit much harder than marijuana or he's starting with a cold.

'When she told me she loved me,' he mutters. 'But it was a lie, so what does it matter?'

'Ethan!' Louise's mouth hangs agape.

I make a quick note, obscuring part of the notebook with my arm: *Jealous? Not happy with their platonic arrangement?*

'It's okay, Louise. I know how hard this is.' I place my pen down, purposefully cover my notebook and direct my attention to Alicia, not needing to hear any more from him.

To my surprise, she stands up, all ready to go with her story, as though she's about to give a report about what she did over the summer. 'Grace and I had this perfect day once. We met up on a Saturday morning and went for brunch in the village. I had scrambled eggs on toast, I think. She had an omelette. Then we went back to mine to practise for a while.' She laughs, and the room echoes with the pleasant jangling of her young voice. 'Neither of us could be bothered though. We were hyped up on coffee and we wanted to go out. We went for this long walk all around the Ash Dale moors, then back into the village. We bought doughnuts from the sweet shop and walked by the river, throwing stones into the water. Grace told me how much she'd always wanted a sister and I told her the same thing. I think I cried.' Alicia rubs a tear from her eye, and I catch Ethan watching her intently. 'I miss her so much.'

At the end of her passionate speech, she dramatically crumples into her chair and allows her dad to loop an arm around her shoulders. As she leans into him, still sniffing, I find myself cringing, and it takes all of my willpower not to let that show. In my notebook I write one word: *LIAR.*

*

After the meeting, I walk down the long corridors to the music room. No matter how many times I come to this building, I'm always taken aback by the grandeur of it. To me, schools are dirty, graffitied places littered with spots of chewing gum that have been worn down beneath scuffed shoes. It's a place where teachers bellow to make themselves heard over the students' din. In contrast, Lady Margaret's is raising well-behaved young people who follow the rules. Sure, there are still hints of the vibrancy of youth, but it isn't anywhere near as chaotic as my old school.

As I make my way towards the music room, the sound of the orchestra fills the hallways, swelling and swelling until I feel as though I'm shrinking down like Alice in Wonderland, and the handsome panelled walls are growing taller and taller. It has been two weeks since I last heard Grace practising her violin part for this particular concerto. Two weeks since I last saw her alive.

There are glass panels on the door, allowing me to stop and watch the students play. One of the violin chairs is empty, probably because I pulled Sasha out of her practice to talk about the memorial. The other chair is occupied by a girl I don't know. She's in a school uniform, which suggests she isn't a sixth former. Sasha will be the first chair now.

A young man stands at the front of the orchestra, conducting the kids. The young, popular teacher who came to Grace's funeral. I remember the card signed by him, too. He'd written a cheesy line about music. What is his name? Daniel, I think.

I can no longer remember why I wanted to come here. The music seeps into all the empty spaces inside me until my eyes burn with unshed tears. Eventually, the kids notice me staring, get distracted, miss their notes and look at me instead of their sheet music. The teacher follows the gaze of the students to find me at the window. He recognises me and nods. I give a small nod in return, step away and make my way out of the school.

When I reach the Land Rover, my phone beeps. I pull it out of my pocket and check the notification to find a new text message.

It's in your best interest to stop coming to the school.

CHAPTER FIFTEEN

An anonymous person with an anonymous number doesn't want me to come to the school. Someone who knows my private mobile phone number – a number I don't give out freely. My first instinct is to call them, but no one answers. I didn't expect them to. I reply: *Why is that?* And then I watch the screen and wait. Nothing. I can't help myself. I text again: *Why isn't it in my best interest?*

And then I stop, because perhaps it isn't in my best interest to let this person get under my skin. Instead, I drive out of the school grounds and into the village, find somewhere to park and then think calmly about what I should do next. Clearly, this person has no idea who they are dealing with. To them, I'm a weakened and grieving mother who can easily be frightened by a vaguely threatening message. The reality is quite different. I'm not frightened at all. Instead, I'm ecstatic. Finally, I have a solid indication that Grace's death wasn't suicide. Why else would someone threaten me? I must be getting too close to the truth.

My screen flashes and another notification pops up.

Don't go to the police.

And then…

I know where you live.

That makes me chuckle, because half of Ash Dale knows where I live – in the big house on the hill, the place that was built to be noticed. Charles and I are part of the community and where we live is not a secret. And now that I think about it, neither is my phone number. Though I don't give out my number to many people, it's listed in the school records as an emergency contact for Grace. Who has access to those records? Most staff members, probably. Could a student hack in to them? Last year a student discovered the admin password for the school's website and redirected it to porn.

And then there are Grace's friends, who could have accessed my number from Grace's phone. In fact, I remember Grace giving Alicia my number after she'd smashed the screen on her old iPhone and sent it to be repaired.

Well, I'm certainly not to be frightened by these messages, and I won't let the threats cloud my judgement about what to do next. The way I see it, I have two choices: I can go to the police or I can keep this to myself and try to put the pieces together on my own. DS Slater has not been much of an ally throughout all of this. He's already dismissed my suspicions about Grace's death. Why would he take me seriously now? On the other hand, the police might be able to trace the number and find out who sent the message. I'm not sure which would be the best option for me, but I need to make the decision soon. The longer I sit on this information, the easier it will be for the police to dismiss me as crazy.

I wait a few minutes to see if any more messages come through, and then I put my phone back in my bag, switch on the engine and drive away.

'Can I speak to DS Slater, please?'

A rotund man with greasy hair regards me with half-closed eyes. The glass partition between us muffles his voice. 'Name?'

'Kat Cavanaugh.'

'What is this about?'

'An ongoing investigation into my daughter's death,' I reply. It's only half a lie.

'I'll see what I can do. Take a seat.'

Ten minutes later, DS Slater strides into the waiting room with his hands pushed down into his trouser pockets. The tight smile on his face tells me he's annoyed about the rude interruption at work. That he's willing enough to tolerate whatever conspiracy theory I'm here to present, but that he has other – more important – things to be doing.

Once he's led me through to a private room, he closes the door and raises an eyebrow. 'Ongoing investigation? You know that the case is closed, Mrs Cavanaugh. Your daughter committed suicide, I'm afraid.'

Carefully, I place my bag on the table, sit on the available chair and cross one leg over the other. 'I have something to show you.'

While DS Slater gets comfortable in the chair across from me, I retrieve my phone, unlock it with my fingerprint and bring up my messages.

'Read this, please.'

He cranes his neck as I tilt the screen towards him.

'Have you tried calling the number?' he asks.

'Yes. There's no answer.'

'What about a voicemail? Any identifying information on the voicemail?'

'No, nothing.' I almost roll my eyes, but I manage to control myself.

'Well, I'll take a note of the number and see what we can do,' he says. 'But I should warn you not to get ahead of yourself here. It would be reckless to assume the sender had anything to do with Grace's death. Unfortunately, when a popular young person dies it can attract a lot of media attention. You've seen the coverage in the local newspaper, and you must have noticed that Grace's passing was mentioned on the BBC news.'

'I have,' I reply, maintaining the same calm exterior as DS Slater.

'Then you know that Grace's death has attracted a lot of interest from the general public. That includes some people who…' He sighs. 'How can I put this delicately?'

'Are a few sandwiches short of a picnic? As the saying goes.'

'Well, I wouldn't put it like that, but there certainly are some delusional and ill people out there. This sort of thing has happened before. Some people crave attention. They want to be caught. They want to feel as though they are part of something bigger. Right now, Grace's death is exactly the kind of situation that would attract a person like that.'

I shake my head as I put my phone back in my bag. 'You're wrong, Detective. I received that message as I was getting in my car to leave the school. Whoever sent me this was watching me. I don't give my number out to many people. Either the sender is a student who knew Grace or they've accessed the school records to find my details.'

'Then it's probably a schoolkid desperate for attention,' he says. 'I'm sorry if that sounds harsh, but trust me, I've seen this before. Killers who have gotten away with it don't tend to make threats. They don't want to draw attention to themselves. There's nothing about this message that makes me believe Grace didn't commit suicide.'

'Well that's your opinion,' I reply, still unruffled on the outside, but alive with fire internally. 'You don't know her and you certainly don't know me.'

He grimaces. 'I know you've seen the inside of a few interview rooms.' His eyes roam the walls of the room in a dramatic fashion, highlighting that I've been in trouble with the police before.

Ah, I've irritated him. He thinks I'm up myself and he wants to bring me back down to where I came from. People often like to remind me that I used to be poor, as though it's some sort of insult. Why would emphasising my improvements be an insult?

Why would drawing attention to the fact that I'm a social climber ever make me cringe? No one chooses where they are born, however much the world likes to pretend otherwise.

'You have a wild past, Mrs Cavanaugh. It was quite unexpected.'

'Was it?'

We lock eyes for a brief instant, but neither of us speak. I certainly don't want to make an enemy of DS Slater, but he's rattled me during this exchange. His instincts must be telling him that I'm different, a little 'off', and I don't want to linger in case he becomes even more suspicious and untrusting. I don't wait for him to show me out.

Someone saw me at the school and decided they didn't want me there. Was it because of who I was talking to at the school? Or is there a vital piece of evidence hidden on the school premises? Grace's locker has already been cleaned out, though I suppose the sender might not be aware of that information.

By now it's almost three and I have barely any time to get back to the school and park somewhere inconspicuous. Perhaps I can catch Alicia as she leaves. I haven't forgotten about her performance in the meeting. Who was that display for? Preeya? Her father? Was she trying to impress me?

Grace and Alicia had been arguing just before she died, but now Alicia can't stop pretending that they were closer than sisters. Little Miss Perfect, queen of the after-school drama club, always on the tennis team, a keen equestrian and a member of the orchestra. She presents herself as squeaky clean, with decent grades and plenty of friends. She was certainly Grace's best friend, but there were tears and fallings-out on a regular basis over the years. I remember one incident, when Grace had been ditched by Alicia because Alicia decided to go to the cinema with a boy. Back then I hadn't quite understood the devastation my daughter felt, but now I do.

I can't deny that my lack of conscience saved me from suffering the brutality of teenage girls in my younger years. I simply didn't care what they did to me.

Parked a street away from the school, I wait for the stream of students to start making their way home. Most are picked up by parents, but some walk, catch a bus or drive. Alicia's parents live away from the school, but I happen to know that she usually heads into the village and buys a coffee to take home with her. Knowing this, I position myself where I can see the road, sinking down in my seat, waiting for that flash of silver hair. As I do so, I realise Grace would find this hilarious. She'd giggle her head off, unable to remain quiet for long enough to complete the mission.

I hear the students' loud, excitable voices before I see them. Footballs bounce against the pavement. Rucksacks hang from shoulders. Nearly all the kids are in school uniform, with a few sixth formers in regular clothing. The sixth formers with cars tend to drive themselves around, but Alicia hasn't passed her test yet. She recently started to learn, passing her theory three weeks ago, something Grace never had the opportunity to do.

Five minutes into my surveillance, a glint of silver catches my attention. It also catches the attention of all the younger lads in uniform, who whisper behind hands, subtly nudging their mates to get a glimpse. Her long, languid limbs must seem goddess-like to these twerps. I imagine the mystery that surrounds her – an untouchable aura. Now I see Alicia's power at Lady Margaret's.

The sea of children parts for her, giving me a better view of who she's with. There's a boy – of course there's a boy – glued to her side, one arm slung around her waist. Her face is relaxed, almost triumphant, as she makes her way through the group. Alicia is obviously part of a secondary-school power couple. I watch them carefully from my car, not at all shocked by who she is with. She passes the car, her hand pressed deep into the back pocket of her boyfriend's jeans. Her head tips back as she laughs at his joke, that silver hair catching the afternoon sun. The tears are gone. The act is gone. This is Alicia without any pretence. This is her with her beau, at ease and happy.

But the boy is Ethan, which means they're both liars.

CHAPTER SIXTEEN

Who was I at seventeen? Was I Alicia? By that point I'd left school with mediocre GCSE results. I was living in a flat above a fish and chip shop and I waitressed at catered events for rich people. To buy my waitressing uniform, I'd had to steal money from my mother's purse, practically while I was stepping over her crap to get out the door. The deposit for the rent had come from saving the few pounds she gave me for dinner money every day, the theft of a few fivers here and there, and the sale of the two items of worth I'd owned – my Discman and a locket given to me by my uncle a few years before he died.

When I worked the weddings held at Chatsworth House, or at charity banquets in private residences the size of my mother's entire council estate, I'd see polished women in ballgowns that draped elegantly around their bodies, their hair artfully arranged, wearing make-up that made their skin glow. They'd been dipped in jewels, wore shoes that cost three months of rent money and cosied up to men in tuxedos.

And there I was, watching from the sidelines, going home to a flat that smelled like grease, with old wallpaper peeling slowly down the damp walls. I lived in silence because I couldn't afford a television. I wanted another life because I'd decided that I deserved it. And when Charles came along, I seized the opportunity for a better life. I prised it out of another woman's hands, someone less deserving. Perhaps someone else would feel guilty about that, but I don't.

I was young, ambitious and ruthless. Alicia might have everyone else fooled, but she doesn't realise what I've done to get myself the life I live. She has no idea who I am and how much I understand who *she* is. Can I imagine her killing my daughter? Yes. Can I picture her standing over Grace's shoulder, forcing her to write that phoney suicide note? Yes. What I don't know is… why? Would a teenage girl murder another teenage girl over a *boy*? The very idea of it is preposterous to me. But as Angela is often telling me, I'm different from everyone else, so perhaps I will never understand.

I'll never know the passionate, all-consuming lust of a teenager. The feelings that made Romeo drink the poison, or that spotty kid in the eighties' film hold a boom box up to a window. It's hard for me to understand, but the truth is, Alicia could easily have killed my daughter over a boy, because people have killed for less all throughout history. Someone was stabbed in London over a perceived slight in a chicken restaurant two weeks ago. Wars are started over money. There are people like me all over the world, killing without conscience, and maybe Alicia is one of them. But I can't know for certain. There isn't enough evidence.

When I tap the keypad on Grace's laptop, my daughter comes to life again. She and Alicia are filming themselves walking the dogs through the fields behind the house, swinging their arms, short skirts flapping in the wind. Alicia keeps pretending to throw the ball and Georgie falls for it every time. When Alicia cackles in amusement, I find myself wanting to hurt her, and my hands clench tightly.

But I've seen these recordings already. I click back into Grace's channel, scrolling through the hundred-odd videos uploaded to the site. She must have been making these almost every day, and yet I had no idea she'd amassed this kind of following.

I've seen all the clips of her with friends, but I haven't watched many of Grace alone. I skip through a few violin tutorials until

I find a video of her talking directly to the camera. Perhaps I can get a better idea of Grace's mindset before she died.

This is a different version of Grace. Her hair is a lighter shade of blonde, meaning that it was recorded recently. I check the upload date and discover that the video is from around five weeks before Grace died. She isn't wearing make-up, which is rare for her. Watching the tutorial videos, I was taken aback by how much foundation was caked onto her already perfect young skin. But in this one she's natural, and the lighting is dim, as though Grace has recorded it at night with the lights off. Everything is tinged blue and there are dark shadows in the corners of the screen. Is she using the light from her laptop screen? Or the flashlight on her phone perhaps? Whatever it is, it reminds me of what I saw that day in the hospital, and the image of her blue fingernails leaps unbidden into my mind.

I click play.

'Hey, everyone. This isn't the kind of video I usually make, but I guess I wanted to chat.' Her face contorts. She quickly brushes away a tear before conquering her emotions and smiling again. She's wearing a grey hoody and pyjama bottoms, and she pulls the hoody closer to her throat. 'Everyone thinks I'm lucky. I live in this big house and I have parents who give me everything I need. But sometimes I feel alone, you know? I guess I'm pretty down right now.' She pauses, glances away from the camera and then turns back. 'Who else feels like that sometimes? Or even right now? I'm here for you. DM me. Us losers need to stick together, right?' She laughs, but it sounds high-pitched, forced. 'No one should suffer alone.' Then she gives another forced smile. 'I'm kind of lost right now, I guess. But I love you all.' She blows a kiss to the viewers and the video stops.

My head swims with the sound of her voice, sending me spiralling back to my memories of her before she died. What did we do the day she made this video? I check the time stamp again.

Charles was in London overnight. I'd gone out to meet Jenny and we'd had cocktails in Bakewell. Now I come to think about it, Grace had pulled me into her arms for a hug as I'd been leaving the house, but I'd put that down to her usual neediness. She'd told me to have a good night and not to come home early. She'd smiled as the door closed and waved to me through the window like nothing was wrong.

Why didn't you talk to me, Grace?

I click on the next video, dated a week later. It isn't the final video she made – a few violin tutorials followed – but it is the last one she made where she was alone, talking to the camera.

'Hey, everyone. I wanted to check in because my last vid was a bit depressing. Sorry, guys! Bad day. I feel a lot better right now, and I have someone to thank for that. Seriously, your friendship is what's keeping me going right now. These last few months of us hanging out have been amazing. You're awesome AF and I love you.'

I play it a second time. *These last few months of us hanging out...* She can't be referring to Alicia or Sasha, because Grace was friends with them for years before she died. Her phrasing makes it sound as though this was a new friend. Did someone else come into Grace's life? Someone I didn't know about? I click play again.

'And, my dad has been surprisingly cool. Who knew dads could be cool? Over the last couple of weeks we've become super close, you know? I think you guys should chat to your dads more often, because they might surprise you. Anyway, see ya, love ya.' She smiles and blows a kiss, and the video ends.

What the hell was that about? Grace and Charles never seemed particularly close to me. They were dad and daughter and they loved each other, but I can't imagine Grace sitting down to chat with Charles about her problems, sharing her secrets about boyfriends or complaining about period cramps. Wasn't listening to that my job?

What did Grace and Charles talk about when I wasn't there? And who was this new friend? Maybe even a boyfriend? Could he be the father of Grace's child?

He buttons the white shirt over the pink expanse of his chest. Watching my husband, my head swims with dark thoughts. My mother injected poison into my mind. *Do you remember how young you were when you met him?* But I'd been twenty-one when I met Charles, who was then thirty-eight. My mother made him out to be some sort of cradle-snatcher, but that's not true.

But what is true is that my relationship with Charles has been, at certain times, quite unusual.

He wasn't married when we met, but he was in a relationship – with a woman who had been *pre-approved* by the great Emily Cavanaugh. A woman I barely remember when I try to picture her in my mind. She was in her thirties, well bred, connected, handsome in a somewhat horsey way.

It was a private function at a rich entrepreneur's house located in the isolated depths of the countryside between Buxton and Edale. Since I had no car, one of the other girls had given me a lift, and we spent the night serving canapés and champagne while ignoring the wandering eyes and hands of the men. Charles wasn't handsy, but he did watch me as I made my way around the rooms with my silver platter. I watched him too. He was the quietest of the bunch, joined at the hip with a very loud woman. She kept patting his arm, interrupting him, laughing at her own jokes.

Working my way around the room, I would hear her cackle as she blurted out another bawdy punchline: *And that was the moment the minister realised his hand was on my backside.*

I remember rolling my eyes at her obnoxious laugh – and Charles caught me in the act. He'd grinned at me and rolled his eyes right back.

I hadn't gone home with him that night, but I had left with his number, and that was when I decided on a plan.

'This fucking thing,' he explodes, pulling me back to the present.

'What is it, darling?' I ask lazily.

'The tie. Can't you see?'

I pad over to him, still in my nightdress, and gently move his hands away from the offending article, slowly looping the material in on itself. *There are rumours*, my mother had said. But about what? I still don't know if she meant about Grace, or about affairs, or about our sex life.

'There.'

He caresses the side of my face, tucking a strand of hair behind my ear. He's gentle. How could I imagine him hurting our daughter? My thoughts drift back to Grace's video, about how *close* they were. What did that mean?

'You're not dressed yet,' he says. 'We need to be at the memorial in an hour.'

'I know, I'm going to get ready now.'

He nods. 'This is the last time.' He slips a jacket over his shirt. 'I can't keep mourning her like this. I can't do it.'

'We'll get through today together,' I say blandly.

His head hangs low. 'Look after me, Kat. Won't you?'

'That's what wives do, isn't it?'

His eyes search mine, as though seeking more from me. He knows that's all he'll get, and I'm sure it's not enough. The realisation hits me and I don't know what to do with it. Now that Grace is gone, there's nothing holding our marriage together.

CHAPTER SEVENTEEN

The April weather breaks on our way there. The sky, which had been an inky indigo and spotted with dark clouds as we'd eaten a rushed breakfast, transforms to black within thirty minutes, and now the rain is gushing down. Charles uses his suit jacket as a shield; I grab the spare umbrella from inside the glovebox. And then I pause. Charles's leather Filofax is in there. I watch him as he runs towards the school building; see him half turn and beckon me to him. Quickly, I slip the organiser into my tote bag and follow him.

The Filofax is an item Charles is never without. Though he does keep electronic copies of his whereabouts, and has a secretary to help organise his appointments, he still prefers to write down everything. He says it helps him remember without having to check. Things aren't real to him unless they are on a hard, tangible surface. Anything inside a computer is inconsequential. Perhaps that's why he always dismissed Grace's vlogging as nothing to worry about.

I shake the umbrella dry and fold it back up as we reach the entrance. It's now that I remember the one time I broached the vlogging issue with him. 'Do you think it's a good idea?' I'd asked. 'What if she's groomed by a weirdo or a paedophile?' In the end, we'd both decided to let her do her own thing, so I can't blame Charles – I was complicit too. We'd both thought that *our* child was different to anyone else's child. Grace would never fall for any of that; she was too intelligent. We'd brought her up right.

We were so sure that she would tell us if she felt uncomfortable. We'd both thought that Grace was the exception to the rule, the sensible teenager who would always come to us first. We shared that delusion together, and it might be the thing that will push us apart.

Charles comes to my side as we step into the entrance to meet the head teacher. Automatically, we put on smiles, albeit half-hearted ones, and show a united front. No one knows that I'm already considering us drifting apart from each other.

'Thank you again for coming, Mr Cavanaugh, Mrs Cavanaugh.'

The woman shaking my husband's hand is as tall as a man, broad-shouldered and wearing heavy make-up. This is Rita Bianchi, the dark-haired, very attractive headmistress. I remember her from the one school-board meeting I attended.

'I know I expressed my sympathies at Grace's funeral, but I need to say it again. She was a bright, beautiful, *lovely* young woman, and we miss her very much at Lady Margaret's.'

'Thank you for saying that, Rita, it's very kind of you.' Charles has evidently forgotten how to let go of her hand, shaking the thing up and down until she finally extracts her fingers from his. His cheeks flush when he realises his faux pas. Playing the good wife, I place a hand on his arm to calm him down.

The funny thing is, I don't remember Rita at the funeral at all, which goes to show how dazed I'd been. That can't happen today. I need to stay sharp.

She moves on to me, grasping both my hands, smothering them with her great paws. 'I can't even imagine, Kat.'

I simply nod, because it's easier.

'The kids are on their way to the hall,' she says. 'They wanted to bring some candles to burn in her memory, but that got a bit out of hand. Instead, I thought you could light a ceremonial candle for everyone.'

'Did you get the photograph I sent?' I ask.

'I did. What a gorgeous photo. We've got it printed out and everything is set up and ready. And yellow tulips? Is that what you said?'

'That's right. Grace loved yellow. She loved all colours, actually.'

Rita smiles broadly. 'She took GCSE art, didn't she? I think I remember a project involving colourful flowers.' Her eyes suddenly fill with tears and she redirects her head sharply away from me. 'If you would follow me into the hall. Alicia's here, too. Alicia!'

We walk into the main hall, where Alicia is sitting with her legs dangling over the edge of the stage. With a phone in one hand and a can of coke in the other, she's innocence and youth personified. We make our way up the steps and onto the stage. Alicia climbs to her feet, slipping her phone into the pocket of her loose trousers. She's wearing a tight, high-neck, possibly cashmere jumper, and her loose-fitting trousers are nipped in at the waist with a chunky belt. Her silver hair is pulled back into a sweet chignon at the nape of her neck, and she's even pared back her make-up to a more natural look.

'Alicia!' I hurry forwards to pull her into a tight hug, but my arm bumps awkwardly against her shoulder, almost knocking her over. I reach down to steady her, placing my hand on her hip. 'Oh, good lord, I'm so sorry.' Once she's regained her balance, I pull her into a gentler hug, holding her slim body tightly. 'Thank you for agreeing to speak at the memorial. I… we' – I gesture to Charles – 'appreciate everything you've done for us since Grace passed away.' While I'm talking, I quickly slip my hand into her bag.

'It's okay,' she says, her eyebrows knitted together. 'You know how much I loved Grace.'

'I do,' I reply.

'Oh look, the students are coming in,' Rita says cheerfully. I narrow my eyes at her, perturbed by her tone at such a sombre event.

They come in holding small posies of wildflowers. Some talk noisily, until they see us on the stage and immediately stop. Their voices incrementally hush as more kids filter in, filling the space below us. Many of the girls clutch each other by the hands for moral support. And as they arrive, I hone in on the ones who are weeping or sniffing, in an attempt to ascertain who could be Grace's new friend. Could it be the tearful girl leaning on her boyfriend's shoulder? Or the quiet girl at the back, dabbing her eyes with a tissue?

There's no way to know, because these children are going through mass hysteria caused by loose lips and gossip. They have whipped each other up into a frenzy, because Grace's death is the most interesting thing that's happened to them in a long time – perhaps ever.

But despite the drama of it all, it's humbling to see a group of young people coming together to pay their respects to a peer. The students form an orderly queue in order to place their posies of flowers next to a blown-up picture of Grace. Some even speak a few words to her image. One girl, around thirteen years old, comes up to the stage to hand me a flower. I stare at it while Rita makes her first announcement. Teenagers can be bad. They can do cruel things without remorse on a daily basis. They can bully and intimidate each other on a level that makes grown men and women wince. Malicious gossip spreads through a school like wildfire. And, yet, they can be gracious and kind and… good.

If only you could see this, Grace, I think. But in reality, she'd probably hate this attention. Thinking of it almost makes me chuckle, and I check myself moments before laughing at an inappropriate interval in Rita's very sad speech. There are a few sniffs in the crowd, and then Alicia takes the microphone to relay her 'sisters' story again.

While she talks, I purposefully look away. Alicia doesn't know what I stole from her – yet. I don't want her to see my expression, for her to see that I know she's full of bullshit. I don't want her suspicions raised.

There's applause for Alicia's speech, and she stands there, drinking it in, wiping fake tears from her eyes, brushing her cheeks with a light touch. She has this performance perfected now. She's a pro at delivering a good eulogy. Jenny should hire her out for events. This time I do let out a tiny laugh, and Charles shoots a gloomy frown in my direction. He shakes his head once, and then steps over to the microphone as Alicia is finishing up.

'Some of you might know me as Grace's dad,' he says, his voice even and clear. 'My wife' – he glances back to me, his expression still cold – 'and I want to thank you all for being here today. We loved Grace' – his voice cracks – 'very much indeed. She was… she was everything to us. We won't be the same without her.' He pauses, letting his head drop. I'm about to approach when he manages to pull himself together and begin speaking again. 'I can't imagine life without her. She was the one good thing…' His shoulders begin to sag, his arms drop to his sides and he sniffs loudly into the microphone. This time I do intervene, walking calmly over and placing a hand on his back. 'I loved her more than… And now she's gone… Gone.' While his high-pitched, broken voice continues on, I try to pull him gently away from the microphone. Below the stage the pale faces gape, horrified by this adult losing his composure before their eyes. This is the kind of thing that horrifies the young – discovering that adults are flawed. That we're breakable.

Finally, he steps away and hurries to the back of the stage. I watch open-mouthed, surprised by this sudden change. He'd seemed fine before the speech. But now I'm left at the microphone, a hundred-odd students staring up at me expectantly, waiting for a profound, moving speech from the grieving mother. And as I stand here, all eyes on me, I find myself floundering, failing to find the words that would come easily to anyone else.

'Thank you,' I say, sweat forming on my brow as I speak. 'This would mean a lot to Grace. She… she would…' My mouth opens and closes, until Rita makes her way towards me.

'Shall we light the candle now?' she asks.

I nod, feeling as young and helpless as the teenagers before me. It isn't often that this happens to me. In fact, I can't remember a time I ever felt this way, helpless as a newborn baby, unable to form coherent sentences. Before Rita hands me the taper to light the candle, I find myself searching for Charles at the back of the stage, smiling sadly, because now I finally understand his difficulty in making the speech. Maybe Charles isn't weak after all. But when I look behind me, I see that Charles is gone.

Rita ushers me down and directs me towards the symbolic candle. Someone places a flower in my hand, a lily, but when I search for the person who did it, they're gone – a glimpse of dark hair and nothing more. Where is Charles? Why has he left me to face this alone?

The flame goes up with a whimper and one of Grace's favourite songs begins to play: 'Lego House' by Ed Sheeran. I say thank you again, with what I hope is a gracious smile on my face, and then I make my excuses and leave. I find Charles slumped against a wall in the hallway leading back to the entrance. Three schoolgirls are staring at him through the window of a nearby classroom. The image of him burns on my retinas, seeps into my mind. Seeing him there strikes me as the most repulsive sight of my husband I've ever experienced, and shame washes over me from head to toe. It's an unusual experience, this embarrassment, but his behaviour today has triggered it.

He stares at me, staggers to his feet, and begins to walk.

My legs shake as I make my way back to the car, but I can't pinpoint why. Charles interprets my silence as anger, walking behind me with his head dropped low to his chest. The truth is, I don't know what to make of Charles's behaviour. His behaviour – the meltdown, swiftly followed by the disappearance – is odd, even given the trauma we've been through. My mother's words echo through my mind, making me question my husband's character once more.

But as I walk, I finger the object hidden in my bag.

Alicia's mobile phone.

CHAPTER EIGHTEEN

'Grace, it's Mum. I went to your school memorial today and now I'm home. Your dad decided to go to work this afternoon and I've reorganised the pantry, because when I stay still I miss you too much. But there was nothing else to do, after that, to stop me thinking about you, so now I'm sitting in the garden alone, allowing myself to miss you. It's raining a bit – that drizzle you like, the kind that makes your hair all frizzy. It used to annoy me that you'd spend hours out in the drizzle and then complain about your hair. I used to think, well, don't go out in the rain then. But I don't think that anymore. Now, I simply want to enjoy it with you.

'I took your friend's phone today. You wouldn't approve of that, I know. You were always such a good girl, but I can't be that way anymore. I need to find out what happened to you.

'I… I took your father's planner, too.

'Grace…' My voice becomes a whisper. 'Did he hurt you?'

Though I want to dive into Charles's planner first, I decide to check Alicia's phone immediately, because she might report it as stolen and it might have some sort of GPS location tracking for all I know. I'm not a complete idiot, but I'm hardly a tech-savvy hacker.

The drizzle wets my cheeks and hair and pools underneath me on the garden chair. It's usually quiet in this corner of the world, but I've allowed the two black labs to have a run around the garden. They're currently growling over a bone. Georgie drops it, runs away, comes back and attacks Porgie's tail. Both of them bark happily. They've moved on so easily from Grace.

But I cannot let her go.

When I try to get into the phone, it becomes apparent that it's password-protected. All phones are these days. I need either the four-digit PIN or a thumbprint. Well, the thumbprint is out, but I do know Alicia's birthday. I type in 0103. Nothing. Then I try 2002, for her birth year. Nothing. I wonder whether there's a limit to how many times I can try, or whether the phone is set up to photograph whoever is trying to guess the code. I've heard of that feature, too, after seeing many pictures of cats captured by laptop webcams as they step all over the keyboard.

Are you sneaky, Alicia? Would you choose a random combination of numbers? Or are you too arrogant to imagine that you would ever lose your phone? I tap in 1234 and the phone unlocks.

I can't help but laugh. Sometimes it truly is the easiest solution. One thing I have heard about hackers is that they don't require thousands of lines of complicated code to override a password. No. They have a list of passwords that they try with thousands of usernames and emails. The reason they hack you, is you.

There's very little in her messages, but teenage girls don't text anymore. I open WhatsApp to find a dozen or more groups, all set up with different members. Surely Grace is involved in at least a few of these. The first thread I open is about Grace.

Can't believe she's gone.
I keep seeing her last messages and crying.
Her dad is weird.
Remember what she said about him?
Yeh.
Fucked up.

My stomach sinks. What did she say about him? My mother's words come back to me. *There are rumours.* I scroll further back but there aren't any more messages about Charles. Instead, I begin to see Grace's name pop into the conversation, and my heart lurches. She was in this group, posting up until the day she died.

Her last message.

See you at school, bitches.

I keep scrolling up and up and up. The messages are frequent. There are hundreds of them and most are complaints about schoolwork or schoolteachers.

And then…

Did you see Lily today? Lord, that girl is a mess.

Skanky AF.

I hope she dies.

I stare at that message for several minutes as the drizzle flecks my face. Next to that last message is my daughter's name. The thought of those words coming from my daughter leaves me reeling. Is this what passes for bitchiness now? I know that I can't allow my mind to run away with itself – I don't know the full context surrounding these messages – but the thought of Grace wishing *anyone* dead is just… alien to me. How could she? My memories of Grace conjure up a kind and gentle human being. This, however, is completely the opposite.

When I've pulled myself back together, I take screenshots of all the mean and disturbing messages on Alicia's WhatsApp. Then I check her Snapchat folder and smile to myself at the saved images and videos there. I fire off a few messages and send as much as I can to my own phone, and then I smash Alicia's phone to pieces. After the dogs are done running around the garden, I hop back into the car, drive out of the village and throw the broken pieces out of the window onto the grass verge of a quiet road.

Alicia, you may be in for a surprise, sweetheart, because you've just sent several bitchy messages about half the members of the orchestra into your WhatsApp group for orchestra practice – by mistake, of course. What a shame those other students are about to find out just what a nasty creature you are.

*

On the drive back to the house, I want to relish in my admittedly rather insignificant victory. Alicia will finally be taken down a peg, which frankly couldn't happen to a nicer girl. Most of the messages I sent to the orchestra are screenshots of conversations between her and Ethan on WhatsApp and Snapchat, bitching about their mutual friends. There were other things that I didn't send, because Grace would've disapproved of me doing so, though I must confess that I did keep them. I am now in possession of a handful of suggestive videos, all filmed while Ethan and Grace were supposedly still a couple. Before, according to Ethan, they'd decided to be just friends. That means Ethan was cheating on Grace with her best friend throughout most of their relationship. I'm not stupid enough to keep anything X-rated, because that would be breaking the law, but they are embarrassing enough that Alicia wouldn't want them sent to her friends, which means I could possibly use them as blackmail, as well as proof of Alicia's lies.

But none of the messages mentioned Grace being in a relationship with anyone else, and that is what holds me back from truly enjoying this victory. I'm no closer to finding out the identity of the father of her unborn child. Despite the Instagram message to Grace confirming Alicia's unpleasant side, there was nothing implicating her in Grace's death, either. But at the same time, I can't stand Alicia's duplicity and I have to admit that I remain suspicious of her.

As I get out of the car, back at home, I reach for my own phone to find another anonymous message. I'd been so lost in concentration that I hadn't noticed. I hurry into the house, sit at the kitchen table and open the message, taking my time to process the words.

You have no idea who your daughter really was.

The drizzle becomes a downpour, battering against the window as I try to make sense of this latest message. It isn't a threat, and it doesn't appear to be attempting to scare me. A very different tone to the others. When I check the number of the first message, it doesn't match. I immediately text back.

Tell me who she was.

Could this be Alicia? Has she already figured out that I stole her phone? I stop my thoughts from running away, determined to keep an open mind. These messages certainly have a different mood and, though I hate to admit it, I can't help but wonder if the sender is correct, because the more I dig into Grace's personal life, the more I come to understand that she was not the person I thought she was.

I hope she dies.

The daughter I'd thought was good and pure wrote that message about another human being. All these years I've been faking my morality in order to set an example, thinking that she would follow my lead. Grace always felt like the burning beacon of *good* in my life. Charles has his faults; he's certainly not working for a charity. I've seen some of his business deals and they aren't contributing to a better world. Then there's me, and my own issues. But Grace was different. Wasn't she?

After staring at the phone screen for a few minutes, I decide that the anonymous messenger probably isn't going to text me back, so I move on to Charles's planner. Perhaps there is something in here that will explain the video diary Grace posted about spending more time with him.

As I open up the diary to the day Grace died, I find myself recalling those first moments after Grace failed to come home from school. All my calls went straight to Charles's voicemail, and later that night, he'd blamed meetings in Derby. But in his planner, there is simply one letter recorded on that date: 'H'.

I flick through the pages and find several instances of this mysterious letter H. What on earth does it mean? Then I begin to notice another pattern. On every Thursday lunchtime, Charles has recorded 'G to T'. What does it mean? G could very well be Grace, but what is T? Charles's other notes aren't written in the same manner. Most of them are filled with detail: *Meeting at 5 p.m. in boardroom @ Derby office*. Or, *Appointment with property developer, Kings Cross, 2 p.m.*

My instincts tell me that these abbreviated notes are different to his usual schedule. After living with this man for two decades, I must have a read of him by now. I must understand him, even if I don't truly love him.

My phone vibrates. The anonymous messenger is back.

I can show you.

The next message is a link to a YouTube video. Surprised, I click on the link and it takes me through to Grace's own channel. My body goes rigid as the video plays. This is a new video uploaded today. Grace is in the middle of the frame, standing outside Lady Margaret's. I enlarge the video to fill my phone screen. The footage begins with laughter in the foreground, followed by my daughter's voice. She's right in the centre of the action.

'Present for you, loser.' Grace grins at the camera before turning to face a girl behind her. The girl is slumped over, her black hair obscuring her face. Grace pulls her upright, and there's a brief glimpse of her pale, surprised face before Grace smashes a brown, squidgy substance all over her nose and mouth.

There's laughter coming from whoever is filming the event. The black-haired girl reels back, scraping the stuff off her face and staring at it on her hands.

'Is it…? Is it dog shit?' the girl says in horror. Her face is pale and small, frightened and disgusted. No one answers her. The other students in the video, none of whom I recognise, continue to laugh, their flushed faces tipped back in hysterics. Eventually the girl runs away.

'Fuck off then.' Grace's expression twists into a sneer that I have never, ever seen before.

I close my eyes.

My heart picks up tempo, fluttering in my chest like bird wings. I've never seen my only child like that, with a hard, cold sneer on her face, basking in the attention of others. That isn't the Grace I knew—the innocent and pure girl I thought she was—which makes me wonder: How did I miss this darker side to my daughter?

Was Grace like me? Did I miss the signs? I had never, ever seen her display any sign of violence, from birth to death, until I watched that video.

There haven't been many moments in my life where I can say I've been surprised. People, on the whole, prove themselves to be entirely predictable, however hard they try to hide their true nature. I've always prided myself on my ability to see through the artificial exterior and delve into the blood and guts beneath. Perhaps that's the privilege of being detached from the rest of the world: we're good judges of character and not often fooled by fakery. But we also seek out the easily manipulated, the weak characters on the edges of society. As a mother, I constantly worried that Grace was the kind of innocent who could be taken advantage of by someone like me. But now I worry the opposite. Now I worry she was *like* me. A sociopath.

After pulling myself together, I log into Grace's YouTube channel, download the video onto my laptop and remove it from the internet. Whoever uploaded this knows her username and password, which means it's someone she was close to. Alicia?

I force myself to watch the offending clip again, and this time I examine the smaller details. Grace was dressed in school uniform, which means it was taken before she went into sixth form. A-level students at Lady Margaret's can wear their own clothes. Her hair is honey hued, and her face is rounder than it was when she died. That's another concern of mine. It's from viewing this old image of Grace that it hits me how much weight she lost. She became a picky eater who went through fads week by week. There was vegetarian week, vegan week, organic week, keto week. Why didn't I see that Grace wanted to lose weight in order to fit in with the other girls at school?

What else do I notice? The dog poo might not be dog poo. Could it be chocolate mousse? I try to believe that it is. The laughter of the person filming the event sounds familiar, but I'm not sure if I'm willing it to be Alicia because of everything else that has happened. Could it be Sasha? I'm not sure. These kinds of videos can spread through a school like wildfire, meaning that the person who filmed it might not be the same person who uploaded it to YouTube.

I estimate that this video was taken when Grace was about fifteen years old, not long before her GCSEs. Fifteen is old enough to understand the consequences of bullying. Unless she didn't care about the consequences, like someone with antisocial personality disorder.

As I close the laptop, I run through what that could mean. According to Angela, most sociopaths see their lack of conscience as a gift, because it allows them to manipulate and hurt others. They can wield their power over other people as part of a sick game of cat and mouse. You don't meet many sociopaths who go to a therapist. I'm in the minority there, and I accept that my *dysfunctional* conscience is a weakness.

And yet sociopaths are high risk for suicide. It's all part of the game. A bored sociopath might kill him or herself in order to get back at a partner, for instance. Back a sociopath up against the wall and they will lash out in the manner that will hurt you the most, even if that means hurting themselves.

When I was in that situation I did the same thing. Thirteen years old and morally bankrupt already, with the world judging me for what I'd done to Annie Robertson and the others. The world against me. A life taken. As I sit there remembering what it was like, I run my fingers along the scars on my forearms. When I was pressing the blade into my wrists, I was thinking about how I'd be getting back at my mother, and Annie, and everyone else in the world. I hadn't been thinking about how I was lonely or depressed or that I wanted to die.

My phone vibrates and a new message appears on the screen. *Nothing to say now?*

Who are you? I text back. *How do you have Grace's YouTube password?*

Pause.

Wouldn't you like to know.

The smug reply raises my hackles. *I asked the question. Answer me. Now.*

No. The response is immediate this time. *Check her feed again.*

I load up the app and go to Grace's channel. Another upload. When I click on play, the video begins with loud voices, laughing and the thump of dance music. The image is dark, blurry, with the twitching movement of drunk people dancing in the foreground. The camera moves through them, allowing me to see that they are in a house. I've been here before. I remember the beige and the 'Live, Laugh, Love'. This is Ethan's house.

The camera moves towards an armchair covered by two entwined bodies. Kissing, groping, writhing. My blood freezes when I see the back of a girl's head with platinum hair. The darkness of the room might make it hard for anyone else to figure out her identity, but I know instantly. It's Grace.

She gets up, clambering down from the lap of the boy in the chair. Ethan. Of course. Neither of them notices that they're being filmed as they kiss standing up before then slinking out of the room. The camera follows them as they begin to make their way upstairs…

The music continues thumping.

So does my heart.

I text, *When was this filmed?*

Hmm, about two months ago, comes the reply.

I download the video and delete it from Grace's channel.

Who are you? Even though I know they won't answer, I can't help myself.

Silence.

You have no idea who you are dealing with, I type.

They counter: *What an original threat.*

Pause.

Then, a reply, *I'm terrified. Come find me, Katie.*

The use of my birth name sends a shiver down my spine.

CHAPTER NINETEEN

Charles comes home late, throwing his jacket over the back of the hallway armchair and abandoning his brogues outside the kitchen. I watch him enter while I stand in the morning room, dressed in a black sheath dress, red lipstick on my mouth. Then I make my way to the dining room to softly call his name.

When he enters the room, it startles him to see me sitting at the table, and his jaw drops slightly. His features crinkle in confusion as he takes in my outfit, the chignon at the nape of my neck, the dress that I wore the last time we had sex, the red mouth, the mascara. Yes, it feels alien to wear these things. Yes, I can see he thinks so too.

'I wanted us to have a nice dinner. There's a lamb tagine keeping warm in the oven. Shall I fetch it?'

'What are you doing?' His voice, low and steady, is more cautious than angry, which gives me hope that this plan might actually work. He tugs at his tie and throws it onto the back of one of the chairs.

The plan is somewhat half-formed – a hasty jumble of ideas that occurred after the video I saw of Grace. Right now, I've decided not to show Charles the video. Instead, I'm going to attempt to find out what he knows about anything and everything that may have happened to our daughter before she died. There are many words spinning around my head as I watch him slowly nod for me to get the food. *Her dad is weird. Remember what she said about him? Yeh. Fucked up.* My mother's lips at my ear. *There are rumours.*

'Sit down, darling. You're making the place look untidy.' The joke is as uneven as I feel. When I rise to go to the kitchen, I place a gentle hand on his shoulder to direct him to his chair.

I wouldn't say that I'm nervous, but for once I'm pushing myself out of my comfort zone. Charles has become unpredictable since Grace died, and I'm not sure whether I'll be able to get the information from him that I want. That I *need*.

The tagine hasn't dried out, which is indeed fortunate since I cooked it, and I'm hardly the world's best chef. I'd considered asking our head housekeeper, Michelle, who often doubles as a chef when we're busy, but I settled on the idea that a home-cooked meal would endear me to Charles. He'll see the gesture as charming. When a drop of sauce hits the lip of the plate, I consider wiping it away, but then leave it. Let him think I'm messy. Let him believe I'm frazzled and clumsy.

When I make my way back into the dining room, Charles rotates his shoulders to watch me. His eyelids are down low, his features crumpled. The tiredness is transforming him into a deflated balloon.

'Kat, I think I know what you're doing,' he says. 'You don't have to.' He pulls at the buttons beneath his shirt collar.

'What am I doing?' I set the plate before him, sauce drip facing him.

'You're trying to go back to normal.'

'"Normal" isn't me cooking.' I raise my eyebrows as I settle into my chair at the opposite end of the table.

Charles tips his head to the side. 'You know what I mean. You're trying to move on, but it's too soon. We still need to grieve.'

I pick up my fork and spear an apricot. 'I'm still grieving. I can put on make-up and still be in pain.'

My eyes remain fixed on the apricot as a pause expands between us. An ever-spreading silence that I cannot imagine will ever stop. Suddenly, this grandiose dining room, with its antique chandelier and table that seats twenty, seems too small for the two of us. But then Charles opens his mouth.

'I know, Kat.'

And we begin to eat.

I soon drain my glass of Merlot, the wine more appealing than the food. With the distance between us, I regret not making our places at the table closer to each other, but we're at the formal dining table and I felt formality would be best. The three of us, when Grace was alive, used to eat dinner at the cosy kitchen table, where we felt like a family. We don't feel like a family anymore.

'Shall I put the radio on?' I suggest. Anything to fill the burgeoning silence.

'That might be nice,' Charles replies. 'This tagine is very good, by the way.'

I shrug and stand up. 'I just followed the recipe.'

'Nigella?'

'Jamie.'

He nods.

I switch on the radio and classical music blares out, strings sweeping like swallows into the room. Both of us freeze and I quickly find a jazz station instead.

'I'm not sure I'll ever be able to hear violins again,' Charles says. On my way back to my seat, I notice that his glass is half empty. I top it up before adding more to my own glass.

'I know I won't be able to. It's as though she played every tune that ever existed. She's everywhere.'

'She was so talented.' Charles places his fork down on his plate.

'No appetite?' I ask.

He shakes his head. 'Not since…'

'Me neither,' I admit, sliding my plate across the table. 'This was a stupid idea, wasn't it?' When I take a swig of the Merlot, the heady taste makes me swoon slightly. Since the funeral, I've been trying to avoid alcohol. Now, the rich red wine plus the lack of food is taking a toll. I gently put the glass back on the table and straighten up in my chair.

'No,' he says, 'it wasn't. It was a nice idea and I'm glad you tried.' He lets out a long sigh and fiddles with the stem of the glass, one fingernail bouncing against the surface. 'One of us should be trying. I haven't been there for you, have I? I'm sorry. Maybe it was too soon to go back to work.'

I shrug. 'There's no handbook for dealing with the death of a child. If it helps, you should do it.'

He offers me a thin smile that fails to reach his eyes. 'Thanks. For everything, Kat. You've been great, since…'

Neither of us can say it. Perhaps it's the situation or perhaps it's the alcohol hitting my bloodstream, but my pulse is pounding.

'That day, when she didn't come home from school…' I shake my head. 'Being here at home waiting for her was… Well, I thought it was the worst day of my life, but then the next day came and they found her.' I rub my eyes, purposefully smudging my mascara. 'When I couldn't reach you, I was in such a panic.'

'I'm sorry, Kat.' He drinks more wine. 'I wish I'd been there with you that day.'

Casually, I sniff and rub my nose, avoiding eye contact. 'Where were you? I can't remember. My head is all over the place.'

'Nottingham,' he replies, absent-mindedly. 'A meeting, I think. Potential buyer for the Chelsea property.'

I nod, circling the rim of my wine glass with my finger. 'That's what I thought.' But we're both lying, because Charles had told me he was in a meeting at his offices in Derby.

When I wake up on the sofa in my black cocktail dress, I can't help but panic. What happened after dinner? We ate ice cream from the tub. Charles and I finished the wine. I asked him if the school had ever contacted him about Grace's behaviour but he said no and I tried to figure out if he was telling the truth but I was too drunk. Then we sat on the sofa in all-consuming silence. Did he open a bottle of whisky?

I creep upstairs and into one of the guest bathrooms, washing my face with cold water, hoping for the sharp shock to bring me back into the real world. Charles had told me that he'd been in the Derby office the day Grace died, but last night he'd changed his story and told me he was in Nottingham. Why had he lied?

Did my husband kill my daughter? Did he rape and murder her? If Charles was abusing our daughter, that could explain why she was lashing out at other students. But it doesn't explain the fact that I never saw that troubled side to Grace.

There's no time to reach the toilet on the other side of the bathroom; my pink puke hits the porcelain sink instead. I run the water and it disappears down the drain.

After a shower and change, it's almost 10 a.m. Charles will probably be at work by now. My head pounds, my abdomen cramps. This time I need to eat, no matter how much my body complains. Dry toast, coffee, water, and then I sit at the kitchen table with my head in my hands.

'Mrs Cavanaugh, are you all right?'

Michelle comes into view as I slowly raise my head, her features slightly blurred by my hangover. 'I'm fine, thank you. Would you mind feeding the dogs and letting them out for a few hours?'

'Of course,' she replies.

I can tell, as she hesitates before leaving, that there's more she wants to say. Slowly, while trying not to aggravate the spreading pain in my skull, I get to my feet and follow her.

'How are you, Michelle?'

'Oh,' she says, as she opens the cupboard with the pet food inside. 'I'm fine.'

'I'm sorry we haven't given you more time off after Grace—'

'I wouldn't dream of it,' she says fiercely. 'You need the help here. You're the ones who…'

Who lost a child.

I nod. 'I know. But still, you must miss her a lot.'

Her chin wobbles, but she's made of tougher stuff than most. I appreciate the way she gets it under control within a few moments. 'I do.'

'Was Grace ever… rude to you?'

Michelle regards me with her eyes narrowed, a question on her lips. 'No, never. She was always extremely courteous and sweet, even when she was in one of her moods.'

We both smile. Ah, the teenage door-slamming. The thunderous expressions and the music blasting from her room. The house is so *quiet* now.

I sigh. 'I don't know… There's a lot I don't know about Grace, about her life before she died. A lot I wish I'd known.'

Michelle fiddles with the dog bowls. 'My daughter is in her twenties and we're finally friends, but when she was a teenager we had no relationship at all. She barely spoke to me between the ages of thirteen and eighteen. You couldn't have known.' The kibble bounces against the metal bowls and I consider that I'll never know what a thirty-year-old Grace would have been like.

'I'm sorry, I shouldn't have—'

'Talked about your daughter? God, Michelle, don't be ridiculous. Are people never going to mention their children to me again?'

'Even still, I…'

I wave a dismissive hand. 'Before Grace died, did you notice her spending time with any new people? It's silly, really, but I watched one of her vlog things and she mentioned a new friend. I thought maybe I could track them down and chat to them. It's hard to piece together her mental state before she died. Maybe this new friend could help me do that.'

Michelle pauses, and I can tell she's thinking carefully. 'There was a girl I saw her with in Ash Dale village. She had dark hair. But I didn't see her again and I don't know her name. Sorry.'

'That's okay,' I reply.

Before the dogs come bounding out of their baskets for food, I make my way back into the family room and pick up the house phone. Charles's Filofax is back in his car, but I have the times and dates of the mysterious 'G to T' sessions written down for reference. All of them occurred during term time, at lunch. Surely, if Charles was picking up Grace from school, her form tutor would have been notified. The sixth formers are allowed to leave school at lunchtime, but visitors to the school need to sign in to access the car park. It's a long shot, but I'm hopeful that Grace would've had to inform her tutor if Charles was picking her up every week.

The receptionist answers and I ask to speak to Preeya. When the receptionist tells me she's teaching, I explain who I am and there's a pause.

'I'll get her right away.'

Whether it's the money connected to the name or the tragedy that has motivated her, I don't know and I don't care.

'Hi, Preeya, just a quick one. Sorry to pull you out of class.'

'Oh, that's fine.'

'I was going through some paperwork here and realised Grace had a standing appointment that took her out of school every Thursday lunchtime. Was this recorded at the school or not?'

'Grace's therapy sessions, you mean? Yes, she told us about them. Charles picked her up every week.'

'Oh yes, I remember now. I'd completely forgotten they were on that day. Thanks, Preeya.'

I swallow thickly to cover up my rising anger and disbelief. Yet another lie hidden by my own family. If it's true, both my husband and my daughter were keeping secrets from me. But worse, it means there was something so wrong with Grace that she needed therapy to cope with the problem. She needed help and she didn't come to me; she went to someone else and then hid it from me.

'Can I ask you another question?'

'Sure,' she replies.

'Were there any behavioural issues that I should have been aware of? There are some rumours flying around her group of friends – you know what teenage girls are like.'

Preeya makes a guttural sound. 'Yes, I certainly do.'

'Some are saying that Grace was a bully.'

'A bully?' Preeya sounds confused. 'No, I haven't heard anything like that.' There's a pause. 'Well…'

'What is it? Look, don't feel awkward – I want to know. It's important.'

'Her group sometimes teased the more… unusual kids.'

'What do you mean by unusual?'

'Oh,' she says, 'you know… The Goth kids. The socially awkward students who don't get along with the rest. I wouldn't say they were *bullies*. As far as I know, they didn't pull down their pants or give them wedgies, but they probably weren't particularly kind to them either.'

'And you didn't step in?'

There's another pause. 'It didn't escalate to that level.'

'As far as you knew,' I reply.

She hesitates again. 'Is there something I need to know, Kat?'

'It's too late now, isn't it?' I sigh. 'You should've told me all of this while she was still alive.'

CHAPTER TWENTY

There are too many threads to pull, so I make a list.

<u>Liars</u>
Charles
Alicia
Ethan
Grace

Grace.

She was a liar and I have to accept it. She lied to me about who she was, pretending to be the perfect daughter when in fact she was a bully, she was in therapy, she had secret friends and she had a secret pregnancy. And then there is my husband, who lied about where he was when my daughter went missing and hid Grace's therapy from me.

Alicia and Ethan went behind Grace's back. Alicia sent her a threatening message. Did she send the unpleasant condolence card? Did she send me those texts? Did she put the videos of Grace on YouTube? But if it was her, how did she find out my real name – Katie? Perhaps her mother told her. We may have talked about my past once or twice. It's not something I mention a lot around Charles's friends, but Jenny likes to probe. Charles may even have mentioned it to Malc. I can imagine Charles complaining about his trashy council-estate mother-in-law.

Or could it be Charles? Has he been doing this to me in order to circumvent the truth? Can I see him buying sets of cheap pay-as-you-go phones and hiding them away? When I received the first text, where was he? Supposedly at work, but for all I know he might have been following me, making me think the school was the key to uncovering the truth. Throwing me off the scent.

And in the middle of all this there's the pregnancy. I still don't know who the father is. This new video of Grace and Ethan is a surprise. Surely, if the message sender is telling the truth about the date of the video, then Ethan as the killer is still a possibility. But I also need to keep in mind that a person sending threatening messages probably isn't the most reliable source. They sent me the videos they wanted me to see, to make me form an opinion of my daughter curated by them. I need to keep that in mind.

I fold up the list and place it in the pocket of my jeans, noticing the extra space around the waistband. My toned, gently muscular frame is wasting away. No, no, no. If I'm going to catch a murderer, I need to start keeping up my strength. Sunlight blooms through the large window and I take a deep breath, making my decision. There is one person who stands out to me, who was closest to Grace, who has lied to me several times. One person who has the means to cover their tracks. I nod to myself.

Finally, I think I know who did this.

What I'm about to do is not going to be easy. It's not a truth I want to accept, but I can't get it out of my head. To finally uncover the secrets hidden within my family, I start with my husband. I make up an email address very similar to one for a top investment company, and then I send an email to Charles's secretary asking her to arrange a meeting at a hotel bar in Derby near Charles's office. For most of my marriage, I've thought of Charles as a mummy's boy, a man who likes to be dominated by women, who needs guidance and comfort. But what if that is his way of hiding his twisted nature? I can't allow myself to forget that he's also a powerful, rich man, used to getting what he wants. If my mother is right – if Charles really did hurt Grace – then I need to be sure he won't respond with violence when I confront him. I want him on neutral ground. I won't be doing what all the wronged wives on TV do, throwing kitchen utensils at him while screaming like a banshee. No, I want a public space, and I want to ensure my safety.

In my email, my fake persona enquires about Charles's Chelsea property, which I know he's been eager to sell for months now. I set up a meeting for tomorrow, which means I have one more night to act like the good wife. One more night to fake it.

Grace, you weren't like me, were you? If I'm right, you were abused and traumatised. That's why you acted out at school. You hid it from me, what he did to you, because you were controlled by him this entire time. He always says that in business he gets what he wants, so why wouldn't he get what he wants at home, too? If I'm right, he's the monster. He's the one who hurt you. If I'm right…

What if I'm wrong?

As I allow my mind to wander, an uneasy tingling sensation spreads across my skin. I see Charles carrying Grace in his arms after she fell asleep in the car. I see him cradling her as a newborn baby. I see him pretending to be a pony on Christmas day, with Grace on his back, giggling and grinning.

And yet… my mother whispered those words into my ear and I saw his every move in a different way. He lied to me. Why would he do that?

If he hurt you, Grace, I will kill him.

My husband sleeps softly next to me, a snore and a snort here and there to break the silence. He rolls onto his back and his mouth gapes open almost comically. We haven't closed the curtains – at my request, because I want to wake up with the sunrise. The earlier tomorrow begins, the sooner our sham marriage can stop.

I lean back against the headboard, unable to quell the rising doubts which are swirling around my mind. The reason sleep alludes me is because I can't stop thinking back to the night we met, at that private function. Charles was a generous tipper and kind to the staff – including me. On one occasion, he chastised a greying, rotund lord who called me a 'cutie' and slapped my backside. He didn't take me around the back of the venue and fuck me standing up – which happened a lot between the waitresses and the clients – instead he'd asked me out on a date, which I found rather endearing. All of the other rich dicks had been much more forward about what they desired, and it was usually a discreet fumble their wives would never know about. Back then I'd been indecisive about what I wanted for myself. A mistress's life could be pleasant enough. Perhaps I could demand hush money or a few pretty jewels. If the right man came along, I could end up with a nice city apartment somewhere.

Charles made me realise I could have more. He was the first man who wanted to take me out where we would be seen. Our first date was to a plush restaurant. I ordered a steak; he ordered lamb. We kissed in his car when he dropped me off outside my old flat. He was never an attractive man – seventeen years older, carrying a bit of weight around the middle, hair balding in one spot at the back and a large red nose that reminded me of the prince he shares a name with – but he wasn't playing a game, which surprised me a lot.

We went on dates together while he took the loud woman in sequins to important events. She was apparently the niece of his mother's friend, and therefore 'approved' by Emily, whose approval was hard to come by. Charles, bless his heart, never stopped aiming for it. He saw me on weeknights, but she had his arm when it mattered, and I didn't like that.

That was when I started playing the game for him.

It helped that I figured out what he liked, and I utilised it. Men with domineering mothers like to be dominated.

Lying there in bed with the cover over my skin, a flush of heat spreads all over me from neck to feet. The emotion rises, quick and all-consuming, too fast and fleeting to understand it. In one fluid motion I throw back the duvet, wrap my legs around Charles's sleeping body and lift myself into a sitting position, resting my hands on his chest. He wakes, his wide eyes illuminated by the security light outside our home.

'Kat, what are you doing?'

My hands slide up his chest, caressing the silk paisley pyjamas he's worn in rotation since we married. A soft *Shhhhh* escapes my lips as my fingertips move upwards, closer and closer...

'Kat, I can't.' His hands grope to find my upper arms, but I push back.

'Isn't this what you want?' I begin to wrap my fingers around his neck, thickened by age and weight.

'No,' he says firmly. 'Not now.'

Shhhhh.

My hands clamp around his neck, tightening and tightening, squeezing dangerously. Am I strong enough to end his life right now? Do I have the physical strength to kill this man? I could watch the life fade from his eyes. I did it once before, back when I was Katie Flack. His hands grasp hold of both my arms, clamping them to my sides. He wriggles underneath me, almost tipping me off.

'Isn't this what you want?' I say, louder now. 'Isn't this why you married me?' Fat tears of frustration fall down my cheeks.

Beneath my hands, his skin is reddening. He grasps my arms, and before I can do anything else, he throws me off, rolls on top of me and pins my arms behind my head.

'Stop playing games, Kat. Stop it.'

'You're only firm with me when we're in bed,' I goad.

He lets go, moving away in disgust. Then he sits up, swings his legs over the side of the bed and sits staring out of the window into the garden.

'I know you're grieving,' he says, 'but that isn't the answer.'

'Just go back to sleep.' My voice is thick with tears that I don't want him to see.

'We should talk tomorrow,' he says, softer now. 'You need to talk.'

'We will,' I reply.

I lie down next to him, but I don't sleep. My mind goes back to the decision I made and the guilt that I have assigned to him. It goes back to the evidence, and I decide that I'm right.

CHAPTER TWENTY-ONE

I don't wake with the sunrise; instead, I sleep right through, until Charles drives away in the Jaguar. Before I get in the shower, I crawl into Grace's bed for a half-hour nap. When I wake again, I wash my hair, apply make-up, put on my form-fitting grey dress with stilettos and a cashmere cardigan and book a taxi to the train station.

My stomach rumbles on the train, but given the options available from the concession stand, I sip water instead. The sleepless night and my sporadic eating have upset my digestive system, leaving me nauseated and hungry at the same time. Eventually, as the train makes its way to Derby, I decide on a few plain biscuits to settle things down.

None of this is like me. I'm not someone who gets nervous or experiences strong emotions. Grace, if you could see me now, you'd laugh. You always used to say that I was perpetually unruffled. I'm a cold fish; that's what everyone thinks.

The memory of Grace makes me feel a little better as I depart the train and jump in another taxi. With careful planning, I've made sure that I'll have plenty of time to settle in at the hotel bar where we're meeting. Charles will have no idea what's going on, and for once I'll get him on the back foot. This is my safe, public space in which to find out exactly what went on between him and Grace, and I have everything I need to take him down.

What if I'm wrong?

I push that thought away. There's no point in doubting myself now. I remind myself of the WhatsApp messages between Grace's friends: *Her dad is weird. Remember what she said about him? Yeh. Fucked up.* And he lied to me. He's been taking Grace out of school every week for therapy. He wasn't where he said he was when Grace first went missing. I remind myself that he's rich, and rich men get what they want. I remind myself of what my mother said to me at the funeral: *There are rumours…*

But then the name Katie Flack pops into my mind.

My old name keeps intruding my thoughts. If it was Charles who sent those texts, why would he use that name? Perhaps he wanted to throw me off? That could be the reason for the anonymous messages – not to threaten, but to misdirect. But why would Charles post that video of Grace at school?

Why are these thoughts coming to me now? It's too late; I've made my decision. I force myself to quash all the niggles telling me that there are alternative explanations. Telling me that Charles couldn't possibly be the one who hurt Grace. My throat turns dry because there's no other choice.

I reach the hotel bar and sit at my table. My bag – which contains everything I need to threaten him – rests by my leg. Charles enters and I let out a long exhale.

This is it.

From my perch next to the table, I cross my legs elegantly and watch as his eyes roam across the bar. His gaze reaches my legs before it does my eyes, and then the shock registers. As his face reddens, I can't stop thinking about last night, when I wrapped my hands around his neck and he pushed me back, pinning me beneath him. The anger was visible on his face, and I'd seen a resolve in him that reminded me that yes, my mild-mannered husband is capable of violence.

He strides over to me, chin angled down, the shape of his skull made evident by the shadows catching him at the right angles. Never has my husband appeared more dangerous. My throat becomes dry and I take a small sip of my wine.

'What are you doing now?' Spit flies from between his teeth as he clenches his jaw. 'I told you last night to stop playing games. I'm about to meet a potential buyer.'

'Yes, I know.' I raise my eyebrows. 'And what does she look like?'

Charles sighs. 'Did you set this entire thing up? Why are you wasting my time, Kat?'

'Why? How precious is your time?'

He grabs hold of my wrist as though to yank me from my seat, but instead I pull him closer to me.

'Try it and I'll scream,' I say. 'Just sit the fuck down, Charles. I brought you here because I want to speak to you.'

'Instead of the seven-bedroom mansion in which we live as husband and wife, you mean?' he retorts.

'I wanted to speak in a public place.'

He pauses, half on the seat, then sinks down onto the leather, crossing one leg over the other. Charles may be balding and slightly red in the face, but he still possesses the presence of a very rich man, which can be quite sexy. My stress nausea returns and I try to ignore it, but Charles notices me wince.

'Are you all right?'

'Fine.' I run my fingers over the soft flesh beneath my eyes and try to pull myself together.

'Shall I get you a glass of water?'

'No.' I can't bear him being kind to me. Not now.

'Kat, what's all this about? Are you all right? You don't seem yourself.'

I let out a low laugh. 'You have no idea who I am.' Then I pause. 'And I don't think I know who you are – not anymore.'

He sighs. 'So, we don't know each other. After eighteen years of marriage.'

I take a sip of my wine and shrug. 'Haven't you always suspected it?'

'No.' He leans forward. 'You're my *wife*.' There's an infantile aspect to the way he pleads with me, and for an instant I'm almost swayed into believing him. But when he reaches for my hand, I snatch it away.

'What did you do to her?' I ask.

'To who?'

'Grace.'

Two sharp glassy eyes find mine. 'Are you serious?'

I force myself to respond with the same ferocious stare. 'You lied to me about where you were when Grace went missing. You told me two different things. I checked your diary and all it said was "H". There were more entries, too. "G to T" every Thursday lunchtime. I called Grace's form tutor and I know you were taking her to therapy. Why? Did you want a therapist to keep tabs on her? To see what she'd say in private? Grace talked about you to her friends and they all think you're weird. Why is that?'

'You are serious.' He leans back in his chair.

Ignoring him, I reach down to my bag and retrieve my laptop, silently placing it on the table between us. I lift the lid. 'You lie about a lot of things, Charles. For instance, you lie about the safety standards employed throughout your business. I have a document here highlighting six serious violations in all of the pubs you own—'

'Kat, stop. Stop this now.' His voice is low, almost a growl, and much angrier than I've ever heard it. 'Are you blackmailing me?'

'I'm pointing out your moral character,' I say calmly. 'I was only twenty-one when you met me, and I looked young for my age—'

'You looked and acted old for your age, Kat.' His lips press into a thin line as though frustrated with me.

'What about our sex life? I've always been willing to do things other women wouldn't do, and yet you don't touch me anymore. Is that because you've been hurting our daughter instead?'

His eyes flash with fury. When he reaches forward to grasp the laptop, I move it away from him. 'Don't forget we're in a public place. You can't touch me here.'

'That's why you lured me here? So that I wouldn't hurt you?'

'Exactly.'

'Don't be so ridiculous,' he scoffs.

'I have copies of everything in case you're planning to snatch the laptop and run away. Let's face it, you wouldn't make a good criminal on the run.'

I've found the upper hand and it's helping to calm my stomach. Moving slowly, and without averting my gaze, I sip my wine. 'All I want to know is what happened to Grace. Was it an accident? Why, Charles? *Why* did you do it?'

I find that my rage is tapping away at a closed door, desperate to break through, but I will remain strong and keep it at bay. There's no way I can make it through this without a cool, collected exterior.

'Tell me, Charles. Get it all out and you'll feel better for it. You've been holding it in, haven't you? The truth is a burden, pressing you down. I know you feel guilt. I know you feel remorse. Just tell me what happened that night.'

He's quiet, his chest rising and falling quickly. Calm and controlled, he adjusts the cuffs of his suit jacket and rests his elbows on the arms of the leather chair, breathing heavily through his nose.

'What's your plan here, Kat? Are you recording me without my consent? What are you going to take to the police?'

'Who said anything about police? I have my own ways of getting justice for what happened to my daughter.'

He laughs softly. 'And what are those?'

No, I think. You won't know about those ways until I deliver them to you.

After a few moments of silence, I say evenly, 'It was clever, making Grace write the suicide note. You have the police fooled. I can't go to them without evidence.'

'Do you have evidence?' he asks.

'That depends,' I say. 'Are you the father of her baby?'

Charles's face contorts into several ugly expressions. He clenches both fists, turning burgundy from the nose downwards. Then he lets out a small laugh, removes his suit jacket and pulls at his tie.

'Am I the father of Grace's baby?' He shakes his head.

'Is that funny?'

He shakes his head again, unbuttoning the collar of his shirt. 'Maybe.'

'I don't think it is.'

'I can see that.'

'Well, are you going to deny it?'

'I think perhaps we should get a divorce,' he says instead.

'That's something of an understatement, don't you think?'

'You're clearly not the person I thought you were. I should've seen it a long time ago, but at least I know your true character now. Your behaviour since Grace died has been nothing short of unnatural. Where are the tears? You've shown so little emotion, I've often questioned whether you even care that she died.'

I let out a snort. 'And this from the man who's been acting the entire time.'

The right side of his mouth lifts up in a smirk. 'Don't you think that if I was abusing our daughter, putting her in therapy would be the stupidest thing I could do?'

'Unless you controlled it all. I'm not you; I don't know what's in your mind. Maybe therapy was a complete lie. Maybe you told Preeya that so she wouldn't question why you kept picking Grace up from school. Maybe "T" isn't therapy at all.'

'No, it is. That's the one thing you've got right. Grace was in therapy for about a year and it has nothing to do with me. It's because of *you*.'

Perhaps it's the wine, or perhaps it's the anger still knocking at that closed door, but my face flushes red-hot. 'You're a liar.'

'You can request the therapist's notes, if you like. Grace was worried that she wasn't developing a connection with other people because she'd never truly felt connected to you.'

'Stop lying and tell me the truth, Charles—'

'You're right. I do need to stop lying to you. It's time for you to face up to what a bad mother you've been all these years.'

Every part of my body tenses with pure rage. 'Take that back.' I pause, desperately trying to control myself. 'I went to every school play, I took her wherever she wanted to go, I spent time with her…' I stop talking as he slowly shakes his head.

'Yeah, when you felt like it. You didn't go to every school play. You'd have months of total disinterest in our daughter, until finally something would click and you'd start paying attention again. I gave you a pass because of what you went through with your own mother, but it's clear that I made the wrong *fucking decision*, because she'd still be here if I hadn't. That's the way I killed her. You wanted to know that, didn't you? I killed her because I allowed you to hurt her.'

Beneath the table, my legs are trembling. This is all wrong. He's all wrong. I was a *good* mother. Grace never wanted for anything. She never knew about the emptiness inside me because I took every precaution to keep it from her. Fake it until you make it, that was me. That was how I became a mother.

'And you're right about another thing: I did lie to you about where I was on the day Grace went missing. I wasn't at the office in Derby and I wasn't in a meeting in Nottingham; I was in Sheffield, speaking to a consultant at Weston Park Hospital.'

All of the pent-up rage drains from my body, leaving me bloodless and limp. H for hospital.

Charles rolls up a sleeve to reveal a bruise on the inside of his forearm. How had I not noticed that? 'In case you wanted proof, here you go. This is from one of several blood tests I've had recently. And I haven't fucked you, Kat, because I have cancer.'

A cold sense of dread hits me in my core and the noise of the bar narrows until all I can hear is a high-pitched buzzing. Charles leans across the table and shakes my arm.

'No, don't you dare. Don't you dare faint on me. You're going to listen to this. I'm dying. My daughter killed herself two weeks ago and I'm dying. She had an illness, Kat. I don't know if it's the same illness you have, because I don't know what's wrong with you, but I know that she wasn't well and that's why she took her own life. Are you listening?'

I limply nod my head.

'I'll send you the records of my hospital visits; I'll send you the emails that record my appointments; and we'll see the consultant together. I'm not lying. I have prostate cancer and perhaps I'll soon be with our daughter again.'

CHAPTER TWENTY-TWO

Charles walks out of the bar and leaves me sitting in front of an open laptop and a half-empty glass of wine. I can't stand up because my legs are trembling all the way from my hips to my toes. All I can do is wait until it passes.

I sit there alone, trying not to picture the expression on Charles's face as he told me about his cancer diagnosis. But when I stop imagining Charles's face, I see Grace, staring at me, judging me for what I did.

But it made sense, Grace. I thought everything pointed to him.

No, that isn't true. My mother got in my head and made me think it was him. I examined the evidence and made it fit what I believed. How could I have got it all so wrong?

After about an hour, I finally feel able to stand. With numb fingers, I slowly pack away the laptop, go to the bathroom, splash cold water on my face and leave.

Georgie and Porgie leap up to my waist, licking my hands, wagging their tails. All I can think about is Emily Cavanaugh, the matriarch, the woman Charles respected more than anyone else. I never met his father; he died in a car accident several years before we began our relationship, which I think made Emily even more protective of her son. If she knew what I'd accused Charles of, I would be out of this house in an instant – back to nothing. Back to poverty.

While Charles's words about divorce were said during a flash of anger, I can't help but think that I should begin to protect myself, in case he was serious. After all, how can we possibly go on after I accused him of abusing our child? That in itself is marriage-ending, isn't it?

My mind runs through practicalities. There's an account with money in it that I can call my own, but the rest is spread around Charles's own accounts. He could try to screw me in the divorce, which means I might need a decent solicitor.

But as I stroke Porgie's head, all those thoughts disappear. None of that matters. I don't care about the money or a possible return to poverty. If what Charles said is true, then my husband of almost eighteen years is ill, and I need to process that, but right now all I can think about is Grace. When I close my eyes, I see her bleeding through her clothes, pawing at the quarry stone, the ghosts of the Suicide Spot terrorising her mind. I still don't know what happened to her, and I'll never find out if Charles kicks me out of the house.

I need to figure out what might happen next. He might insist I find a hotel or stay with a friend, or he might go down to London and stay there. Maybe he'll cool down enough for us to stay in the house together – temporarily, at least. I push Porgie away and he whimpers, but it's all a show. He merely wants more food. Greedy.

My feet ache; my belly is empty; I'm weakened by the stress of the day. Perhaps it's time to concede that I cannot do this in the clinical way I thought I could. This emotional wound is opening up. I thought I could force it to clot with my anger, but I can't.

The dogs follow me through the house as I collect the laptop and take it through to the family room. I'm in the process of booting up the computer when the house phone rings. I shoo a barking Georgie away and snatch the phone from the coffee table.

'Hello?'

'Hi, this is Chloe from the Waterford catering company. We're calling about the event next week.'

'What event? Sorry, there's been a family tragedy and I've been all over the place. You'll have to remind me.'

'I'm so sorry…' She hesitates. 'It's the charity clay-pigeon shoot that you're hosting at Farleigh Hall – proceeds going to the Prince's Countryside Fund. We're arranging the catering…'

'I'd forgotten all about it,' I admit. 'Can I call you back?' With everything going on, I'm not sure I'll even be here next week.

Just as I'm hanging up the phone, I hear the front door opening, and while the person makes their way through the hallway, I consider heading upstairs in case it's Charles. But then Michelle walks into the family room, her usual easy smile brightening the gloomy atmosphere.

'Afternoon, Mrs Cavanaugh,' she says. 'Want me to let the dogs out for a run?'

'That would be great, thanks.'

'Oh, you don't look at all well.' She stops in her tracks, frowning like a disapproving mother. 'Have you eaten?'

'No,' I confess. 'I'm a bit under the weather, to be honest.'

'Let me make you some toast,' she suggests. 'Toast and butter. It's what my mother always used to make for me when I was sick.' When she smiles, her grey eyes twinkle. In her fifties now, Michelle is still an attractive woman. I envy her warmth. Some people exude goodness, and that can't be faked – no matter how much I try.

'I'm not sick. But I don't feel well either.'

'I know,' she says, already on her way out of the room. 'But you need to keep your strength up.'

I lean back on the sofa with the laptop open on my thighs. The document detailing Charles's wrongdoings is open on the screen. It would be tacky, but I can still threaten him with its release. If a journalist found out about these health-and-safety violations, the chain of pubs Charles inherited when his father died would be closed down pretty swiftly. Perhaps I still have the upper hand here, if not the moral high ground. The thought of using this information against Grace's father is one of the many causes of my nausea. But then I have a second thought: I haven't checked the validity of Charles's story yet. What if the cancer is nothing more than a fabrication?

Who would lie about having cancer? Someone without remorse. *A killer.*

I need to be careful if I'm to uncover the truth, and I need to make sure I'm not too hasty in accepting excuses and stories. Even now, after the day I've had, I can't trust Charles. I can't trust anyone.

By the time he comes home, it's dark, Michelle is gone and I'm alone in the family room, feet curled under my body, the grey dress loose around my disappearing frame. Even though I want to self-medicate, I am forcing myself to avoid any kind of alcohol in order to keep my faculties sharp and fresh. This is not going to be easy.

Charles stumbles into the house, tripping over the umbrella stand – I hear it crashing onto the tiles – then bumping against the hallway wall. He falls over his feet as he comes into the room and sees me snuggled up on the sofa.

'I thought you'd be gone.'

'No,' I say carefully. 'I'm still here. And for what it's worth, I'm sorry about earlier.'

Charles collapses into a chair and begins removing his shoes. 'It's worth nothing, Kat. Nothing at all.'

'Someone murdered our daughter. Aren't you angry about that?'

He throws his brogue to the floor and it thuds against the thick carpet. 'Our daughter was ill and she killed herself. She was depressed. Here.' He pulls a small square of card from his trouser pocket and throws it down at my feet. 'Call her therapist if you don't believe me. She was lost, and we failed her.' He crumples in, face reddening, nose streaming. But there's a hardness to him now. He pulls himself together with a lot more ease than before. 'I want you gone. I won't live with a woman who thinks I could rape and murder my own daughter.'

'No,' I say softly. 'We're going to work through this.'

He regards me with complete incredulity. 'Are you insane?'

'Maybe.' I smile at him through the darkness. 'I don't care what you say, Charles. Someone killed our only child and I'm going to find out who. Here.' I toss him my phone. 'Look at the texts I've been getting.'

Charles has to hold the phone at arm's length to read it. 'What are these? Are they threats?'

'Yes.'

'What was the link in this one? I click on it and it doesn't go anywhere.'

I switch on the laptop and open the video of Grace bullying the dark-haired girl. Charles watches with his hand over his mouth. 'Play it again.' I do and he shakes his head. 'If someone told me about this, I wouldn't believe them.'

'Me neither.'

He sighs, passes me the phone, then leans back against the chair, his greasy, thinning hair creating a halo. 'This is all so fucked up.'

'And we haven't even got to your cancer yet.'

He begins to laugh, and a low chuckle reverberates around the room.

'You know, whatever happens, I'll always be grateful for what you did for me,' I say. 'Without you, I'd be working behind a bar, or on drugs and living with my mother.'

He shakes his head. 'No, you wouldn't.'

'I was convinced that the one thing I did right in this world was Grace, but now I'm not so sure.' I shake my head. 'Do you think Grace had, I don't know, a personality disorder or something?'

He turns to me sharply. 'The therapist would have told me.'

'How did you get the therapist to tell you about Grace's sessions?' I ask.

'I paid her.' He shrugs. 'Everyone has a price.' When he sees the surprise on my face, he adds, 'It's the way the world works.'

'How unremorseful of you.' But he's right, as much as I hate to admit it. 'Do you think most rich people don't care about other people? If you grow up getting whatever you want, does it stop you empathising with others?'

He stares out into the distance. 'I don't know. I don't think so.'

CHAPTER TWENTY-THREE

A reluctant agreement is made, because even though Charles hasn't quite come around to my thinking, he at least wants to understand what happened to Grace just before she died. Our truce is fragile, with broken trust on both sides. I would like to trust him again, if only to have an ally to help me get through this, but I'm not there yet. Proof of both the therapy and the cancer would help.

Charles moves into one of the spare rooms, but we decide to remain living together as part of our pact to find out what happened to Grace. Part of that agreement involves having a daily conversation about what I've discovered. Our truce includes going ahead with the charity event, which is now fast approaching. I even tell Charles some of the things I've learned about Alicia and Ethan – missing out my little misdemeanours, like sending the orchestra all of Alicia's bitchy messages and saving her cosy videos with Ethan in case I need them for leverage in the future.

The text messages have ceased for now, which makes me wonder why the sender has stopped. I haven't been to the school, therefore inadvertently complying with the threat about poking my nose in where it isn't wanted. What could I possibly have learned at Lady Margaret's that day? The messages came from two numbers, but were they from the same person? Or two separate people with two separate agendas? Staying away from the school doesn't have any link to me seeing who Grace 'really was'.

I decide to take Charles's advice and call Grace's therapist. A woman called Dr Bruner, who insists that I call her Mandy, answers the phone and agrees to answer my questions.

'I was so sorry to hear about Grace passing away,' she gushes. 'I wanted to come to the funeral, but I'm afraid I didn't feel up to it. When a patient, and such a young patient, passes away, it's...' She drifts off, as though recognising that there's no good way to end that sentence. 'She was a lovely girl.'

I can't bring myself to play this game, to acknowledge all the virtues my daughter possessed, to explain my grief to another person and wait for their pity or judgement. Instead, I dive in. 'My husband paid you extra to tell him about Grace's sessions.'

'Oh, I… Well, it wasn't quite like that.'

'It was, Dr Bruner. Mandy. It was exactly like that.'

She sniffs. I ignore it.

'Was Grace depressed?'

'I never made that diagnosis,' she admits. 'But I would say that she was suffering from anxiety. She was very concerned about school and she showed signs of stress. I told Mr Cavanaugh all of this.'

'When was the last time you saw her?' I ask.

'Let me think,' she replies. 'It would have been the Thursday before…'

'She died,' I finish, aware that my voice is unemotional and that dear old Mandy is probably diagnosing me already.

'She was upset as soon as she walked in the room. I asked her to tell me what was wrong, but she wasn't communicative that day. I remember it well because she was out of sorts. She left early, in fact, because she didn't want to talk.'

I press a hand to my abdomen, sickened by the thought of Grace lost and tearful, storming out of her therapy session. 'Was she behaving in a way that would be consistent with her taking her own life?'

'Oh, well now, Mrs Cavanaugh, that isn't a question I can answer. People behave in all different manners before they commit suicide. Some are very distressed, others are in fact very amenable and happy. To be honest, a lot of people who commit suicide show relief, because they've made the decision and that alleviates some of their pain.'

Pain. There's that word again. How it creeps into our lives, sometimes treading softly and sneakily, other times stomping its great feet. I never imagined that I would ever experience as much pain as I do right now, listening to this woman describe my smiley, enthusiastic daughter as someone who could have committed suicide. Someone who was in *pain.* To me she's still the same eight-year-old who sang karaoke all through Christmas, who even managed to force Emily Cavanaugh into a duet for 'Rockin' Around the Christmas Tree'.

'Okay, thank you.' She's still speaking as I put down the phone, but all I want is silence.

I'm awake at night again, staring at my outfit for the shoot tomorrow: a cream cashmere V-neck, Marc Jacobs trousers in camel and a tweed hunting jacket. Later, for the dinner, I'll change into a white knee-length dress with a cropped pink jacket. Soft, malleable, approachable. All the hard edges are gone, and I'll be rounded off, like a shark with its teeth filed.

It's been five days since I accused Charles of killing Grace and I'm still not even close to uncovering what happened to her. But Charles took me to see the consultant who diagnosed his prostate cancer, which took place in the correct hospital, in the right department. It all adds up, except for the fact that I can't stop thinking about one thing Charles said: everyone has a price.

Do I trust him? Not fully. Not completely. I still don't trust anyone on this earth.

*

The next morning, I complete the look with a slick of lip gloss and two long curls framing my face. As soon as my outfit is on and my hair and make-up are complete, the tired and stressed Kat fades away and I become someone reborn. I even eat breakfast as the caterers set up, this time without any hint of nausea. The house bustles with excitement, and yet Charles and I are silent.

His agreement was grudging – the text messages his one reason for carrying on. But at least he's entertaining the idea that Grace was killed. As he sits cleaning his shotgun ready for the shoot later, I notice his jaw is set with determination. Today, our house will be a battleground.

When I move to the morning-room window to watch the cars arrive, all I can think about is the day of Grace's funeral as we'd lined up in this spot, waiting for the coffin. If I close my eyes, I can see the deep mahogany of the wooden box and imagine her lying in the soft cream interior. I pull out my phone and call her again, suddenly remembering that I still haven't found her missing phone.

After the beep of her voicemail message, I freeze, staring through the latticed window, mouth opening and closing but nothing coming out. I don't know what to say anymore because I have to admit to myself that I don't know who Grace was. She wasn't the bright, shining spark of goodness I'd always thought. She wasn't even the *person* I thought she was. My memory of her is of a cheerful, happy girl. But it's all a lie.

She went to a therapist because of me. She was ill because I didn't show her enough love.

Can a sociopath love?

Not usually.

The doorbell rings, pulling me out of my thoughts. I hadn't even noticed the large 4 x 4 pulling into the drive. After jolting in surprise at the sound, I see Jenny is waving her arm manically, tottering across the drive with her long scarf blowing in the wind. I hurry through the house and into the hallway to greet them, but Michelle already has the door open.

'Kat! How are you?' Malc embraces me as always, planting a kiss on each cheek.

'Oh, you know, still holding up.'

'Listen, it's so brave of you, hosting this. You know we would've taken on those duties for you if you'd needed us.'

'It's okay,' I reply. 'To be honest, I needed the distraction. And having everyone here is another way to honour her, you know?'

'I get it.' He nods. 'And, hey, you look sickeningly good in that hunting jacket. Are you a secret equestrian?'

'Emily Cavanaugh would turn in her grave if she thought I'd stepped even a toe into a stirrup.'

The quip makes me grin and Malc laugh heartily. We've always shared a dark sense of humour, and this is the first time since Grace died that I've found myself making a joke. Making someone else laugh feels wrong and right at the same time.

Before I can process that feeling, Jenny rushes in, with Alicia trailing behind. 'Kat, *darling*, how are you? How *are* you?'

She grabs me with both hands as usual, holding me at arm's length.

I offer her a sheepish smile. 'I'm okay. It's good to see you. Your hair looks gorgeous.'

'Oh,' she says, tucking a ringlet of strawberry blonde behind one ear. 'I popped into Derby this morning for a makeover. But look at you. You look *fantastic*.'

She continues holding my arms, looking at me intently. 'Did you call the psychic? I have a strong feeling that it would be good for you.'

Malc's shoulders sag. 'Jen, don't.' He flashes me a guilty smile.

Jenny raises her hands in apology. 'I'm not; I'm just checking in.'

'I haven't called,' I say, and then I add, 'not yet, anyway.' I may as well keep Jenny onside. Who knows, I might need her at some point. 'Why don't you come out into the estate? They're setting up the shoot.'

'Perfect.'

As Jenny links her arm with my own, I watch Alicia cautiously as she trails behind us with her flute case. Ethan is probably already here, setting up with the rest of the waitstaff, though he's managed to avoid me. The thought brings back a memory of Grace asking me to hire this specific catering company, those puppy-dog eyes of hers widening, and a shiver runs down my back.

'You know, I didn't think you'd go through with today,' Jenny says. 'You're so brave, Kat. *I* would've been a gibbering wreck these last few weeks, but you've almost managed to carry on as normal. I don't know *how* you do it.' Jenny is talking at rapid-fire pace, which usually means she's had a few glasses of Prosecco. I'm also not too stupid to hear the slight dig in her tone.

'I thought about cancelling,' I admit, leading her out to the patio. 'But I thought this might be another good way to honour Grace. She loved these events.'

'Oh, she did,' Jenny agrees. 'She was such a social butterfly. Just like Lissy. Where are you, Liss?' Jenny wafts her head back and forth to find her daughter, as though she's afraid to lose her.

'I'm here,' Alicia says in a bored voice.

When Jenny glances at Alicia, I do the same. Our eyes meet and Alicia stares me down, her expression cold and emotionless.

CHAPTER TWENTY-FOUR

The richest people in the north step out of their Range Rovers to join the shoot. A photographer from Tatler sets up next to the stables to take a few pics of those arriving, then moves around to the south field where canapés and champagne are being served.

The crack of gunfire sounds out and the men slap each other on the back as clay discs are obliterated in the air. Charles is a good shot, having been given lessons as a boy, and I can hear him ribbing the other competitors as he moves into the lead.

While the men compete, the women hang back, quaffing champagne and playing their own hunting games. Who can deliver the most efficient backhanded compliment? One of my favourites is to walk up to the Instagram influencers invited to the party and say, 'I love how you don't care how you come across on social media.' Nearly all of them reply 'Thank you.'

'Kat, there you are.' Malc pats me gently on the back and hands me another glass of champagne. 'Where have you been?'

'Annoying the Instagram models.' I nod across to a blonde taking a selfie next to a bottle of champagne, with a Formula One driver at her side. 'Look at her eyebrows. A toddler could do a better job with a Sharpie.'

Malc laughs. 'Did you set a dress code for tonight? Only *that* is certainly an unusual dress to wear to a shoot.'

'Yes, "surprised escort" wasn't exactly what I had in mind when I suggested "Sloane chic".' I bite my lip, that same sense of good and bad squirming inside me. It feels wrong to make someone laugh, to laugh myself, but at the same time it feels good to let loose. I hadn't realised quite how tightly wound I've been since Grace died, though the pain of missing her never goes away, not even for a second.

Malc's voice softens. 'It's good to have your sense of humour back. I've missed it.'

I take another sip of champagne. 'It does always seem to be us at the back during these events, cracking jokes about the guests, doesn't it? When we used to have parties here, Grace would come out and we'd be tipsy and joking and she'd pretend to understand what we were laughing about.'

'She looked up to you,' Malc says. 'Everyone saw it.'

My throat becomes thick with emotion, but I chase the sensation away with my champagne. Now isn't the time to crack.

Malc nudges me in the ribs and I get the impression he's about to lighten the mood. 'Hey, those Instagram models reminded me of something. What was that joke you told me at the parent-teacher mixer last year? About narcissists?'

I frown, trying to remember. Then a laugh bubbles up from my throat. 'Oh, the one my therapist told me? A narcissist and a sociopath walk into a bar. The narcissist starts telling the bartender stories about how great he is. The sociopath isn't talking; instead he's planning how to steal the narcissist's watch.'

'Shall we go steal their watches?' he says, a wicked grin spreading across his face.

'I already have,' I reply, finishing the last of my champagne. At that parent-teacher event, Grace's maths teacher had told me she was getting straight A's. We'd been talking about her possibilities regarding higher education. It feels like a lifetime ago.

'Another?'

But I shake my head, forcing away my memories and the desire to drink even more. I need to focus. 'How is Alicia doing? I'm sorry I haven't been to the house much.'

'Honestly, I'm worried about her,' Malc says. 'She's bottling something up. She goes around like everything is normal, and she never talks about Grace, then all of a sudden she'll be in floods of tears about it. She lost her phone, which is very unlike her. And' – he glances left and right, as though checking there's no one around – 'don't tell Jen this.'

I mime my lips being sealed.

'Well, Jen isn't helping at all. Lissy only gets upset after Jen has been winding her up. First of all, that psychic thing? Well, she made Alicia do it. I was furious, Kat, I can't even tell you.' He shakes his head and grips the champagne stem tight enough to turn his fingernails white. 'She had Alicia walking around saying that, according to the psychic, Grace forgives her. It's plain wrong.'

I glance away, considering whether there were any important nuggets of information to be mined from that or whether Alicia is bullshitting again. Does Alicia *want* forgiveness? And if so, what does she want to be forgiven for?

'Oh God, I'm such an insensitive arsehole. I shouldn't be talking about this to you.'

'Don't be ridiculous, Malc.' I place a hand on his arm to reassure him. 'I asked you how she was and I wanted to know. The psychic business doesn't faze me at all. I know it's a load of rubbish, but I don't have the heart to tell Jenny what I think about it.'

'Me neither.' He drains his glass then glances down at my hand, which I've purposefully left on his arm for a moment too long.

I clear my throat as I remove my hand, blinking a few times to make my eyes shine, all the while aware of Malc watching me intently. Oh, I'm no idiot. I've seen his lingering gaze and the way his eyes trail my body. I know that he's turned on by my spontaneity and wicked sense of humour. But I've never acted on it before, perhaps because I've never needed to. Or perhaps I'm simply a very loyal friend and wife. But now I'm going to use every means available to discover what happened to my daughter.

Both of us look away awkwardly, and I find Alicia staring at me from behind the patio doors, her eyes narrowing.

After the shoot, the guests make their way upstairs to change out of their wax jackets and boots. The thought of people using the guest rooms on Grace's floor is horrifying to me, but I've locked her door to prevent anyone going in there. While the staff prepare for the evening festivities, I head up to the bedroom to change into my evening dress.

I'm fiddling with an earring and making my way back down the stairs when a man passes me. His face is instantly familiar but I can't place him. He gently places a hand on my shoulder and says, 'I'm sorry. About Grace.'

But I instinctively move away, dropping the back of my earring. I mutter a curse word and glance around for it, lifting up my tight skirt to allow me to bend down.

'Sorry,' he says, reaching down to help me. 'I didn't mean to startle you.'

The tiny piece of metal eludes me. 'You didn't. It's a fiddly little thing.'

'Here.' The man holds up the butterfly clip triumphantly.

'Thank you.'

As I press the clip onto the stud, he regards me with friendly brown eyes. 'I was Grace's music teacher. Daniel Hawthorne.'

'Oh, Mr Hawthorne, hello.' Daniel Hawthorne, the young, attractive teacher whom all the girls fancied. He wrote a sweet message on her condolence card. I take his extended hand. 'You must be here with the orchestra then.'

He nods. 'Our first event since Grace passed away. We all miss her an awful lot.'

'The house is too quiet without the sound of her violin. I'm not sure I'll ever get used to that. Whenever I walk in the front door, I expect to hear her practising.'

'I'm so sorry.' He takes half a step back, as though repelled by the grief emanating from me. 'I didn't mean to bring up painful memories.'

'You haven't,' I say. 'They're happy memories. Or at least they'll get less painful over time. She talked about you much more than her other teachers. You were definitely her favourite.'

'She was a great student. Unbelievably talented. The entire orchestra misses her.'

'Thank you for the card. That was very kind.'

'We all meant every word. Grace touched all of our lives in some way.'

I understand that by nature I am suspicious about other people and their motives, which means I can't always trust my own instincts; but at the same time, I find it difficult to shake the notion that Daniel Hawthorne's words sound rehearsed in some way. However, as I'm thinking of a response, my name is called by someone downstairs.

'Would you excuse me?' I say.

He smiles. 'Of course.'

As I walk away, I can't help but look back at the handsome young man on the stairs. Now I know why Grace talked about him so often. Teenage girls easily become fixated on young, good-looking teachers, but there are times when that fixation can develop into more.

'Kat, there you are.' Charles appears from the kitchen and, to my surprise, wraps an arm around my waist, leading me into the vast dining room where Cavanaughs have hosted events for generations. The pared-down ensemble from the school orchestra is all set up, and a microphone is waiting at the end of the room. 'It's time for your speech.'

When I nod to him, acknowledging his reminder, he smiles, as though our relationship is as rock solid as ever. No one warns you, when you step into a different social class, that there are rules and expectations. Putting on a smile and pretending everything is fine is one of those rules that the upper classes follow exceedingly closely. I quietly clear my throat and make my way towards the microphone. It was agreed that I would toast Grace before the dinner began. We can't go through an event like this without referencing her.

I grab a glass of champagne from a tray and tap it gently with a knife. All at once, the room hushes and glamorous faces regard me from the crowd. Now isn't a good time to falter, like I did at Grace's memorial. This is the time to fake a smile and share heartfelt words.

'Thank you for coming, everyone. Charles and I almost cancelled this event…' I pause and put on a brave smile. 'But then we decided to carry on. It's not in us to hide away behind these walls. We want to share this house with our friends and family, and that's what we're doing tonight. The house has been particularly quiet recently – many of you know about the terrible, awful tragedy we suffered just a few weeks ago.' I stop and clear my throat. 'Grace meant the world to us. She was bright, loud, always playing the violin. She filled every room in this house with laughter, and that is what I want you all to do tonight. I want you to honour her. Think of Grace at her best, at her most beautiful, at her funniest. I know most of you knew her. Think of her and give generously, because Grace picked this charity. She picked this food and she chose for her own orchestra to provide us with entertainment while we eat. Remember the amazing, clever and beautiful person she was – and for God's sake crack a smile, you lot, will you?' I pause for laughter. 'To Grace, who is definitely cracking a smile right now, wherever she is.'

The room fills with gentle laughter and the guests echo my words: 'To Grace.'

I nod towards the orchestra. Daniel Hawthorne smiles, before facing the girls and their instruments. The music begins to play.

CHAPTER TWENTY-FIVE

For the first time since Grace died, there is laughter in the house. No one knows that I'm completely numb all the way through as I eat, make conversation and even find some of my sense of humour again. The night is going surprisingly well, and even Charles manages to hide his disgust for me by occasionally putting his arm around my waist or holding my hand. I'm impressed with him. I never knew he had this steely, determined side.

Some of the day guests have already left. Not everyone at the shoot would have been able to fit into the dining room for the banquet. But I don't cry any tears for the Instagram models who have gone home with their sportsmen, or the low-level politicians who have other events to attend, other people to schmooze. Our dinner-party guest list is winnowed down to close friends and those with the most money, at least until the food is over and a second wave of attendees arrives for the dancing afterwards.

Finally, Ethan has crawled out of the woodwork. He moves up and down the dining table, serving wine and avoiding eye contact with me. Alicia is playing the flute in the orchestra. Sasha's violin melody soars. All the while I continue to speculate: did one of you hurt my daughter? The answer is still: I don't know.

'Kat, you okay?' Jenny tugs at my sleeve. Her eyebrows are lifted to form an almost triangular shape.

'Hmm? Yeah, fine.' I subtly begin to move away from her, somewhat sickened by the pity on her face.

'I noticed you talking to Malc earlier,' she says. 'Did you have a nice chat?'

I glance across at Malc, positioned between my husband and one of the lords Charles invited. I've forgotten his name already.

'Sure,' I say, paying more attention to the pheasant breast on my plate than Jenny.

'I know you're grieving, Kat, but you can't steal other people's husbands away.'

I almost spit out a piece of gamey meat in shock. 'Excuse me?'

'I won't be Debbie Reynolds,' she rasps in a loud whisper, making me realise how drunk she is.

Her sudden accusation is so ridiculous that I can't stop the manic giggle escaping from my throat. I quickly take a sip of red wine to try and drown out the sound. 'What on earth are you talking about?' I try to keep my voice even as I put my glass back down.

'You know what I mean. I won't be dumped for a pretty face. Look at you, all wounded and vulnerable and beautiful.' She slurs her words. 'You know *exactly* what you're doing. I've seen the way he stares at you, like something he wants to fix, and I know you can't help that, but you *can* help leading him on. Just because your marriage is broken, it doesn't mean you can find comfort in the arms of a married man. I won't sit here and watch you become Elizabeth Taylor and him Eddie Fisher.'

Aware of the people around me, I speak in a low voice to try and avoid making a scene. 'Jenny, do you have any iota of how absurd you sound? I lost my *child*. The last thing I want is another man in my life.'

'Yeah, because women never find comfort in men other than their husbands, do they?' She sloshes her wine around while she talks. I reach for the glass but she pulls it away from me. 'Whatever. Stay away from him.'

'Why don't you stop worrying about me and work harder to keep him then? We all know about his affairs. You're just paranoid because he's strayed in the past. You know I'd never do anything with your husband—'

'Oh, fuck off. You came from scum and you're still scum. No amount of Chanel can class you up.' The attempt at a whisper is abandoned as she drops her knife to the table. Almost the entire table of guests redirect their attention to us, slightly bored and craving the drama. Jenny's pitiful expression is gone and now she's all cat, her lips retracted and her cheeks flushed. Good on you, Jenny. Get angry for a change.

The guests turn politely away after noticing how drunk Jenny is, but I can tell they're listening. Heads tilted slightly towards us, they pretend to continue their conversations.

'No, probably not,' I reply with a shrug. 'But at least I know who I am. At least I know where I came from and what I want out of life.'

'Meaning?' Jenny is vibrating with anger now, her breath coming out slow and laboured.

I raise an eyebrow to show I'm not afraid of her, but I lower my voice so that the eavesdroppers don't hear what I'm about to say. 'One day, Jenny, you'll grow up and realise exactly how much of an imbecile you really are.'

She brought it upon herself, lashing out at me like that, coaxing my anger to the surface. Did she really think I would sit here and take it? Still, it's unpleasant to see the bravado drain out of her, to see her head drop and her eyes lose their shine. The pheasant's pink centre is unappetising and too rare all of a sudden. I smile politely at the other guests, pick up my glass of Merlot and make my way outside.

As I leave the room, the music stops and the quietness of the house returns. I can hear chattering voices and the occasional burst of laughter, but I miss the music and I want them to carry on. However, it's time for the orchestra's scheduled break, and asking them to keep going would create another scene. With the cool wind on my back and the rustle of the neatly trimmed yew bushes, the weight of silence is almost unbearable. This evening has been pointless. All I've learned is that Malc is a horny bugger and his wife is a paranoid old cow. I take out my phone and call Grace's number, needing to hear the reassuring sound of her voice again.

Hey, this is Grace. Leave a message!

I hang up and call again.

Hey, this is Grace. Leave a message!

This time I speak. 'Who did you love, Grace?' Then I hang up and stare out into the dark.

'Kat? Aren't you cold out here?'

The sound of Malc's voice makes my stomach drop with disappointment. This is truly the last encounter I need right now, but before I can protest, he's removing his jacket and placing it on my shoulders. He takes a lock of my hair and twists it around his finger. I sigh and remove the jacket, handing it back to him.

'Your wife thinks that I'm Elizabeth Taylor and you're Eddie Fisher,' I say. 'Can you sort that out, please? I don't have time for her hysterics.'

'I mean... Sure,' he says, his eyes flashing with lust. I hate that this weak, flawed man is who Jenny has chosen to spend her life with. The eager, greedy expression in his eyes is unbearable. Before he can say anything else, I walk away, shivering, contemplating my failures. Attempting to keep Malc on my side has backfired dramatically. What else is going to go wrong tonight?

Who did you love, Grace? I love you. I do. I'm not supposed to, as Angela tells me, but I do and no one can tell me otherwise. Your dad claims you were worried that you didn't love anyone, but I know you better and I know you loved too much. No one can fake that kind of warmth. Can they?

I wish you were here right now, so I could see your face and find the answers in your eyes.

As I make my way around the side of the house, I begin to regret giving Malc his jacket back. The wind brings a chill that makes my eyes water.

There are abandoned napkins and plates dotted around the low walls of the garden, and I absent-mindedly pick them up, as though I'm still a waitress. Jenny was drunk, and, quite frankly, off her rocker tonight, but she wasn't wrong about me. No matter what I wear or how much I cover up my accent, I'll never fit in with these people. I can read to better myself and make jokes about psychology, but I'll still be the kid from the council estate.

Before tonight, Malc's wandering eye never struck me as anything to worry about, even when it happened to move in my direction. To me he comes across as a philanderer bored by his current wife, always open to other opportunities, rather than someone who has a fixation on me. But that move with the jacket and the lustful expression… What if Malc is more dangerous than I thought? What if his wandering eye has found more than one target? The thought makes the pheasant and red wine churn. How old have Malc's previous lovers been? I try to think back to the social-media pictures that Jenny has shared about his affairs. Were the women younger than Jenny? As young as Grace…? But when I think about Malc's interactions with Grace, I don't remember any signs that might indicate an attraction to younger girls.

Paranoia is seeping into my every thought, directing me to the darkness in everyone I meet. But is it justified?

One of the catering staff scuttles past, glances at me, sees the plates and appears mortified.

'Oh, I'll take them,' she offers.

'That's okay,' I reply. 'You're already carrying a load.' I nod towards the pitcher of water in her hand. 'I'll leave them outside the door.'

'I'll come back for them,' she promises.

She's pretty, with her glossy hair tied back, a similar shade to Grace's natural colouring. She must be the same age as Grace, which is a punch to the gut. If I saw her walking from behind, it would be easy to mistake her for Grace, and now I know that I'll never go another day without seeing shadows of my daughter in other people.

As I leave the plates by the front door, I hear the bustle of the caterers inside and a sudden wave of jealousy hits me. I used to be part of a group like that, with a sense of camaraderie on nights like this. Though no doubt I'm romanticising the memories, especially as most of the other waiting staff hated me. I was known for charming the men, in more ways than one. The other girls thought I was a slut, and the lads were annoyed that I offered the rich men certain pleasures that I denied to them.

A movement near the stables catches my eye as I'm about to make my way back to the dining room. The orchestra's break should be over in a few minutes and hopefully Jenny will have excused herself by now to cry in the bathroom. More likely she'll simply pretend that nothing happened and start going on about her psychic again.

A young woman giggles and makes a shushing sound. Even in the dim light of the yard, I can tell that two excited young people are heading into the stables. Quietly, I decide to follow them and find out what they're doing down there. I can't have catering staff fraternising on the grounds. If one of the journalists found out, it might hurt our family's reputation. Charles certainly wouldn't want that for his business, and I don't particularly want any more gossip following us around like a bad smell.

'Hurry up,' says the girl as they open one of the stable doors. 'It's fucking dark in here. I can't see a thing.'

'I'll use the light from my phone.' The other voice is male.

'Put the platter down on the water trough; we can do it there,' the girl whispers. 'God, I need a hit. I can't believe that bitch hired the school orchestra for tonight. After everything with Grace.'

'She's a nutter,' the boy agrees. 'Who would even go ahead with something like this after their fucking *daughter* died?'

'Someone with a screw loose.'

They share a laugh about me.

'I know it was her who took my phone. I never lose my shit. And then she sent those messages to everyone. Sasha won't even look at me now. One of these days I'm going to fucking kill her.'

'Why would she want your phone though? And why would she send those messages?' The boy sounds dubious, which makes me smile.

'I dunno. She's probably a psychopath like her daughter.'

There's silence except for the rustling of paper – or perhaps plastic, I can't tell. Then there's a tapping sound. I activate the camera app on my phone, waiting for the perfect opportunity.

'You're quiet,' the girl says. 'Thinking about her, are you? Thinking about your hands all over sweet Grace?'

'Shut up,' the boy replies. 'You know I didn't do anything with Grace. It was all for show. She had some other guy.'

'That's a lie, though, isn't it Ethan?' I ask, as I swing open the stable door and begin taking photos. 'Hi, Alicia. Hi, Ethan. I wanted to thank you both for doing such a great job tonight.' *Flash. Flash.* 'You've dropped some white powder on that tray, Ethan, and on your trousers.' *Flash. Flash.*

'Shit.' Ethan tries to wipe the cocaine from his thighs.

'Oh, *fuck*,' Alicia says, running her hands through her hair.

I ignore her and look at Ethan. 'Someone sent me a video of you and Grace kissing at a party two months ago. Did you have sex?'

'Jesus,' Ethan says, staring forlornly at the tray of cocaine resting on the old water trough.

'He's not here, Ethan. No one is absolving your sins tonight,' I quip.

'Look, it was nothing,' he says, staring at Alicia, whose jaw has dropped. 'We messed around a bit but we never…' He turns to me. 'We didn't have sex, okay?'

'Was it really two months ago?' Alicia asks, her eyes like two hard marbles in her pretty face.

'Yeah,' he says. 'But it was nothing. I promise—'

'That's enough fake apologising, Ethan. Tell me the name of the other boy Grace was seeing.'

'I dunno,' he says. 'She wouldn't tell me. But…'

I open and close my mouth like a fish. 'But? But?'

'You should talk to the music teacher,' he says. 'There was some talk…'

Alicia stares at me with cold, damp eyes. 'There. Now leave us alone, would you? You just keep wrecking everything. *I hate you.*'

I briefly let my mask slip. 'Fine, I'll go,' I say icily. 'It's been a pleasure – as always, Alicia.'

CHAPTER TWENTY-SIX

I searched for him, the music teacher, after the dinner ended and the orchestra stopped playing, but he left before the party began. Then the rest of the evening went by in a flash and soon I had guests to say goodbye to and a clear-up to organise. Charles stumbled up the stairs to bed after midnight, drunk and sad.

As the weekend progressed, all I could think about was the brief conversation I'd had with Daniel Hawthorne, and the way Grace used to talk about him. Had she talked about him more than she'd talked about her boyfriend? Had the signs been there all along?

It's Monday morning and I still haven't told Charles about what I managed to get out of Ethan at the party. This new version of my husband is too unpredictable, and if he finds out there's a chance that Grace was having sex with a teacher, he could lose his temper and ruin my plans. The truth is my priority now, and Charles's volatility is a problem I must account for.

He's already at work, whereas I'm still trying to drag myself out of bed. It's almost ten, and I should be motivated to act on this new information, but instead it's dragged down my mood. Perhaps thinking of Grace with an older man reminds me too much of myself. I never wanted Grace to be like me. I wanted more for her.

There are things I want to do today, but first I check out Daniel Hawthorne on social media. All his accounts are set to private, but I do discover from his 'about' section on Facebook that he's married to a woman called Sophie, whose page is not as private. When I click onto her profile, I see a pretty, baby-faced young woman who likes to use Snapchat filters of animal ears. Her smooth, soft skin does nothing to comfort me. For one thing, she's blonde, with a smattering of freckles across her nose and big blue eyes, like Grace. She's very attractive and has an open, friendly look. According to Facebook, she's in her mid-twenties – around the same age as Daniel Hawthorne himself, and there's nothing wrong with that. She's the kind of young woman that many men would find desirable, but I find her striking resemblance to Grace particularly disturbing.

I could continue digging into the Hawthornes, but instead I need to get ready for another appointment with my therapist, for which I'm running late. Luckily, the daytime traffic is light, but I still find myself creeping over the speed limit and having to force myself to slow down, to follow the rules. I park the car under a magnolia tree in full spring bloom and make my way to the building, somehow two minutes early.

In Angela's office, she smiles as calmly as always and it immediately helps to ground me. In times of turmoil, the mundane repetitions in our lives can be comforting. As a thrill-seeking sociopath, that's a strange thought to admit.

'How did your party go?' she asks.

'Well. I discovered that there's a rumour at Lady Margaret's that my daughter was having an affair with her music teacher.'

For once, Angela appears taken aback. She gapes at me before saying, 'Goodness! That must have been quite a shock.'

'It was,' I admit.

'How does this rumour make you feel?'

It strikes me as a strange question with an all too obvious answer. But I know that I should voice all my emotions in therapy, otherwise what's the point in paying for it?

'Angry. Sickened. If it's true, then he took advantage of her.'

The thought of that man being the father of her child… There is the flicker of anger, building up again. As I haven't told Charles about my findings yet, it means I could be the only one who suspects Daniel Hawthorne of impregnating Grace, and possibly killing her, too. But rumours are one thing. Truth is another.

'That's perfectly understandable. Teachers are always in a position of power, even if the student is over the legal age of consent.'

'Are you trying to teach me about morality?' I snap. 'I know that.'

Angela merely smiles sweetly in response. 'I was only demonstrating to you that I understand how you feel. Your anger is valid.'

'But?' I prompt, knowing her well enough to recognise that she has more to say about the matter.

'Be careful you don't allow your anger to propagate. It's toxic and it spreads far too easily. You may experience an urge to get revenge for what happened to Grace, but the best thing you can do is work on yourself instead.' She taps the top of the pen against her notebook and shuffles in her seat, as though uncomfortable talking to me about this subject. Does she think I might lose my temper now? Here?

'Anger can be a difficult emotion for people with antisocial personality disorder, because they don't feel remorse for anything they do while angry.'

'Isn't that the fun part?' I suggest.

'You're doing so well with your therapy,' she says. 'You wouldn't want to jeopardise all of that hard work for a few moments of pleasure, would you?'

After my therapy, I drive straight to the school, make my way to the administration office and ask for Preeya and Rita to meet me during lunch break. I'm still the grieving mother, and people are still willing to bend over backwards to help me when I need it. It's not long before I'm sitting in Rita's office with Preeya in the chair on my right, both obviously eager to know why I'm there.

'I held a charity event at Farleigh this weekend, and both Alicia and Ethan were there,' I say, not bothering with pleasantries. 'While they were on my property, I found them both taking drugs in the stables. Here; I have photographic proof.' I show them the pictures on my phone. 'Not only have Alicia and Ethan been taking drugs, they're in a relationship that I think went on while Grace was still alive. Alicia also sent Grace some very unpleasant messages before she died. I thought it best to come straight to you both about this. Something needs to be done about their behaviour. Honestly, I think they're both out of control.'

'That's… shocking.' Rita leans back in her chair after examining the photographs. 'This is a real disappointment. They've never been in any serious trouble before.'

'Yes, it is. And I think they both deserve to be removed from the sixth form.'

Preeya lets out a long exhale while Rita remains impassive.

'That's… quite a reaction,' Rita says eventually. 'Quite a *severe* reaction.'

'They were taking drugs,' I protest, 'and bullying a student.'

'Kat,' Preeya jumps in, 'I know this is hard, but the girls fell out all the time at school. I'm sure Grace sent messages to Alicia that she wasn't proud of. I'm not sure bullying is the correct term here.'

'How about drug addicts, then?'

'Mrs Cavanaugh.' Rita's formal tone has me sitting up straight in my chair. 'I know you've been through a lot and I understand that you're angry, but you can't come in here and tell us to remove two students for drug use outside school. They're both adults, or thereabouts. If we were to expel every sixth former for taking drugs, we'd be left with about half a dozen sitting their final exams. If they'd been arrested then that would be different, but they haven't. However, I will be talking to them both and contacting their parents for a serious meeting about this.'

'Is this anything to do with the amount of funding that Malc throws to the school? You know that Charles and I match it.'

She shakes her head. 'It's nothing to do with that, and, frankly, that's offensive.'

I shrug. 'I don't care if you're offended. What I care about is those two getting away with whatever they want because their parents are loaded.'

Preeya lets out a derisive snort.

I direct a cold glare in Preeya's direction. 'What was that noise for?'

She angles her body away from me. 'Nothing.'

'No, you have more to say, so say it.'

'Perhaps we should leave this meeting here,' Rita suggests, getting to her feet.

'Preeya?' I ask again. 'Just tell me.'

There's a moment where Preeya and Rita exchange a glance, as though trying to decide whether to tell me or not. It's obvious that Rita is against it, but Preeya appears compelled to get something off her chest. Eventually, Rita sits back down and raises her hands, as though giving her permission.

'It's pretty rich, you coming in here with these demands, when Grace was found with drugs on school property six months ago. We tried to call you that day but you didn't answer your phone. Instead we spoke with Charles. Ethan claimed they were his and took the blame, but Grace was no saint, Kat.' She laughs. 'Charles even offered us a bribe to keep it all quiet.'

'I didn't know anything about this. You should have told me.'

'Yes, we probably should've,' Rita admits.

'This school is a fucking joke.' As I snatch my bag from the floor and storm out of the office, all I can think about is Grace letting me down again.

*

I'm not too proud to admit that I'm riled. Grace with drugs. Grace pregnant. Grace a bully. Grace in therapy. Oh, my perfect daughter, you had far to fall and you're falling a long, long way. Almost instinctively my fingers reach for my phone and dial her number, desperate to hear that sweet, innocent voice once more.

But it's a lie.

Part of me thinks I should have accepted her death as suicide and never started any of this. Then Grace's memory would've remained untainted. She would still be pure. But now I've started, I can't stop.

On my way out of the school I pause and watch the kids as they mess around on the steps leading to the entrance. They're a world apart from the kids I went to school with. Happier, glossier, like teenage models in a clothing catalogue. But deep down they all have the same issues. Drugs. Meanness. Boredom. Insecurity.

Over by the school gates I notice a flick of curly hair that I recognise. Sasha is here. I'd hoped to speak to her after my meeting, by asking for her to be taken out of class if necessary, but then Preeya's revelation left me reeling and I'd forgotten. If anything, finding her here is better because it doesn't involve a fuss. I hurry over to where she's standing with her friends.

'Sasha, hi!' She's a quiet girl, easily spooked. I put on my most amenable smile in an attempt to put her at ease. 'How are you? I meant to say thank you the other night. The orchestra were brilliant – as always. All the guests remarked on how good you were.'

'Thank you, Mrs Cavanaugh,' she says shyly.

'Have you got a moment? I wanted to ask you a question about Grace. It won't take long. Promise.'

'Okay,' she says. I can tell that she's agreeing out of politeness. I want to tell her not to be polite, because people will take advantage of that politeness for the rest of her life. But right now I'm going to be one of the people taking advantage instead.

We walk away from her group of friends towards the car park to find a quiet spot.

'I wanted to ask you about Mr Hawthorne.'

'Okay,' she says. It might be my eagerness to read cues, but I swear her smile becomes tense.

'Alicia told me about a disturbing rumour. She said the students at school were gossiping about Grace and Mr Hawthorne having an affair.'

Sasha's eyes immediately fall to her shoes and she begins to fumble with her shirt sleeve. The girl doesn't hide her nerves well, which is something else I can take advantage of. When the bell rings she spins on her heel and lifts her big brown eyes towards the school entrance, longing to be anywhere but here answering my awkward questions.

'I should get to class,' she says.

'Please, Sasha.' I place a gentle hand on her arm. 'If you know more, tell me. It's incredibly important for me to understand what was going on with Grace before she died.'

Sasha continues to stare at the school, but she says, 'Grace once told me that they were together. But no one believed her. She used to make up all kinds of stuff.'

'Like what, Sasha?'

'I need to go now.'

I want to push her further, but I know that I can't. I allow my hand to drop and she hurries away from me. With a sigh, I run my fingers through my hair, trying to make sense of all the things Grace was involved in before she died, when another girl steps out from behind a nearby car. Surprised, I gawp at her, not grasping why she's there or why her dark eyes are fixed on mine.

'I can tell you everything you need to know about Grace,' the girl says.

She has a familiar face that I can't place. I know that I recognise her, but I don't know *how* I recognise her.

'Are you one of Grace's friends?' I ask.

'Yeah,' she replies. 'I guess it wasn't for long though. She… she died too soon.' She shakes out her glossy black hair and smiles sadly.

The new friend. The one she talked about in her video diary.

'What's your name?'

'Lily.' She glances up at the school building, squinting in the afternoon sun. 'I have psychology now, but I can meet you in Ash Dale later.'

'At the café?'

'Sure.' She hovers awkwardly before saying, 'Bye then.'

I frown as she walks away, her black hair bouncing along with her steps. Then I remember exactly who she is. She's the girl from the video. She's the girl Grace was bullying.

CHAPTER TWENTY-SEVEN

A few minutes before 3 p.m., I ask for the Wi-Fi password in Ash Dale café, take my macchiato and sit by the window. After a sip of my coffee, I upload a few photos I believe might be in the public interest to the front page of Lady Margaret's website. While Preeya and Rita were busy with their outrage, I'd slipped a slim address book into the palm of my hand. It contains not only all of Rita's contacts, but the passwords to her various accounts, including the website administration password.

If I hadn't found the password like that, I would've found it another way. But Rita struck me as the kind of woman who would need to write down the passwords she doesn't use often enough to memorise. Most people my age and over do. It hadn't been my intention to steal the book during our meeting, but I could see that my pleas were getting nowhere, and the book caught my eye.

I have to do something to ensure that Alicia and Ethan understand the repercussions of their actions. Perhaps with the photo caption – 'Look what Lady Margaret's condones' – both the kids and the school will find themselves facing consequences. And why shouldn't they? My daughter was failed by that school. They dismissed the way Alicia bullied her and they failed to tell me about the drugs. Everybody let her down, including me.

The door to the café opens and a small group of kids arrive, staring at their phones and giggling. As I'd been uploading the photos, I must admit that I'd worried no one would check the school website before the pictures were removed by staff. It's obvious, however, that news has already spread, and no doubt all these kids are screenshotting the evidence already. My macchiato tastes good today.

'Hey, um, Mrs Cavanaugh?' The girl from the car park shuffles over to my table, thumbing the strap of her rucksack as it rests on her shoulder. I can tell by the frayed edge of the material that this is a common tic of hers.

'Lily, isn't it?' I gesture at the empty chair for her to sit. 'Would you like me to buy you a hot chocolate or a coffee?'

She places the rucksack down on the ground and sits in the chair. 'That's okay; I have money.'

'Oh, I don't mind treating.' My voice is honey, my expression warm. I know how to come across as sweet, especially to a nervous teenage girl like Lily.

'Okay, well a hot chocolate would be good,' she agrees.

'This weather is rather gloomy, isn't it? We need comforting hot drinks in this weather.'

She nods.

The waitress comes by and takes our order, then disappears back to the counter. All the while, Lily twirls her hair and shuffles her feet underneath the table. Now that she's closer, I notice she's lost much of the 'alternative' style I saw in the video of Grace bullying her. No thick black eyeliner and no bead bracelets. But she is wearing Doc Martens and her rucksack is decorated with band badges and song lyrics, which I see clearly when she lifts it onto the table to take out her phone. At the same time, she removes a few notebooks to get to the bottom of the bag.

'Grace had a book almost exactly like that,' I point out. 'Is it a school book?'

'Oh, no,' she says. 'We bought matching books one day.' She hurries to jam everything back into her bag and then unlocks her phone. 'Sorry, I need to text Mum and tell her I'll be home late. She doesn't like it when I don't tell her where I am.'

'Good girl,' I say, perhaps too patronisingly. 'Don't stop telling your mum things.'

Lily appears uncomfortable as she puts down her phone and frowns. As the waitress comes back with her hot chocolate, I can't help but deliberate whether the sudden paleness in her expression is guilt or fear, or something completely different.

'Thank you for talking to me, Lily. I'm sorry we never met while Grace was alive. Did you hang out with her a lot?'

She drops her marshmallows into the drink and nods. 'I think Grace was sick of Alicia's drama. She wanted to talk to someone outside that group. Outside of the orchestra, I guess.'

'I never saw you on Grace's vlogs.'

'Nah, I guess not. I don't like my photograph being taken.'

'Why not? You're a beautiful girl.'

Lily's pale cheeks flush and her shoulders lift like a much younger girl pretending to be shy. 'Really not.'

'You don't have to be a Barbie clone to be beautiful.' I quickly change the subject, seeing her discomfort. 'You mentioned that Grace told you things? Like what happened with Mr Hawthorne.'

Lily nods. 'Sasha said Grace was lying, but that's not true. I saw the text messages.'

'Between Grace and Mr Hawthorne?'

Another nod. She tugs at her sleeve, pulling it back to scratch her inner arm, at the same time revealing a red scar along her forearm that concerns me. But as soon as I frown, she pulls her sleeve back down to cover it up.

'Yeah, she showed them to me. He was going to leave his wife for her.'

'Lily, do you have Grace's phone?'

She shakes her head. 'Don't you have it?'

'No, it's missing.'

'Oh, okay,' she says. 'That's a shame, because then you'd see all the messages. He used to tell her that he loved her and all that kind of thing.'

I close my eyes for a second, trying to control the tidal wave of emotion threatening to knock me off my feet. How did this happen?

'Are you all right?' Lily asks.

'I'm just shocked that this was going on and I didn't know.'

Lily sips her hot chocolate and then says, in a quiet voice, 'I feel horrible for not saying anything. At the time it didn't seem that bad. She was happy with him and she was always talking about how amazing he was. I mean, he's not that much older than us, so I guess I didn't think it was that bad. Though I knew he was a teacher and that was wrong.' Her gaze wanders to the café window. 'But then…'

'What?'

'Then she was frightened. There was…' She grips the end of the table and blinks away tears. 'Oh God, I don't want to say.'

'Please do, Lily. I need to know.'

But she shakes her head. 'You'll hate me. You'll think I'm awful.'

'No I won't. You're not in any trouble, but I need to know what happened to Grace.'

Lily whispers, 'She was pregnant.'

I let out the breath I didn't realise I was holding. 'I know. It came up during the post-mortem.' So Grace did know she was pregnant, and she chose not to tell me.

Her face pales again. 'That poor little baby.' Her hand flies to her mouth and she blinks a few more tears away.

'Are you okay?' I reach across the table and gently stroke her arm. 'I know it's a lot to take in. You've been carrying this alone for a long time, haven't you?'

She nods. 'I guess so. No one knew we were friends. It took me by surprise because Grace was popular and I'm… not. But I really miss her.'

'I know.'

She wipes her eyes and sniffs.

'I know Grace bullied you once. Someone sent me the video of her doing it.'

Her jaw drops.

'How did the two of you become friends?' I ask.

'She came to apologise. She said... she said that she'd been going to therapy and it'd made her evaluate some stuff, you know? She had regrets about what she'd done. She stayed and talked to me for a bit, and we got on, and then we started hanging out.'

If Grace felt guilty for what she'd done to Lily, it means she wasn't a sociopath after all. She wasn't like me.

'And... she seemed genuine?'

Lily nods.

Oh, I want to believe it. I want to know that my Grace had a conscience, and that she loved, and she felt remorse, and that she cared about the world. But what if she was faking it, like I'm faking concern for Lily right now?

'Did Grace tell Mr Hawthorne she was pregnant?' I ask.

'Yeah, she did. That didn't go well.' Lily glares at her spoon as she stirs the hot chocolate, and I can see that she's unimpressed with the way the teacher behaved.

'How so?'

'He was a total arsehole to her. Everything he told her about leaving his wife turned out to be bullshit. He wanted her to get an abortion.'

My heart hurts for Grace. She went through all that rejection alone.

'Oh, wait – I just remembered. Grace sent me a screenshot of that conversation. Let me see if it's still in my phone.'

While I wait for Lily to find the right message, I shake my head, thinking about the scumbag who impregnated my daughter and then rejected her. Of all the lowest creatures in the world, a man who takes advantage of a young, innocent girl and then abandons her in her time of need must be the worst. I'm convinced that hatred is seeping out of my pores as I sit here in the café. Mr Hawthorne is going to pay. He had no idea who he messed with when he hurt the one person I've ever loved.

'Here it is.'

The sound of Lily's voice makes me start. I pull myself back from the violence in my mind and concentrate on the image on the screen. It's a picture message sent via WhatsApp from my daughter's account.

Grace: I want you, Dan. Why are you making it so hard? You said you'd leave your wife and be with me. Now we have a baby to look after. I know it's scary but we can get through it together.
Dan: I'm sorry, Grace. I can't. I have to stay with my wife because she's sick. You can't message me anymore.
Grace: It isn't fair! You're punishing me!
Dan: I'm not. This is just the way it has to be. I'm sorry.
Grace: I can't believe you're doing this to me.
Grace: Will you at least come to the clinic?
Dan: Yeah, I guess. Make an appointment.

The most disturbing part of the exchange to me is Grace's use of emojis throughout. A crying face; a sad face; two hands pressed together as though begging him. It hammers home how young she was, and I can hardly bear it. When I pass Lily the phone, my hands are shaking.

'He's an awful human being,' Lily says. 'I wish I'd gone to you back then. If I'd known you were nice, I might have.'

The atmosphere in the café is stifling. A prickle of sweat breaks out along my hairline, but I manage to pull myself together enough to think straight.

'I'm going to write down my email address,' I say, grabbing a napkin and retrieving a biro from my bag. 'Send me any message that you think is important. In fact, send me that screenshot right now.'

'Okay,' she says.

'Here's the money for the hot chocolate. I'm sorry to rush off, Lily, but I have to go. Thank you for telling me all of this.'

'It's okay,' she says. 'I hope he loses his job. Creep.'

'Don't worry; he'll get what's coming to him.'

On the way out of the café, I turn back to see Lily drumming her fingers against the table, a long sheet of black hair obscuring half of her face.

I'm close now, Grace. I can feel it. I'm close to finding out what happened to you that night.

CHAPTER TWENTY-EIGHT

My phone starts ringing before I even make it to my car. The school's number flashes up on the screen. Rita isn't an idiot. I showed her the pictures of Alicia and Ethan before I put them up on the website. This was never supposed to be the crime of the century.

'Rita, I know why you're calling me, but I want to let you know I'm on my way back to the school.'

'What the hell were you thinking? How did you even get those photos onto the website?'

'There's something more important to talk about. I'll explain when I get there.'

I have too much going on to care about the high pitch of Rita's angry voice. What Alicia and Ethan did is nothing compared to the sick relationship Daniel Hawthorne had with my daughter, and since Lily has already sent me the screenshot, I have proof.

My windscreen wipers swish back and forth against the April showers as I head back to the school, passing groups of chattering students queuing outside the newsagent. They know who Alicia is now. They know who Ethan is, too. But what they don't know is that there is someone more dangerous walking the school halls. They don't know about a man who might take advantage of them.

I swing into the car park, quickly find a bay and hurry through the entrance to Rita's office. For the first time, it hits me that my relationship with Lady Margaret's school is over. Grace is gone; we have no connection here; we won't be sending them donations anymore. We won't come to the board meetings. We won't be in their list of contacts. Especially after what I've done today. This is over.

On my way to the office my phone beeps: *Why are you here?*

Another anonymous text. This time from the *first* number to text me.

You should get out.

I stop to reply: *Why? What are you going to do?*

Make you pay for not keeping your nose out of my business.

My response: *Is this Daniel?*

Who's Daniel?

If it is, I think you're the one who should be worried. You have no idea what you've started.

When the text messages stop, I carry on down the hall to the head teacher's office.

'Get in here, Mrs Cavanaugh.' Rita is on her feet. She ushers me in and shuts the door.

'I have your address book.' I take the slim book out of my bag and drop it on her desk. 'I made a few notes. You should probably change those passwords; they aren't particularly strong.' I dump my bag on the carpet and sit down in the chair opposite her desk, waiting for her to get back to her seat.

'Did you know that hackers start with the password? They use common passwords, like colours and flowers, and then they try different combinations with thousands of email addresses. The more unusual and complicated your password, the more secure your account is. Could I possibly get a glass of water? It's very dry in here.'

Rita stares at me open-mouthed, which is good, because I want her attention. 'Did you seriously steal my address book and use my password for the school's website?'

'Yes, I did.'

'That's… a crime.'

'Are you going to phone the police?'

'I… I'm not sure,' she says.

'Let me tell you exactly why you're not going to do that.' I hold up one finger to instruct her to wait while I pull up the screenshot on my phone. 'The music teacher, Mr Hawthorne, was having sex with my daughter. She was pregnant with his baby at the time of her death, and when she told him about it, he tried to make her abort the child. One of your students told me all about it, which she had to do because Grace never talked to me herself. You see? This is proof.' I show her the phone. 'So what's going to happen is that you're going to tell me where Daniel Hawthorne lives, and I'm going to go there now and explain to him why fucking my *seventeen-year-old daughter* was a very, very bad idea. I'll also be talking to his wife.'

Rita sighs. 'Kat, wait.'

'You don't seem surprised, Rita. Did you know?'

'It's not that,' she says. 'It's this screenshot. There's no profile picture and the name is "Dan", without a surname. You can't see the mobile number. There's no way of knowing for sure if this is Daniel Hawthorne.'

'Oh, come on, Rita!'

'This is an extremely serious allegation against a teacher. For one thing, I'm not giving you his address while you're worked up like this. For another, I need to see the original texts to figure out if it really is Daniel. I won't act without that, or at least the testimony of a credible witness.'

'I'll bring Lily in to speak to you.'

'Lily who?' she asks.

Then it dawns on me that I never asked for her last name. 'Shit. I don't know. Hold on.' I check the email address she used to forward the screenshot, but there's no surname. 'Look, I heard it from Ethan *and* Sasha that there were rumours about this relationship going around the school. Don't you think that's a pretty huge coincidence? Dan is Mr Hawthorne's first name.'

Rita speaks slowly, as though she's dealing with one of the students. 'It is, and it's certainly an investigation that the school needs to make. We may even need to bring the police into this. But kids tell lies and make up stories, Kat. They always have and they always will. Daniel is barely twenty-four. He has a long career ahead of him, and he's a target for these kinds of rumours because he's young. You know that as well as I do. It could be a completely different Dan, anyway.'

'Jesus.' I put my head in my hands. 'I don't know what to believe anymore.'

'Kat, you know I'm on your side,' Rita says in a gentle voice. 'Just give me some time before you act, okay? I'll look into it.'

I snatch my bag from the ground for the second time this afternoon. 'An investigation by you isn't good enough. If I find out that one of your teachers was involved in the death of my child, you'll pay – along with Daniel Hawthorne. And that's a promise.' I lean over the desk and I let my guard down. I let all the emotion slip from my face. Rita takes a step away, her expression unsure and frightened.

All I want is to know what happened to her. All I want is to be able to visit Grace's grave and know that I did right by her, that I fought for her. Nothing I do will bring her back, I know that, but there must be a reason she was taken away from me. All of this has to make sense, otherwise I'm not sure I can carry on living and breathing. How can I live with the nightmare of her chipped blue nails and her cold, stiff body? What's the point in anything?

In my dream there are two deaths. One where I see the light fade from a pair of brown eyes. Another where desperate fingers scrape against stone until they come back bloody and broken. I wake as a mouth opens to scream, the blackness of it threatening to swallow me whole. That's no way to live, dreaming these things over and over.

There is blame for the things that happened to my daughter, and if I can find a place to direct that blame, maybe the nightmare will stop. Maybe I can finally lay her to rest once and for all.

Rita's reaction to my concerns is a wake-up call. I know what I need to do next. It's time to make use of the incredible wealth I married into.

One thing that rich people sometimes like to do is find out what their lovers or spouses are up to behind their backs. I know at least one woman who hired a private investigator during a divorce to find proof that her husband was cheating on her. She got the house and custody of the children. When I call her, she gives me the name of the person she hired, telling me with glee that he's very good in bed, apparently.

'Thanks, Vanessa,' I reply, 'but I just want him for the investigative services.'

Vanessa's testimonial is perhaps a bit alarming, but without her recommendation I wouldn't know where to begin. Who knows what kind of charlatans there are out there, ready and willing to take my money any way they can get it.

Matthew Gould is the investigator's name. We arrange a meeting for 2 p.m., and as I wait for that time to come around, I find myself pacing the library in Farleigh Hall, Georgie and Porgie knocking their tails against my legs, shedding black hairs over the antique rug. I take a glass of Pinot Noir with me, sipping it slowly, not wanting to consume too much alcohol before I leave. This is merely to help me relax, to reduce the anxiety building in my chest.

I didn't redecorate after Emily passed away three years ago, which is strange now that I think of it. She was this looming figure in Charles's life and I resented her almost every minute. She chose the heavy curtains in the dining room and the red carpet in the bedrooms. The antique furniture is all either hers or has been inherited from Charles's ancestors. The few modern rooms at Farleigh are the family room, which was once the billiard room, and the kitchen, which is the one place Emily allowed me free rein. 'A wife should control her kitchen,' she'd said, while delegating all of the cooking to our staff.

As I pace back and forth in front of the many shelves of old books, I keep thinking back to the moment Charles and I told Emily I was pregnant. It was early into our 'relationship', if you can call it that. We'd been seeing each other for about nine weeks, and he still hadn't broken things off with the other woman. I hadn't been nervous as I'd arrived at the house with Charles. Instead, I remember thinking to myself that all of this could be mine if I played the game well. Charles was a man I felt I could easily manipulate. The only obstacle was his mother.

She'd taken me into the kitchen to make tea and patted me gently on the arm.

'You must be very clever, dear, to get pregnant this fast. What did you do? Did you lie to him? How do I even know that the child is my son's?'

I made sure to act incredibly shocked and offended. 'It was an accident.'

But she'd just chuckled. 'Oh yes, of course. You keep playing that act and don't let it slip.' She poured boiling water into the teapot, splashing a few droplets onto my hand. 'If I'm honest, I'm struggling to be angry. Charles hasn't had much luck with relationships and I was beginning to think I'd never have grandchildren.' She paused and licked her lips. 'There will be a paternity test once the child is born. I'm no fool.'

Her threat didn't worry me; I knew the baby was Charles's, having never cheated on him. 'I think it's a boy,' I'd said, hoping to win her over with the promise of an heir to the Cavanaugh business. Women like her always wanted boys.

'Remember, Katie—'

'Kat,' I'd corrected, hoping to distance myself from everything that had happened with Annie Robertson at my old school.

'Remember to keep that act up, dear, because I'll be watching you. My son deserves a good wife.' She'd lifted her pointed chin and raised her eyes – the same slate grey as her son's – and fixed me with a long stare.

It was at that moment I decided my life would be easier without Emily in it.

Unfortunately, it took a long time to reach that point, and now I find myself wishing she were here. Emily Cavanaugh would have moved heaven and earth to find out why her grandchild died. And I could do with an ally as ruthless as myself.

CHAPTER TWENTY-NINE

Matthew Gould hands me a latte when I meet him at his office in Buxton. He's tall, relatively handsome, with wavy brown hair that catches on his stubbled jaw. He leans back in his chair, resting his ankle against his knee. Dressed casually in jeans and a flannel shirt, he reminds me of the kind of man cast as the love interest in a movie. A man at ease with who he is. Good on you, Vanessa. She goes up in my estimation.

'Vanessa Richards recommended you,' I say, as I sip on the excellent coffee. '*Highly* recommended you.'

At that he grins, and his face becomes almost boyish. 'How is she? We haven't spoken in a while.'

'She's good. Filthy rich, thanks to you.'

He performs a faux bow, tipping his chest forward slightly. 'I try my best. Are you here to get rich too?'

I shake my head, becoming more sombre. 'My daughter died and I want to know what happened.'

'I'm so sorry,' he says.

I bite my bottom lip, unsure how much to tell him right away. I don't want to scare him away with my suspicions or with information about my past, but I know that I need to tell him enough so that he can investigate every possible avenue.

'What happened to your daughter, if you don't mind me asking?'

'Not at all,' I say cautiously. 'It's why I'm here. She fell, or was pushed, down Stonecliffe Quarry. The police conducted a short investigation, but because there was a note in her pocket, and because she was found in the "Suicide Spot" and there were no witnesses, her death was ruled a suicide. She bled out, alone and freezing cold, at the bottom of the quarry.' When my voice cracks, he reaches down for a box of tissues, but I shake my head.

'Would you like a glass of water?' he asks.

'No, thank you,' I say, regaining control of my voice. I clear my throat as he waits patiently. 'I don't believe that my daughter did commit suicide. She had… issues – I can't deny that – but the letter she left for us was odd, nothing like how she usually sounded. The police, however, decided that I was wrong. I have nowhere else to turn. That's why I'm here.'

He nods. 'Let me quickly tell you what I do here. I listen, I investigate and I give you an honest report. I don't judge people and I don't make decisions without investigating the evidence first. You won't be dismissed here, Mrs Cavanaugh.'

Relief floods through my body. I didn't realise how much I needed to be believed until this moment. I launch into the rest of my tale, telling him all about the pregnancy, the back-stabbing between her friends, my husband's sneaking around, finishing with the text messages I believe are from Daniel Hawthorne to my daughter. After I'm done talking, I finally understand the expression 'warts and all' because I've laid it all bare. For once, it makes me feel vulnerable, and a little nervous of his reaction. As I wait for him to speak, I try to ignore these uncomfortable, and fleeting, emotions which I'm not used to experiencing.

'I'm so sorry,' he says. 'Losing a child is… Well, there aren't any words…' His easy bravado is gone, and I see him adjust his weight, obviously trying to work out what to say. 'You only found out about her pregnancy after she died? That's…' He shakes his head.

'You don't need to worry about me.' I pick up one of the complimentary pens from his desk and tap it against the wood. 'I'm tough; I can handle anything life throws at me. Even when life has decided to lob razor blades my way.' I hope the tone of my voice doesn't undermine the strength of my words. The truth is that the last few weeks have been the worst of my life, but until I find Grace's killer, I'll keep going. *Tap. Tap. Tap.* The Pinot Noir has failed at keeping me calm. I inhale deeply to steady myself. 'There's more that I need to tell you. I don't know for sure that this is linked – in fact, it probably isn't – but there's some stuff in my past.'

'Okay.'

'I've been receiving these threats.' I show Matthew the texts on my phone. 'In one of them, the sender addressed me by my maiden name, Flack, which suggests that they know about my background. My birth name was Katie Flack. I prefer Kat now, and my married name is Cavanaugh.'

'I'll make a note of the number.' Matthew takes a pen and scribbles it down in a notebook.

'Using my maiden name might be nothing more than a ploy to rattle me. Some of the snootier people around here have never accepted me into the fold because of my poor upbringing. I grew up on a council estate. But…'

Matthew lifts his head. 'Go on.'

'I had anger issues at school. It's possible that there's someone out there, from my past, with a grudge. Perhaps Grace's death, with the report on the news, brought me some unwanted attention. The text messages came from different numbers. Some focused on Grace, whereas others threatened me. What if they're different people? Honestly, I'm confused and I don't know what to think. I've shown some of these messages to the police as well. They think that because of the high-profile nature of Grace's death, it's someone's idea of having a laugh. It wouldn't be hard to figure out that I'm Katie Flack. It's not a secret that I've hidden away. You can pull up my police record, too. It'll tell you all about my…' I search for the right word. 'Difficult past.'

Matthew raises an eyebrow. 'I'm sorry. You don't seem…'

'The type?' I suggest. 'Trust me, I am. No matter how hard I try to escape Katie Flack, she keeps finding me.'

She's screaming as she rolls around on the dirty ground, her eyes bloodshot and red-rimmed, her mouth cavernous. Her desperate fingers claw the dirt, but it does nothing to help her and a blue nail peels from her finger. I'm forced to watch as her head is slammed into the soil, knowing I can't do anything to stop this from happening. Her head is smashed down for a second time. When she lifts her chin I see the red blood trickling from her nose. She screams but no one can hear her – except me. Her eyes find mine and there is nothing but hate in her expression. Pure hate.

I don't know what's worse: the scream, or the silence that comes after. Within the silence hangs the suspense, because I know what's going to happen next, and I know that I can't stop it. When my arms are pinned down behind me, I realise that my lips are moving and I'm begging for it to stop. Fear takes control of my body. I care about nothing and no one except getting away and surviving. I want to survive, and I will at all costs.

I jolt awake as though electrocuted, sitting straight up, my chest rising and falling, my heart knocking hard against my ribs. My body is hot all over, and for the first few seconds, I'm almost positive that I can smell dirt and blood mingled together. But that's impossible, because I'm here in my room, staring at the wall, staring at my dress on its hanger, ready for the day ahead.

The door to the room opens and Charles stands in the doorway, hair mussed, eyelids drooping.

'What is it?' My husband has that thick, drowsy voice that everyone has when they wake from a deep sleep. 'Nightmare?'

'Yes. How did you…?'

'You were screaming,' he says.

'Oh.'

'I thought they'd stopped.'

'No. They haven't stopped.'

They will never stop. They will only get worse.

In the movie version, the mother would sit back and cry and accept her daughter's suicide. She'd be at home with mascara-stained eyes while the father is out there with a baseball bat, threatening anyone who hurt his daughter. I'm not the movie mum and I'm not the movie dad either. This is how I fight. I use my brain and I use the charm I was given. I'm going to fight back with everything I have. Maybe, if my investigation fails, I might get out the baseball bat and give it a go. One thing I do know is that the person who hurt my daughter will be found.

Since seeing Matthew Gould a few days ago, my nightmares are even more intense than before, and I'm beginning to consider that the cause is my lack of trust in Charles. He doesn't trust me either. Since our tentative truce, we've lived in our own spaces. I tell him my suspicions about Grace and he nods along, not giving much away about his thoughts. The thorny issue of divorce hasn't come up since the day I confronted him. But this lack of trust is the reason for my next move.

Matthew is in the process of uncovering the dirt on Daniel, as well as researching Grace's school friends. But Charles is my territory. He's the man I married, and because I don't trust him, I need to make sure he isn't lying to me. Yes, he took me to see his doctor, and yes, he has started to look ill recently, and he certainly spends a lot longer in the bathroom. But can I be sure that he hasn't orchestrated all of this?

No, because I wasn't there when he had the blood test. And Charles is a rich man who has already claimed to have bought people off. He even offered a bribe to Grace's school to get her out of trouble. I can't trust him at all. I need to see where he goes. I need to know whether he's lying to me.

As soon as I hear Charles's car leave the grounds, I go to my phone and open the app I installed to trace him. It's a simple GPS tracker that shows exactly where he is on Google Maps. Charles isn't the best with technology, and I'm confident that he won't even notice this new app, let alone figure out what it does.

I get out of bed, shower and throw on jeans and a shirt. On the way out of the house, I leave a note for Michelle, feed the dogs and down a cup of coffee. This new idea has me energised. I'm finally in control. I have a private investigator on my side and I have a way of keeping tabs on my husband. I'm closer than ever to finding out what happened to Grace, even if my nightmares are haunting me, even if my clothes hang from my body and anxiety grips my chest, refusing to let go. They won't make me surrender.

My nightmares are mine and mine alone to experience, and for that reason I've never mentioned them to my therapist. Perhaps it's a bad idea to keep recurring dreams from your therapist, or maybe that dream-analysis Freudian bullshit is pointless anyway. Either way, no one knows what I dream about and no one ever will.

The screaming girl sometimes comes to me in the middle of the day, the black space between her bloodied teeth opening wider and wider. I often think about what I need to do to stop her from finding me. Atone for my sins? Or maybe it's inevitable that one day she will swallow me whole, and every struggle, every difficult choice, every painful experience will finally come to an end.

Since Grace died, my dreams have elaborately expanded. Too often I dream of the Suicide Spot, waking up with the scent of Grace's shampoo on my pillow, wondering if my illusion of her will be shattered irreparably by the time I find out the truth.

CHAPTER THIRTY

When Charles's car comes to a stop between home and Derby, I decide to get into the Land Rover and follow him. What's the point in having this app if I'm not going to act on it? I make my way out through Ash Dale, navigating towards the tiny icon that represents Charles's car. He isn't near his office, and I want to find out what he's up to. Of course, it could be a business meeting, or he's stopped for breakfast – who knows? Zooming in on the map isn't giving me much of a reading.

Thirty minutes into my journey, he drives away from wherever he was, moving in the direction of the office. I consider going home but then decide to keep following. As I'm keeping one eye on the phone screen, a text message comes through, and the hands-free function reads it out loud to me.

You're dead. How could you do that to me?

And yet again, the number is different. I shake my head, frustrated by this unknown stalker who won't reveal their identity to me. Using speech to text, I reply.

'Why don't you grow up and tell me who this is.'

Two words ping back.

Fuck you.

I take a left turn too fast and I'm forced to slam on the brakes when I see parked cars ahead and another car coming in the opposite direction. As much as I hate to admit it, my stalker has rattled me and I need to calm down.

As the driver on the opposite side of the road glowers, I lift my hand to apologise, like a good citizen would. After driving on for a few minutes, my phone rings and I answer it via the speaker, not paying much attention to the name on the screen.

'Kat, how could you do that to Alicia?'

'Jenny?'

'Have you decided to destroy my family? First you flirt with my husband and then you ruin my child's future. I thought we were friends. I was there for you. I *defended* you when everyone was blaming you for Grace's suicide.'

'Who blamed me?'

'Everyone! We all thought you were a terrible mother. We all know that Grace was pregnant.'

'When did you find out? Before or after she died?' Pinpricks make their way up and down my arms. Was I the last to know that my daughter was pregnant?

'You know Alicia and Ethan have been thrown out of the sixth form?'

'No, I didn't know that.'

'Well, they have. We found out today.' I can tell Jenny is crying. 'That's her chance of going to Oxford ruined.'

I almost laugh. Considering the fact that Alicia is a B student at best, Jenny's plans for Oxford University were pretty ridiculous. But I manage to stop myself, knowing that laughter at this moment is not going to get me the information I need.

'Alicia and Ethan are suffering the consequences of their actions,' I remind Jenny, forcing myself to stay calm. 'That's not my problem. If you want to know more about your sweet daughter, you should see some of the awful texts she sent to Grace before she died.'

'Oh, get off your high fucking horse, Kat. Grace was the worst of them all. You keep acting like she was some kind of angel but she was a real bitch. A spoilt brat.'

'That's hilarious considering how much you spoil your brat.'

'Alicia is hardworking—'

'You're delusional!'

'Loyal—'

'She was screwing Grace's boyfriend!'

'Fuck off, Kat. Everyone knows what you did to get where you are. You got pregnant on purpose and tricked Charles into a lifetime of misery. You're nothing but a chavvy little gold-digger so don't you *dare* act high and mighty with me.'

I tighten my grip on the steering wheel to allow my hot skin a moment to cool.

'Jenny,' I say, calmly and quietly, 'you have no idea who you are talking to. You're right about one thing: I came from nothing. The way I grew up, this conversation wouldn't happen, because we'd have already started throwing punches. I'm more than a bitch, Jenny. You don't know who I am or what I've done. I've had blood on my hands before. I understand how fragile bones are because I've seen them break. I know what sound a skull makes when it's crushed.' I pause for a few seconds, letting my words sink in. 'Now, I would never do anything as uncouth as threaten you with violence, because when I married Charles and had Grace I vowed to be a different person. But it might be an idea to modify the way you talk to me, because as a better person, I've decided that I value respectful discourse. Seeing as you've chosen to be disrespectful, I think I'm going to hang up now. Okay, Jenny?'

Her voice is a breathy whisper. 'Okay.'

'Also, I think it's best that our families stop socialising from now on. Don't you?'

'Yes.'

'Goodbye, Jenny.'

She hangs up. I loosen my grip on the wheel then tighten it again. My forehead has broken out in tiny beads of sweat. I turn down the heat and lean back against the car seat. I hadn't intended to say that to her. Usually nothing on earth can make me dredge up those memories, and now I need to fold them away and return them to the envelope I keep at the back of my mind.

Angela helps me compartmentalise the bad things I did when I was a teenager. That day with Annie Robertson is the one I never allow myself to think about. The blood on my hands, the surge of adrenaline running through me, Annie's eyes meeting mine. I can't linger on those images. I need to keep my attention on the road ahead. I check back on Charles's movements to see that he's still heading towards his office. Maybe following him like this was a bad idea. Am I going to uncover anything suspicious, or is all this a complete waste of time?

I take a left, travelling towards Charles's office, followed by a right, avoiding bad traffic on the A road. It's as I make the right turn that I notice a blue Volkswagen Golf behind me. It was a few vehicles back when I was coming out of Ash Dale. Could they be heading in a similar direction, or are they following me? Perhaps this route is a popular shortcut on the way to Derby?

As an experiment, I decide to go off track, taking a left followed by another left. After a few more turns I'm back into the countryside, and the Volkswagen is still behind me. I try to see who is driving the vehicle using my rear-view mirror, but whoever it is has a hat pulled down low over their face. I'm pretty sure the driver is male, but I can't be certain.

With all my impromptu turns, I've ended up on an unfamiliar road full of bends. I'm forced to slow down in order to traverse the corners on this narrow road, but the Volkswagen doesn't slow down at all. In fact, it speeds up. There's no one else around, and for once, fear rushes through my veins, like a drug in my bloodstream. Part of me craves this kind of adrenaline rush, but knowing how easily things could end badly for me doesn't give me a thrill.

The car is right behind mine, almost bumper-to-bumper, and I find myself travelling at a much faster speed than is comfortable. More than once, my left tyre clips the grass verge. I'm glad the ground isn't wet today. When the car bumps me from behind, I aggressively beep the horn. The Volkswagen beeps back, then there's another thud from behind and my body is thrown forward, and this time I lose my temper, slamming on the brakes to come to an emergency stop, letting the car behind crash into the back of my vehicle.

As metal crunches against metal, my airbag deploys and my face slams into the fabric, taking my breath away. My ribs smash into the seatbelt, leaving me bruised and dazed.

Get out of the car, Kat. Open the door and get out.

I unclick my seatbelt with shaky fingers, open the door and step onto the road, trying very hard not to show that my body is trembling. My ribs throb with pain and my legs could buckle at any moment, but I need to know who has been following me. Fuelled by the adrenaline coursing through me, I stumble down to the Golf to find the driver fighting with his own airbag. I open the driver's door, lean across his lap to unclick the seatbelt and drag him out, ignoring his bloody nose and dazed expression. When I swat the hat from his head, I see straight away that it's Daniel Hawthorne.

As I raise my fist, he cowers away. 'Don't, please don't!'

'Why are you following me?' I keep my fist raised, rage shuddering through me, burning me from head to toe.

'I thought…' His mouth gapes open and then snaps shut. 'Why doesn't anything frighten you?'

'Stop whining and tell me why you're following me.'

To my horror, he begins to cry. He slides slowly down the side of the car, forming a misshapen puddle on the road. There's no way I can get answers from him in this position, which means I'm forced to hoist him back onto his feet, propping him up with my weight until he supports himself again.

'It's all gone wrong,' he utters between sobs. 'None of this was meant to happen.'

My hands stay clenched at my sides; fist still longing to smash into his teeth. 'Why are you following me?'

'I thought it'd scare you off. Nothing scares you off. Not the messages... You wouldn't stop coming to the school, so I thought if I frightened you on the road... I'm such a – a – *fucking* idiot.' He hits himself with the palm of his hand, missing his injured nose and lightly slapping his forehead instead. 'I just didn't want the school to find out.'

'That you were having an affair with my daughter?'

He stares down at the ground with his mouth gaping, tears running down his face. I'm sick of watching other people cry about my daughter.

'You impregnated her.'

A loud moan escapes from his open mouth and a long line of drool runs down his chin. But I don't care about his feelings.

'You told her to get an abortion?'

He nods his head.

My hands ball back into fists and I raise my right arm again. Somewhere, in the background, there's the sound of another car coming towards us, but I don't bother to move, even though we're blocking part of the road.

'Did you kill her?'

His head snaps up and his eyes meet mine. 'What? No!'

'Why should I believe you? You're the one who sent those threatening messages to me, aren't you?'

He lifts his hands as though begging. 'Why couldn't you leave it alone?'

Somewhere behind me a car door opens and slams shut.

'Because you killed my daughter!'

His lip trembles as he stutters, 'I – I didn't. She killed herself.'

As I'm about to finally release, to hit this pathetic mess of a man, someone catches my fist and holds me tight. I whip around to see Matthew Gould holding me back.

'Don't do it, Kat. It's not worth it.'

'But he—'

'I've already gathered a stack of evidence against him. He's going to lose his job and possibly face prison time,' Matthew says. 'Don't do anything you can be arrested for.' He gently lowers my hand down to my waist and manoeuvres me away from Daniel. Then he takes his phone from his pocket and makes a call.

CHAPTER THIRTY-ONE

Matthew had been following Daniel, that was how he'd found me preparing to break Daniel's face with my fist. After preventing me from committing a crime, he called the emergency services and an ambulance arrived for us both.

What I'll never know, since Matthew stopped me, is what I would've done to Daniel if he hadn't. There's no doubt in my mind that I would've allowed that punch to launch, but would I have gone even further? We were on a quiet country road with no CCTV and possibly no witnesses. Could I have killed Daniel Hawthorne? Wrapped my fingers around his neck and squeezed tight? Do I possess the strength to do that? After all, I'm not sure what a person like Daniel contributes to this world. I taught myself how to stop leaving oily footprints where I stepped, but people like Daniel Hawthorne are too weak-willed to change.

What I learn, after speaking with Matthew, is that Daniel was with his wife at the time Grace died, which is perhaps the oldest alibi of all time. Would she lie for a cheating, morally bankrupt scumbag like Daniel Hawthorne? Would she stand by her man? Some women do. Some people are so broken and manipulated that they don't see the alternative. I hope Sophie Hawthorne realises that she can dump that pathetic man and start a better life on her own.

After my nose and ribs are checked over, I'm not sure what to think anymore. While still at the hospital Matthew shows me – along with the police – the evidence that Daniel was sleeping with

Grace. After these last few weeks, it's almost a relief to uncover a piece of the puzzle. But at the same time, when I think about the way Daniel abused his power over my daughter, I find it hard to stay still as I listen to Matthew. All I want to do is storm into the police station, fight my way through to whatever interview room Daniel's in and beat him senseless. Is it unladylike of me to visualise revenge through violence? Is it wrong? I close my eyes and imagine that moment I had with him by the car. I'd come so close…

It was Daniel's wife who allowed Matthew to search his laptop, which means she can't be completely on her husband's side. Matthew uncovered many emails Daniel obviously thought he'd deleted. Those emails reveal a romantic relationship between him and Grace. I glance at one or two examples while I'm waiting to be released by the doctor, but I find it difficult to read them, so he hands them over to the police officers taking our statements.

Daniel Hawthorne, to no surprise, is not a criminal mastermind. He's actually pretty stupid. He thought sending threatening messages to me would stop me from coming to the school, when all it did was make me more suspicious. He knew there were rumours about him and Grace, which he didn't want the faculty to discover, but the way he went about everything was wrong-headed. Now he'll be fired from his part-time job at the school, will lose all of his private clients and will be arrested.

But none of that sounds like true punishment. Even if he didn't push my daughter over the quarry cliff, he had a hand in her death. He made her sad and vulnerable. He made her feel hurt and alone. Daniel Hawthorne deserves pain.

'Mrs Cavanaugh, can I come in for a moment?' DS Slater has his hands shoved deep into his pockets, and an expression on his face that says entering my house is something he does not want to do at all.

I match his unenthused expression. 'Please, come in. Make yourself at home. Can I get you a drink?'

'A tea would be appreciated. Is your husband home as well?'

'No, but you can talk to me. Milk and sugar?' It's lucky that Charles isn't home because when I told him about the crash, I didn't mention the driver of the other car involved in the collision, or what was discovered about Daniel and Grace.

'Two sugars please.' He shrugs. 'I have a sweet tooth.'

The detective follows me into the kitchen with his usual striding gait, though I do note a slight slump of his shoulders. Perhaps he's here to apologise for dismissing my concerns, which would explain the puckered lips, like a Bulldog and a wasp, or so the saying goes.

Michelle puts the kettle on while I gesture for DS Slater to sit at the kitchen table with me. I don't particularly want to lounge on a sofa with him. I want this conversation over and done with.

'We're investigating Daniel Hawthorne following the collision with your vehicle yesterday,' he says. 'Can you talk me through what happened?'

'I was driving towards Derby to surprise my husband at his office when I noticed a blue Volkswagen Golf following me. I decided to try redirecting away from the main roads to get rid of the follower, but I lost my way and ended up on a very quiet country road. The road where I was picked up in the ambulance.' I gently touch the bridge of my nose, which is still swollen and sore.

'Yes.' DS Slater checks his notes. 'Fern Lane.'

'Right. Well I ended up on Fern Lane and the car was still visible in my mirror. Daniel Hawthorne was the driver, though I didn't know it at the time. He was wearing a hat to conceal his identity. Then he rammed into me.'

'Did you brake?' he asks.

'Yes. I was scared.'

He makes a note.

'You know he was having sex with my daughter, his student?'

DS Slater nods. 'Yes, you hired a private investigator.' He exhales slowly through his nose and raises his eyebrows, but fails to meet my gaze.

'The baby was his.'

He nods again, not saying a word.

'He was sending me those threatening messages.'

'We're going to check those messages. Mr Hawthorne will certainly be facing harassment charges if there's enough evidence. You're within your rights to file a restraining order against him.'

I shake my head. 'He doesn't scare me. He's an idiot.'

DS Slater puts down his pen and observes me closely, his expression both thoughtful and serious. 'Idiots are capable of a lot, Mrs Cavanaugh. Go visit a prison sometime and see what I mean.'

'If he's willing to break the law to try and hurt me, I'm not sure what good a restraining order will do.'

'Very well. I was just saying that it's an option.'

I smile. 'Okay.'

He scribbles in his notebook again.

'Do you believe his alibi?' I ask. 'Or are you beginning to understand that I'm right, and my daughter didn't kill herself?'

'I do believe his alibi,' he replies, 'because his wife doesn't have any reason to lie. For one thing, she's left him. Also, he made a phone call at home that would make it almost impossible for him to have got to the quarry at the time of your daughter's death. I'm sorry; I know that must be disappointing for you.'

There's no triumph in his voice. DS Slater is genuinely sorry, and I can see clearly that he pities me. He thinks I'm delusional.

'So you're not going to reopen the investigation into my daughter's death?' I ask.

He lifts his palms, not so much in a shrug but in a gesture almost like an apology. 'Not unless we receive some concrete evidence that Grace was murdered. This affair with the teacher – well, I'm afraid it suggests to me that she was under even more stress than perhaps anyone could have imagined.'

'And her phone?'

'We searched the area,' he says. 'There was nothing at the quarry, nothing at the school.'

'But did you look thoroughly? Her phone could be important,' I insist.

He sighs. 'We did. But we need our resources elsewhere now.'

Michelle brings over two mugs of tea as the detective continues with his questions, asking for boring, minute details about the positions of the cars as I find my attention drifting back to Grace. Finally, I've uncovered the identity of the father, but it hasn't answered all of my questions. If Daniel Hawthorne didn't kill my daughter, who did? Or did Grace commit suicide after all?

CHAPTER THIRTY-TWO

My most overwhelming emotion is in fact a colour. Blue. The blue tinge of the hospital lights. The blue gown my husband is wearing. This is the first time, since he admitted to me that he has cancer, that it feels real. Charles has a biopsy to suffer through today and I decided to come with him. Now that I see the fear in his eyes, I can't believe I ever doubted him. And that doesn't come from a place of love or naiveté or delusion. This is real. There's no way he'd go this far to lie to me.

This is the last step in the diagnostic process, apparently, and it's also to determine the level of aggression of the cancer. The doctor mentions a Gleason score.

'Are you all right? Comfortable?' I ask.

'Well, I'm about to have a needle plunged into my rectum.' He shakes his head and lets out a laugh. 'To be honest, I feel terrible. Like I might be sick, or, I don't know, cry.'

'I'm sorry.' For once I mean it. For our situation, for the fact that Grace isn't here to comfort him. I feel sorry for all of it, which in some ways takes me by surprise. These last few weeks have revealed a depth to my emotions that I hadn't known existed.

His hand wraps around mine as we wait for the doctor to come into the room. Then Charles will be taken somewhere private. We didn't marry for love, Charles and I, and the gold-digger insult that Jenny threw in my face isn't far from the truth, but we've been through a lot together since then. Charles is all I have left in the world, and I don't want him to leave me.

'That day, when I came to Derby and I set up that fake meeting, I…' I'm not sure what to say in order to make things right. My apologies aren't usually sincere; they're constructed to make me come across like a normal person with a conscience. 'I was very wrong and I'm sorry. It was unforgivable, but I want you to know that I feel closer to you now than I ever have before. I know things have been… strained since then. But I want to move on. I want to make this work.'

He shakes his head and lets out a strangled laugh. 'You know what's ridiculous? It took me a fortnight to forgive you.'

We're silent for a few moments, until Charles says, 'But you weren't wrong about everything. My company have cut corners. For the sake of making more money, we took unnecessary risks.' He lifts his hand and wafts it in front of his chest. 'What do we need more money for? Money didn't stop me getting cancer, did it? It didn't stop Grace from dying.'

'No, it didn't. And if she were here, she'd tell you to stop being a bastard and do the right thing.' But I falter. My voice drops. 'Wouldn't she? God, Charles, that video of her bullying the girl. That wasn't the real her. I won't remember her like that.' I stare up at the fluorescent light until my eyes burn. 'Grace would hate seeing you like this. But she would love seeing us still together after everything that's happened.'

He nods.

'Do you think she picked up on it? I mean, we don't fight, but I don't think we have the most conventional marriage. We never married for love, did we? Do you think that's why she was concerned she didn't feel love?'

'I loved you. I still love you.'

I blink in surprise, shocked by the tingling sensation spreading all over my body. 'You can't love someone if you don't know who they are. I've been hiding—'

He taps my hand twice with his finger. 'I know you, Kat. You keep thinking that you're different from the rest of the world and that no one could possibly care for you. But that isn't true. I see who you are, and I love you.'

But I shake my head. 'No, no, I'm a terrible person. How could you possibly love me? After what I accused you of…'

'Tell me why you think you're a terrible person. Tell me now.'

I'm about to open my mouth and reply when the doctor walks in. He begins to inform Charles all about the procedure he's about to undergo. Charles's hand wraps around my fingers and squeezes. It's only after at least five minutes of listening to the doctor that I realise Charles is comforting *me*.

Once home, I sit with Charles in the bedroom for a while, but he drifts off to sleep, resting from the stress and pain of the day. The age difference has never been an issue in our relationship, but as I see him curled up in bed, his head thrown back on the pillow, I can't help but think about how age has changed his face, his body. And that in itself makes him more vulnerable to me.

I can't stop thinking about what he said to me in the hospital. Was it the circumstances that made all those raw emotions come to the surface? Angela always tells me that true sociopaths cannot love, and I have always rebutted this with the certainty that I love my daughter. Now I'm experiencing warmth towards another human being: my husband. This fragile man in my bed. Being a good person means caring for the vulnerable. That's what I need to do. I need to care for him.

But what is this? Is it growth? Is my conscience like a bladder that fills with goodness, overflowing with empathy? Or is it a pocket-sized creature that needs to be fed in order to grow? One thing I know is that my conscience-creature was starved of empathy when I was growing up. My mother starved it first, and then I took a life and starved it even more.

I back out of the room slowly, trying not to wake him. No matter how much I feed my conscience and allow it to grow, I'll always be a murderer. I can't take that back. No one can erase their past. And I'll always be the mother who could have given more to her daughter, who could have saved her.

I decide to fill the rest of the day with dull chores, starting with feeding the dogs and sending thank-you letters out to the attendees of our charity shoot, and then I sit down to check my emails. Most are spam – a sale at Net-a-Porter, new films released on Netflix, another invitation to a function in London – but then… Lily. An email sent this morning while Charles was in the hospital.

Hi Mrs Cavanaugh,

I'm so sorry to bother you. I'm not sure why I'm sending this email to you of all people. Maybe it's because there isn't anyone else for me to talk to. My mum doesn't listen to me. Grace was my only friend and now she's gone. When we talked the other day, you were nice to me, and you seemed like someone I could talk to.

I'm having a tough time right now. It's like I'm stuck in mud and I can't move. Everything is pressing down on me. I can't breathe. I can't do anything. When I'm alone all I think about is ending things once and for all. It's too hard.

This is stupid. I shouldn't be saying these things. My mum is out and I started drinking her vodka and it's all so stupid.

Lily

There's a sincerity in the way she rambles that makes me believe this is a cry for help. This girl wants to die but she's fighting to live, and her fear of both of those emotions shines through her words. As soon as I finish reading the email, I close the laptop and take a moment to think. My first thought is that Lily is a connection to

Grace, and I can't lose another connection to my daughter. I must help this girl if I can. I lift the lid of the laptop and begin my reply:

Hi Lily,

You can talk to me whenever you like. I'm so sorry that you're feeling this way and I'm sorry that your mum isn't helping you. Would you like to meet in the café again?

Kat

This girl might need more help than I can give, but I don't want to fob her off with the number for a hotline or the name of a counsellor. She reached out to *me*, and I owe it to Grace to follow through. After all, I let Grace down.

Can we meet today?

The immediate reply doesn't surprise me. Lily is probably never more than a few inches away from her phone, like most teenagers.

I can meet you now, if you like.

Okay.

I shut down the computer, brush my hair, leave a list of instructions for Michelle and make my way out of the front door. Charles will be asleep for a while yet and I'll only be an hour or so, even if I do end up stuck in the school traffic through the village.

It may be selfish of me, but I can't help but hope that this meeting with Lily might uncover more about Grace. Were Lily and Grace drawn to each other because they were both troubled? Perhaps Lily was a bad influence on Grace. Or the other way around. Maybe they bonded over their bad relationships with their mothers, as much as it pains me to consider it.

The scent of coffee hits me as I make my way into the café. Lily is immediately visible to me, hunched at the back of the room with long tendrils of hair falling to the table. Was she the person who sent lilies to the house? I hadn't thought of that, but it's possible. Perhaps she and Grace joked about her name. Grace never liked lilies, but I could understand why Lily would send them if it was a private joke between the two of them.

Before I make my way to the table, someone close by clears her throat, catching my attention. When I turn around, I see Alicia standing by the counter, a cardboard coffee cup in her hand. There's no hint of a smile on her frozen face; instead, her eyes glint like smooth pebbles washed up on the beach.

'Hi, Mrs Cavanaugh,' she says, in a sarcastically sweet voice. 'Did you get my message the other day?'

'What message?'

'Ah, that's right,' she says. 'You won't recognise the number because I got a new phone. Someone stole my old one. I think my mother called you right after I sent it.'

'Oh, that one was from *you*, was it? What did you say to me? That I'm dead? I'm sorry to disappoint you, Alicia, but it would appear that I'm still breathing.'

She leans closer, talking quieter. 'You threatened my mum with some bullshit. I just want you to know I'm not afraid of you.'

Before I have a chance to reply, Alicia leaves with a flick of her silver hair, turning to look at me through the café window before folding into Ethan's arms when they meet outside. All I can think is poor Grace; no wonder she needed to find a new friend. I shake my head and move to the back of the café.

'Hi, Lily. Can I get you anything?' I place my coat over the back of the chair and sit opposite her, suddenly full of nerves. I've never had to talk to someone in the throes of depression before. I don't know whether I'll be able to say anything comforting or not. People like me aren't known for their compassion. But as soon as she begins to cry, I instinctively reach out and hold her hand. 'Are you okay?'

Between sniffs she nods her head up and down. 'This is embarrassing.'

'No, it isn't. It's absolutely fine. Here, let me get you a tissue.' I let go of her hand to find the small packet of tissues I brought with me. They weren't packed for Lily; I just got into the habit of doing it when Grace was a toddler, and now I think I'll do it forever, despite not having any toddler snot to wipe away.

She dabs her eyes and lifts her head.

'Oh no. Whoever he is, he isn't worth it. What can I get you both?'

I hadn't noticed the waitress approach while Lily was crying. A big part of me wants to snap at her and tell her to get lost, but I don't want to make a scene in front of a distraught teenager and I definitely don't want the waitress sneezing in my coffee.

'Latte, please. Lily?'

She shakes her head as she blows her nose.

'All right. Won't be a minute.' The waitress smiles with pity at Lily and disappears.

When Lily is finished with her tears, she crumples up the tissue in the palm of her hand. 'Urgh, I can't believe I cried in public. I'm such a mess.'

'If it makes you feel any better, I've seen several grown men cry in public recently. I almost punched one of them.'

She cracks a smile. 'Yeah?'

'To be fair, he deserved it. But that's not the point.' I place both hands on the table between us and try to figure out what to say. 'Your email was very distressing to read. You're in pain, Lily, and I hate the thought of you being in pain. Grace would… well, she'd be upset to see you like this, and she'd want to be there for you. That's why I'm here now. I want to be there for you too.'

Her smile widens. 'Thank you.'

'I saw the scars on your wrists last time we met. I know you're hurting yourself.'

She fumbles with the sleeve of her cardigan. 'It's the only thing that makes me feel better.'

'You know, I'm here for you if you want to talk, but there's only so much I can do. Lily, you could have an illness, like depression, and you might need to speak to a professional.' As I talk, she's unresponsive, staring down at the table. I decide to take a different direction. 'I see a therapist every week. We talk through my issues and ways for me to improve. We spend time going over what kind of thoughts I need to ignore and how to redirect my behaviour.'

Now she lifts her head to regard me. 'Do you have depression?'

'No, I have something else. But what we talk about in therapy helps me every day. My therapist, Angela, tells me the kinds of thoughts I should ignore.'

The waitress comes back with my drink and a small plate with a chocolate chip cookie on it. She winks. 'On the house.'

Lily smiles gratefully, but she pushes the plate towards me. 'I'm not hungry.'

'I'll take it home for my husband.'

'Grace talked about him,' Lily says. 'She said he was a billionaire like Bill Gates.'

I can't help but laugh. 'He's not. He's rich, but not Bill Gates rich. And he certainly didn't make it himself; he inherited it.'

Lily nods. 'And she said that once he held her hand over a flame on the cooker.'

I frown. 'That never happened. I would've seen it.' As far as I remember, Grace never had a burn on her hand.

'She said he touched her, too, in a bad way. But then later she said that he didn't. I think she used to lie to get attention.'

Tension ripples through my body. 'I think she did too. But I don't know why.'

Lily leans forward and licks her lips slightly. She lowers her voice as though telling me a secret. 'Mrs Cavanaugh, I didn't want to say this before. Grace was my best friend and everything, but sometimes I kind of hated her.'

CHAPTER THIRTY-THREE

'I didn't want you to get the wrong idea,' she continues. 'Grace was my friend – honestly, she was. I know she did that awful thing to me, but she felt bad about it after, and then we started talking and hanging out and she was so sweet. We shared everything. But…'

'Go on, Lily, it's okay.'

'I think I understand why she did what she did.'

'What do you mean?'

'I know why she killed herself. It wasn't because she was pregnant or because she fell out with Alicia or anything like that. Grace was *dark*. She could be a bully. She lied all the time. And it was super-obvious shit, like she said her grandmother killed her grandfather, and that her dad's family helped Nazi officers in World War Two, that one of her cousins in America was in the *Spider-Man* movie. Stupid stuff. You could maybe believe one or two of them, but she lied constantly.'

The blood drains from my face as Lily keeps talking. I hate to imagine Grace making up these things, but from the messages I saw on WhatsApp, it does make sense. *Her dad is weird. Remember what she said about him? Yeh. Fucked up.* What if Grace had started some sort of rumour about Charles for attention? I don't want to think about her like this, lying and bullying. I steady my spiralling thoughts, remembering that she had requested to go to therapy – probably as a way of becoming a better person. She made that choice.

'She wasn't like that at home at all,' I say. 'She never seemed to have the kind of confidence it takes to lie.' My mind is flooded with memories of her smiling, and I desperately attempt to marry the idea of Grace as a compulsive liar with the Grace I knew at home. Why is it that everyone knew a different version of her to the version I knew?

'I wasn't going to show you this, because I didn't think it would be fair. But I can't stop thinking about it. Before Grace killed herself, she wasn't… I dunno. She wasn't herself, I guess. She turned on me again and started being nasty.' Lily pulls open her rucksack and reaches deep into the bottom to retrieve her phone. While the bag is open, I can't help but notice the notebook again. The one that Lily said she and Grace bought together. 'I need to show you these messages.'

While I wait for her to retrieve the messages, my mind runs through several awful possibilities. What has Grace done now? What did she say to this girl? The last time I met Lily, she'd painted Grace to be regretful of her past behaviour, but now she's telling a new story. Why doesn't anything about my daughter make sense?

When Lily finds what she's searching for, her eyes fill with tears. 'I… I've been having a tough time with my mum. She drinks too much and she's never around. I'm on my own all the time and everyone at school hates me. Grace was good for me for a while and then she just… changed. I don't know what it was. Maybe it was the stress of being pregnant. The hormones or… I dunno.' A shudder works through her body as she cries. 'I don't want to think of her like that because I know it's not who she was.' Finally, she holds out the phone and I view what's on the screen.

Lily: I don't know what I'm going to do. It's too much. I want to end it all.

Grace: If you feel like that then embrace it. What's the point in living if you're miserable? Sometimes the only thing you can do is die.

Carefully, I lean back in my chair and try not to scream. Lily puts the phone away.

'Mrs Cavanaugh? Are you all right?'

'I'm fine, Lily. But I think perhaps that I should go.'

'Oh no. I didn't mean to upset you!'

I can't cope with her tear-filled eyes anymore.

'Don't go,' she begs. 'Please stay and finish your drink. I'm sorry I showed you that message. It wasn't her. She wasn't well.'

Before I can put on my coat, I find myself sinking back down into my chair. 'Do you honestly believe that Grace killed herself?'

She nods. 'I do. I don't have any doubts. When she sent me that message, I think she was talking about herself. Projecting. Is that the word?'

I nod.

Lily wipes her eyes on her sleeve and clears her throat. 'I couldn't stop thinking about it. That message was one of the last things she said to me. I hate that she sent it, but after talking to you, I understand it better. She wanted to die because she didn't see a way out. She was stuck, like I was saying in my email. She felt trapped.'

I offer to give Lily a lift home but she refuses. And, strangely, she's cagey about telling me where she lives, rushing out of the café as soon as our conversation is over. But the impression I get from her is that she isn't from a family as affluent as others in the area and could be embarrassed by her humble background. Especially if her mother is an alcoholic.

But the real reason I offered Lily a lift home was to avoid being alone for a while, because I knew where my thoughts would go as soon as I stepped into the car. Since Grace died, everyone has been telling me that I'm wrong, that she did commit suicide. All this time I've been searching for answers, and they keep pointing me towards her death being at her own hands. Daniel Hawthorne was threatening me, but he was trying to keep his affair secret, which explains the nasty messages. Grace had issues with bullying at school, but everything points to this being related to a darker side of her personality. She had difficulty fitting in at school, regularly fell out with her friends, made up lies for attention and posted dozens of videos online for whatever validation she didn't get at school or from me and Charles. She felt disconnected enough to want therapy. And then she fell pregnant and she didn't have anyone to turn to.

According to everyone else, I was a distant mother, and despite how much I try to tell myself that I hid who I am from her, I can't argue that they're wrong. She couldn't tell me she was pregnant, and when she went to the father of the baby, he rejected her.

We all failed her, but I failed her the most because I didn't raise her with the tools she needed to be able to cope with this world. For that I'll never forgive myself.

As soon as I get home, I pull off my shoes, swat away the two dogs, ignore Michelle asking me if I'm okay and pour myself a large glass of red wine. I walk up the grand staircase, lined with oil paintings of Charles's ancestors, and make my way into Grace's room. Here it is. Untouched, uncleaned, gathering dust. There's a lingering smell of dirty laundry. Soon I will be forced to wash those clothes. They don't smell like her anyway; they smell like old underwear.

This is where she came to get away from me and Charles. This is the place we allowed her to be alone. Is this where we failed her? I gulp down half my glass, then I open her laptop and go back to her YouTube channel. Grace was happy here – or at least she pretended to be. I skip through some of her tutorial videos and her voice fills the room: *This is a B-flat chord… This part is tricky, but concentrate and you'll be fine…* God, my body aches from missing her.

But I still can't cry for her.

I move on to her outdoor videos. There's Grace hiking a trail through the fields, clutching a selfie stick in one hand and Georgie's lead in the other. She stops and says hello to other hikers on the way, making everyone smile with her easy nature.

No. Stop!

How can this be the same Grace who sent Lily the message telling her to die? I slam down the laptop, almost shattering the screen, and glug the rest of my wine.

Throughout all of this, Grace's phone has never appeared, which means I might never know the context for all these messages that I've seen on other people's phones. Where is it? What did Grace do with it before she… Can I even think it?

Before she committed suicide.

The word sickens me, but even I can't deny that all the evidence points to Grace killing herself. Maybe I rejected the idea because I couldn't accept that my daughter would do that. Now it's time to face facts.

But as I pick up my glass and decide to go and check in on Charles, I change my mind again. Grace and Lily bought matching notebooks while they were friends. I remember the way Grace carried around that notebook, and I especially remember her slamming it shut if I entered the room. I might not be able to find Grace's phone, but there's a chance that I can learn more about Grace's state of mind if I can find that book. And if the book is here somewhere, it must be in her room.

Imbued with a new sense of purpose, I put Grace's laptop back on her bed and begin with her desk drawers. There's no rhyme or reason to the way Grace stored her belongings. The notebook could be mixed up with sheet music, or kept under a pile of clothes, or thrown in the back of a drawer. I searched through Grace's things soon after she died, but now I'm questioning whether I did a good job of it the first time around.

One by one, I pull out each drawer and rummage through. I open the ottoman, filled with sheet music, and remove every single piece of paper. I upend her bedside-table drawer and spread the contents out on the carpet. When I don't find anything, I move to her walk-in wardrobe, emptying every box, tipping out photographs and old pens. The notebook isn't to be found.

The notebook, along with Grace's phone, is missing. There must be a reason why they are both gone.

CHAPTER THIRTY-FOUR

Angela plunges the end of her pen into her ear and wiggles it around. I have no patience for it today; the sight of her constant scratching and fidgeting grates on me, and it takes nearly all my willpower to prevent myself from blurting out the rude thoughts in my mind. If I did that, I might have to find a new therapist, and that would mean starting afresh after twelve years. Learning to feed my starved conscience is hard enough without having to find a new therapist too.

'Did you hear what I said?' I ask, speaking gently to avoid sounding rude.

There's a split second where Angela's eyes narrow, as though she's trying to suss me out. She rarely does this, usually maintaining such a neutral expression that I find myself aggravated by it.

'I did,' she replies. 'I thought there was going to be more, which is why I decided to give you time to say what's on your mind.'

'What is there to say? According to this girl, Grace believed that death is the best option if you can't find happiness in life. She told another girl to kill herself. I even saw the message.'

'What are your thoughts about what Grace said in those messages?'

'All this time I assumed that Grace was murdered, because I could never imagine her wanting to die. But now I don't know what to think. Throughout this whole process, this *vengeful* need to learn the truth, I've done things that could be described as morally wrong. I got Alicia and Ethan kicked out of school because I disliked the way they treated my daughter. I accused my husband of terrible things without enough evidence to believe those things were true. I almost hit a man because of what he did to my daughter. I've manipulated people to get answers out of them. I threatened my friend Jenny and called her names. If Grace was still here, I wouldn't have done any of those things.' As I finish speaking, I glance down at my hands, now realising that I've been clutching them tightly onto my knees.

'You sound remorseful,' Angela says. 'When we first met, I don't think you would have had any remorse for those actions.'

'I don't think I am. I did all those things to help me find out what happened to Grace. I believed that someone took her away from me. But if she *did* kill herself, then everything I've done was for nothing. There was no *point* to me behaving that way. And that makes me… Well, I don't know what it makes me feel.'

Angela simply says, 'Hmm,' as though she doesn't know either.

'Fake it until you make it,' I say quietly. 'I've been pretending for so long that I don't know what's real and what's fake anymore. All these years I've been doing good deeds, but inside I'm rotten. I'm bad. At least that's what I used to think. Now I just feel empty.'

'Why do you think that is?'

I shake my head. 'Because Grace is gone. Because she wasn't the person I thought she was. Because nothing makes sense anymore.'

Angela scribbles into her notebook. She shuffles again and I have to stare out of the window to distract myself from her. There's no rain today; instead, a muted sun casts a gentle glow on the world. And yet I'm always in the shade.

'To answer your question from earlier,' I say. 'I think that Grace was right. Maybe death is the best option for people who find no happiness in life. Maybe sometimes you can't keep trying anymore.'

*

The sun peeks out between the gathering clouds as I sit in the Land Rover with my phone in my hand. It's on speakerphone. I keep hitting the redial button.

Hey, this is Grace. Leave a message!

I close my eyes and pull myself back to that memory of us on the sofa, bundled up together, watching reality shows, me trying to suppress the mounting boredom building up from my easy, upper-class life. All those lies. Walking around like a declawed cat, pretending to be a mother, pretending to be a wife. Giving to charity. Brushing my daughter's hair. Doing the school run. I'll be the woman who puts out an extra plate each mealtime because for a split second she forgot that the tiny baby she gave birth to all those years ago is gone.

And what do I want to do about any of this? Continue to walk through life with my canines filed? Claws retracted? Learn how to be remorseful for the things I've done?

Hey, this is Grace. Leave a message!

'How could you? After I fought to be a better person for you. You lied to me and you lied to your dad. You lied to the world. You pretended to be someone you weren't, and now I'm angry and I don't want to be. But I can't stop it growing inside me. How could you, Grace? How could you say those things?'

But saying the words out loud brings me no satisfaction. I hang up, hit my head against the steering wheel. Nothing takes away my sense of pointlessness. Nothing.

From somewhere, I find the strength to start the ignition, let off the handbrake and drive away. I take one turning and then another, and then I drive up the hill towards Farleigh Hall. All the while, I hear my mother's voice in my mind: *What did you say to her?* My mother is right: I'm the bad parent who screwed up my daughter.

This is all my fault. All of it. From the moment she was born she rejected me. I should've walked away then and done everyone a favour, but my hubris told me I could become someone else – a loving mother, a good wife, a good friend. Who was I trying to kid? While it pains me to think about Grace taking her own life – and I keep fighting the possibility that she *did* commit suicide – I can't help but consider that it was my illness that caused it all. If I had a deeper capacity for love, would she have gone down those dark routes?

Charles is still at home, having taken some time off from work. When I enter the house, I find him on the sofa with the dogs all over him, his wrinkles and greys more prominent than ever.

'How was therapy?' he asks.

'I feel worse.'

'Ah, that's exactly the reason why I don't go.' He pats the sofa next to him and I sit down, allowing Porgie to collapse on my lap. 'I'm watching a TV show about people who find antiques in their attic and sell them. Imagine what's in this old house.'

'You can start with that portrait of Emily if you want,' I say.

Charles takes this as a joke and laughs heartily. As I watch him, I can't decide if I did mean it as a joke or whether it was spite. My motivations aren't clear to me anymore and I'm exhausted from trying to figure everything out.

The programme waffles on, I'm absent-mindedly stroking Porgie behind the ears, then my phone beeps. Another text message from another anonymous number.

You're right. She is a liar. If I was her mother, I'd be angry with her too. How dare she pretend to be someone she isn't? Then again, you know all about that, don't you, Katie?

I read the message twice in order to allow my brain to process what it says. This person listened to my voicemail to Grace. This person *has Grace's phone*. I sit up straight, causing Porgie to almost fall off my knee.

'Everything all right?' Charles asks.

'Yeah, fine. Just had a bit of cramp.'

'Do you want me to move?'

I shake my head, and glance back at my phone. They called me Katie again. I'd thought that was a tactic to throw me off, but what if this is someone from my past after all?

You have my daughter's phone? I text back.

I've very much enjoyed listening to your messages.

There's a pause, but three dots on the screen tell me this person is typing another message.

You loved her, didn't you?

Who is this? I text. Watching the messages come through has my heart pounding so hard that I'm afraid it might burst. The dots appear again, wiggling up and down like a Mexican wave. Then they stop, and my pounding pulse stops with it. A moment later, they start up again and my body grows hot all over. I'm surprised Charles hasn't noticed me breathing faster, but he's absorbed in the show, oblivious to everything else.

The message finally comes through: *Want to meet?*

I text back: *Where?*

Stonecliffe Quarry. The Suicide Spot.

When?

Tonight.

CHAPTER THIRTY-FIVE

The anonymous texter suggests a time to meet at the quarry and I agree. They want to wait until after dark. Midnight. This person has Grace's phone. If they have her phone, they must be her killer. And now I believe they want to kill me. They tell me to come alone. They'll be watching to make sure I am alone. If they see the police, they'll leave, and they assure me that the police will not find them.

None of that matters to me. I don't want to involve the police, because I have no interest in the way the police deliver justice. I have no interest in watching this person go to prison for a few years. That isn't going to happen to the person who killed my daughter.

I'm still on the sofa, my body hot all over, nerves on edge. Porgie is whimpering. Perhaps he smells the adrenaline pumping through my veins. Maybe, like Jenny said, he knows that I'm agitated. I pat his head and then slip the phone back into the pocket of my jeans.

'I may have to go out later,' I say to Charles, still patting Porgie. 'And I'll probably be home late.'

'Oh yeah? Going out for a drink with the girls?'

'Takeaway night at Jenny's,' I lie. He doesn't know about my row with her yet.

He nods with approval. 'Good. You haven't seen much of the girls recently.'

'Do you think you'll be all right on your own? Shall I get Michelle to pop in and check on you?'

'Oh, don't be silly,' he says. 'I'm fine. The only thing I can't do is take a piss, and Michelle isn't going to want to help with that!'

I shrug. 'Maybe she's into that kind of thing.'

Charles laughs. Then he reaches out and grasps my hand in a casual but loving gesture. The shock of it is a dull pain to my core, similar to the ache I feel when I miss Grace.

'When we were talking the other day in the hospital, I never got to finish what I was saying,' he says.

'Oh, it doesn't matter.'

But he shakes his head. 'No, it matters. When you first accused me of hurting Grace, I told you that you were a bad mother, that you tended to lose interest in her. Look, I exaggerated all of that. I saw you holding it together day after day, and I saw you hiding your issues from her. Grace did want to go to therapy, that's true, and she was worried about the way she handled emotion. But what I didn't tell you was that Grace was worried about letting you down. That's why she didn't tell you about it. I knew a bit about the bullying, and there were some drugs involved at the time. She thought you always knew how to be a good person, and she didn't want to disappoint you.'

'God, she was wrong.' My skin burns.

'Kat, I know what you did. I know you lied to me when you told me you were on the pill. I know that you fell pregnant on purpose. And I know you did it to get away from your mother and out of that horrible flat. You still think you're a bad person because of that, but you're not. You walk around with this weight on your shoulders. You're not a bad person, Kat. You're a *good* person. I never cared about what you did, because it gave me Grace. Perhaps I should've been angry about it – most men would be, obviously – but I understood why you did it, and I forgave you. Maybe now you should forgive yourself.'

I snatch my hand away from him. 'You don't know… You're wrong. You just… You have no idea who I am.' I find myself on my feet, pacing the length of the family room. He doesn't know what I did all those years ago.

'I didn't want to upset you,' he says. 'Hey, come on. Sit back down with me. Chill out for a few hours before you have to go.'

I sit back down next to my sick husband and I think about what I'm about to do to the person who killed our daughter. And as I sit there waiting for time to tick away, I realise that I know who did it.

Since Grace died, I've learned a few things. She wasn't as perfect as I thought she was, and that's okay, because she was real, and now I understand why she did those things. I've learned that I wasn't a terrible mother, but I was a flawed mother, and I could have done more to steer her well. I've learned that I married a good man, even though the circumstances around that marriage were less than ideal, and I've learned that my life isn't everything that I hoped it would be.

I gather my things and go to the car. It's still hours before midnight, but I can't leave any later or Charles will be suspicious. Instead, I decide to drive around for a while to clear my head and work out what I'm going to do. On the way out of the house, I picked up Charles's hunting knife, and now I slip it into the glovebox.

There are things that don't add up. I'm sure about who's behind everything, but there are loose ends I'm eager to tie, and I don't think I'll be able to until I go to the quarry and get some answers.

As I loop Ash Dale village, I call Grace's phone one last time. *Hey, this is Grace, leave a message!*

'Since you sent me your text message, I've thought a great deal about why you want to meet me. You've done what is almost impossible to achieve – you have managed to get away with murder – and yet you're risking it all because you want to see me. You want to tell me your side of the story. Do you feel guilty about what you've done? No, I don't think you do. Do you understand who I am and what I'm capable of? Yes, I think you do. This need to tell me *why* is strong for you, isn't it? Tread carefully, because that kind of arrogance can be problematic. Pride, fall – you know the saying. I can't wait to meet you for real. Shall we take our masks off and be ourselves? I want to see you.'

This time, the message comes from Grace's phone.

I'll be home soon, Mum. Love you xoxo

They're playing a good game, I have to hand it to them, but they've surely underestimated my love for Grace. Now my rage is as cold as ice as it traverses through my body.

I have one more hour to wait. I fill up the car with petrol, drive around some more, watch a group of drunk people spill out of one of the few pubs in the village.

Grace should be with a group like this. She should be on her way to university, celebrating her A-level results. No one will ever send me a text message like that ever again: *I'll be home soon, Mum. Love you xoxo.*

Part of me wants to stop at that pub to buy an enormous bottle of whisky, to chug it down and pass out and pretend Grace is still alive.

I turn the car around and I drive out of the village, away from the street lights and the pavements, onto the isolated country roads, like the one where Daniel Hawthorne followed me. Out here I'm alone, with no private detective to save me. A shiver runs down my spine, so I pull over and call Matthew. Adrenaline rushes through me and the reality of what I'm about to do finally hits. Matthew's phone goes to voicemail and I leave him a rushed message telling him where I'm going, leaving out the why, but suggesting that I need his help. After hanging up the phone, I find myself glancing at the glovebox, where Charles's knife is waiting, forcing my fear back into resolve.

You won't get away with murdering my daughter. There's no way I'm backing down now, even if doing this alone is incredibly dangerous.

The darkness swallows the car. I press the accelerator, eagerly leaning forward as though willing the car to go faster. And then I reach the sign for Stonecliffe Quarry, graffitied with the word 'DIE'. My tyres crunch against the gravel as I pull the Land Rover off the road and onto the long path that runs up to the quarry. When my lights touch the figure standing ahead of me, a little gasp leaves my body. I brake, reach into the glovebox and take out the knife.

She stands with her back to the car, staring out into the cavernous black hole of the old limestone quarry. There is still yellow police tape ahead, flapping in the wind, dusty and tangled because no one bothered to collect it. She's slightly hunched, as though gazing into the abyss. Her black hair swirls around her, beautiful under the yellow glow of the lights. Then she slowly turns around and smiles.

Lily.

CHAPTER THIRTY-SIX

Behind Lily the suicide spot basks in light. When I cut the engine, I leave the headlights on. I want to see what she's doing, and I can't do that in the dark. She waves to me, wiggling her fingers in coquettish delight. Well, we did agree to remove our masks.

It was the missing notebook in the end. When I failed to find the notebook in Grace's room, it finally hit me: they didn't buy two at the same time; Lily stole Grace's notebook and then kept taunting me with it. I would do the same thing if I wanted to mess with someone's head. Her act in the café was a good one, but it didn't take much effort to peel away the layers.

Lily sent lilies to our house and wrote the nasty message about Grace. She was the one who gave me a flower at Grace's memorial. She found out about my past and she sent me the messages calling me Katie, and the ones that focused on Grace as a bad person. She never forgave Grace for bullying her.

She became Grace's friend in order to get close enough to kill her.

And now I hate her, and I'm angry, and I want to end this. I slip the knife into my jacket pocket and climb out of my vehicle, heading closer to the quarry, my hair gently lifted by the cool night-time breeze. She steps slightly to the side, and lifts a small object into the air. Grace's phone.

'Those voicemails were very sweet.' She taps the screen and I hear my voice: *Hi, Grace. It's Mum. I wanted to call yesterday, because I wanted to talk you through everything…*

I almost don't recognise myself. Who have I been kidding about my grief? The pain is clear in my trembling voice. I'd thought myself detached and emotionless. I was wrong.

'Poor Katie.' Lily sticks out her bottom lip as she stops the voicemail.

I can't stomach the way she's standing there with her head tilted to the left, a broad grin on her face, exuding arrogance. Without warning, I charge her, grabbing the knife from my pocket. Lily's expression changes to one of shock, but she reacts quickly, ducking away from me. I take a swing at her with the knife, barely a centimetre away from her arm as she arches back, catlike in the way she moves her body. I ready myself to take another swing, but she rushes forward and shoves me into the dirt, climbing on top of me to grab the wrist holding the knife.

'You can't win, old woman. I'm younger and fitter than you.' Then she lowers her head and bites down hard on my arm, forcing me to open my hand and drop my weapon. I cry out in pain as her teeth chomp down on my skin, almost drawing blood.

Lily is on her feet in an instant, eyes on the sharp object. While I scramble to recover the knife, she kicks it and it goes flying into the quarry.

'No!'

She faces me, nodding her head. 'It's just you and me now, Katie.'

'Why do you keep calling me that?' I say. 'What has my past got to do with you? You weren't even born then.'

But Lily doesn't say a word. She walks nonchalantly over to where I lie on the ground, cradling my damaged arm. I assess whether I have the strength to push her into the quarry, but I'm not sure I do, and it's not a risk I'm willing to take. She could too easily dodge me or throw me down there herself.

'I decided to learn everything I could about you,' she says. 'And I learned that you came from a dingy council house, that you had a boringly regular name, that you were arrested quite a few times before the age of sixteen – and that you *killed someone*.' She says the last part in dramatic fashion, like Poirot with his big reveal.

'Then you know what you're doing right now is dangerous,' I say, lifting myself from the ground into a crouch.

She laughs. 'Please stop kidding yourself, Katie. You make all these dramatic threats but you have no follow-through. I'm not even armed, yet you gave up trying to kill me with barely a fight.'

Pathetically, I take the bait and rush at her again. She kicks me straight in the mouth and my lip splits. Both blood and hot pain blossom from my lips and teeth, and I fall onto my backside.

'Why did you want me to come here?' I ask, holding my face with my hand, watching the blood trickle through my fingers.

'It wasn't fun anymore. No one knew how clever I'd been.' As she speaks, she glances off to the side, as though searching through the shadows.

'Did you just want to boast? Are you going to kill me? This is the Suicide Spot, after all. You might get away with it. Have you got a taste for blood now? It never ends well for serial killers, you know. You could murder me, but you'd then want to do it again and again. You'll get sloppy and mess up.'

As I sit there, injured and pitiful, she stands over me with her feet splayed wide and her shoulders back. She leans down, like an adult does with a child. 'I don't know why you keep assuming that I killed your daughter. She wanted to die.' She crouches and places a hand on my cheek, keeping it there even when I flinch away from her. A sense of shame washes over me when it becomes obvious that I'm afraid of her. 'Just like you.' She strokes my face once, and then reaches back into her pocket for Grace's phone. 'Here, let me show you.' She sits cross-legged on the ground next to me and unlocks the phone with Grace's passcode. Then she opens her messages app and scrolls down.

There on the screen, I see the exact same messages that Lily showed me in the café, except that they are reversed. Now I understand. Lily cleverly photoshopped the messages to make it appear as though Grace was the one urging her to die, when in actual fact it was Lily trying to convince Grace to commit suicide. When she held out her phone to me, she was showing me a screenshot. I didn't touch the phone. I didn't scroll up or down. Now that the proof is here in front of me, it all seems so obvious.

> **Grace**: Sometimes I think things will get better. But then I get so lost and things keep getting worse and worse. Should I talk to my mum?
> **Lily**: You think she'll understand? You're pregnant with a teacher's baby! She'll be so disappointed in you.
> **Grace**: I know. I let her down and I hate myself.
> **Lily**: I know what it's like to let someone down. Remember what I said at the quarry? I understand what you're going through. I want to die, too. I hate it here.
> **Grace**: ((hugs))
> **Grace**: Death is so final though.
> **Lily**: It makes the suffering stop.
> **Lily**: We could do it together.
> **Grace**: I want to see you. We should talk about this. It's crazy. I have the baby to think about.
> **Lily**: It solves all your problems in one go.

I shake my head. 'She didn't want to die. You found her at her most vulnerable and you twisted every emotion she was going through until it was ugly and desperate. You killed her.'

'I made her wake up to what she wanted to do.'

'No. You manipulated her and you lied to her. You isolated her, taking her away from her friends and her parents, making her believe you were the only one who understood what she was going through. Why did you do it, Lily? Was it because Grace bullied you? Was this all some sort of sick revenge?'

Lily's throat bobs as she swallows. 'Yes. But it wasn't revenge for that.' She reaches into her coat pocket and pulls out the notebook I've seen several times in her rucksack. 'I think you need to read this before I tell you everything else.' She holds it out to me, then snatches it away at the last moment. 'But first you need to give me your phone, and any other weapons you might have concealed in your clothing.'

She has the upper hand and we both know it. I hand over my phone and then take the notebook from Lily's hands. Finally, I get to read Grace's own words.

'The last entry is her suicide note,' Lily says. 'The real one.'

CHAPTER THIRTY-SEVEN

Lily licks her lips as I open the notebook and begin to read.

Dear Mum and Dad,
   I think I've let you both down. Especially you, Mum.

'Read it aloud,' Lily demands. 'I want to hear your voice.'

'No.' Her arrogance is beginning to get on my nerves. I can't stand her smirk, or the dark eyes I'd once considered so wounded.

When she snatches the book from me, I throw my weight towards her to get it back, but she brings her knee up, knocking me down. And then she begins to read.

'At least I'll never have to see the expressions on your faces when you read this. I'll never see the disappointment in your eyes when you find out how awful I've been. It started a long time ago, when I told a lie and everyone at school listened to me for a change. And then I discovered that I couldn't stop lying, because I wanted them to go on listening. But keeping up with my lies proved to be harder than I thought, and the more I lied, the more mistakes I made. Now I'm drowning in them and I can't keep my head above the water—'

'Give it to me.' I reach out for the book. 'I'll read it to you.' I can't stand hearing Grace's words coming out of her mouth.

Lily tosses the book down in the dirt where I collect it with bloodied fingers, attempting, and failing, to keep the blood from the pages.

Lily plops down beside me and gestures for me to read.

'The first lie I told was on my first day at secondary school.' I pause to catch my breath. These are Grace's words coming through my mouth. Her truth at last. 'The girls were horrible – they kept calling me chubby because I wasn't slim like them. One of them held her foot out to trip me over and then she laughed at me. It was Alicia. When I got up, I told her that I had a thyroid problem but that I was going to get surgery to help me lose weight. And then I told her you were a supermodel who tried to force me into those weird beauty pageants for kids. We started chatting and we were kinda friends by the end of the day. Over the next few months I lost some weight and Alicia never asked me about the surgery again. You and Dad made friends with her parents and we kept hanging out with each other.'

'Alicia is a bitch.' Lily places her chin in her hands and gazes at me.

'I can't blame Alicia for everything. She was mean, but she didn't make me bully Lily. She didn't force me to tell lies or start my vlog or do any of the stupid, attention-seeking shit I did.'

'Also true,' Lily says. 'Get to the good bit, will you?'

I hate this. I hate that Lily is forcing me to read this out loud. The cool night, the dark sky, the quarry stretching out beyond – this is where Grace suffered, and I cannot stop thinking about her body, about the identification in the morgue.

I owe it to my daughter to find out what she went through. 'Dad, you suggested that I try therapy. And that was when we both started lying to you, Mum. You always do the right thing and I didn't want you to find out how horrible I am inside.

'I thought it was going to be like taking a magic pill – that I'd talk to someone in a room and we'd figure out what's wrong with me and then fix it. After a few weeks, I didn't understand why I was still doing things to get Alicia's attention, like dieting. I'm a different person at school than I am at home, and I don't know which version is real anymore.

'One day, Daniel asked me to stay behind after orchestra practice to work on a tricky piece. Nothing happened that day, but I still remember the way he made me, Grace, the girl who can't stop lying, the person no one notices unless I make them – feel like I mattered. He saw me. He told me that I was a "bright spark". He made me feel like I was a firework, pretty and colourful, not just a spoilt rich girl with no personality of her own. He decided that I needed a solo piece, and we worked on it alone, in the music room. His hand on mine as I played the notes. Moving the bow together. I'm sorry, Dad.'

'Keep going,' Lily says.

My bottom lip trembles as I try to continue. It isn't my cut that prevents me from speaking; it's the all-encompassing sadness that has wrapped around my body, squeezing tight.

Finally, my voice comes back. 'Everyone at school is pretty and I don't think that I am. At least I didn't until Daniel started to make me feel that way. Then that all went wrong and now I feel like pond scum.

'Then Lily came up to me one day and told me that she forgave me for the bullying. Can you imagine that? She forgave me, like it was nothing. Like I hadn't humiliated her in front of everyone at school. No one liked Lily. She was this weird freak girl who dyed her hair black and came to school wearing dark eyeliner, never speaking to anyone, always with headphones in, listening to loud music. We were nasty to her because we were ignorant. Once I got to know Lily, she made me understand that Alicia and her gang are nothing but entitled little rich girls who tear each other down instead of building each other up. They're the worst kind of girls. They fight and spread insecurity, splitting us down the middle with their nastiness. I grew to hate it all, and as I began to hate them, I realised that I hate myself, too.

'Lily had to fight against the things that happened to her as a child. I saw the scars on her arms and she told me about how she does it to make the pain stop. I'm full of pain, too. I'm drowning in it and I can't figure out how to float back up to the surface. She told me all about her adopted mum's alcoholism and I felt horrible because I have you guys and you're nothing like her mum. I should be grateful for everything I have, but I'm not. I'm suffocating inside, like my lungs are full of water.

'Lily reminds me of you, Mum. We all know how horrible Grandma is, though we don't talk about it. And you grew up to be a good person, like Lily. I'm sorry you two didn't get to meet.'

'But we did get to meet,' Lily says brightly. 'And look how close we've become. You're my hero, Katie. My mother figure in shining armour. You dropped everything when I sent you that email and you came to meet me, to offer me a shoulder to cry on.' She places a hand on my knee. 'Do you think we're alike? Do you think Grace is right?'

'I don't know,' I mumble. 'I don't know you.'

She tucks a strand of hair behind my ear. 'Keep reading.'

'After making friends with Lily, I began to believe that things could get better for me. I had Daniel and I had Lily – two real relationships for me to cling onto, not frenemies like Alicia. And then I found out I was pregnant, and everything changed.

'I still love him. You can't blame Daniel for what happened because it's all my fault. I should've gone on the pill like he told me to, but I was too scared to go to the doctor's alone, so I lied to Daniel, thinking that everything would work out ok. It didn't.

'Lily helped me through it all. She hugged me when I cried, she gave me advice when I needed it. But there is a person growing inside me and I can't nurture him or her. I can't give this baby anything, because I'm empty inside. I'm lost. What can I do when I'm sinking to the bottom of the ocean? Babies deserve love and I have none to give. I could force myself to carry on, to give away this child to someone else, but sometimes I think it's the baby pulling me down. I can't tell if I'm being pushed or pulled, and I can't tell who is doing the pushing and who is pulling me. Everyone and no one, I think.

'When I first found out, I thought Daniel would leave his wife and we could be together. I figured that at least if he was by my side, the little one would have love from him, and then he or she could have a happy life. Mum, I'm not right. I lie to people and I bully people. I'm not a good person and I have to accept that. I'm sorry. I need to make it all stop once and for all, because I can't do this anymore.

'If I come to you, I have to own up to all the things I've done, and I can't do that. Lily's right – death is the way out. If I die, then all of this ends.'

I pause, clear my throat, try to compose myself. I'm not sure I can keep going, but I force myself to. 'Lily can't see any other way out either and we know that we're stronger together. After I've finished writing this, we're going to go to the quarry together, and we're going to hold hands and jump.

'Please don't be angry or upset. With me gone, you can carry on without me as a burden, without me and my failures dragging you into the water with me. But most of all, I'll never let you down again. I love you both, I truly do. You're everything to me. I'm sorry. Grace.'

As I close the notebook, invisible fingers work their way between my ribs, tugging my heart down to my abdomen, down to my hips. Down. Down. Every part of my body is a lead weight and I can barely breathe. Pain dripped from her every word. Loneliness came through every line. I can't stand the thought of her suffering. I close my eyes and picture her smile. She kept up that smile throughout the worst of her anguish, hiding her true feelings from us. How can I ever accept this?

More than anything, I'm surprised and saddened to see that Grace thought I was such a moral person, that I'd hold her to a higher standard. Grace, how could you get everything twisted up like that? It was you who made me hold myself to a higher standard. It was you who made me want to be better, to fight against the person I was born to be. It was all for you, but it led to you doubting yourself.

I wish I could hold her and tell her that none of the things she talked about made her horrible or terrible or bad. No one is complete at seventeen. You lied – so what? Work on yourself and learn not to lie. You fell pregnant – so what? It's an accident, and humans resolve accidents every day of the week.

Grace, I did a terrible thing when I was a teenager, and I carried on. I kept on living.

'What about the suicide note found by the police?' I ask, pulling myself back to Lily and her watchful eyes.

'That was Grace's first draft,' Lily says. 'It took a bit of warming up to get her feelings out. But I didn't want you to find everything out right away, so I slipped her first draft into her pocket on the night. Of course, I had to scribble out the part about me in it.'

'You're obviously here,' I say. 'Did you ever plan to kill yourself? Or was it all some sick game to enable you to commit murder?'

'I keep telling you – I didn't murder anyone.'

'Did you make friends with her to get revenge? I don't understand why you did any of this.'

Lily smiles, like she possesses a secret I want to know.

'Tell me, or I'll rip you limb from limb.'

'You're all bark, Katie,' she says. 'I'll tell you what we arranged. Grace came to my house after school and we had some dinner while my mum was out. No one saw us, because no one ever sees me. No one cares about me and no one cares who I'm with. Then we went upstairs to my bedroom and we wrote our suicide notes. We waited until dark, then I drove us here to the quarry. It was agreed that I'd leave our things on the cliff for the police to find.' She pats the ground to indicate where that was. 'We were going to jump together at the Suicide Spot.' She points to the area in front of us, where the police tape flaps in the wind.

'But you didn't jump?'

'No,' she says slowly. 'I didn't jump.'

Lily is choosing her words carefully, avoiding important details. Since reading Grace's suicide note, a lot of the fight has seeped from me, like I'm a balloon pricked by a needle, but I still want answers.

'Did Grace jump?'

A smile. No answer.

'Fine. Then tell me why you did this. Tell me what all of this was for.'

'It's all been about *you*, Katie. I'm surprised you didn't guess. There were plenty of clues in the messages. We used your real name so many times.'

'I've never hidden who I am. Plenty of people know that I used the name Katie before. I thought it was a taunt.' As I'm speaking, the blood drains from my face. I finally focus on the one important word from her statement: *we*.

'Katie, I need to tell you something,' Lily says. 'You're a bit of an inspiration to me. You were the original bad girl at school, weren't you? I mean, there's one killer here and it isn't me, is it? You're the one who bashed in a skull. What was it like to see the life leave someone's eyes? Did it make you feel powerful?'

'Someone put you up to this.' The headlights of the car only highlight a small portion of the quarry. There are plenty of other places for someone to hide in the shadows. Is this why Lily wanted to meet at night? A dark place where she could hide her accomplice? Who is out there, concealed in the shadows? Who would want to hurt me like this?

And then I know. Of course I know. Why didn't I see it sooner?

She is the one person I hurt more than anyone else in this world. She witnessed my worst act, was the victim of my most heinous crime. It's her. It must be her.

'I guess it's time you met my mum,' Lily says. She places her fingers between her lips and whistles. The high-pitched sound echoes around the quarry.

My skin prickles with anticipation, as though the thin twigs of a tree are scraping up and down my arms and legs. The breeze seems to still and the world goes deathly quiet, until I hear footsteps coming towards us. There is a shadow in the distance. All I can see is her frame, wider than the average person, perhaps slightly shorter than other women. She walks agonisingly slowly, dragging out the reveal. I climb to my feet, not wanting to meet her while on the ground, and Lily stands with me.

All the time I'm thinking that Grace died because of what I did when I was a teenager. Her suicide note is full of remorse for her own behaviour as a young person, but it's me, my consequence, my burden to carry. I'm the one to blame, not her.

The woman finally moves close enough for the light of my car headlights to brush her light brown hair, and I hold my breath.

'Hi, Katie.'

That voice. I recognise that voice.

She walks a few more steps, standing at the edge of the light, her hair frizzy and wild. But this isn't Annie Robertson – not as I remember her.

When we were thirteen years old, she always wore her hair in a bun tied with a purple scrunchy. But now that I concentrate hard, I remember that her hair came loose that day, and it was curly and wild.

'Let me see you.' My voice is low. My fingertips tingle. I can't pinpoint the emotions building up inside me. Anger. Regret. Fear. 'I want to see your face.'

'You already know my face,' she replies.

And then she steps into the light and I nod my head. There is the doughy face with the bad nose job that I remember. I recognised her voice because I hear it every single week. She's the person who tells me what I should be thinking, who helps me be a better person. She's the person I have trusted with my most private thoughts. She's the person who confirmed my diagnosis of antisocial personality disorder, and she is the person who has told me, week after week, that I'm a sociopath. She has been my therapist for twelve years. But only now do I realise Angela is also the girl from my past.

'How are you today, Kat?' Angela says, without a trace of a smile on her lips. 'How does that make you feel?'

'How could it possibly be you? I've known you for years… I don't understand. What happened to you after… after school?'

'God,' she says, venom in her voice. 'You can't even say it, can you? You can't admit that it happened.' Angela glares down at the ground and back up, as though trying to reel in her temper. 'I moved away with my parents after leaving the hospital. At that point, my face was wrecked. I looked like a bag of oranges. After two years of reconstructive surgery, I started to resemble a human being again.'

'I'm sorry,' I reply. 'I wanted to talk to you – after – but you left.'

Angela laughs. 'Look at you and your guilt. Anyone would doubt that you're a sociopath at all.'

The words, so casually thrown at me, hit me like a bucket of ice-cold water. I stand there staring at her in complete and utter disbelief.

'Are you even a therapist? How did you end up as *my* therapist? *Twelve years*, Angela. Why?' The questions tumble from my lips.

'Some luck here and there,' she answers, 'along with plenty of hard work. Yes, I am a therapist, trained and qualified. When I read about your marriage to Charles Cavanaugh, I happened to move closer to you. At that point, I was curious to see if what happened to us had affected you too. You see, I desperately wanted you to be suffering, but you were thriving. So I joined the same gym as some of your friends and started talking to them. Eventually, one of them mentioned that her friend Kat Cavanaugh had asked her for a recommendation for a good therapist. It was too good an opportunity to miss. I told her that I'm a therapist and asked her to recommend me to you. The rest you know.'

When the realisation hits that this woman has been after me my entire life, hot rage comes flooding in to heat the icy shock of her revelation. 'So you stalked me and ruined my life? Then you went after my *kid*. You used your own daughter to kill my child? You're a fucking psychopath, and you made me believe that *I'm* the sociopath?'

Annie or Angela, or whoever she is, lifts one finger. 'Are you completely sure that you *aren't* a sociopath, Kat? I gave you my professional opinion over and over again.'

'Liar.'

She shrugs.

'And what about Lily? You've not only destroyed my life and my husband's, my daughter's and my potential grandchild's lives, you've tormented your own child.'

'Oh, Lily isn't my daughter. I can't have children of my own. Lily is adopted.'

I glance across at Lily, who isn't smiling anymore. Her expression seems hurt, as though she was hoping that Angela loved her deep down.

'And to answer your previous question, I went after your kid because she deserved it. Did you see what she did to Lily? All these years later and you raised a spoilt brat who bullied other kids. A clone of yourself. Don't you remember how you bullied everyone at school?'

'You sent me the messages,' I say. Then, to Lily, 'You worked with her. You're both murderers. You took advantage of my vulnerable child and encouraged her to take her own life.'

'Maybe,' Angela says. 'But we weren't the only ones to fail her. You didn't see that she was hurting. Your husband failed to tell you she was in therapy. And pretty much all of her friends made her feel like total shit. *Both* the guys she was in relationships with abandoned her. And do you know why?'

I don't give her the satisfaction of asking.

'Because everyone knew she wasn't worth it.'

There's a snapping sound in my head. I heard it once before, a long time ago, when I saw a cavernous mouth and heard a scream so loud it imprinted on my mind forever. In that moment I lunge for Angela, almost taking her by surprise, but not quite. As she steps to the left, another set of hands shove me forwards. With my body tilted over at the waist and my weight completely unbalanced, it takes one more push from whoever is behind me to ensure that I tip over the edge of the quarry and plunge down into the depths below.

CHAPTER THIRTY-EIGHT
Chesterfield, 1993

It's not easy to step quietly through my place. I need to make sure I don't trip over the pile of magazines or stumble face first into the glass cabinet, full of half-empty bottles of booze. I definitely need to not upend the stack of boot-sale trinkets still piled up on the living room carpet. Miniature porcelain clown faces watch me from below.

I'm pretty sure I'm a master at finding my way through this obstacle course. Blindfold me, let me loose – I could do it all without waking up the booze-soaked monster unconscious on the sofa. Because tiptoeing through the mess is far easier than waking her up. She'll be angry and mean, honing in on whatever I've done wrong this week. She'll wind me up and make me so full of fury that I'll end up smacking someone again. There are days when some other kid will look at me funny and I can't stop myself. I don't like them staring at me like that, because that's when they see who I am, and I can't stand it. Then I have to hit them, to stop them seeing the real me, but afterwards it's worse.

Here comes Katie Flack, deliverer of pain, the girl with bruises on her knuckles because she can't stop pounding you in the face. The teachers say that one day someone will teach me a real lesson and then I'll stop being such a little shit. They keep suspending me, but they don't expel me. I think that's because they're scared of Mum.

After sneaking through the mess, thankfully without waking the monster, I can't resist slamming the front door and legging it down the alley behind our house. I'll be halfway to school before those glued-shut eyelids begin to flutter open. And it'll serve her right if she has 'one of her headaches' for the rest of the day.

Some of the kids at school call me and Mum dole scroungers. Not that they're any better. *Fuck you, Stacey, your mum works at Wynsors World of Shoes. Get lost, Heather, your dad drinks away his wages in the Nag's Head.* They all think they're better than me, but they're not. I hate all of them. Well, except for Annie. She's all right. We're hanging out after school today.

By the time I'm down the street, I have a sweat on and I'm running late for registration. Still, what does it matter? The teachers think I'm scum anyway. I slow to a saunter and allow the morning breeze to cool me down. All the other kids are at school by now, leaving the streets nice and quiet.

As I begin to relax into the silence around me, a rough voice disrupts the peace.

'Mornin', scrubber!'

I don't even turn around, just keep on walking. On this estate, being heckled by a nearby weirdo isn't an unusual occurrence.

'Oi, bitch. I'm talking to you.'

It's probably some dosser off his face on drugs, but still, I quicken my pace to get away from him. People like that are unpredictable. I hear the footsteps behind me shuffle faster to keep up, which makes my muscles tense with fear.

'You late for school too?'

A hand grips my shoulder and spins me round. The tall boy smirks with satisfaction and his eyes gaze up and down my body, slowly taking in my shape.

'Better than I expected.' His smile widens and his blue eyes twinkle with mischief. 'Never thought a girl with dull hair like yours would have such a good rack.'

'Don't touch what you can't afford.' I wrench myself away from his grasp. But when I move away from him, ready to carry on walking to school, I can't deny a certain thrill running up and down my body. He noticed me and thinks I'm sexy.

'I like 'em feisty,' he says, walking quickly to keep up. 'What year you in?'

I consider lying because he's obviously older than me. But then I shrug and blurt out, 'Year 8.'

'I'm Year 10, so you should respect your elders. That's what my mum always says. Before I kick her teeth in anyway.' He laughs.

'As if. I bet you've never kicked anyone.'

He grins again and then his eyes narrow, their pale blue colour kind of nice to look at. 'Hey, I know you. You're that kid that's always scrapping. You're all right, you. You can hold your own.'

'Yeah?' Hearing an older boy tell me I'm all right fills me with a sense of pride, and I find myself walking a bit taller, smiling a little wider.

'Yeah. You got any friends?'

'I guess there's Annie.' I shrug.

'You and your friend should come hang out with us tonight. My brother got his driver's licence a few months ago. We'll pick you up after school if you want. By the shop.'

I know the one he means: the newsagent near the school that gets bombarded every lunchtime by teenagers wanting penny sweets and Mars bars.

'What's your name?' I ask.

'Gav. You?'

'Katie.'

He winks at me, then leans across and pinches my bum. I swat away his hand with a frown, but Gav doesn't seem bothered by my discomfort. He just laughs.

'See you later, Katie with the nice rack.' As he jogs away, he makes kissing noises at me.

All the way to school, I think about Gav. I'm not sure what to make of him. On the one hand, I like that he noticed me and that he thinks I'm all right. On the other hand, now that he's gone, my tummy is all crampy, like when Mum's about to bollock me. I wrap my arms protectively around my breasts. I guess I hadn't noticed that they'd grown before today.

Annie lives on the estate too, which is probably why we became friends. She's pretty, I guess. Not like me. The boys sometimes stare at her and make comments. They ask her what sort of bra she's wearing and what colour knickers she has on, but they don't ask me. Sometimes, when we're hanging out, I want them to ask me those questions too, but then I see Annie's face flash red and I wonder whether it's worth it.

'I don't think we should be hanging round with anyone old enough to drive a car,' Annie says, chewing on the end of her pen and somehow managing to make it look incredibly grown up.

She's pretty and she doesn't have the kind of temper that gets her in trouble. She could have way more friends. I don't know why she even hangs around with me.

'Are you kidding? It'll be cool.'

We're in RE and I'm bored, and convincing Annie to come out with me later is more fun than learning about how many days there are in Lent.

'We don't know anything about them.' Annie leans back in her chair and glares at me. She has a way of looking at you like she's better than you. For some reason it doesn't bother me when she does it. But if anyone else does the same, then I lose it.

'Well, they go here.'

Annie rolls her eyes. 'The lads from this shithole are awful. Yesterday in maths, Simon stuck a pencil under my boob to see if I "passed the test".'

'What test?'

'Apparently, perfect boobs shouldn't be able to fit a pencil underneath them or something. The dickhead didn't realise I have to be naked first.' She pulls a lock of hair free from her bun and twirls it around her finger. 'I pass it, obviously.'

'What, when naked?'

'Yeah.'

'Cool. Gav said I have a nice rack.'

'Is he fit?'

'Yeah.'

'Hmm.' She scrunches up her mouth and moves her lips to one side, as though considering her options.

When Miss Rowe comes walking by our desk, we lean over the textbook and pretend to be studiously examining the passage before us. Someone has drawn a squirting penis in the corner.

When Rowe is gone, Annie lifts her head. 'I don't know. We could get in trouble.'

'Your mum'll be at work. Mine'll be drinking gin at the miner's club.'

'True.'

'I'm going on my own if you don't come.' When I stick out my chin, she knows I'm serious. That's what I do before starting a fight. Across the room, Susie P glances in my direction and I flash her a 'what you looking at' glare. She turns away.

'Fine.'

'Nice one.'

I tap her on the knee with my pencil in celebration, and then we get on with the reading.

The twenty minutes we wait for them after school goes on forever. I spend most of the time holding up a mirror for Annie as she spreads on thick lipstick and neatens her bun. She pulls out two thin locks of hair to frame her face, and after she's finished I tie my hair up into a ponytail and do the same. When she offers me the lipstick, I decide to try it. The shade doesn't suit me particularly well, but I do look older and I like that.

'They're not coming. We should go,' Annie says.

'Wait, wait. That's them.' I nod across the street as a beat-up Vauxhall Nova pulls up, blasting happy hardcore at full volume.

Gav leans out of the passenger window and waves to us. 'Get in.'

Annie rolls her eyes in disdain, but she still follows me as I hurry over to the car.

'Get in then,' Gav instructs, nodding especially to Annie, who hangs back at first.

We have to squash into the back with two other guys. Their names are Steve and Mark, we're told. Gav informs us that the driver is Jamie, Gav's older brother, an eighteen-year-old fairground worker who lives in Wingerworth with some housemates.

For a while, Jamie drives aimlessly around town, circling the Donut Car Park while the boys lean out of the windows and whistle at people walking by. Someone thrusts a can of Carlsberg into my hand and I take a gulp, screwing my face up at the sour taste. But when I get halfway down the can, I find a warmth coming up from my belly, and some of my worries fade away. Even Annie starts to chill out after finishing her beer. She grins when Steve leans over and tells her she's fit as fuck.

After an hour of driving around the town, Jamie takes us away from the centre and out into the countryside. Annie's too busy giggling with Steve and chugging her second can to notice the change in direction. Mark has his hand on my knee, which is making my face feel warm, but I'm not sure if it's good or bad. I haven't finished my first can yet, and he's encouraging me to drink more.

I lean forward between the front seats. 'Where are we going?' I ask Gav, noticing a sign for Littlemoor, which I know is quite isolated and might not have a bus service if we need to get away.

'A good spot for getting wasted,' Gav says. 'Don't worry, Jamie knows what he's doing.'

As the roads get windier and narrower, we pass a group of tiny holiday bungalows next to a sign saying 'Barn Close' and then continue driving for another mile or so. Jamie pulls over and Gav grabs a stereo system and a few CDs. I'm trailing behind as everyone climbs a five-bar gate to get into a field. By now Annie is stumbling a bit and Steve has to help her. Mark puts his hand on my bum as I climb over, and they all stare up our skirts and laugh.

There are horses in the field but they ignore us, keeping their distance further out. One of them looks up from its grazing and lazily nods its head up and down. It has kind brown eyes, and I want to go up to it and stroke its velvety nose, but the others are moving on.

Further down the field, Jamie and Gav stop by a small shelter, putting down the portable stereo and turning on the music: more happy hardcore, which is definitely getting repetitive and annoying.

This isn't going how I'd hoped. I thought it would be grown up to hang out with older boys, but the stuff they want to do isn't interesting to me. I don't care about beer or loud music or coming to fields in the middle of nowhere. For once, I want to be at home on my own, or at school – where there are adults in control.

Scrapping with the other girls has always made me feel strong and powerful, but now I'm the opposite. The temper inside me has fizzled out until it's nothing but a tiny, dampened wick trying desperately to ignite. For some reason, I can't find my voice to tell them that I want to leave. Instead, I sit down on the hardened soil and fold my arms. I notice a lot of rocks lying about. Maybe the farmer threw them in here to get them out of the grass. The ground is packed down, made hard from the dry summer we've had. In the corners of the building I see old syringes and a condom.

I hate it here.

'Why don't you come and dance?' Gav asks. 'Or have another drink and chill out.'

'No, thanks.'

'You've got a face like a slapped arse, love,' Jamie shouts from across the shelter, and then he laughs loudly. They all join in, even Annie. And yet still I shrink into myself. I haven't cried since Uncle Bob died, but now I want to cry again. When no one is looking, I reach inside my school shirt and touch the gold locket that I'm wearing. Mum never buys me presents, but Uncle Bob did, and it's the only object I own that's actually worth anything. He was nice and he'd know what to do if he was here right now. But I haven't got a clue. I just want to go home.

Three of the boys surround Annie, grinding against her, but she's still laughing and smiling. Jamie puts his hands on her waist, lets them trail up to her chest. She shrieks in a good-natured way and bats him away. Then he spins her around, grabs roughly and picks her up, his arms pulling up her shirt a little.

'Put me down! Put me down!' she laughs, patting his arms and squealing.

'Maybe we should go, Annie. Won't your mum get home soon?'

Jamie glances over and shushes me. The hard glint in his eyes makes me shudder. Gav places an arm around my shoulder, but I'm too distracted by Jamie and Annie to notice. In one quick motion, he has Annie down on the ground.

'Hey.' She wriggles underneath him. 'Hey, stop that.'

I try to stand, not liking this at all, but Gav holds me tightly. When I try to wrestle him off me, he waves Mark over, and the two of them hold me down, arms across my chest and waist, pinning me. Panic builds. I can't move. I can hardly breathe.

Annie screams. Jamie has hold of both of her wrists. Steve gets down on the floor with him and takes her arms while Jamie starts to pull down her underwear.

'Stop it,' I say. 'Stop.' But my voice is a whisper beneath Annie's screams.

I close my eyes. I don't want to see.

My heart thuds.

Someone grunts.

I force myself to look. Annie's mouth is open wide; she's screaming. Tears run down her face. There's soil on her cheeks.

Jamie calls her a whore, but she can't be, because whores do this willingly. Whores aren't held down by two men. Are they?

My chest tightens. I want to touch the locket again but I can't move so I shut my eyes again for a second, wishing I was anywhere else but here. There's a wheezing sound. It's coming from me. I make myself look.

Annie bites Steve and he pulls one hand back. She tries to claw herself away but Jamie bashes her face into the compacted ground. There's a crunch, and when she raises her head, her nose is broken. Blood runs down her face. Foul-smelling liquid spews out of my mouth. I think it's beer.

'Jesus, Jamie. Did you have to mess up her face? I can't do it with her looking like that.'

I don't want to see. When I squeeze my eyes closed, the world goes black. Annie's face isn't beaten up anymore. Someone will come and help us. Someone will make it stop. They have to.

I open my eyes.

Gav wrinkles his nose when he sees the stain down my shirt. 'Urgh, she's puked.'

'I don't care – I'm doing her,' Steve says. 'I'm not doing this one now. Bring her over here, will you?'

No.

'What did I say, Steve?' Jamie says. 'I'm first.'

No.

'Fine.'

I'm pulled to my feet. I don't want to see what's happening and screw my eyes tightly together. There's a high-pitched whimpering sound coming from my lips. Every part of my body grows cold.

Someone forces me down onto the ground where the soil is hard like concrete, and then someone else tugs at my clothes.

No.

I go still.

Someone laughs at the old, grey pants I'm wearing. I'm spun onto my back, and when I finally force my eyes open, Jamie's smirking face stares down at me.

'She's willing,' he says. 'Be a good girl and we won't hurt you.'

Out of the four faces, I find Gav, pleading silently with him. But I find no sympathy, no saviour, no decency here. There's four of them and they're stronger and there's no point in me fighting back. I want to give up, let it happen, but that damp wick deep inside me somehow ignites, and a spark of heat explodes into flame.

Jamie lets go of my arms, because he thinks I'm a 'good girl'. Mark wanders over to the entrance to the shelter to keep an eye out for anyone who might have heard Annie's screams. Steve goes over to Annie and starts touching her breasts. Gav's attention wanders over to Annie, too. It's just me and Jamie. His weight is heavy on top of me, but he hasn't started yet. He's clawing at my stained school shirt. Rough fingers catch on the chain of my locket. I have some time. I search for a weapon, edging my hand away from my side, towards a rock. Jamie's hands travel up my chest to my neck, and fear grips hold of me. I have only seconds. I reach out and grasp the rock and swing my arm with as much force as I possibly can. Before Jamie even understands what I'm doing, the rock bashes into the side of his head, knocking him off balance. He rolls onto the ground and the heavy stone falls from my grasp. Quickly, I scramble away as the others all look at me in surprise. I pick up another – heavier – rock with both hands, lift it and let go. Gav tries to tackle me. We stumble away, the crack of Jamie's skull a sickening sound amidst the chaos.

'Fuck.' Mark drops to his knees next to Jamie. He gazes up at me. 'Fuck.'

Gav's fist meets my face. He sits astride me. Pain explodes along my cheekbone, but I still manage to hit him hard enough in the nose for blood to spurt out.

'Gav, he's dead,' Mark cries. 'He's fucking dead.'

Gav gets to his feet, spins around and stares at his lifeless brother spread across the centre of the shelter. His trousers are down, exposing his genitals. There's blood and soil on his hands from when he hurt Annie. I crawl over to the dead boy and gently place my hand on his head. When I touch the warm blood and the broken skull, I scream, and then I scream again. Gav stands there staring at me.

'We've got to get out of here,' Steve says.

The thudding in my mind is the sound of my pulse. It's like the ocean. A tide of blood.

'You killed my brother.' Gav stares down at me in disbelief.

I don't want to see, but I have to look. Jamie lies there, his lifeless arms out wide, blood pooling underneath him, underneath my knees. I can't stop staring at the blood and I can't move as it touches me, gets on my skin. Warm. It's still warm.

Somewhere, in the background, I hear the footsteps of the other boys hurrying away. Annie is moving as though in slow motion, trying to sit up. Her nose isn't where it's supposed to be, her eyes are swollen and her jaw doesn't look right.

She strains to form words. 'You. Brought me. Here.'

I nod my head and forget how to stop nodding. Then, one last time, I screw my eyes shut and allow the world to go black. My heart continues to race, and the air wheezes out of my body when I try to breathe. I open them at last, get to my feet, legs shaking, blood on my hands and shirt, and stumble out of the shelter. I continue stumbling – past the horses, over the gate, onto the road. I keep going and going, wondering if I'll die on this road. Maybe I'll stop existing here. Keel over and suddenly stop.

But instead, a car pulls over.

CHAPTER THIRTY-NINE

I've been forever lost in a black, cavernous mouth.

When I wake, I lift my body, inhaling deeply and discovering pain in my ribs and the stench of blood. My fingers grope around me, touching the slimy stone of the quarry underneath. My ribs and my ankle throb; my head is reeling; there's blood on my temple.

I'm not dead.

Jamie is dead. I killed him when he tried to rape me. That's the ending to the story that I've kept tucked away in a sealed envelope at the back of my mind. Annie Robertson, with her open mouth and broken face, has haunted my dreams ever since, though I've never admitted it to anyone.

What happened to us that day was all my fault. If I allow myself to think back to my first meeting with Gav, I can see that he was awful. The things he said to me were disgusting, but because I was stupid, I took them as compliments. Stupid Katie. She messed up everything. She failed to save her friend. Katie knew how to fight, and yet she allowed Gav and Mark to hold her down and make her watch.

I roll over and vomit, which hurts my aching back. After I'm done, I gasp in pain, trying desperately to stand. My eyes slowly adjust to the dark, allowing me to see that I'm on a ridge, low down in the quarry. I didn't fall all the way to the bottom. Not like Grace.

That day in Littlemoor with Annie, I'd limped to the road and flagged down a car. Together, the driver and I had gone back to the shelter, picked up her crumpled body and taken her to the hospital. It was the early nineties, so no one had a mobile phone, and we decided it was quicker to drive rather than find a payphone and wait for an ambulance. All that time I was thinking about my lost underwear. There was vomit on my school shirt, too. I had buttons missing and I couldn't cover my training bra.

Later, after the police interrogation and my recounting of the moment where Jamie's skull smashed under the weight of the rock, I found myself relieved that Annie was visibly hurt. The monster in me was glad that Jamie had smashed Annie's face, because then the police were forced to believe us. Otherwise how would it look? We'd been drinking. We went voluntarily with the boys. Without the violence towards Annie, they might not have believed that it was self-defence.

But my mother had no such illusions.

'You were asking for it, Katie. And you dragged that girl into it. You're disgusting. You're a murderer.'

A murderer.

A killer.

I saw a psychologist and they took into account all of my past violence as well as the self-defence killing, and they suggested to my mum that I might have a disorder. *She could have antisocial personality disorder. It's difficult to diagnose...* And that was it. I've been a sociopath my entire life. I am. That's who I am. Isn't it?

Angela, Annie, a wolf in sheep's clothing, told me that sociopaths can't love. Have her words denied me love all this time?

It's easier to accept a label, to have a term slapped onto your skin to explain all the strange thoughts and behaviours that crop up over a lifetime. You're a sociopath, that's why you took a life. That's why you fell pregnant on purpose. That's why you stole that parking spot from the nice lady. That's why you're different to everyone else.

The quarry is a silent, black hole, and I'm in the centre. Pushing my body against the stony wall, I gaze up the cliff, trying to find the spot where I was pushed. Are they still there? The place is silent.

This is where Grace lost her fingernail, where she bled to death as she tried to pull herself out of the quarry depths. She should've been the one to land luckily, to have a chance, but instead it's me.

I grope for my phone, but it's gone. That's right, Lily took it. At this moment, I'd call Grace rather than an ambulance, desperate to hear her voice one last time.

Hey, this is Grace. Leave a message!

There, I don't need the phone. It's in my head.

'Grace. I thought I wanted to die, but I don't. I read your real suicide note today, and I'm sorry. I missed everything, didn't I? Another parent failing their kid. I always said I wouldn't.' I manoeuvre myself onto my hands and knees and slowly, very slowly, begin to crawl.

'Remember when I had to pick you up early from that birthday party? It was rock climbing. You hated the heights and kept crying. The supervisor had to help you down because you froze up near the top of the wall. Well, you were brave when you fell down here. You tried to pull yourself back up. If you hadn't been so hurt, I know you would have made it to the top.'

I'm inching forwards, with my hands groping for every ridge. The steps were built in 1982. The council were going to transform the place into a park with a trail leading to the bottom. There was going to be a pond and all kinds of flowers. Then they lost funding and gave up.

'You were searching for the steps when you were down here, weren't you? That means you changed your mind. I don't care if you jumped, fell or were pushed. You didn't want to die. You changed your mind and you wanted to live. You fought to live.' My palm reaches a flat surface of stone perpendicular to another flat surface. I let out a laugh that echoes around the quarry. 'I think I found them. Grace, I found the steps.'

When I attempt to stand, my ankle buckles beneath me and I fall back down. It's too risky to try and climb the steps with a twisted ankle. I can't risk toppling all the way to the bottom. But I can crawl by propping myself up on my elbows and taking my weight with my arms. Every tiny movement is an effort and every part of my body aches. I don't want to think about the damage. There must be bruises all over me. My head is throbbing. My ribs are sore. Pain radiates up and down my spine. Sweating profusely, I somehow manage to pull myself up one step. And now I need to move on to the next.

The steps plunge me into a shadowed part of the quarry with no light to guide my way. I find no comfort in keeping my eyes open. Instead I close them, like I did that day with Annie. But this time I think about Grace stuck down here with her broken leg and her torn fingernails. My elbow scrapes over the sharp edge of stone and some of my skin rubs away. It doesn't matter; all that matters is that I keep going. The muscles in my forearms burn with the effort of heaving the weight of my body and my knees press painfully against rough stone, propping up the weight of my legs.

On the third step, the pain in my ribs intensifies and a wave of dizziness almost knocks me out. That would be it for me. If I fell from this ledge, I doubt I'd make it back up. The thought of shivering down there in the darkness with my hurt ankle and bloody head injury spurs me to get over the third step and onto the fourth. But then I take a break, and I place my cheek on the stone, trying to find a rhythmic breath. I'm exhausted.

When my consciousness starts drifting away, I force my eyes open again. I could have concussion. I can't trust my body right now, not with a head injury. *Keep going.*

Up the fifth step, with sweat running down my back. My jeans are wet around the knees and my top is ripped. I can't tell if my hands are wet from the damp ground or whether it's my own blood. All I know is that I need to concentrate, and I need to hold on to this stone. Any slip or trip or mistimed effort could see me plunging back down to the ground below. How close am I to the top? I don't know. The headlights from my car are too high up to highlight what's down here with me, but I can see a hint of them now, which means that my car is still there. I won't be able to drive it with this ankle, though.

After a few more steps, my hands start to numb. I take a break and slap some life into them. Pins and needles spread up and down my legs. Is it from the injury? Or is it because they're at a strange angle? I'm not sure, but it's not a good sign. Every now and then my vision becomes blurry and I have to take a moment to recover. The problem is, when I stop, I want to sleep.

Up above, I notice that the glow from the headlights is brighter than before. But on the tenth – or maybe twelfth – step, I slip and fall backwards. The jolt to my ankle makes me scream in pain. Then nausea rises, and I'm forced to use my own willpower to stop myself from throwing up. That would be wasted energy. *Keep going.* These steps won't beat me. Fuck therapy, and labels, and bad psychology. I'm Kat Cavanaugh. I'm relentless, ruthless, robust. A steel plate around my heart. Conscience starved in a cage. A knock to the head and a few broken ribs aren't going to kill me.

I'm sorry, Annie Robertson, that you've continued to feed your hatred through all these years. There was no thank you after I killed your rapist, was there? You blamed me because it was easier. You made the choice to come, but it was my idea, so it was all my fault. Wasn't it? I was forcibly held back, and I couldn't help you, but I *wouldn't* help you, would I? Gav, Steve and Mark all went to prison because I testified for you, but it was all my fault in the first place. I'm the guilty one.

You stalked me, got in my head, made me think I was someone else. You found an acolyte for your cause and trained her to hate me and to hate my daughter.

You made Grace think she wanted to die. You isolated her from me. You stopped me from helping my own daughter.

You broke me down into pieces, tortured my mind and killed the one person I loved, and then you threw me down a quarry. But I got up, and I always will get up.

Here I am, at the point where the headlights are touching the cliff edge.

Annie, if you think you can hurt my child and not suffer the consequences, you messed with the wrong mother.

I drag myself out of the quarry, sweat running into my eyes, the taste of dirt in my mouth. Relief floods over me as I turn onto my back and pant, allowing myself to slowly recover. The exhaustion descends like a dark cloud, flattening all my adrenaline, but I refuse to allow myself to sleep. I need to get out of here, in case Angela and Lily come back to finish me off. Surely they must think I'm dead, but I can't risk it.

Using the light from my car, I search the area for my phone, but of course they've taken it with them. There's nothing to indicate they were ever here, except perhaps for the knife at the bottom of the quarry. My ribs and ankle ache, but I begin the slow task of pulling my woozy, damaged body towards the Land Rover. It's tough going. There's no strength left in my arms or legs and all I want to do is sleep.

Halfway between the quarry and the car, I scream in frustration and anger, about ready to give up, when I hear the sound of tyres on the gravel road. Matthew's truck pulls up next to mine and he hurries out, sprinting over to me.

'Jesus Christ, what happened?'

I could almost laugh, but I don't. 'I pulled myself out of the quarry. Can you take me to a hospital, please?'

'I'm not sure I should move you, Kat. Let me phone for an ambulance.' He bends down to wrap his leather jacket around my cold shoulders.

'You can't be here when the ambulance gets here,' I say.

Finally, I rest back on the cold ground, and find myself drifting into sleep. Before I lose consciousness completely, Angela's twisted expression forces itself into my mind. Then, in a heartbeat, it's replaced by Grace. I know what I need to do.

CHAPTER FORTY

My body feels pleasantly numb, and I could swear that I'm floating. But when I touch starched sheets with my fingertips, I know that I'm not floating at all. I'm in a hospital bed.

The colour blue pops into my mind, but I swiftly force it away.

There's a dry, rasping feeling at the back of my throat, and I long for a glass of water. Maybe if I press one of these buttons, someone will come along.

But then the door opens and Charles walks through. 'Kat.' He smiles, hurries towards me and takes my hand. 'You're awake.'

'I don't remember sleeping,' I admit.

'You've been asleep for almost a day.'

'I have?'

'That's right. I should go and get a doctor. You wait here for a minute.' He places a takeaway cup of coffee and a Snickers on the table next to my bed and leaves the room.

His absence gives me a moment to assess where I am and what's going on. There are other people in this room, which means I'm in a bay on a hospital ward. The curtain that extends around my bed isn't closed. I'm on view. The old lady on the opposite side snores softly and her left foot twitches.

The door opens again and Charles strides in with a short doctor behind him. And behind the doctor I recognise the faces of DS Slater and PC Mullen. It hits me all over again that Grace is dead; I'd forgotten for those few seconds.

I'd forgotten.

Now I look at DS Slater's sharp chin and remember the chipped blue nail polish, the colour of her lips, the stillness in the room as we identified her body. I remember DS Slater talking to us, telling us that Grace had committed suicide, showing us her suicide note. I remember the pain and the disbelief. The anger. The injustice of it all.

'Why are the police here?' I ask Charles.

It's DS Slater who answers. 'We just want to ask you a few questions, if you think you're up to it, Mrs Cavanaugh?'

'I'm not up to it,' I snap.

'Perhaps we should let the doctor be the judge,' he replies.

'Yes, I'll give my opinion after spending a bit of time with Mrs Cavanaugh.' He offers the police a thin smile.

'Of course,' DS Slater says. 'We'll be right outside.'

I roll my eyes after they're gone. 'Do I have to speak to them? I can't stand that detective.'

'I'm afraid so,' Charles replies. 'Kat, what were you doing at that quarry?'

'It's... complicated.'

The doctor shines lights in my eyes, asks questions, checks vitals and pokes and prods me for a few minutes. He explains that I have a badly sprained ankle, a bad knock on the head with some concussion, a bruised, but thankfully not broken, spine and a couple of broken ribs.

'You were lucky,' he says, and I get the impression he's trying very hard not to judge me.

'I know,' I say.

'What happened, Kat?' Charles takes one of my hands in both of his and draws it close to his face. There are new lines around his eyes. His own personal stressors are weighing him down, and pulling his skin with them. Cancer, grief, fear.

'I...' I sigh. 'You should bring the detective and his sidekick back in. I suppose I need to give them a statement too.'

Charles nods towards the doctor, who opens the door to allow the police back in and then disappears from the ward. DS Slater offers me an impassive stare before pulling the curtain around the bed.

'Thought you might prefer some privacy, Mrs Cavanaugh,' he says by way of explanation. 'How are you feeling?'

'I'm fine. Let's get this done so I can carry on with getting better.'

'That sounds excellent.' He pulls his notebook out of his coat pocket and skips through a few pages. 'Can you tell me what happened, Mrs Cavanaugh? And please, take your time.'

'Honestly, I don't remember much. I went to the quarry because that was where my daughter died. And then...' Every part of me wants to stop talking, to be silent. Every part of me wants to be alone, or at least away from these police officers. But I can't. I have to tell them.

'Please continue when you're ready.' DS Slater uses his gentle, understanding voice.

I bite my lip and regard my husband. 'I think I was there to kill myself. I'd been feeling low and stressed, and everything got on top of me. I'm sorry, darling.'

He squeezes my hand but stares at a spot above my head rather than meet my eyes.

'I woke up on a ridge after falling some way. I knew my ankle was badly hurt and that I'd hit my head. From my position on the cliff, I managed to pull myself up the steps to climb out.'

'I'm surprised you were physically able to do that, given your injuries,' DS Slater says.

'That's how much I wanted to survive,' I reply. 'I knew I'd made a mistake.'

'Was anyone else there that night?' he asks.

I shake my head. 'As far as I remember, I was alone.'

'What about the person who made the call to the emergency services? Why did they leave before the ambulance arrived?'

'I don't know, you'd have to ask them,' I say.

'Why wouldn't they leave a name?' he prods.

'I don't even know who they are, so how would I know?'

He moves on. 'You didn't leave a suicide note.'

'Is that a question?'

DS Slater's lip twitches. 'More of an observation.'

'I'm feeling quite tired,' I say. 'And I need to talk everything through with my husband.'

'I'll leave you to it then.' He backs away from the bed. 'You should speak to someone about this, though. Your doctor will be able to recommend someone.'

'I have a therapist. But thank you.'

There is much discussion about my care following the suicide attempt. Should I spend time on a psychiatric ward? I obviously refuse this. Charles offers to care for me at home, as though I'm a kid with the flu. But with his failing health, the doctors are reluctant. In the end, they decide to keep me under observation for a few days. During that time, I talk to various professionals and take a few questionnaires. Eventually I'm able to leave, after three days, limping around the car park on my bandaged ankle.

'How are the dogs?' I ask as I climb into the car, trying not to put weight on the bad foot or twinge my ribs.

'Porgie has a dicky tummy.' He jams the car into reverse, shoulders set tightly. 'All these changes have stressed him out. You know, I think they can smell the cancer on me.'

'Charles, you're reversing out of this space rather quickly. Charles!'

He slams on the brakes as a Mazda swings past us.

'Arsehole! He wasn't looking where he was going.'

'Charles.' I place a gentle hand on his arm. The motion gives me a sense of déjà vu. When I withdraw it, I see us very clearly in the hospital, Grace's body cold and lifeless on the gurney.

He pulls the car back into the bay and switches off the ignition. 'I'm dying, Kat—'

'We don't know that,' I interrupt. 'We get the biopsy results in the next few days and then we can discuss treatment…'

He holds up a hand. 'I'm dying, and I don't care what the doctors will say when the results come back. I can feel it. Maybe not this week or month or even year, but sooner than I ever planned, I'm dying.'

I shut my mouth and nod, allowing him to speak.

'Grace's death has left a bigger hole in my life than I ever thought possible, and yet I still want to live.'

'I know,' I say softly.

'You chose…' He leans his forehead against the steering wheel and I place a palm on his back.

'Let's go home.'

Farleigh Hall sits proudly atop its hill of green fields. We drive past the empty stables – wooden doors marred by horse's teeth, the ground still littered with stalks of hay. The cross house comes into view, with the ivy hanging over the door and the white gables covered in black beams. Inside the house, there's an antique tapestry in the smoking room and a grand piano in the library. These are the luxuries that many covet. This is what I dreamed of when I was living above a chippy on my own, fighting the smell of grease seeping up through the floor.

But it means nothing.

Because I built a family here by accident. It wasn't my life's goal to be a mother and a wife, because I'd convinced myself that I didn't care about people. They weren't supposed to be family members, they were supposed to be pawns in my games. What I'd never considered was the fact that there was no game, and my life has been little more than a series of moments to survive. First, I survived my childhood, then I survived the attack, then I survived poverty, before surviving a new life surrounded by people who looked down on me. I survived being a mother and I survived the death of my daughter.

I survived the Suicide Spot. What else is there to survive?

We get out of the car and Michelle opens the front doors to let out the dogs. I stumble up the drive while Charles distracts Georgie and Porgie, to prevent them from knocking me clean off my feet.

There is time for more survival. To rebuild and make a new life.

But there is one more event that I need to go through in order to be able to do that.

Hidden away from Charles and Michelle is an anger I'm carefully stoking. It's true that I never played the game, merely survived the one I was thrust into as a child, but now a new game is about to begin, and I will win.

CHAPTER FORTY-ONE

The first part of the game is waiting, and it's this part that generates the most frustration. There's a delay on getting the results back from Charles's biopsy, which adds to my impatience, to the limbo we currently inhabit. Not only does he stay home from work for several days, but he has Michelle around me all the time, fussing over cushions and making me sandwiches and cups of tea. I'd rather be alone with my thoughts, or up in Grace's bedroom watching her vlogs.

Still, I know that waiting is essential, and I can live with that. At first, I worried that my anger would fizzle out. But it hasn't. Not even after a week.

Anger is the one human emotion we don't tolerate as a species. Sadness, happiness, emptiness – all are treated with the respect they deserve, but anger is shunted away. From a young age, we're told that our anger is not valid. *Tommy stole my toy and I'm angry at him.* Well, kiddo, you're the one who should be ashamed of those feelings. Suck it up, kid, and get over it.

And we do get over it. We stop ourselves shouting at the person who cuts in front of us in the queue, and we ignore rude people in the street. Worse, we shrug when our politicians let us down, and we change the channel when injustice occurs around the world. Maybe the reason why we do all of those things is because, a long time ago, you were shamed when Tommy stole your fucking truck and you screamed at him.

Now that I know the truth about Angela, I consider whether I was so ready to believe what she told me about myself because

I was too afraid to confront my anger. When I hit Jamie over the head with that rock, I'd been in the midst of a rage that burned through me as fast as a firework. When Grace died, I finally allowed myself to feel angry again.

I spent my entire life feeling disconnected and cold because of the opinions of others. I believed the child psychologist who diagnosed me when I was thirteen and traumatised. I believed Angela as she told me over and over again that I was a sociopath. Grace was the one person who could penetrate my hard exterior, and when she died, she became the one person who could reignite that suppressed anger.

There is a hardness in me that I can't deny, and it will take me a long time to figure out who I am, to introspect without Angela's voice telling me what to think. I'm tough, I'm spontaneous, I do things and make decisions that other people might not be comfortable with. But am I truly a sociopath, devoid of any conscience? Self-serving, manipulative and charming? I don't know. Perhaps my final plans will answer that question.

Finally, Charles goes back to work, and I can arrange a meeting with Matthew Gould at the house. By now I've learned I can hobble around more easily with my ankle tightly bandaged. My ribs are less sore and my back no longer hurts at all. Still, I decide that he can come to the house, as long as Michelle stays out of the way.

'Mrs Cavanaugh, it's good to see you again.' He follows me as I limp through to the family room. 'How are you feeling?'

'Well, alive to tell the tale, thanks to you,' I say. 'Really, thank you for what you did.'

'You're welcome, and I hope I can help again.' He pats me gently on the arm and it feels good to have an ally.

'Would you like a cup of tea?'

'Oh no,' he says. 'I'm good.'

He's sparing me the annoyance of having to arrange a drink with my injuries. Could someone diagnosed with a personality disorder, who is supposed to have no conscience, *understand* such a kind gesture? I'm not sure I know anymore.

'Did you find the address for me?' I ask.

'I did.' He places a folder down on the ottoman between us. 'But they're not there.'

'Really?'

'No, they up and left about a week ago. But they haven't gone far. They're in a holiday cottage on the edge of Edale.'

I lift the folder and flick through it. 'That's very interesting. Lily isn't going to school and Angela hasn't resumed her therapy?'

'No, she's taken two weeks off work, according to her receptionist.'

They're running scared, I think, hoping that they can distance themselves in case I remember everything and tell the police. What will happen after two weeks? Will they come back, hoping that things have died down? Or will they disappear to a new town with new identities? They know they've made a mistake. No doubt they're considering their options right now, which means that I need to act quickly, before they decide to run away.

My sore ankle makes this less than ideal, but I slowly begin to piece together what I want to do. First, I write my husband a note to explain everything, then I put it in an envelope and give it to Michelle.

'You're not to give this to him until tomorrow,' I tell her.

She stares at me with wide eyes. 'Why? What's going on? You know that I can't allow you to do anything stupid. I'll have to tell him.' She knows all about my 'suicide attempt' at the quarry and isn't about to allow me to try again.

I grasp her by the shoulders, catching her by surprise with the strength of my grip. 'Listen to me. I'm not going to kill myself. Look at me. I didn't try before, but I couldn't tell you the truth.'

'Why not?'

I've thought about whether to do this many times over. I've considered all the options, wondering what a good person would do in the same situation. In the end, I sit Michelle down and I tell her everything, from the very beginning. Her face pales, and then she shakes her head angrily.

'You need to go to the police,' she says.

'I have a better way to deal with this.'

'Kat, I don't think I can let you go through with this.'

'I have to. For Grace.'

She nods her head slowly, and I leave her with my letter to Charles.

The car comes later that afternoon, before Charles gets home from work. I've already sent him a text message to say that I'm meeting Vanessa for dinner and will be home late. His reply is quick and panicky, worrying about how I'll manage to get there and back. But I reassure him that I've hired a driver and that relaxes him. He sends me a message telling me to have fun, and I contemplate whether the lie makes me feel guilty or not. I shake it away. Guilt won't help me now. At least I have Michelle on hand to make sure he has a bit of whisky and relaxes on the sofa tonight.

My insides feel like a bag of squirming snakes, but I keep on stoking the fury spreading beneath my skin. Anger often burns itself out in a fiery burst, unless we allow it to build and build, pushing it down until there are hundreds of scorched layers wrapped around our bones and organs. I can barely breathe with all that fire inside me.

The sun drops as we make our way out of Ash Dale village, and the distant hills and valleys fade away into the shadows. Instead I see the street lights and houses of nearby towns. Every dot represents people going about their evening: cooking, watching television, holding their loved ones.

Neither Grace nor I was perfect. I'm still figuring out who I am, but I think I may have pieced together some of who Grace was. My daughter. Flawed inside and out, part of my body, uniquely mine, uniquely herself.

We continue on in darkness until we reach Edale, and the driver takes me to my cottage. He lifts my suitcase and carries it through to the bedroom. I didn't pack much. A change of clothes. A toothbrush. A lighter. A small can of gasoline.

CHAPTER FORTY-TWO

The holiday cottage in front of me is in darkness, and for a split second I think I'm at the wrong place. But then I see Angela's car in the driveway. The same red Fiat was always parked next to her office. I used to remark on the grubby windows. In adulthood, Angela appears to have difficulty with making changes for herself – the chair that's too small, the car that's never clean. I wander closer and peer in through the grubby windows. There are old food wrappers and bottles littering the floor.

I grip the can in my hand. My plan was simple. I was going to come here and stuff a rag through the front door, covered in gasoline, and set it on fire. Then I was going to do the same at the back of the house. Whatever pity I once felt, because of what happened to us in the past, was eradicated when Angela targeted my vulnerable daughter and took her away from me. But now that I'm here, I'm all too aware that Angela is not alone in this house. Lily is here with her.

Since the night at Stonecliffe Quarry, I've thought of Lily many times. I've thought of her smirk, her knee in my face, the sneer in her voice, and I've thought of her hurt expression when Angela began to talk. The arrogance I saw from that young girl reminded me of something else: bravado. As much as I want to hate them both, all I can think is that Lily is the same age as Grace. Just seventeen.

And then there's Angela. I want to see her one last time, and I want to talk to her. I want to get answers from her, face-to-face. But I have a sore ankle and ribs, and I've never broken into a house before. All Angela needs to do is call the police and this whole thing is over. But I know she won't do that.

As I move around the house, the outside light flickers on and off, triggered by my movement. The lights within are off, suggesting they're both asleep. It's 1 a.m. – surely they're asleep by now. I gently test the windows on the ground floor as I make my way around the building. When in an unfamiliar house it's easy to forget to check all the doors and windows. Sure enough, Angela has locked them all except one. It's small, and I'm not sure if I can fit through it, but I jimmy open the stiff hinges, which were no doubt what tricked Angela into thinking it was locked. When I lean in, I see that it opens into the downstairs toilet, and I'll have to negotiate my way over the toilet to get in. Staring down at my sprained ankle, I deliberate how exactly I'm going to do that. First, I push the can through the window and place it on the closed toilet seat. Then I take the rag, already coated in gas from when I stood outside the house pondering my plan, and shove it in one pocket. I put the lighter in the other pocket.

With my hands now free, I place both on the bottom of the window and attempt to push myself up, resting my weight against the house. This is not a good move for my ribs, and after one attempt I'm forced to lower myself down. It's as I land on my feet that I begin to laugh. It's a quiet, manic laugh that builds up from my belly. I need to pull myself together.

Then I hear footsteps inside the house and freeze. A light goes on, and then there's the unmistakable sound of a key scraping in the lock on the front door of the house. I edge quietly towards the noise, my back to the wall. All manic laughter gone. Soon I'm standing next to the front door, but it doesn't open.

Instead, a voice drifts through the wood. 'Katie?'

I move to face the door. 'Angela?' A few options run through my mind. Forcing the door open and tackling Angela to the ground. Running her down and searching for a weapon.

She speaks again, interrupting my thoughts. 'What are you doing here, Katie?'

'I want to talk.'

The door opens, and her hand reaches out and grasps me by the shoulder of my jacket. She shoves a knife to my face, stopping a centimetre from my left eyeball. She regards me carefully, taking everything in – from the wince when I lean on my right foot to the bruises on my face.

'You probably should've waited until you'd healed,' she says.

'You'd have been gone by then.'

She pulls me roughly into the house, lowering the knife to my throat. 'That's true.'

'Have you called the police?' I ask.

'Not yet.'

'Why not?'

She shrugs. 'I guess we do need to talk.'

Angela shoves me away from her while she locks the door. There's the sound of movement behind me and I spin around, carefully avoiding the knife, to find Lily rubbing sleep from her eyes, dressed in blue striped pyjamas. When she sees me, her face pales.

'Sorry I woke you.'

She nods. Her jaw is clenched and her eyes are furtive, constantly flicking back to Angela. Where is the arrogance of the girl at the quarry? This is off script for her. Everything else has been orchestrated by her mother, but neither of them expected me to come here. They didn't expect me to survive.

'I guess you decided on a holiday,' I say. 'It's nice. Quaint. Better than the homes we grew up in. Isn't that right, Angela?'

'How did you find us?' She moves the knife to my lower back. Gently, she pushes me through the hallway, past Lily and into the small living-room area.

'The same way I found out Daniel Hawthorne was having sex with my daughter. I hired a private detective.'

'Always using your money these days, Katie. Remember when you actually had to work?'

I scoff at that. 'I never worked.'

'No, that's right, you didn't.' She pushes me down onto the floor and sits over me on the sofa, the knife never far away. 'I was the one who worked. I read the textbooks, achieved my A's, paid for university with a part-time job, created my practice from nothing.'

I can't help but roll my eyes. 'Everyone got loans for university fees back then.'

She shoves the knife in my face. 'At least I didn't get pregnant to marry rich.'

Fire smoulders underneath my skin. 'Then I guess we both worked for what we have.'

While she seethes, I take a quick scan of the room. There's a log fire in the hearth, two armchairs, a large sofa and long curtains that extend to the plush carpet. A lot of flammable items in this room. Lily sits opposite us on one of the chairs, her mobile phone in her hand.

'Are you going to call the police, Lily?' I ask.

Lily glances at Angela, rather than answer.

'What have you done to that girl, Annie?' I say. 'You've used her every step of the way. Lily, did you really want to kill my daughter? Or did your mother make you? Did you want to do any of this?'

'It was my choice,' Lily says. 'She shoved dog shit in my face.'

I redirect my attention to Angela. 'You've been creating socio-paths for twelve years, haven't you? You messed with my head, and you've starved this girl of love, tricking her into doing your bidding so you get to keep your hands clean.'

'What makes you think you're not a sociopath, Katie? You did plenty of bad things before we started our therapy sessions. Do you remember knocking out Susie P's front tooth with a headbutt? What did she do to you? Do you remember? She looked at you funny. That was her crime.'

'I was a troubled kid. You know the stuff I went through with my mother.'

'Even after you left your mother behind, you orchestrated a pregnancy and tricked a man into marriage.'

'Charles loves me.'

She chuckles to herself, staring at the logs in the hearth, and for a split second I deliberate whether I have an opportunity to take the knife, but then she turns back to me and the moment is gone. 'You keep forgetting how well I know you. You've paid, weekly, to come to my office and tell me your thoughts. And you know what? Your thoughts are black. Every week, I sit there and I listen to you berate your friends and family. Every week. It's not just your mother that you complain about; you constantly complain about your husband, your daughter, your friend Jenny. According to you, no one is as good as you. No one lives up to your expectations, and you don't want them to. You're a wall, Katie. Nothing gets through. Is that any different to being a sociopath? You talk about trying to be better, about giving to charity, doing the right thing, being a decent parent, but your thoughts are who you are, and they are rotten.'

A sick feeling builds in the pit of my stomach. My voice is quiet. 'No. My thoughts were dark because of what you told me I was.' Not wanting to gaze at Angela's hateful face any longer, I seek out Lily and watch in surprise as she wipes a tear from her eye.

'I wasn't the one who diagnosed you with antisocial personality disorder, was I?' she points out.

'Maybe they got it wrong.' My voice sounds uneven, because how can I be sure? I was a kid then, and I'd been through a lot. But what those psychologists said to me shaped me well into my adult life, before I even started therapy.

It was a mistake to come here. Stupidly, I'd thought that I could win, and now I know how ridiculous that sounds. I keep fooling myself that I'm in control. In reality, I never am, and I never have been.

'Let's talk about that day,' Angela says.

'Go on. Tell me how it was all my fault.' I can't keep the bitterness out of my voice. 'You can't confront Jamie anymore, can you? I'm the best you've got.'

'They got less than ten years for what they did to me.'

My insides twist and I fight the urge to vomit. 'I know, I was there when they read out the verdict.'

'They left prison years ago, and since then they've been out there living their lives as though nothing happened.'

'What does that have to do with me? They hurt me too, remember? I know your face was bashed in, but you had to notice Jamie pinning me down and ripping off my underwear.' Out of the corner of my eye, I catch Lily looking away in fear.

'Yes, I saw. I saw how you fought for yourself, but you didn't fight for me.'

'I was held down by two men!' I yell.

'Not the whole time, you weren't. You're remembering it wrong. You were drunk. Slumped in the corner. Jamie started raping me while you were barely conscious. I needed you and you weren't there.'

I shake my head. 'That's not true. I… I didn't drink much of the beer. You were the one who…'

Angela shakes her head very slowly, and this time I can't stop the urge to vomit.

CHAPTER FORTY-THREE

I cough up thick yellow bile onto the carpet, and a foul stench fills the room. Sweat breaks out on my forehead and my abdomen cramps up one more time before it releases. Everything about the smell and the shame and the sweat takes me back to that day. I remember sitting on Mark's lap in the back of the car, swigging beer, bouncing along to happy hardcore, shouting out the repetitive lyrics in a slurred voice. I hear myself inform Annie in an obnoxious voice that she's uptight, twirling my way through the field towards the shelter. I see myself spinning around and around with the boys until I stagger over to a corner and throw up, half collapsed, and pass out for a minute or two.

When I woke, Jamie was on top of Annie. Her mouth was that same cavernous expanse I've imagined all these years, and her screaming made my ears ring.

'Katie, help me!' she screamed.

But I couldn't wake myself. I think my drunken mind was convinced I was having a nightmare. Instead of going over there to help her, I closed my eyes. When I opened them again, I was restrained, Annie's face was being smashed into the ground and Jamie was yelling at her. That's why I kept closing my eyes, because I was drunk and slipping in and out of consciousness.

Then they dragged me out of the corner. Jamie tugged at my clothes, his thick, dry fingers fiddling with the stiff buttons on my cheap school shirt, tugging on my necklace. Something snapped inside me. I found the rock. It was over in a matter of minutes.

'It's funny. Every time you told me your version of that day in our therapy sessions, I thought you were deliberately lying to me in order to make yourself sound better. But then I began to understand that you truly believed your own lies. I'm not sure what made me angrier. In the end, I got sick of listening to you. While I still feel the pain of that day, you've moved on. You've protected your precious psyche by inventing a different story. You've even managed to find a rich man and maintain a *marriage*.' She chews on her bottom lip and her eyes open wide. 'While I'm barren and will never give birth to a child, you had a beautiful daughter. *Grace.* My relationships never lasted because I could hardly bear to have a man touch me. I never got back that size-eight figure; instead I hid my body under these layers of fat, ashamed of who I used to be. Not that I'll ever be attractive again, with this botched face. While I was fighting for my life, you were passed out in the corner of that shelter. It's still all I can see when I close my eyes, even after all these years.' She wipes away tears. 'I can't punish them. I could never be within a mile's radius of them because of the sheer terror of it. But you... well, you're different. I thought it would be enough to watch, and plant seeds, and manipulate you however I pleased. But then my life kept getting worse while yours got better and better and I wanted more than just being your therapist. Grace's bullying of Lily was the last straw. Neither of you deserve the life you were given.'

'Mum,' Lily says quietly. 'Don't you think we should stop now?' Her eyes glance across to me. 'It wasn't dog poo. It was this prank stuff from a joke shop.'

'None of that matters now,' Angela says. It's the first time that she has acknowledged her adopted daughter's presence since dragging me into the living room. 'We talked about why we're doing this, honey. It's because of what she allowed to happen to me.' Angela jabs the knife in my direction.

'I don't want to keep doing this. I don't want to keep lying.' Lily's eyes plead with me instead of Angela, suddenly reminding me of Grace when she'd come home from school after a fight with Alicia, forlorn and crumpled. 'We pushed her into the quarry. That was enough.'

I watch as Angela's face contorts, bringing out every ugly line and wrinkle on her forehead. 'She survived! She always survives.' The knife carves through the air as she waves her arms back and forth.

'But you did too, Mum!' Lily stands, opening her palms. 'She's sorry for what happened. You told me that she wasn't sorry, but she is!'

Angela paces the room, still brandishing her knife, swiping it back and forth between us both. 'It's not enough.'

'You killed her daughter,' Lily whispers. 'You pushed her over the edge and she died.'

'What?' As Angela paces towards the fireplace, I climb to my feet, the pain in my ribs and ankle inconsequential compared to the impact of Lily's words. 'What did you just say?'

Lily's eyes are round and oddly innocent as she faces me. 'Grace did write that suicide note, but when we got to the quarry, she changed her mind. The plan was for us to stand on the edge together. I'd promised her I was going to jump, but the plan was that I wouldn't jump at the last minute, letting her go alone. But Grace got cold feet. She decided she wanted to live. She was going to go home and tell you everything. But Mum was watching nearby, like she was that night you met me at the Suicide Spot. She saw Grace change her mind.' Lily falters, staring at her mother.

I clench my fists tightly before I demand, 'Then what happened?'

'Mum rushed over, and everything happened so quickly.'

'Lily?' I take a step towards the girl, but Angela comes closer, the knife held aloft.

'Just tell her,' Angela insists.

'Mum pushed Grace into the quarry. I'm sorry. I'm so sorry. Everything went too far. I did what she told me because she said you both deserved it, but I don't think you did deserve any of it.'

Angela steps away, puts one hand on the mantelpiece above the fire and pauses there.

I'm not sure what to make of the tears wetting Lily's cheeks. Yes, she reminds me of Grace. Youthful skin, young voice, quivering bottom lip, big eyes. She's a teen, not yet grown, still soft clay to be moulded – and Angela has moulded her into a dark and destructive creature. But do I feel sorry for her? Do I believe her pleas for contrition? Or is this more pretence?

'It's true, I did push her into the quarry. I grabbed her by the arm and we both looked at each other. My God, Katie, she had your eyes. It was like looking at a polished version of teenage you. You were beautiful, in a rough kind of way. You dressed like a boy, never washed your hair, always had spots – but the beauty was there underneath.' Angela moves back towards me, lifting the knife higher. 'The girl deserved it. She was a bully and a liar. She was prepared to kill herself anyway, along with her unborn child. I would do anything to be able to carry a child.' Lost in an imaginary world, Angela strokes her belly as though there's a child in there now. 'I whispered to her… "I'm coming for your mother next." And then I pushed her.'

Before I can let those words sink in, she crosses the room, grabs me by the hair and puts the knife to my throat. 'Let's end this now,' she says. 'You and me. Let's finish it together. You survived the fall for a reason. We're meant to die together. Look at us: we're the same. I've watched you for twelve years; I know you. I know *us*. We both changed our names and pretended to be new people, and then we found each other. We should die together.'

'Mum!'

As Angela pulls my head back to slice my flesh, I twist my body away, somehow wrenching free from her grip. Lily throws herself onto Angela and the knife goes flying. A flash of red-hot anger courses through me. This woman murdered my daughter. I pull Lily away and push her towards the door to the kitchen. In one quick motion, I pull the rag from my coat, flick on the lighter, light one end of the rag and toss it at Angela. While she tries to bat the burning cloth away from her body, I hurry out of the room and towards the front door. On my way, the small can of gasoline on the downstairs toilet catches my attention. I grab it and limp back to the living room, where I witness Angela desperately trying to remove her burning dressing gown, screeching almost as loudly as she does in my nightmares. Flames dance along the fluffy material, licking at the ends of her hair. Before I can change my mind, I toss the can at the sofa and watch as the gas spills out and the fire spreads. Soon it's travelling across the carpets towards the door. I get away, limping as fast as I can.

'Help me!'

The desperate voice forces me to stop. It isn't Angela shouting to me, it's Lily. I'd thought she'd got out, but when I glance over my shoulder, the view is one of chaos: a room almost completely filled with flames, black smoke building into a cloud of noxious gas. Lily is in Angela's clutches, held back by this half-crazed, burning human being, unable to get away.

A sociopath would leave Lily to burn in that room with the madwoman. Self-preservation is a sociopath's first concern; no one else truly matters to them. I could hobble over to the exit, turn the key, stagger out and survive another day. But Lily would die along with Angela.

When Grace was born, I decided to be a better person for her, and she died believing I was that person.

'Fake it until you make it,' I mutter to myself, rushing into that burning room, feeling the smoke clog in my throat, the flames searing my exposed skin.

'Take my hand!' I shout.

Lily grasps hold of me and I shove Angela away, throwing her back into the room. Her shrieks die down as her throat rasps through the smoke. There's an expression on her face that will join my nightmares, but I have Lily and we make our way out of the house. She props me up as much as I help her. Both of us are coughing through the black smoke, choking on it.

As we stagger out of the house, people begin to spill out of the nearby cottages. A man in paisley pyjamas hurries over and helps us onto the driveway.

'I've called 999,' he says. 'Are you all right? Let's get you away from the house.'

Someone else hands us both glasses of water.

Soon the sirens blare. A large fire truck struggles up the dirt track to the isolated cottages. Fire fighters climb down from the cab, barking orders to each other as they unravel their hoses.

'Is there anyone else inside?' someone shouts.

'Yes – my mum,' Lily replies.

The man stares at the house and his shoulders sag. He knows as well as we do that she's dead.

Annie Robertson and Angela Mardell are both dead. And so is Katie Flack.

Lily stays close to me in the hospital, clinging to my side like a frightened puppy. Not long after our arrival, a confused Charles appears, clutching the letter I told Michelle not to give him until tomorrow. I can see it is still sealed, and I whisper to him not to open it when the doctor is examining Lily. No one else comes to support Lily. Then the police show up to take statements, and I'm relieved to see DS Slater isn't among them for a change.

'I'm sorry for your loss,' the police officer says. 'I know this is a difficult time, but I need to ask you a few questions about the fire.'

It's Lily who answers, before I can even open my mouth. 'It was all Mum.' Her voice shakes with emotion. 'Kat is Mum's friend. Well, she's Mum's patient, but they were friends, too. I called her because Mum was acting weird, and she came in the night to make sure everything was okay.' Lily takes a sip of water and slowly swallows. I can't keep my eyes from her. 'Mum had this small can of petrol and a lighter, and she was threatening to kill herself. Kat was really brave. She tried to talk Mum out of it, but Mum wouldn't listen. She lit this rag and set the sofa on fire. Then she grabbed me and tried to make me stay in the room with her. It was Kat who managed to get me free. She saved my life.'

The police officer makes a note of all of this.

Lily grips my hand and leans her head against my shoulder. 'Thank you, Kat. Thank you for helping me.'

EPILOGUE

Mrs Nash hangs over the garden wall as I make my way down the back alley, her low breasts squashed between the cheap fabric of her T-shirt and the bricks. A cigarette hangs out of the corner of her mouth, but as she sees me approach, limping, she pulls it from her lips and exclaims.

'Oh, Katie, what have you done to your leg?'

'I fell down a quarry.'

When the shock registers on her face, I let out a laugh, enjoying the way her jaw hangs open.

She takes a long, slow drag. 'Well, I never. Susan didn't mention it at bridge night last week.'

I just shrug. 'That's because I didn't tell her.'

She waves a limp-wristed hand in my direction and the cigarette smoke wafts over. 'I'm sure you didn't want to worry her. Are you here to visit your mum? Course you are, aren't you, love?'

'Who else would I be visiting?' I say, leaning away to avoid her cigarette smoke. 'Unless I've come to visit you.'

'You can come in for a cuppa if you want.' She cups her mouth and lowers her voice. 'Or, I've got a bottle of gin open.'

'Nice one, Mrs Nash. But I'd better go.'

'Good to see you, Katie.'

'It's Kat now.'

She frowns. 'It is?'

'I got married eighteen years ago. I've been Kat ever since.'

'Oh, you silly beggar. Why didn't you tell me?'

I shrug. 'I guess it didn't occur to me until now.'

Her eyes follow me as I limp along the rest of the alley to my mother's house. As the ghostly wisps of Mrs Nash's cigarette smoke fade away, I find myself imagining cold fingers reaching inside me, grasping my lungs, squeezing tight. After everything that has happened since Grace died, I can finally admit to myself that I am afraid of walking down this street. When Angela managed to convince me that I'm a sociopath, I in turn convinced myself that I don't feel fear. That it was hatred making me feel this way, because I'm a hateful person. But now I know that it was weak of me to never acknowledge, to never own, the fear that I've always had of my mother. There is strength in acknowledgement and weakness in avoidance.

My mother frightens me more than anyone else in the world, even more than Jamie, Gav, Steve and Mark, the idiots who thought they were entitled to my body. The fear of my mother isn't a physical one. She never hurts me in that way. It's a deeply ingrained emotional pain. Those fingers around my lungs, squeezing the air out of my body...

Fear of Gav and the others is physical. Since leaving the hospital, I've done some research into those three – Mathew Gould came in handy again – and discovered that Mark ended up in and out of prison for assault, currently located in HMP Wakefield. Steve is a born-again Christian who works for a Christian charity. Gav is an alcoholic living in Old Barrow on a zero-hour contract.

After a brief knock on the door, she answers. Shock registers on her face when she sees my bruises, but it's fleeting, replaced by a smug satisfaction that I've fucked up again. She opens her mouth to speak but I cut her off almost immediately.

'Grace didn't tell you anything, did she? She probably didn't even come to visit you. The only reason you said that was to get in my head and under my skin. You're poison, Mother. This is the last time I speak to you, I want you to know that. I came here to say it to your face. Our last connection is severed and there's no reason for me to stay in your life, and vice versa. After I saved my own life by killing Jamie Sutton, you called me a murderer, but I was never a murderer. You told me I was worthless, and you were wrong. I saved my life that day, and I saved the life of another. I fought back even when I was drunk and afraid. The worst mistake I ever made was believing what you told me. We're done.'

When I turn away from her and limp through her concrete garden, she calls my name once. It's half-hearted, thin as her sinewy body. Then she stops. She doesn't follow me into the alley, and goodness knows I'm moving slowly enough for her to catch me up with ease.

One down.

At the end of the alley, I take a right and pass a number of snarling dogs straining at their chains to try and reach me. In the next garden, a kid in nothing but a nappy toddles over to wave at me from the garden gate. Two teenage girls sitting on the wall outside the youth centre laugh at my limp. All in all, even with my bad ankle, the walk takes three minutes.

The house is a terrace. There are no dogs in the garden, but there is an empty rabbit hutch and underwear on the clothes line. I open a squeaking gate into the garden, taking care on the paving slabs, slick with moss. After three blasts of the doorbell, a woman with greasy grey hair opens the door. 'Yes?' Her eyes trail my body, taking in my appearance. I don't blame her unease; I'm dressed in expensive clothes, but I have bruises and scratches on my face and burns on my hands.

'Can I speak to Gav, please?'

'Who are you?' she asks. I've learned from Matthew Gould that Gav lives with his aunt Eileen.

'An old friend.'

Without breaking eye contact, she shouts Gav's name and leans against the door frame. Her feet are bare; chipped red polish on the toes, cracks in the skin around her bunions.

'What?'

Hearing his voice after all these years sends an involuntary shiver down my body. Eileen's brow knits as she notices my reaction. She scrutinises me, trying to suss me out.

Thumping steps come down the stairs at the back of the house, and a moment later, a tubby, middle-aged man lumbers into view. He knows who I am as soon as he sees my face. I, on the other hand, would never have recognised this man as the attractive boy with blue eyes who had caught my attention with his charm offensive all those years ago.

Eileen takes a few steps back and allows Gav to move closer. He doesn't say a word, simply stares at me, and I do the same back.

'Give us a minute, will you?' he grunts at his aunt.

She regards me one more time and then shuffles back into the house, scooping up a tabby cat on her way.

'Jesus, what happened to you?'

'Annie Robertson found me.'

The sound of her name has an effect on him. He reels back, and his eyes flick away from mine. Would this have been easier if he had no remorse?

'She still had a grudge,' I say. 'Against me.'

He shakes his head in disbelief. 'Why?'

I shrug. 'I guess in some ways I was easier to blame.'

'I always expected her to knock on my door, but for some reason I didn't expect you would.'

'Why is that?' I ask.

'You seemed like the type to draw a line. Move on.'

'Is that what you've done?'

He lets out a breathy laugh. No humour in it. 'No. No, I haven't.'

'No one told me you were living near my mother.'

He rubs his stubble. 'I would've contacted you, but I didn't know what to say.'

'"Sorry" not in your vocabulary?'

'Yes. But it's not enough, is it?'

'No.'

'For what it's worth, I am sorry.' He pulls at the sleeve of his Adidas hoody. 'I was a different person then.'

'So was I.'

'I see her face every night. And every night I see myself not helping either of you.' His voice cracks.

A modicum of that fire sparks up again, and I push him, taking him by surprise and knocking him to the hallway carpet. 'Don't you dare suffer. It's *my* suffering and you don't deserve to share it. You are not haunted by that day, *I am*. Don't you dare grieve for me.'

'Katie, I'm—'

'No. Shut it. I wanted to see you, and now I have. Now I can go.'

As he nods once more, it feels like an acceptance. 'All right.'

'Do you think she'd like it?'

I don't have the heart to tell him that I hate it and that I wish we'd had Grace cremated, her ashes thrown into the air to be taken by the breeze. Instead Grace ended up in the family plot, next to her grandmother. Charles felt that Emily's presence would bring comfort to Grace, and I'd been too spaced out with grief, and too consumed with the idea of revenge, to say no to him.

'She'd love it.'

'It's her, isn't it? Simple. Unique.'

The headstone is black, smooth marble with gold lettering. A violin and musical notes are etched beneath her obituary.

Grace Cavanaugh
5 February 2002 – 15 March 2019
Beloved daughter. Forever loved.

No words could ever summarise her. She was flawed and she made mistakes, but I loved her more than anything in the world and there will always be a hole in our lives, the shape of her, the sound of her. She died *unfinished* without a chance to right her wrongs.

And, oh, Grace, those wrongs were not so bad. We could've overcome them together if you'd talked to me.

I take a deep breath to steady myself, thinking about the kisses she used to plant our cheeks in the morning, the way she laughed with her whole body, the dance-party sleepovers. The way my love for her made me want to be a good person.

'Kat? Are you all right?' Charles wraps an arm around my waist and pulls me in.

It's hard to be close to him, to be close to anyone. There's a doctor's appointment hanging over both our heads. Later today, we'll discover how advanced Charles's cancer is. But I can't think about that now.

'You've been distant.' His tone is careful. Since the fire he's treated me with kid gloves. Not much physical contact; short conversations that are never too heavy. The ever patient husband. He deserves to know everything, and now is as good a time as any. Grace always did bring us closer together, it feels fitting that I tell Charles my story here, in front of her grave.

'That night at the cottage in Edale didn't happen the way Lily told the police,' I begin. 'I wrote what I had planned to do in the letter I gave to Michelle.'

'It's still unopened,' he says.

'Well, it's, umm…' My body is fighting off tears, but I regain control and continue. 'It wasn't Angela who started the fire that night. It was me. Angela wasn't who she claimed to be. She was someone from my past, but she hid her identity so that she could be my therapist – for years. She was Annie Robertson.'

Charles keeps his arm around my waist, but he frowns when his eyes meet mine, and I find it difficult to read his expression. Is he angry? 'Who's Annie Robertson?'

'It's a… long story.' My breath refuses to steady and the tears are winning.

'I have time.' A gentle squeeze of my waist. Patience.

'I never told you this, because I wasn't sure how to say the words. Angela was the only one I ever spoke to about it, and that was mainly because I was paying her. But you see, she'd changed her appearance. I never…'

'Take your time, Kat.'

'We were thirteen. There were four older boys. They wanted us to go out with them, so we did.' Slowly, in a trembling voice, I tell him everything. 'Somehow, I don't know exactly… I lifted the stone and I smashed it into Jamie's head. I killed the man on top of me.'

There's silence between us. That protective arm still around my waist, keeping my knees from buckling.

'I always said that I didn't hide my violent background. That's not strictly true. You knew about the school fights and the arrests, but you didn't know about the time I killed someone.'

He's silent again. This time it stretches out, as though hours pass.

'Those nightmares…' He shakes his head. 'I always suspected. Perhaps I should have asked you.'

When I double over and finally allow myself to cry – for Grace, for Annie and for me – he holds me and stops me from falling down. It takes a while. Maybe two minutes, or five, or ten, I can't tell. Eventually, I bring myself under control.

'Annie pretended to be my therapist and she convinced me that I'm a sociopath. She made me believe that I can't love. But I knew I loved Grace.'

'I know you did.'

And then I tell him about Lily, and the bullying, and how Lily manipulated Grace. I tell him about Daniel Hawthorne and the baby, and Angela's arrival at the quarry.

'Lily showed me an alternative suicide note written by Grace, but I think it probably burned in the fire. I wish I could show it to you.'

Charles's eyelashes are wet. I clutch his hands in mine.

'That night when I told you I tried to kill myself, I met them both. They admitted it all to me. Annie pushed Grace into the quarry, and she was the one who pushed me too.'

'Fuck, Kat.' He shakes his head in disbelief. 'Why didn't you tell me?'

'You believe me, don't you?' My thumb finds a curve in his palm and strokes back and forth.

'You're not a liar. Eighteen years and you've always told me straight, either with your words or your eyes.'

'Well, I had to lie to you in the hospital. I didn't think anyone would believe me otherwise.'

'I knew something was off. I know I got angry with you, but I still thought it didn't add up.' He lets out a long, heavy sigh, his head bobbing low. 'Jesus Christ, poor Grace. God, I'm so fucking angry. Why didn't you tell me? I could've helped you.'

'It was my battle,' I reply.

We stand there in silence and I sense Charles mulling over my words, digesting them, coming to terms with them.

'She loved us,' I say. 'She truly did.'

He squeezes my hand.

After another moment of silence, I ask, 'Do you think a person can be good if they have bad thoughts?'

He glances at me in surprise. 'What sort of thoughts?'

'Ones that see the bad in people. That sometimes wish bad things on people. Getting annoyed by insignificant things and mentally berating people, even loved ones.'

Charles's eyebrows pull together at first, but then his face relaxes. 'We're all bad people, then. Every single one of us. You know, thoughts are fleeting and fickle, changing from day to day, just as we change. What we do is what lasts forever. That's what makes a difference. You can't take back what you say or do, but you can allow your thoughts to exist and then let them go. I suppose thoughts are the ghosts of what we do. In some ways they aren't even real.'

'I've done terrible things, too. The fire.' I stare down at Grace's grave, trying desperately to ignore the throbbing burns on my forearms. 'I swear she was out of control, she was going to attack me, but… Charles, I went there with a can of gas. I went there intending to kill them.'

'You did,' he says. 'And you can never take that back. But in the end, the circumstances absolve your intentions. Not only did you wait until it became self-defence, but you saved one of the people who conspired to kill your daughter. Kat, this woman stalked you for over a decade, messed with your head and murdered our daughter. Christ, if I'd known any of this, I would've cut her into tiny pieces.'

I shake my head. 'No, you wouldn't.' As aged and frail as my husband has become since the cancer began to take its toll, his wisdom and patience shine through. There's Grace in him, and I was stupid not to see it sooner. 'We're going to be okay, you know. We're going to get through it together.'

He pats my hand. 'Of course.'

One last look at the headstone. Grace isn't here. 'She wouldn't want us to stay.' I bend down and place a yellow rose on the grave. 'Let's go.'

Charles leads the way as we step around the other graves to head back to the car. But a minute or so after leaving the grave, I have the strange urge to glance back over my shoulder. As I do, I catch a glimpse of a dark head of black hair hurrying in the opposite direction. I let go of Charles's hand and make my way back to Grace's grave. There, on the marble plinth, is a single white lily.

A LETTER FROM SARAH

I want to say a huge thank you for choosing to read *Only Daughter*. If you did enjoy it, and want to keep up-to-date with all my latest releases, just sign up at the following link. Your email address will never be shared and you can unsubscribe at any time.

www.bookouture.com/sarah-denzil

This book has been one of my favourites to write, and I am so thrilled to be able to share it with you all.

I hope you loved *Only Daughter* and if you did I would be very grateful if you could write a review. I'd love to hear what you think, and it makes such a difference helping new readers to discover one of my books for the first time.

I love hearing from my readers – you can get in touch on my Facebook page, through Twitter, Goodreads or my website.

Thanks,
Sarah A. Denzil

 sarahadenzil

 @sarahdenzil

 www.sarahdenzil.com

 @marmiteandbooks

ACKNOWLEDGEMENTS

As always, a big thank you to family and friends for your support. An extra big thank you to my husband, who not only reads each and every book but also listens patiently to all of my worries and frustrations along the way.

Another big thank you to the team at Bookouture, especially my editor, Natasha, and publicity whizzes Noelle and Kim. You guys put my work ethic to shame!

And last but not least, thank you to each and every reader. Without you, I wouldn't have my dream job right now.